"Debut author Alyssa Alexander captivates with a potently drawn Regency suspense that will keep you turning pages far into the night . . . Her delightful protagonists—including a lovely and lethal mathematician-smuggling heroine—will charm readers, while the sensual romance with an ultra-alpha spy provides the heat. Packed dialogue and action . . . Alexander is clearly an author we ought to watch *and* read."

—Jennifer McQuiston, author of
*What Happens in Scotland*

## THE LADY REMEMBERS . . .

He leaned in farther, lips close to hers. He hesitated, giving her the chance to run. She knew what would happen, knew the inevitability of it. And she wanted it—wanted him—in a way that was both foreign and familiar, and filled her with the same fire as the ride.

She didn't run. Instead, she gripped his biceps and lifted to her toes to meet his lips. When his mouth touched hers, it wasn't gentle or demanding. Instead, it was simply there for her to take from, to use as she wanted.

Emboldened, filled with her own recklessness, she pushed her hands to his shoulders and pressed her lips more fully to his. His mouth opened beneath hers and she darted her tongue between his lips. He tasted hot and salty and male.

He groaned and pushed his hands into her loose hair, taking control of the kiss. The demand was there now, the need clear in his foraging tongue and agile lips. His hands worked through her hair, then cupped her cheeks as he drew her against him. She obeyed, hungry for the forbidden. As their bodies met and breath mingled, Grace knew what she had been missing for so long . . .

# The Smuggler Wore Silk

## ALYSSA ALEXANDER

**B**
BERKLEY SENSATION, NEW YORK

**THE BERKLEY PUBLISHING GROUP**
Published by the Penguin Group
Penguin Group (USA) LLC
375 Hudson Street, New York, New York 10014

USA • Canada • UK • Ireland • Australia • New Zealand • India • South Africa • China

penguin.com

A Penguin Random House Company

THE SMUGGLER WORE SILK

A Berkley Sensation Book / published by arrangement with the author

For information, address: The Berkley Publishing Group,
a division of Penguin Group (USA) LLC,
375 Hudson Street, New York, New York 10014.

ISBN: 978-0-425-26952-7

PUBLISHING HISTORY
Berkley Sensation mass-market edition / January 2014

PRINTED IN THE UNITED STATES OF AMERICA

10  9  8  7  6  5  4  3  2  1

Cover illustration by Aleta Rafton.
Cover design by Diana Kolsky.
Interior text design by Tiffany Estreicher.

*To Joe*
*For knowing I'm crazy and loving me anyway*

# ACKNOWLEDGMENTS

The number of people who help a novel move from dream to reality cannot be counted. They are infinite, and for me, started somewhere in the vicinity of fourth grade. But I will do my best to list everyone and hope I do not leave anyone out. I no doubt will, and I apologize in advance.

Thank you to my amazing agent, Nikki Terpilowski of the Holloway Literary Agency, for her tireless efforts on my behalf and for believing in me and my work. Thank you to my editor, Julie Mianecki, and the copyeditors, artists and promotions team at Berkley for giving me this wonderful opportunity and seeing it through to fruition.

Thank you to my Three Cheeka Honey Badgers: Tracy Brogan, Jennifer McQuiston and Kimberly Kincaid. Without you, my daily life would be very drab indeed. So would my writing. And I would never have learned there was somethin' about a truck. May your flasks be ever full and your fingers be ever quick on the keyboard.

Thank you to the Romance Writers of America and the Mid-Michigan Romance Writers of America. I didn't know it was normal to have voices in your head until I started to attend meetings with other writers. I must also thank the Beau Monde, a special interest chapter of RWA, for their combined wealth of knowledge and their willingness to share it.

And my deepest gratitude to all those people who touched my life and book along the way:

To The Side Saddle Lady, for patiently answering my questions. Turns out that first kiss scene would not have worked on a side saddle.

To Avis Hewitt, the professor who told me writing romance was a viable option. Yours was the first encouragement I received outside of my family, at a time I needed it most.

To the friends who didn't look at me like I'd grown two heads when I said I wanted to write books, and to the friends who listened to me talk about my characters as though they were real people. You know who you are.

To Bruce, for not firing me when I sold my first book. Thanks for the time off to write!

To my family: Mom and Dad, for always encouraging me in this foolish idea I had to be a writer. To Susie, for reading those horrible first handwritten pages nearly twenty years ago. To Kelsey and Kara, for playing dress up with me. All the stories started there.

To Josh, for being five years old and a delight in my life. I have no idea how you went from being my baby to being a little man. I didn't notice it happening, and now you're all scraped knees and sharp elbows and gangly limbs. I hope your dreams are bigger and better than mine, and I hope you obtain them.

And most of all, thank you to Joe. For dreaming this dream with me. For eating pizza for dinner when I don't feel like cooking. For waking me up when I fall asleep at the computer, taking the small child out of the house when I need to write, and working hard so I could go to conferences and chapter meetings. For being my IT guy and setting the coffeepot for four thirty a.m. and preheating the bed. For giving me the upstairs carpeted office and putting your computer in the concrete dungeon. For believing in me, even when I didn't believe in myself.

# Chapter 1

HE COULDN'T SPEAK, couldn't think. Couldn't *breathe*.

In front of him, the spymaster's lips moved, but the sound issuing from them was tinny and thin. He struggled to focus on the words.

The man couldn't have said *retire*. Impossible. Spies did not die as old men in soft beds. Death took them in the field. A knife to the throat. A bullet. Even poison was preferable to this.

"With respect, sir, I cannot retire."

Julian Travers, Earl of Langford, uncurled clenched fists. Blood roared in his ears. He was being *asked* to retire. As though the request did not decimate the life he had carefully rebuilt. As though ten years of atonement meant nothing.

"There are no other options." Sir Charles Flint's voice was brisk. If the spymaster was disappointed to be losing an agent, he didn't show it by a flicker of an eyelash. "The French know you are the Shadow."

Julian's hands jerked reflexively. "Sir—"

"The traitor gave your identity to the French. You and two other agents have been compromised." The lines around Sir Charles's mouth deepened. He pushed aside a stack of documents and leaned over his worn oak desktop. "If we send you to the Continent and the French capture you, they'll use every method of torture in their arsenal to extract information from you. You *must* retire."

The words punched into Julian's belly. He pushed to his feet to pace the cramped government office. "Austria has officially declared war on France. I could travel to—"

"No. You're the best agent I have, but I can't send you on a mission abroad." Finality rang in Sir Charles's tone. "It's time for the Wandering Earl to return home."

Julian ignored the moniker. He much preferred the Shadow, his alias among the other spies, to the ton's pet name for him. Still, the Wandering Earl's bored and spoiled persona served as a useful cover for his frequent trips to the Continent.

"The other compromised agents are also being forced into retirement," Sir Charles continued. "The threat to our network of spies in France and on the Continent is simply too great to allow any of you to continue."

"I still have a job to do, sir." Julian stopped pacing to stand in front of the room's only window. He gripped the smooth wooden windowsill and stared down at the cobblestones of Crown Street.

"Langford, you're an unofficial agent. Assignment to an official position is not possible. Unless you want to work within this building, behind a desk—"

"That would be worse than rusticating in the country or haunting the drawing rooms of the ton, which are my other choices." Julian suppressed a disgusted snort. His gaze fell to his knuckles, the flesh white where his fingers gripped the windowsill.

"The Shadow served king and country for ten years." Cloth rustled against leather. The chair beneath Sir Charles creaked. "During those ten years, the Earl of Langford turned his back on his title and his heritage."

"I never wanted the title," Julian said flatly. Beyond the window, gray fog drifted around carriages and buildings. Diplomats and clerks and secretaries scurried to and from their offices. They went about their business, blithely unaware that only a few feet away, the earth was shifting beneath Julian.

"Nevertheless, you are an earl. You belong in the London

drawing rooms. Your duty is to marry and create heirs. It's the way of things."

Julian's gut turned to ice. The world did not need another Travers. Therefore, Julian needed no heir. The logic was inescapable. He couldn't change the past, but he could ensure the Travers legacy did not continue.

He forced his fingers to release the windowsill. The war continued. Napoleon was a threat. He could prove to Sir Charles he was still useful and return to active duty. All he needed was the right leverage. The right mission. He thanked whatever fate had sent him to the filthy pubs lining the docks of France on his return home.

"I have information that may lead us to the traitor, sir." Julian faced his commander. He knew how to give a report. Straight shoulders. Steady gaze. No emotion. Only the facts mattered. "I may have found one of his contacts."

Sir Charles let out a resigned sigh. "How did you receive this information, Langford?" Impatient fingers tapped the scarred surface of the desk.

"From another British agent. Our paths crossed in Cherbourg." He stared steadily down at the spymaster. The desk seemed like an ocean of oak between them.

"Sit down, Langford." Sir Charles rubbed the back of his neck and sent Julian a baleful look. "My neck is beginning to ache from looking up at you."

"Yes, sir." Julian settled himself into the armchair facing the desk and resisted the urge to stretch out his long legs.

"Now give me your report."

"The agent overheard a conversation in a tavern while waiting for his vessel to sail. Two men were arguing about secret documents and whether they should be delivered to Cherbourg."

Sir Charles's brows rose. "What type of documents?"

"I don't have specific information. The agent was unable to pursue the men without compromising his own mission. However, he did overhear that the documents contained military information and the two men would talk to a Miss Gracie about the documents."

"Miss Gracie? Is that an alias?"

"With a few inquiries, the agent discovered Miss Gracie is Miss Grace Hannah. She lives in Devon with her uncle, Lord

Thaddeus Cannon. They live near Beer." Julian paused. "She is definitely not an innocent. Miss Hannah has strong ties to Jack Blackbourn."

"Blackbourn? I thought he had retired from smuggling."

"He has, sir. For now, at any rate. He's running a public house."

"I can't believe Blackbourn would abandon smuggling to be a publican." Sir Charles frowned, brows drawing together over cool brown eyes.

"I was surprised myself."

"Still, it would be easy enough to transfer military information to France through the smuggling channels," Sir Charles mused, absently reaching for his quill and tapping it against the desktop.

"If the documents were smuggled out of Devon by Grace Hannah, then someone in the War Office or Foreign Office gave her that information. There must be a channel of communication between them." Julian leaned forward, resting his elbows on his knees. "I believe we can flush out the traitor in London by pressuring the smugglers in Devon."

"A reasonable strategy." Sir Charles pursed his lips as he considered the feathers of the quill. Then, with a frustrated grunt, he tossed the quill down. "My best agents are all on the Continent. With so many agents compromised to the French, I don't have anyone I can send." He broke off, eyes narrowed as they focused on Julian. "Which you are perfectly aware of."

"Sir." He didn't shy away from the commander's gaze. Lying would be useless.

"Your family seat is in Devon."

"Yes." Childhood memories crowded Julian's mind. He gritted his teeth and willed the images away.

"Damn if I don't have a final assignment for you, Langford." Sir Charles steepled his fingers and regarded Julian over their tips. "I can't send you to France, but I can send you to Devon."

"Sir." His muscles tightened. Anticipation snaked through him. He had the opportunity he needed to prove himself. To avoid a slow and meaningless death by boredom. To prove he wasn't like his father. The mission hung before him, plump and ripe and as easy to pluck as any red apple.

Coiled muscles twitched at the perfunctory knock on the office door. Julian's head jerked toward the sound. He stared at the young man peering around the doorframe. Fashionably tousled brown curls topped a handsome face dominated by long-lashed brown eyes. The face, however, held a decidedly apprehensive expression.

"Sir?" Miles Butler's voice cracked on the word. "A dispatch has arrived for you from the foreign secretary."

"Thank you." Sir Charles held out his hand without looking at Mr. Butler. When the clerk did nothing, he glanced up. "The dispatch?"

"Oh, of course." The young man hastily crossed the room and laid the folded letter in Sir Charles's hand.

"Excuse me, Langford. I must read this before we continue," Sir Charles said distractedly as he broke the wax seal and perused the communication. Then he reached for his quill, dipped it in ink and began to scratch out a reply. He glanced at Julian as the quill bobbed across the page. "The circumstances in Devon require further inquiry. I expect you to conduct an expeditious investigation of Miss Hannah." Sir Charles ended the note with a flourish and blotted the ink.

"Yes, sir." Julian struggled to keep his voice calm. Success. He could taste it. If he found the traitor, Sir Charles would reinstate him. He knew it.

"Mr. Butler," Sir Charles said as he folded the note and sealed it. "See that my answer is delivered to the foreign secretary. Also, I'm sending the Shadow on a mission in Devon. I need you to inform him of the channels of communication for that area before he departs."

"I will, sir," Mr. Butler said, beaming. "Is there anything else I can assist you with? Any correspondence I can answer, sir?"

Sir Charles waved him away. "I'll notify you when I have another task for you."

Miles Butler backed out of the room. His shoulders had wilted, poor sod. Julian sent him an encouraging smile. He'd been just as young and earnest once. A lifetime ago.

"I expect to be informed of your progress in Devon at regular intervals," Sir Charles said after the door closed. "Use your discretion regarding what information should be relayed in person and what can be sent in writing. If we discover any new information in London, I will send word. In fact"—Sir Charles glanced at the door to the hall—"if anything new arises I'll send Mr. Butler to Devon as my emissary. You'll keep an eye on him and see he doesn't get into trouble, won't you?"

"Yes, sir." And he would send Mr. Butler back to London as quickly as he could.

"This is your final mission, Langford." Holding Julian's gaze steadily, Sir Charles leaned back in his chair. "When the investigation is complete, you may consider your service to His Majesty concluded and attend to your estates."

An angry protest rose in his throat, but he swallowed it. He'd bought a reprieve. "Understood, sir." He pushed himself out of the armchair to stand in front of Sir Charles's desk, waiting for dismissal.

Within minutes, Julian was flicking the reins to spur the matched bays harnessed to his high-perch phaeton. Instinct navigated him through the busy streets of London, but his mind was on treason.

Innocent soldiers fighting for England had died because of this traitor. The country was at risk, and the bastard had betrayed Julian. Fury lanced through him, hot and sharp. Retirement was simply not tolerable. *Retribution*, he thought. *Redemption*. He would pursue Miss Hannah, find the traitor, and turn him over to Sir Charles. Or kill the bastard.

Sir Charles would reinstate him if he found the traitor. He had to.

There was no alternative to spying.

# Chapter 2

"MOST UNFORTUNATE, MY lord." The valet's nasal tones cut through summer birdsong. He poked his head out of the open carriage door as the vehicle rolled to a stop in front of the Traverses' ancestral home.

"What is unfortunate, Roberts?" Julian shifted in the saddle as he reined in his mount. Beneath him, the horse's hooves danced over gravel, then stilled. Dust puffed up to hang in the humid air. "The heat or the dust?"

"Neither, my lord." Roberts squinted up at Julian's mount. "If I may say, the dust would not be such a difficulty if you traveled *inside* the carriage instead of on that ill-tempered beast."

"I'd rather be covered in dust than baking in that stifling carriage." Julian studied his valet and fought back a grin. The man's heat-flushed face resembled a bright red posy on the skinny stalk of his neck. Roberts stubbornly insisted on traveling inside the carriage, but that same stubbornness made him the perfect loyal assistant for a spy. "Besides, this ill-tempered beast carried me through enemy lines and back again. Come to think of it, Roberts, this beast saved your hide a time or two."

"True enough, my lord." Roberts sniffed and stepped gingerly onto the carriage step.

"In fact, I recall an escape from a jealous husband in Italy."

"My lord, I—she—" Roberts sputtered. "She had information necessary to the mission—"

"Oh, cheese it." Julian laughed. "You're an easy mark."

"Well." Roberts's lips twitched into a smile before he could hide it. He brushed a speck of nonexistent dust from his sleeve. "To return to our initial subject of unfortunate happenings, I was referring to our location. It's quite unfortunate your mission brought us to the wilds of Devon."

"Devon isn't wild, Roberts. A Parisian salon is considerably wilder these days." Julian dismounted to stand beside the valet. A groom jumped down from the carriage to take the reins.

"Perhaps," Roberts conceded. "Still, Devon isn't London or Brussels or Lisbon."

"Indeed not, but my informant tells me the traitor isn't in London or Brussels or Lisbon. The traitor is in Devon." He narrowed his eyes at the Jacobean architecture of his ancestral estate. He had intended to go the whole of his life without ever seeing it again. "She has much to answer for," he added softly.

"Quite." Roberts straightened his waistcoat, sent his thin nose into the air and turned to the carriage. "I shall see to the trunks, my lord."

"Good. I was beginning to wonder if the coachman would be required to hold the horses here indefinitely." He set his hand on Roberts's shoulder to take the sting from the words.

While Roberts grunted and muttered behind him, Julian stepped back to study the façade of the home he hadn't seen in twenty-three years.

Thistledown spread its wings across acres of green lawns and gardens brimming with bright summer blooms. Towers speared toward the vivid blue sky, long fingers reaching for the clouds. Mullioned windows caught the August sunlight and reflected it in a thousand tiny rays.

He hated the very sight of it.

It was unfortunate that Thistledown was only a few miles away from Grace Hannah. The traitor had sent him to the one place he'd vowed never to return to.

Wheels crunched over gravel as the carriage trundled toward the stables. Julian glanced at the wide front steps of Thistledown and sucked in a breath as memory flashed, as clear and focused as though it had happened yesterday. His father dragging him by the collar down those steps, kicking and screaming. Being tossed into the carriage and held down.

It was the last day either one of them had been there.

The day of his mother's funeral.

Anger stabbed through him. He did not have the choice to turn away. He could not climb onto his horse and ignore the memories.

He forced himself to take the front steps two at a time. Pushing open the heavy paneled front door, he stepped into the dark, cool interior and breathed deep. It smelled of home. Grief rose in him, bittersweet and raw. The clean scents of linseed oil and beeswax mingled with aged wood and dust. But the sweet scent of fresh flowers he remembered from his childhood was missing.

Julian let the door fall closed. Brooding silence surrounded him. He wasn't surprised at the lack of life. There were no residents at Thistledown aside from the butler and housekeeper, Mr. and Mrs. Starkweather. The other servants came only to do the necessary tasks to keep the house from falling into neglect and left again.

He poked his head into nearby rooms in search of the caretakers. Silence rang in the empty chambers. Fireplaces were bare and curtains were drawn. Furniture and paintings were draped in wraithlike dust covers, as though life had stopped and only ghosts remained.

As he turned away from the great hall, he heard laughter echoing. *Finally*, Julian thought. *Signs of life.* He followed the sound through the halls toward the upper kitchens. The air here carried the delicious scent of roasting meat. Savory herbs mingled with it and set his mouth watering.

Cautiously, Julian pushed open the door to the kitchen and paused on the threshold to scan the room. Mr. Starkweather, older and plumper around the midsection than Julian remembered, sat in his shirtsleeves at the kitchen table, a cup of tea and an empty plate before him. His feet were propped on an adjacent chair and he was gazing fixedly at the roasting oven.

Rather, he was gazing at what was in *front* of the roasting oven.

Two derrieres bobbed side by side. One was wide with ample hips that shook as its owner made a movement inside the oven.

The second, however, had slimmer hips with a bottom that was lush and rounded, and clad in a light wool riding habit that pulled tantalizingly against the curves it covered. A pair of serviceable leather ankle boots extended from the long skirts.

Yes, a fascinating view, thought Julian, eyeing the shapely bottom. And not bad as far as homecomings went.

"I think it could use a touch more rosemary. What do you think?"

Julian assumed the voice belonged to Mrs. Starkweather, the caretaker's wife.

"I agree. Perhaps basil might be added as well?" The second voice was younger, smoother, with the clear, modulated tones of an aristocrat. He could just make out a shining coronet of white-blond hair floating above the lady's shoulders.

"You know, basil might be just the trick," the older woman agreed. "Mr. Starkweather? Your preference?"

"I think your roast is superb, dear. But you should add whatever you think best."

"A diplomatic answer." The young woman's laugh bounced through the kitchen like a beam of silvered light on the air. "Clearly, you are the wisest of husbands, Mr. Starkweather."

Julian glimpsed a full, smiling mouth and delicate features as the young woman swung to face the butler. Her smiled died when her gaze lit on Julian. To his regret, the pretty features blanked.

Vaguely discomfited, as though he'd been revealed as a voyeur, he infused his smile with charm. "What incredible feast do I smell?"

The comment resulted in a flurry of movement. Mrs. Starkweather backed up and whirled around, narrowing her eyes for one long, appraising look. Mr. Starkweather jumped to his feet, frantically snatched his coat from the back of his chair and shrugged into it.

The young woman, however, exhibited no such distress. She didn't smile in greeting, but rather regarded him with the polite indifference of an ancient statue, pale as marble and carved of stone.

Unlike Mrs. Starkweather, who planted her hands on her hips and beamed at him. "Well, young master! I barely recognized you—it's been three years since you last had us brought up to London for an accounting. You are a sight for these old eyes!"

Julian plucked up the woman's hand and brought it to his lips. "Never old, my darling Mrs. Starkweather. Why, you're as lovely as ever." He bowed, adding a flourish to amuse her.

"Go on with you, Master Julian." Her round cheeks pinked. "Though I suppose you're 'his lordship' now. You should have told us you were coming. We would have readied everything for you. Instead, you give us not a word of warning."

"I do beg your pardon." Julian laughed. "I didn't know I would be taking up residence until the day I left London."

"Welcome home, my lord," Starkweather added to his wife's greeting, tugging his coat into place.

"Thank you." Julian sent an appreciative smile toward the caretaker.

Turning to the pretty blonde, he warmed his smile. She remained in precisely the same position, fingers linked together in front of her, quietly watching. Her eyes were silver gray, a perfect complement to the fair hair.

"I quite forgot myself!" Mrs. Starkweather gestured to the young woman. "My lord, may I present Miss Grace Hannah? She lives a few miles away."

Surprise had him quirking a brow before he slipped his mask into place.

How convenient to find Miss Hannah's head in his oven.

———

"Welcome home, my lord." Grace hoped her voice didn't crack. She hated to be caught unprepared. Forcing her fingers to loosen, she extended her hand to the earl in greeting.

"Miss Hannah, a delight to meet you." His lips curved, at once beguiling and sensual.

On purpose, she was certain.

She sent him a polite half smile as their gazes met over their linked hands. His eyes were the bright blue of a cloudless sky in midsummer, a color that would have been attractive if not for the calculating light behind them. Her pulse skittered as those shrewd eyes scanned her face.

"Had I known such a fair lady would greet my homecoming I would have returned fifteen years ago," he said.

"I would not have been here fifteen years ago." The words sounded stilted. She struggled to add something witty and engaging. "Your homecoming would have been bereft of my presence."

"Ah, then I shall be content with today, and count myself fortunate to be honored with your charming company."

He looked truly disappointed. But she knew the reputation of the Wandering Earl, as well as the reputation of his father, grandfather and great-grandfather. Wastrels, gamesters and womanizers, every one. A lady couldn't trust a rake and wastrel.

Then again, she wasn't a lady.

She schooled her features into the polite, expressionless face she had mastered for dealing with aristocrats and their ilk. "Regrettably, my company is about to end, as I must be on my way."

"Alas, must I be deprived of such beauty so soon?"

Her instincts leapt again as his watchful and cunning eyes continued to hold her gaze. The hair on her nape rose, sending a shiver down the line of her back. She suddenly felt like prey.

Uneasy, Grace collected her riding hat, more than ready to depart. She secured the plain hat by its long ribbons beneath her chin and wished it had been fashionable even three years ago, instead of five.

"Mrs. Starkweather, Mr. Starkweather, thank you for your hospitality. If you will excuse me, my lord? I must return home." Acknowledging the earl with a nod she hoped appeared regal, she turned toward the door to depart.

"I shall return as soon as I have escorted our guest to her carriage, Starkweather," the earl said.

"My lord, there's no need—" Grace began.

"There is every need. My afternoon would be incomplete without a few additional minutes of your delightful company." He offered his arm, extending it with a short half bow.

Nearly ten years of being the poor relation had taught her when to hide behind the pretense of submission. Resigned, she nodded in acquiescence and took his arm. It was strong and hard beneath her fingers. Their shoulders brushed, just the lightest touch as he steered her through the house. She felt the heat of him, and rising with it was the scent of man and leather and outdoors. Fresh, earthy and oddly appealing.

They left the silent interior of Thistledown and emerged into the bright August sun beyond. Grace glanced over at the earl, studying him quickly. His gaze absorbed the lawns, the drive, even the horizon in one quick glance. A breeze teased his light brown hair. The tips faded to gold at the ends, as though they had been dipped in sunlight. Lean and handsome features held a subtle tan that set off those blue eyes.

She turned away, refocused her attention on the grounds of Thistledown. It wouldn't do to be caught staring.

"Thank you for escorting me to the stables, my lord," she said.

"I take my duties as host quite seriously. Courtyards are dangerous places, you know." He smiled at her in that way people did when they shared a private jest. Flirtation came easily to him. "And I'm ever a gentleman, Miss Hannah."

Absurd. And amusing. She should remain quiet. She should refrain from responding to his banter. And yet—"It's quite difficult to traverse a courtyard, is it not?"

"Extremely. One must be forever on guard against wayward guests interrupting your walk."

"Or wayward residents." Gravel crunched beneath her feet.

"Residents as well," he agreed. "In fact, residents may be worse than guests, since they never leave." He paused, glanced around. "But where is your carriage?"

"I rode from my uncle's."

"What did you ride?" he asked, turning smiling eyes toward her. "A dainty palfrey so delicate her feet barely touch the ground? A proud, high-stepping mare? But no." He laughed. "Something more fantastic—a dragon covered in jewel-toned scales, perhaps? Or did you use your own exquisite wings? For surely only an angel could be so beautiful."

Hard-pressed not to laugh at the sheer nonsense of his words, she tried to keep her features bland. "None of those, my lord. I arrived on an ordinary horse."

"Alas. My enchanted visions dashed. Well, an ordinary

horse can be raised to extraordinary by its rider, as must be the situation here. I trust you do not have a difficult journey home?"

"I have lived at my uncle's estate for the last ten years. I probably will not lose my way," she said drily.

"I hope not." He slid a glance in her direction. "I may be a gentleman, Miss Hannah, but a few miles across the Devon countryside may be beyond my escort skills."

"Gentlemen are just not what they used to be." She sighed. Despite his amused smile, her mind chastised her tongue. What devil was pricking her sense of humor?

"Having lived here for so many years you are probably familiar with the people in the community and countryside," he said. "No doubt there would be any number of friends to help you find your way."

Grace cast a glance at the earl. The calculating, watchful look returned to his eyes, turning a rogue into a predator. "Indeed, my lord," she answered warily. "One can meet any number of people in ten years."

"I've met a fair number myself."

"In London?"

"And on the Continent."

"The Wandering Earl. I have heard the sobriquet."

"My reputation precedes me."

"You are an earl, my lord. The only one in these parts, in fact, which makes your various activities interesting."

"I haven't been to this part of Devon in years."

"That doesn't negate the fact that you are the only earl. The others are merely barons, knights, honorables, or, as in my case, mere misters and misses."

His eyes gleamed. "Somehow, I don't think you are a mere miss."

"I'd like to think you're correct."

The earl pulled open the stable doors and stood aside for her to enter. The faint scents of horse and hay drifted on the air. Grace let her eyes adjust to the dim light as he closed the door behind them. In the first stalls she saw what must be the earl's horses busily munching their feed. They passed the animals and Grace pointed to a large stall near the end of the row. "My mount is there."

As they approached the stall, a massive black horse thrust its head over the door. The stallion's head was huge, his eyes a little wild. Grace watched man and beast eye each other with distrust. The horse snorted, nostrils flaring, and a hoof pawed the ground. His ears pricked forward and a decidedly irritated glint appeared in his eyes.

"An ordinary horse, Miss Hannah? That horse is definitely not ordinary. In fact, he looks to be a Thoroughbred."

"Demon is descended from the Darley Arabian." She crossed the few feet to the stall that housed her stallion. The animal whinnied softly at her.

"I assume he earned the name *Demon*."

"Would you expect otherwise?" Grace stroked the stallion's muzzle. "Demon has the speed and stamina for racing, but not the temperament, poor fellow. He has trouble following directions. Which is why my uncle dislikes him and handed him off to me." She was lucky, really. If he didn't bring in a fee for acting as stud, her uncle would have sold him years ago.

The earl eyed the horse again. "I would be remiss, Miss Hannah, if I did not ask whether you could handle this animal. I don't believe I've met a lady that would ride a stallion."

"Such ladies are rare, I'm sure." She tilted her head, met his gaze. "But she only needs to know how best to handle the stallion."

He paused. The blue of his eyes was intense. "An interesting theory."

Grace glanced at the watch pinned to her riding habit. It was nearly five, and she was allowing herself to be caught up in a conversation she shouldn't have. She schooled her features. "It is past time for me to depart, my lord. I must return home to—" To what, she thought frantically. What could she tell him? To oversee dinner preparations? To ensure the linens were properly washed and aired?

"Beggin' yer pardon, Miss Gracie," a voice called out. A young groom hurried between the stalls, carrying Demon's saddle and other tack. "I would've 'ad Demon ready for you, but 'is lordship came home and is—"

"Right beside me," she said quickly.

"Milord." He acknowledged the earl with a nod before hurrying to saddle Demon. The horse shied away from the groom, as usual.

"I'll hold him steady." She slipped into the stall to murmur to Demon, stroking his forehead. When the groom stepped back she took the reins and led the horse through the stable and into the sunlit courtyard beyond.

She approached the mounting block, but the earl stayed her course.

"Allow me to assist." He linked his fingers together and offered her a leg up.

She couldn't politely refuse and leave him standing there. With an inward sigh, she placed her foot in his linked fingers and boosted herself onto the sidesaddle. Her breath caught, then rushed out again when he gripped her waist to steady her. His fingers, hot and strong, lingered for a moment, imprinting their heat onto her waist. He squeezed gently, then let his hands glide down her hips and drop away.

Breathing seemed impossible. The caress was intimate. Too intimate. Worse, her reaction—the sudden awareness of her body, the drumming of her pulse—was discomforting. She struggled to keep her expression serene.

"Welcome home, my lord. And good-bye."

She sprung the stallion into action, cantered down the graveled lane and through the iron gates.

---

JULIAN HELD UP his brandy glass and studied the liquor swirling within. An exceptional French brandy, probably smuggled. Perhaps by the lovely Miss Hannah herself.

She seemed an unlikely candidate for a smuggler. She was slender, even delicate despite her considerable height, with fine bones and nearly translucent skin. He knew she was the niece of a minor baron. Polite, refined, well educated. Yet she was connected to two smugglers in a tavern arguing about treasonous documents. Then there was the serene and composed expression. He found himself wondering what it concealed.

If anyone knew about masks, it was the Shadow.

He would peel away the outer layers of Grace Hannah to discover what lay beneath. What did Miss Hannah know, and how involved was she? Someone was smuggling more than spirits and tobacco, and the evidence indicated it was she.

He sipped the brandy, letting the liquid heat settle in his belly as he considered how best to approach her. Every suspect had a weakness. Hers just had to be found.

A knock sounded at the door. He tensed, reached automatically for a weapon, before deliberately relaxing his muscles.

"Enter."

"I've brought your supper, my lord." Mrs. Starkweather bustled into the room, a large tray in her arms. "I've a hearty roast and good fresh bread for your meal. Not as fancy as in London, I'm sure."

"It looks delicious."

She set the tray on a table near his armchair and busied herself straightening the cutlery and repositioning the plates.

"For dessert, there are Miss Gracie's blackberry tarts." She lifted the cloth covering them and revealed golden crust and deep purple-black filling. "I'm afraid there's only the two, though. Mr. Starkweather and I ate most of them when she was here earlier." She dropped the cloth over the pastries again.

"I've a fondness for pastries myself." He set down his brandy. "Do Miss Hannah and her tarts visit often?"

"About once a week for nearly—why, it must be six or seven years at least. I've near forgotten what it was like before Miss Gracie came, as that was probably ten years ago now." Mrs. Starkweather fluttered across the room to the fireplace. "You'll want light soon. The sun is starting to set."

"Yes, thank you. Miss Hannah must have been young when she came to Devon," he prompted. Information was as much a weapon as the knife in his boot.

"She was." Lighting the candelabra on the mantel, she continued her chattering monologue. "I remember seeing her in church that first time and thinking what a sad little thing she was. Those big gray eyes just brimming over with melancholy—then again, her parents had died and she'd been sent to Cannon Manor. A worse fate I can't think of, what with Lady Cannon just dead and no one to take the children in hand or direct the staff. The staff—" She broke off as she set the candles near the tray of food. "Forgive me, my lord. I didn't mean to forget my place."

"You've known me since birth, Mrs. Starkweather." He shook his head lightly. "You've no place to worry about."

"Well." She smiled at him and leaned forward in the manner of gossips everywhere. "The staff had been doing their best, of course, as staff always does, but with no mistress and Lord Cannon concerned with his own affairs, the manor was in a muddle. Miss Gracie soon put it to rights and that's that."

"Miss Hannah sounds resourceful."

"She is, my lord," Mrs. Starkweather chirped. "Why, she was Miss Cannon's governess after Miss Cannon drove away the last one—and what a chore *that* was. Miss Cannon is Miss Gracie's cousin, but she was no easier on Miss Gracie than she'd been on the other governesses. Neither were his lordship's sons. Miss Gracie had to mind them as well." Mrs. Starkweather shrugged philosophically. "Now she minds Cannon Manor, his lordship and the rest of us when called for. That's just Miss Gracie."

"A paragon of virtue." Except, of course, for the smuggling. And possible treason.

"Beg pardon, my lord?"

"It's not important, Mrs. Starkweather." He speared a bite of meat and swirled it around in the accompanying dark sauce before sampling it. The refreshing taste of basil lingered on his tongue, tempered by the sharp tang of rosemary and the bite of pepper. "The roast is delicious."

"Thank you, my lord." Beaming, she fluttered her hands at him. "Now, you just sit and enjoy your supper while Mr. Starkweather and I open the master's suite for you."

"Not the master's suite," he snapped. He would not sleep in that monstrosity of a bedroom. "Pick another bedchamber. Any other bedchamber."

"Yes, my lord." She sent him a questioning look. "What of the countess's chamber? It's been closed since . . . for a number of years."

His stomach churned, the roast burning like acid in his gut.

"Leave it." His voice was sharper than he'd intended. He softened it. "For now."

"Yes, my lord." Her chin lifted. They became servant and master again. She strode from the room, leaving Julian alone with his dinner.

He pushed away the half-full plate. An itch formed between his shoulder blades. He shrugged out of his coat, tugged at his cravat. He slid the knife from his boot and set it beside his brandy glass. Both glinted gold in the candlelight, mirror images of dancing flames.

Comfort and death, side by side. Much like his life. Right from the very beginning.

He picked up the brandy. Even that tasted foul, burning his throat and stomach. He set the glass down with a sharp snap.

He must face it, either now or later.

His footsteps echoed in the hushed and empty halls. The walk to the master suite felt long, but he could have done it in his sleep. He faltered outside the bedchamber door, unable to enter.

Buzzing filled in his ears and his heart began to pound. He shoved open the door, stepped through and snapped it shut, blocking out reality. He craved silence and space as he battled memory.

The centerpiece of the room was a massive four-poster bed wreathed in dark crimson hangings. He could remember his father taking his mistress to this room well before his mother's death.

An elaborate marble fireplace dominated one wall of the room. Again, the ghost of his father hovered. In his mind's eye, Julian saw him standing near the fireplace, tall and lean, with cruel blue eyes and a sharp-featured face. Memories surfaced of a glass thrown into the fireplace, the shards bouncing back into the room and slicing across his mother's face. It was only one of a hundred injuries she had suffered.

Julian turned from the fireplace and scanned the remainder of the room. A tall wardrobe hulked in one corner. Thick, dark rugs covered the floor and bulky curtains hung at the windows. His father had believed the heavy furniture and dark crimson and brown fabrics were masculine. Julian only found them oppressive.

He pulled open the door leading to the dressing room that adjoined these chambers with the countess's chambers. He strode through, intent on entering his mother's old rooms. But when his fingers grasped the handle of the chamber door he stopped, unable to turn the knob and step through.

His mother's image flooded his memory. He could remember her eyes bright and laughing, as well as wide with fear and shock. He could see her crying, even pleading with his father. And he could see her lying dead on the cold parquet floor.

Julian backed away from the countess's bedchamber, leaving the door shut tight. He couldn't enter, couldn't face it. Stumbling through the halls, he retreated to the library where his brandy glass waited. Crystal clinked as his shaking hands refilled the glass.

He picked up the knife. The hilt was cool against his palm. Solid. As familiar as the fingers gripping it. The symbol of what he'd become to prove he was not his father. To atone. Except death could not be undone.

If he had been stronger, braver, he might have stopped her death. He would never know, and that tortured him more than the fact that his father murdered his mother.

# Chapter 3

"MISS GRACIE! MISS Gracie! He's done it again."
Grace started, spilling powdered comfrey root onto her worktable. "Who's done what?" Using her fingertips, Grace delicately scraped the fine powder into a pile.

Cook bustled into Cannon Manor's stillroom, her flushed and shining face set into disgruntled lines. "His lordship."

Grace's fingers jerked. "His lordship?" Who? The Earl of Langford? What had he done?

"Your uncle. He's invited the gentlemen over without any notice. *Again*. How am I to plan dinner for six guests without proper notice?" Cook's ample bosom heaved with indignity. The ladle she carried sliced through the air, coming perilously close to Grace's face.

"I'm sure you'll manage, Cook. You always do." Of course it was Uncle. Why on earth had she thought of the earl?

"Common courtesy, I tell you." Cook attempted to shove her flaming red hair back into its haphazard bun. "It's common courtesy to give a body proper notice. What will the gentlemen think if they arrive for dinner and there's nothing to eat?"

Grace set aside the mortar and pestle. The comfrey root would have to wait. "What was planned for dinner tonight?"

"Fresh trout and venison, Miss Gracie, but there isn't enough trout for all the gentlemen. The gamekeeper offered to go fishing, but he might not catch anything—" The ladle arced again as Cook started tugging at her hair, setting the flames loose.

"Didn't farmer Cragman butcher a lamb yesterday?" She used her cotton apron to wipe the powder from her fingers. "As I recall he planned to bring by a leg of lamb."

"He brought two, Miss Gracie, in payment for you birthing their little one."

"Yes, I thought so." She tapped her forefinger against her upper lip as she formulated a menu. "Use the trout in the first course—trout en matelot, I think. Roasted leg of lamb can join the second course. For the third, perhaps a pudding or a cream. Do we still have blackberries?"

"We have enough for blackberry cream."

"Good. I shall arrange the proper wines for each course and provide Binkle with the list."

"Thank you, Miss Gracie. I knew you would know what to do." Cook bustled out in the same manner she had come in, waving the ladle and muttering about proper notice.

With a fond smile, Grace returned her attention to the mortar and pestle containing the comfrey root. With each pass of the pestle, she leaned into the tough root until she found the familiar measured rhythm. The monotonous task turned her thoughts inward.

What was wrong with her? The Earl of Langford arrived in Devon less than a week ago. She'd met him once. He shouldn't have entered her thoughts so quickly.

It must be that the local gossips, both gentry and laborers, discussed the earl continuously. The prodigal son returning to his ancestral home after twenty-three years was sensational news and would no doubt keep tongues busy for months.

With a vicious thrust of the pestle, Grace reminded herself there was no reason for her mind to dwell on him. No reason why her body should remember the feel of his hands or the heat of his fingers on her waist. She had learned long ago that physical desire meant nothing.

Of course he was a rake and a rogue. He was a Travers. What more did she need to know? Still, it wasn't her place to criticize the Earl of Langford. She was only the Cannon family's poor relation.

She pushed a loose strand of hair out of her eyes and

looked out the window at the bouncing blooms delineating Cannon Manor's pathways. Her eyes didn't see the delicate white clusters of yarrow, the bloodred amaranthus, or the pale purple nigella that bordered the walkways.

She rubbed a hand over her chest, as though doing so would ease the lonely ache that had settled there. Why did she feel this way? Why did the darkness so often drag her down, like cold fingers tugging at her?

She shrieked when a shadow blocked the light from the ancient window. Her heart gave a terrified leap that had her gasping for air. It was a moment before she recognized the grotesque mask as a face blurred by the glass's impurities. The abundance of whiskers pressed against the window told Grace it was the village cabinetmaker. She gestured him in through the door to the kitchen gardens, still trying to catch her breath.

"Beg pardon, Miss Gracie." The man whipped his hat from his head as he stepped over the threshold.

"It's all right," she said, still patting her chest lightly. "What can I do for you?"

The cabinetmaker began running the worn brim of his hat nervously through his fingers. "It's young Ben, Miss Gracie. He's got the croup, I think."

Concern washed through her. "Is he having trouble breathing?"

"Some. It's not too bad yet. I remember when my oldest girl had the croup and it's not near that bad, but the missus is worried sick."

"I'm sure she is," Grace murmured, moving toward her cabinets. She began to sort through jars and bottles, measuring out roots and dried leaves as she spoke. "Try to keep him sitting up. It will ease his breathing. He may have an attack in the middle of the night. If he does, I want you to come straight here and wake me, no matter what time it is. You know the nighttime procedure?" She glanced at him, brows raised in question.

"Knock on the third window from the right of the kitchen door to wake the butler."

"Correct. Binkle will know where to find me." She handed him the small packet of dry ingredients she had mixed. "This is marshmallow root, mullein, elm and licorice. Use the blend to make tea and give it to Ben twice a day. The tea doesn't taste particularly good so he may not like it, but try to make him drink it. Add honey for flavor if you have it."

"I will. Thank you." He cleared his throat awkwardly. "I know you need new doors for the cabinet in his lordship's pantry. I'll have those made for you by next week."

Grace desperately wanted to tell him that no payment was necessary, but she knew he would insist.

"I'll see you next week then," she replied. "Remember, come to the manor and wake me if Ben has any problems in the night, no matter what time it is."

"I will, Miss Gracie," he repeated, disappearing through the door.

Grace returned to the crushed comfrey root. She emptied the powder onto a battered set of silver scales for proper measurement. After measuring out an acceptable portion, she brushed the fine granules into a muslin sachet and set it aside. She hadn't finished measuring the second batch when there was another knock, this time from the door inside the manor.

"Miss Gracie?" The butler's reedy voice issued from a thin face perched upon a long neck and narrow shoulders.

"Yes, Binkle?"

"A messenger arrived from Lord and Lady Hammond with an invitation. Lord Cannon stated he will attend the Hammonds' gathering and bade you to formulate the appropriate response."

He held out the invitation. Grace wiped her hands on her apron before accepting it. As usual, it was addressed to Thaddeus Cannon as well as to Grace, though she hadn't attended an assembly in years. The occasion was a ball, with the Earl of Langford as the guest of honor to welcome him back to the community.

"I'll write the response, Binkle."

"Certainly. I will see that it is delivered to Lady Hammond."

She stepped into the hall and used the heavy ring of keys she always carried at her waist to lock the door. With its comforting mix of spices, sweet flowers and earthy herbs, the stillroom tucked in the rear of Cannon Manor often served as her refuge, but it contained expensive herbs and spices and even substances that were poisonous.

Grace slipped through the hall, Binkle at her heels, intending to go to her tiny personal sitting room. But her uncle, Lord Cannon, appeared in the hall before her. He was dressed in his usual riding breeches and coat. Buttons gaped and seams strained, so that he appeared to be a little round sausage stuffed into the casing of his clothing.

Grace automatically moved to the side of the hall to allow Lord Cannon to pass, Binkle doing the same behind her. But Lord Cannon stopped in the hall and turned to face her.

"You will answer Lady Hammond's invitation as directed." The thick brown mustache that bisected his face twitched as he spoke.

"Yes, Uncle." Grace folded her hands in front of her and bowed her head slightly in the manner her uncle deemed proper.

"You will see to it that my guests have every comfort available to them this evening."

"Of course, Uncle. I have already made arrangements—"

"Just see that it's done," he interrupted, rocking back on his heels.

The crunch of gravel came through the open windows in the rooms beyond. Cannon frowned. "Who's calling?" he demanded of Grace.

"I don't know, Uncle."

"Well. Get the door, Binkle." Cannon waved his riding crop toward the butler as if to shoo him along.

"Of course, my lord." Binkle jerked, a quick spasm as though his body suddenly realized he was supposed to be manning the door. He spun on his heel and dashed toward the front of the manor.

Grace would not, of course, be invited to greet the caller. She *should* leave her uncle to his guest and go about her duties, but curiosity had her trotting behind Lord Cannon, staring at the bald circle on the top of his head while he stomped along behind Binkle. It was so rare for Lord Cannon to have an unplanned caller.

They reached the front hall. Binkle tugged his coat into place, then drew a deep breath and straightened his narrow shoulders. Grace could hear Lord Cannon's riding crop thwacking lightly against his thigh and knew he was becoming impatient. She opened her mouth to tell Binkle to hurry, but subsided when she saw Binkle reach for the polished door handle. The butler swung the door open and Grace craned her neck to see past Lord Cannon.

A carriage was rolling to a stop before the steps, the wheels grinding and tumbling the gravel beneath them. A groom hopped down from his position in the rear and lowered the steps. One Hessian boot landed on the top step. The second planted itself beside the first. Grace could see the austere front of Cannon Manor reflected in their glossy shine. Her eyes followed the length of the boots up to light breeches covering well-muscled legs.

Shaking her head at her own audacity, Grace looked away. She shouldn't have noticed the man's legs. Grace tried to concentrate again on the little bald circle on the back of Lord Cannon's head. Her uncle's presence alone should deter her from improper stares. She'd suffer yet another lecture if he caught her.

Grace faded into the doorway of the nearest salon. The visitor would certainly be calling on her uncle. She should go about her household duties.

Yet she didn't move. Rooted to the spot, she worried Lady Hammond's invitation in her hands and listened to the Hessians crunching on gravel as they approached the door. She could only see the hall table and its vase of summer flowers through the open salon door, but she could hear a murmur from Binkle, then an answering murmur.

"My Lord Cannon, may I present the Earl of Langford," Binkle called out.

Her heart bumped, one quick knock against her ribs. What was the Earl of Langford doing at Cannon Manor? Perhaps he'd decided to complain about her impertinent conversation. Her tongue so often let loose at inappropriate moments.

Looking down at the invitation twisted between her fingers, she waited for Lord Cannon's angry bellow. It didn't come. She smoothed the expensive paper and forced her shoulders to relax. Until she heard her uncle's words.

"Come into the salon, my lord."

Now her heart pounded in earnest. Ignoring it, she forced her breathing to remain even and pasted a polite smile on her face. There was no escaping the earl now.

*He's so handsome.*

It was her first thought when the earl stepped into the room. Handsome and charming in fashionable breeches and a dark coat. He smiled in greeting when his eyes landed on her.

Heat flooded her cheeks. Why couldn't she have removed her apron? The dress beneath was years out of fashion, but at least it wasn't as ragged as the cotton apron.

"Miss Hannah! A delight to see you again." He bowed with as much flourish as he had in the kitchens of Thistledown.

Lord Cannon visibly started. His brows drew together and she could almost hear him wondering how the earl had met her before. A tirade was imminent, though she hoped Lord Cannon would wait until the Earl of Langford departed.

"I won't be staying but a few minutes, Lord Cannon." The earl's long fingers reached for his watch chain and ran the gold through his fingers. "I wanted to make a brief social call and reacquaint myself with my neighbors. May I also say, Miss Hannah, how much I enjoyed our conversation the other day?"

Lord Cannon's mustache bristled. "Well now, Langford, my niece has never been to London. I'm certain you haven't met her."

"But I have." His eyes twinkled as they met Grace's. "She was in my oven when I arrived at Thistledown."

Grace closed her eyes, taking a long moment to collect herself before attempting to explain the meeting to Lord Cannon in a manner that would not anger him. "I was advising his housekeeper on the proper technique for preparing a roast."

Lord Cannon narrowed his eyes but didn't query further.

"Um. If you'll excuse me, Uncle? My lord?" She edged toward the door. Perhaps she could escape without saying something utterly ridiculous.

"Forgive me for being improperly inquisitive, Miss Hannah," the earl said. "I recognize the crest atop that stationery in your hand. I received an invitation to Lady Hammond's ball as well."

Looking down, Grace again read the elegant script. "I'm sure you did, my lord. You are the guest of honor, of course, and one mustn't forget to send an invitation to the guest of honor."

"It would be a monumental oversight in the planning stages of a ball, I imagine," the earl replied, "and quite embarrassing when the remaining guests arrived and the guest of honor was mysteriously absent."

*Thwack!* The riding crop slapped against Lord Cannon's leg. Grace knew the sound. Disapproval. Impatience.

"I must go," Grace said. "Please excuse me."

"Please tell me that you will be attending the ball, Miss Hannah."

*Thwack! Thwack!* The riding crop's rhythm increased and the sound sharpened. Grace could feel her uncle's cold brown eyes boring into her. She forced herself to keep her gaze on the earl.

"No, I'm sorry. I can't attend."

"But you must, fair lady. The ball would be nothing without your enchanting presence."

"I—"

"She cannot, Langford," Lord Cannon interjected.

"Please say you will," the earl cajoled, ignoring Lord Cannon. "Or I shall not attend myself. And as you said, the guest of honor must attend."

"Er. Well." Her fingers twisted the invitation of their own accord. She couldn't possibly attend. She hadn't attended any social function in nearly seven years. Not since the fiasco she'd caused. Uncle would be furious.

Then the earl smiled and oh, it was full of temptation. All caution died in the light of that smile.

"Yes, my lord."

*Thwack-thwack-thwack-thwack-thwack!*

"Wonderful, Miss Hannah!" The earl reached for her hand again. "You must save me the first dance."

His fingers were long, the pads interestingly callused. He rubbed his thumb against her palm, tickling the sensitive skin. The movement was so intimate, so shocking, she struggled to hold back the gasp.

His eyes gleamed. He *knew* what his touch had done to her. The delighted quirk of his lips proved it.

"Of course, my lord. I would be pleased to dance with you." Flustered, the words tumbled out of her. "If you will excuse me?"

"Grace has urgent duties she must attend to," her uncle said. His eyes snapped with fury as looked at her. "Please excuse her."

"Of course. Miss Hannah, the pleasure has been mine. I look forward to our dance." The earl squeezed her fingers before letting her hand slide away. "Lord Cannon, I would be happy to further our acquaintance."

As Grace quit the room, she heard her uncle say, "A brandy, then."

*What had she gotten herself into?*

She strode to her sitting room and shut the door carefully behind her. Sighing, Grace paced to the escritoire. She propped the wrinkled invitation against a stack of ledgers and stared at it.

Withdrawing her acceptance would be wiser than attending. She wouldn't embarrass her uncle, nor would she make a fool of herself. She wouldn't have to struggle to find the appropriate pleasantries for the neighbors. Nor would she see Michael—her former betrothed—and his gorgeous wife, who would certainly attend.

Closing her eyes, Grace breathed slowly in and out to calm her pounding heart. If she went, she would have to be on the dance floor, with the earl, in front of everyone. Naturally, her conversation would be stilted, her comments gauche. She'd trip over her own feet or trod on the earl's toes, and every one of the guests would observe her clumsiness.

A low groan sounded in the room and Grace's eyes popped open. Looking around, she saw she was alone. The groan had been hers. Of course.

Voices carried down the hall. She heard the earl murmur something unintelligible at this distance. Her uncle responded and she heard a distinct "good-bye." Then footsteps pounded down the hall, rhythmic, sharp, and growing louder every moment. She held her breath and prepared for the storm.

The door flew open, hinges squeaking in protest. Lord Cannon rounded on her. His skin was mottled and purple right up to the crown of his head. "What are you about?" he roared. "You don't belong at Lady Hammond's ball!"

"I know, Uncle." Grace gripped her fingers together and looked at the crumpled invitation propped on her desk. "But you heard the earl. He wouldn't attend if I didn't—"

"He doesn't know who you are, so he doesn't know better. But *you* do."

"I couldn't refuse." Of course she could have. She hadn't wanted to.

"He was *flirting* with you. It cannot be tolerated." His riding crop flicked through the air. "This will be your first assembly since Michael Wargell jilted you. You'll likely meet his wife. Don't embarrass me."

"No, Uncle. I won't." What would she say to the Wargells? To anyone?

"And for God's sake, *don't* make a fool of yourself with the earl!" Lord Cannon stalked out, his stride matching the furious rhythm of the riding crop.

She knew most of the gentry, visited their homes with various poultices and tonics and advice. But she didn't *socialize* with them. Certainly not since Michael had left her two steps from the altar. She simply didn't belong.

Unfortunately, she had foolishly agreed to attend and, worse, promised her first dance.

The image of the Earl of Langford's laughing eyes bloomed in her mind, and with it, all the promise of excitement and the social suicide of breaking her promise of the first dance. No, she would have to attend.

Before she had time to think, she opened a small drawer. One by one she retrieved a quill, paper and an inkwell, before scratching her reply to the invitation.

*Lord Thaddeus Cannon and Miss Grace Hannah gratefully accept your invitation.*

She blotted the response, sealed it and strode into the hall. On a delicate wooden table near the door lay two letters, waiting to be mailed. She set her reply onto the table for a footman to deliver to Lady Hammond, but her hand refused to drop away. It hovered above the response, fingers poised to pluck it off the table and shove it into her apron pocket.

No. Her hand flew back, leaving the crisp cream stationery in the salver. She'd made a promise, so she would attend and pretend she knew what she was doing.

Heaven help her.

She fingered her apron as she continued to stare at the dried ink and rounded letters of her response. Edginess crept in, sending a rush of nervous energy through her. She needed to move. To breathe.

# Chapter 4

"I'M GOING TO walk from here," Julian called to the coachman, pounding a fist lightly on the ceiling of the carriage. The brilliant sky—so much larger here than in London—had sent out fluffy white clouds to tempt and tease him into the fields.

"Are you sure, milord? It's nearly two miles to Thistledown," the coachman called back.

"Yes." Julian jumped from the carriage and waved the vehicle away before turning to the vista that rolled out before him. Field melded with field, creating a patchwork of green and gold bordered by dry stone fences or hedgerows.

If his memory was correct, some of the land before him belonged to other landowners in the area, but he was certain the farther fields were part of his own estate. He wondered where his own borders were. He had never wanted to know before. He didn't want to know now, either, particularly. He would be returning to London as soon as the traitor was flushed out.

He stepped from the dirt lane and onto the springy turf. Breathing deep, he took in the tangy scent of grass and damp earth. He tramped through a field, then another, listening only to the drone of bees and bleating of sheep.

Much of the terrain had changed in the past quarter century. Flashes of memory accompanied particular views, but they were so brief he only retained impressions. Then he recognized a large oak, its branches spreading over a stone fence swathed in blooming pink clematis and dark green moss.

He'd sat in the dappled sunlight on this fence as a child. Nostalgia rose in him, a bittersweet pang that burned his throat and caught him by surprise. He settled beneath the oak, leaning against the rough stones. The ground was dry but soft, the earth warm from the summer heat. Around him, flowers rioted over the wall, their sweet scent filling the air.

Fingering the delicate blossoms, Julian contemplated his strategy. He'd thought of simply forcing information from Grace Hannah. If she were innocent, however, it would do her a disservice. If she was involved and fled because of the pressure he put on her, it might also alert the traitor in London. Similarly, he couldn't directly demand an answer from her. She could inform the traitor, who could go to ground indefinitely. That was something he could not tolerate.

He needed to determine what avenue he could explore. There were numerous smugglers in the area who might have information, but penetrating their ranks without some leverage or an idea of who might be involved would be a futile exercise or, once again, alert the traitor. But it was a risk he'd have to take.

He would pursue Miss Hannah. It would be no hardship to further that acquaintance. A light flirtation, a hint of courtship. Perhaps something more carnal, though he'd never been one to take flirtation too far in his work. To use a woman's body, to use his own that way—even for the good of the country— would make him no better than his father.

The sound of hooves thudding against earth interrupted his solitude. Julian turned to see the oncoming rider. His lips curved when he realized it was the subject of his thoughts, fast approaching on her magnificent stallion.

"Why, Miss Hannah," he murmured to himself as he watched the pair race over the ground. "Whatever are you doing riding astride?"

Not only was she riding astride, she was galloping across the field as though all the demons of hell chased her. Her skirts billowed and whipped behind her. Surely the rules of propriety weren't so lax in the country that a lady's ankles and calves were a common sight? She wore no hat and the sun glinted on her hair.

Julian *knew* there was more beneath the serene mask she hid behind. No one could take such a tumultuous, reckless ride and throw propriety to the wind without passion. Julian admired the melding of woman and horse, their lean bodies moving as one as they approached a low hedgerow. Together, they seemed to gather their energy before soaring gracefully over the earth and shrubs.

Their unity spoke of an affinity that surpassed mere horsemanship or even innate skill. Horse and rider shared a bond, some understanding or connection. He continued to study Miss Hannah as her words about the magnificent stallion at their first meeting echoed through his memory. *Demon has the speed and stamina for racing, but not the temperament, poor fellow. He has trouble following directions.*

Horse and rider were now close to the wide oak he sat under. Miss Hannah showed little sign of slowing. She may not see him and take the stone fence as a jump. If so, he would lose an opportunity that might lead him to the traitor.

With a quick push, Julian drew himself up to standing and raised a hand in greeting. He knew the moment she noticed him. Her face tensed with surprise. She leaned forward in the saddle, as though to urge the stallion on past man and tree. Then her shoulders slumped and she turned the stallion toward him. Julian could all but hear her resigned sigh. Propriety won out. This time. If he was any judge of character, it didn't win every time.

That would be his advantage.

She slowed, drew close. He could see her repositioning her leg, sliding it from the stirrup, around the old-fashioned high pommel and to the other side. Amused, he watched her spread her skirt to cover the saddle, as though she thought the lack of sidesaddle would go unnoticed.

"Good afternoon, my lord." Breathless from the ride, her words came out between light gasps. Her cheeks were flushed from the heat and loose tendrils of hair trailed around her face. He found her mussed appearance even more tempting than the mask that begged to be stripped away.

"Good afternoon, Miss Hannah. I must be favored by the gods to be given the gift of your beauty twice in one day. Out for a ride in the warm summer air before it fades to autumn?" He gestured vaguely in the direction of the sky.

"Indeed. Demon needed a good run." She patted the stallion's neck.

The horse, too, panted from the gallop, but his sounds weren't nearly as interesting as the little pants coming from Miss Hannah. Her breasts rose and fell in the most delightful manner with each inhalation. The action combined with her mussed appearance brought all sorts of erotic images to mind, most particularly of the serene Miss Hannah rising above him, her white-blond hair spilling over her shoulders and breasts.

He couldn't stop the wicked smile.

———————

GRACE DREW IN a deep breath to slow her ragged gasps. She tried to smooth her skirts over the saddle once more before abandoning the effort. He would know she wasn't on a sidesaddle. By attempting to hide it she'd probably drawn more attention to the fact.

Worse, she was certain she looked disheveled, windblown and, given her fair skin, flushed from the heat. Her fingers ached to dive into her hair and tuck the loose ends back in place, but the action would emphasize the disordered mass.

The earl, of course, looked both handsome and relaxed, leaning against the old stone fence as though he were in no more an unusual place than his own drawing room. Jacketed arms were crossed over his chest and booted feet were crossed at the ankles. The wind ruffled the hair around his lean face, highlighting the seductive smile.

She cast around her mind for polite conversation. "Are you enjoying your afternoon, my lord?"

"Very much. I have been reacquainting myself with Thistledown's lands, as I did with the inhabitants of Beer this morning," the earl said. He looked into the distance as he spoke, as though seeing something in his memory. "I'd forgotten how close Thistledown is to the sea. Do you ever get to the seaside, Miss Hannah?"

"Often," she replied. Unease rippled up her spine as his eyes met hers, intense and focused. His tongue might be gilded, but his watchful eyes gave him away. He was seeking information. But what, and why? "The sea is only a few miles from here."

"Not everyone enjoys the water. Do you?"

"I do."

"I imagine the smugglers do as well."

"Smugglers, my lord?" Grace struggled to keep her face expressionless as her heart thumped. "I imagine they must enjoy the water, given their profession, but I wouldn't know for certain." *Except that she knew nearly every smuggler from Seaton to Sidmouth.*

"I've heard the coast is rife with smugglers," the earl continued easily. "I'd be most disappointed if it isn't true. I had hoped for some excitement down here in the country."

"Looking to join the smugglers, my lord?"

"Would that thrill you? Would you find me dashing and dangerous and attractive?" The melodramatic tone of his question made her smile.

"I'd certainly keep the information in mind," she answered tartly. "If the customs officers appear at my door I can turn you in for the reward money." Even as the words left her lips, she wished she could take them back.

The earl didn't seem to mind her wayward tongue. "You wound me, fair lady." With overdramatic flair, he placed his free hand over his heart.

She nearly snorted, but managed to keep her features bland. "Hopefully it's not too deep a wound, as I've nothing to stanch it."

He laughed, long and loud, letting his head fall back. The sound filled her, sending warmth all the way down to her toes.

Demon pranced to the side, reminding Grace of her precarious position on his back. She easily brought him under control again. When she looked up, the earl was watching her intently, his gaze full of admiration.

"Demon truly is a magnificent animal," the earl said. "In fact, I expect he could outrun the customs officers."

"Are you thinking of taking him out on loan when you join the smugglers?"

"I would, but I'd lose my dashing reputation among the ladies if I'm riding one of their horses. I'm certain the famous smuggler Jack Blackbourn would never borrow a horse from a lady."

"Jack would borrow anything if it meant escape, including his wife's petticoats," she said wryly. "Escape *is* escape, after all."

"A smuggler must be prepared for every eventuality and use what comes to hand." He propped one booted foot on the stone fence and rested his arms on his knee.

"It sounds as though you have given this a great deal of thought."

"I *have* been looking to take on a career." He tapped a finger against pursed lips, appearing deep in thought.

"The Wandering Earl isn't a career?"

"A gentleman must have some excitement in his life. Smuggling would be just the thing, don't you think?" He plucked a pink clematis from the blooms trailing across the stone wall. Stepping forward, he offered it to her. "As I asked before, would that thrill you?"

This time there was no melodramatic hand over his heart or laugh in his voice. Instead, he purred the words, his tone silky and low. The sound slid along her senses, soft and seductive, even as the petals of the clematis slid along her skin as she accepted his offering.

"I doubt it would thrill me, my lord. Smugglers are plentiful along the coastline and I'm certain I've met a few already." The flower fluttered in the breeze as she tucked it into the bodice of her simple gown.

"Ah, but I would be a different sort of smuggler," he answered, raising a hand and settling it on Demon's neck. The horse's hide rippled beneath the earl's hand as though the animal luxuriated in the man's touch. "I would no longer be the Wandering Earl. I'd be the Smuggling Earl. The wild rake that took on the high seas, outrunning the customs officers and Boney's ships."

Grace watched the long, strong fingers caressing Demon's dark hide. Fascinated, she continued to stare as his fingers moved down the horse's neck and came to rest inches from the saddle. Inches from her.

She cleared her throat. "I doubt anyone could compete with Jack Blackbourn."

"A challenge?" He raised his brows and sent her a slow, considering smile. "Perhaps I should join and see if I can't be more exciting than the famous Blackbourn. Perhaps I will be able to turn your head. Perhaps I'll sweep you away to sea and prove just how exciting I could be."

His tone continued in that silky purr that shivered up her spine. She knew now the tales of the Wandering Earl were true. A man who looked like that, spoke like that, had certainly captivated dozens of women. He apparently wanted to add her to his list of accomplishments.

Despite knowing of his skill with women and his reputation, she still found herself drawn to him. She angled her head, pursed her lips. "Are you certain I haven't been swept away to sea already, my lord? Perhaps I've had my fill of excitement."

"Not the type of excitement I could show you." His honey-eyed words swirled about her, seducing her.

"I'm certain I don't need your particular sort of excitement." The words sounded more confident than she felt. Inside, deep inside, she felt warm and taut and urgent.

"No? After witnessing your reckless ride, I'm not so certain." His hand slid once more across Demon's broad shoulder. Only a breath away from her thigh. "Let me escort you back to Cannon Manor."

The sensuous caress of his voice sent a shudder through her. *Yes.* Her body all but screamed it. Every inch of her seemed enlivened so that even the air gliding over her skin inflamed.

She needed to ride once more, to relieve the energy pent up within her. Frantic for some release from the spell woven around her, she glanced around for the earl's horse.

"Your mount, my lord?"

"I don't have one, Miss Hannah. I'm on foot. But you wouldn't leave me stranded here, would you?"

Her hands tightened on the reins. "I might."

"Forcing me to walk all the way back to Thistledown in this stifling heat? What if I were to overheat? Go into convulsions or the vapors?" A melodramatic hand wiped imaginary sweat from his brow and Grace couldn't stop the little smile that pulled at her lips.

"For an aspiring smuggler you're not very hardy, my lord."

"Again you wound me, fair lady! Striking at the heart of my manhood!"

This time she laughed, unable to keep the sound at bay when he clutched at his heart.

"You must rescue me, Miss Hannah. Carry me to the safety of Thistledown where my wounds may be ministered to." His dramatic expression turned wily. "Unless, of course, you're afraid of my sort of excitement?"

She sucked in a breath. It was a challenge. Did she dare? He'd know that she was riding astride—if he didn't already, given the lack of a slipper stirrup. It would be the most improper position, together on a horse. What if someone saw them?

The earl remained beside the stallion, his gazed fixated on her. The calculating look had returned to his eyes and she knew he was after something. Still, she couldn't ride away without answering his challenge.

"Very well, my lord." She tossed her head. "Mount."

She moved forward on the saddle as far as possible, grateful for the high pommel of her uncle's out-of-date saddle as she hooked her knee around it. The earl placed a foot in the stirrup. A moment later he was seated behind her in the saddle.

Demon danced sideways at the additional weight and she focused on controlling the uneasy stallion. Even as she fought to calm the animal, a part of her was focused on the earl. There was barely enough room for them both and Grace could feel the heat from his chest against her back. His hands circled her waist, resting there as she calmed Demon.

The earl leaned forward and murmured in her ear, "There would be more room if you rode astride. I won't tell and I promise not to look at your ankles—even though I'll be tempted." His husky voice echoed through her, the dare heating her blood.

*Oh, dear God, please let no one see me*, she prayed.

She hitched up the skirts of her simple gown and swung her leg over the horse's broad back. She knew her ankles and calves were exposed. She didn't care.

She slid forward until her front pressed against the pommel of the saddle. Even with the additional space, they were fitted together in the same position. She could feel him pressed intimately against her backside, his hard, muscular thighs aligned with hers. The earl's strong hands curled around her waist as a steadying hold, fingers splayed across her belly. Over it all was the knowledge that her legs were opened wide, with his body straddling hers.

The earl leaned forward once more, hot breath tickling her ear. "Ride," he commanded.

She didn't hesitate. The thrill of the adventure drove her forward as she spurred the horse.

They flew across the fallow field, both Grace and the earl bent low across the saddle, bodies nearly united as they moved in tandem with the rhythm of the horse. Limb brushed limb and the heat from their bodies mingled. The earl's fingers gripped her waist, digging into the pliant skin beneath the light cotton. Wind whipped around and between them, pulling at Grace's hair and whistling in her ears.

A low hedgerow appeared before them. Without even a moment's deliberation, she sent the horse soaring over it. Time seemed to stop as they hung suspended in the air. She felt the earl's body brace for the landing even as her own body tensed. Demon thudded to the ground on the other side of the hedgerow before continuing across the next field.

Exhilarated, Grace laughed loud and long, all sense of decorum abandoned. Her braided hair finally loosed from its pins and she could feel the wind whipping through the long strands. Lost in the moment and uncaring that her unbound hair would be streaming into the earl's face, she leaned forward over the pommel. The earl did the same until his face was over her shoulder. His breath was ragged in her ear, but she could feel the pleasure in her body echoing in his. He seemed to vibrate with energy behind her.

She urged Demon faster, then faster still, and even the animal seemed to relish the sheer abandon of the moment.

Grace wished she could go on forever. The freedom and joy of the ride bubbled in her blood until she was full of heat and light and energy. But the aged brick of Thistledown came into view on the horizon and she knew she must stop. She couldn't be this woman, this free spirit.

She reined in and the horse slowed to a canter, then a walk. When the horse stopped, they sat still for a moment.

She swore she could feel the earl's heart pounding against her back.

He swung to the ground, then eased her from the saddle before she had a chance to protest. She braced herself on his shoulders.

"The horse needs to rest." He was breathing hard. She saw the same exhilaration in him that coursed through her veins. His hands were on her waist, hers resting on his biceps. He leaned in, breathed deep. "My God—"

He broke off, drew in another breath. Lost in the thrill of the ride she could only stare at his eyes, as blue as the August sky behind him. He leaned in farther, lips close to hers. He hesitated, giving her the chance to run. She knew what would happen, knew the inevitability of it. And she wanted it— wanted him—in a way that was both foreign and familiar, and filled her with the same fire as the ride.

She didn't run. Instead, she gripped his arms and lifted to her toes to meet his lips. When his mouth touched hers, it was neither gentle nor demanding. Instead, it was simply there for her to take from, to use as she wanted.

Emboldened, filled with her own recklessness, she pushed her hands to his shoulders and pressed her lips more fully to his. His mouth opened beneath hers and she darted her tongue between his lips. He tasted hot and salty and male.

He groaned and pushed his hands into her loose hair, taking control of the kiss. The demand was there now, the need clear in his foraging tongue and agile lips. His hands worked through her hair, then cupped her cheeks as he drew her against him. She obeyed, hungry for the forbidden. As their bodies met and breath mingled, Grace knew what she had been missing for so long. The *something* she could never define but that left a hole within her. It was this heat, the fire in the blood and the lust that pooled in her belly.

But even as she craved more he pulled away. His fingers still lay against her flushed cheeks, his breath coming in sharp puffs.

"Miss Hannah, I—"

"Don't apologize, my lord." She wouldn't be able to bear it. Grace managed to keep her tone light despite the fire that raged within her. "Smugglers never apologize."

She stepped back and his fingers dropped away. Gathering her skirts, she whirled around. Without waiting for assistance—what did propriety matter now?—she mounted Demon astride. She wheeled the horse around and set off at a canter, leaving the earl standing in the empty field behind her.

She knew he watched her go, could feel his gaze on her back. But she refused to turn around and glance behind. Somehow that would cost her the challenge, and she knew she'd won this round between them.

*Chapter 5*

THE BEST TIME for espionage was the deepest part of the night.

A sliver of the waxing crescent moon shone through light clouds and onto Cannon Manor. Its windows should have been dark and silent, its inhabitants asleep. But they were not.

At the edge of the graveled drive, Julian rolled his shoulders and studied the pathetic, swaybacked nag standing in front of the manor house. Its rider had dismounted and was even now standing at the side kitchen door. The door itself was open, revealing a single candle and the silhouette of a second man.

The visitor gestured impatiently, the resident responded in kind, and the door swung closed again. The rider returned to his mount and cantered away from the manor, his body bent low over the saddle and rigid with urgency.

Now why, wondered Julian, was a clandestine visitor at Cannon Manor an hour past midnight?

Candlelight sparked to life in a second-floor room. He could see a shadowed figure flitting across the window, then back again. He grinned delightedly when the figure drew off a piece of clothing, revealing the outline of a womanly shape beneath. Regrettably, he was too far away to see clearly, but he glimpsed enough of the curves of breast and hip to know the lady's shape was pleasing.

He sighed when the figure disappeared from view. That tantalizing peek at Miss Hannah was not going to help his sleep. He'd kissed her just that afternoon, and had lost himself in her honeyed taste and the exhilaration that hummed beneath it. Was it any wonder? There was so much vibrant passion and life behind that cool exterior. He'd been powerless to resist her. Now he was left feeling edgy.

The light in her room went dark. He waited, certain there would be more, and was rewarded when a groom led Demon from the stable toward the kitchen door.

Finally, the lady herself stood silhouetted in the doorway, the glow from the kitchen outlining her shape. He almost failed to recognize her, dressed as she was in men's clothing. The breeches emphasized long, shapely legs and a trim waist while the coat concealed her torso. The crown of white-blond hair gave her away before she tucked it beneath a laborer's cap.

She strode to the stallion, placed her foot in the stirrup and threw her other leg over his broad back. Her movements were fluid, graceful—and practiced. Clearly, Miss Hannah needed no mounting block.

The lady was riding astride. Again.

His blood began to heat as he remembered their gallop across the countryside. The memory conjured up a vision of the lady riding astride something else. Namely, him. The image of that cool, serene woman, her head thrown back in passionate abandon as she rode him, had him shifting uncomfortably in his saddle.

He fought back the vision. There was no room for attraction in this mission. She was his assignment. Nothing more than a lead to the traitor.

By the time she trotted Demon past his hiding place, Julian had tamped down any lingering desire and forced himself to study her clinically. Her features were indistinguishable in the darkness, but her shoulders had tensed and her movements were erratic. Not her usual demeanor.

When she urged Demon into a trot and left the graveled drive, he wheeled his horse around and followed at a safe distance. Eventually the windows of Beer's main street began to glow in the darkness ahead. He expected her to skirt the town, but she rode straight through the village, staying on the nearly empty main street.

The only signs of life in the village were in the various pubs and inns still doing a brisk business. Light and sound spilled out of those establishments as the customers shared ale, cider and smuggled spirits.

She drew to a stop in front of the sign of the Jolly Smuggler. Julian narrowed his eyes as he scanned the pub's façade, pleased to be making progress in the investigation. The Jolly Smuggler was Jack Blackbourn's pub.

Still, a lady did not enter a public house owned by a smuggler and catering to the lower classes, even if she was wearing breeches. Did Miss Hannah care nothing for her reputation?

A thin, gangly lad just shy of manhood darted forward to claim Demon's reins.

"Be careful. He's frisky tonight." Her voice floated through the darkness.

"I'll be careful, Miss Gracie," the lad answered as he led the animal away.

Julian's eyes narrowed as he watched his quarry stride to the door of the public house. Miss Hannah's gait was sure, her chin held confidently high, her shoulders at ease. She looked more comfortable wearing breeches into a smuggler's pub than wearing a lady's gown in a salon.

Interesting.

Warm light and raucous laughter spilled out of the open door. Julian saw a man behind the bar raise his hand in greeting and beam out a delighted smile. Then the door slammed closed behind Miss Hannah and Julian was shut out.

———————

THE COMMON ROOM smelled of ale and tobacco. Beneath that was the ever-present scent of fish and ocean, as most of the patrons made their living on the water—by means both legal and clandestine. It was a pungent mix, but comforting in its familiarity. The tension at the base of Grace's neck eased slightly as she scanned the room.

The man behind the bar was stout, with a square face and a prominent nose. Wild hair sprung from his scalp in tufts that Grace knew he tried desperately to control with the queue at the base of his neck. He was a man with many roles: fisherman, pilot, sailor, publican—and smuggler.

"Hello, Jack," she said.

"Now there's a lovely lass come into my pub. A drink on the house? I have your favorite French wine." Jack Blackbourn wiped the counter with a well-used rag, clearing a space for her.

"Thank you, Jack, but no. I've business tonight." She held herself away from the counter even as Jack leaned companionably on it. She recognized his posture and knew he was preparing to settle in for a long talk.

"All work and no play again, my lovely?"

"I'm afraid so."

"Spend a few hours in my pub, and Jack will show you how to play," he said with a wink.

"Your wife might object and skin you alive. Then where would I buy my wine?" she replied blandly.

"She might, Miss Gracie, she might indeed." Jack guffawed and slapped his thigh before gesturing across the room. "Your business is in the corner, my lovely. But come back soon and share a bottle with Jack."

"I will." Giving in to affection, she rose to her toes and leaned over the counter to drop a kiss on Jack's cheek.

"It's just as I always tell my Anna. The ladies love me."

With another laugh, Grace turned in the direction he'd pointed. The village blacksmith and two other men sat at a table, heads together, talking in low voices. She threaded through the throng in the common room while patrons hailed her from all directions. Even as she answered the greetings from the fishermen and laborers, her focus was on the trio in the corner. She knew their expressions like her own and understood something was wrong. Her muscles tightened again as the tension that had drained away upon entering the pub roared back.

Three faces peered up at her as she approached. Each man stood as she reached the table, and one drew out a chair for her before they all sat again. There the propriety ended. Etiquette between the sexes was only a nuisance when it came to smuggling.

"Hello, Jem," she said to the young man across the table. "How is Fanny?"

"Tired, and ready for the babe to be born." Jem's shock of

flame-colored hair was mussed, no doubt by the sea wind given his occupation as a fisherman.

"There's a few months left, I'm afraid, Jem." She smiled, though her heart clutched. His brilliant green eyes were too anxious.

She looked to the side and studied the round, bewhiskered face of John the blacksmith. He leaned close to the narrow face of Thomas, a tenant farmer from a nearby estate. Worry etched both of their faces, carving deep lines around their mouths.

"What's happened?" she asked sharply. "Your wife is well, John? Your children, Thomas?"

"They're all well enough, Miss Gracie," John said, his voice low and urgent. He scratched at the stubble on his chin. "We found something in the smuggling caves, and don't think as how it's quite right." He glanced at the other two men in turn. Each nodded in confirmation.

She, too, kept her voice low. "What did you find?" she asked, brows drawing together.

"This." John reached into his homespun coat and pulled out a leather folio tied with a thong. "We found it inside a trunk of lace."

He handed the folio to Grace. She untied the thong and opened the trifolded leather. Inside was a sheaf of papers covered with thick, heavy writing.

What she read had her mouth dropping open.

*San Sebastian . . . Wellington to join . . . battering train traveling through Spain . . . appropriate siege guns, short on ammunition . . . troop count . . .*

Then, on the next page:

*Alastair Whitmore, code name Angel, 13 stone, over 6 feet, blond hair, brown eyes . . . Safe houses . . . 14 Avenue de la République, Paris . . . 22 Rue Carnot, Cherbourg . . . 4 Rue Delacroix, Calais . . .*

At the close of the document was a French revolutionary call. *Liberty, Equality, Brotherhood, or Death.* Her ears buzzed and she could feel the color drain from her cheeks.

"I can read some," the blacksmith said, bringing Grace out of her shock. "Though it's harder when the words are joined. But I can tell it's not right, is it, Miss Gracie? What's on that paper, it's not right."

"No," she answered. "No, John, it's not right. It's military information. Troop counts, munitions information." *It's treason*, she wanted to shout. Fear strangled the words in her throat.

"S'what we thought, Miss Gracie." John nodded with grim satisfaction. "What's on there shouldn't be going to Cherbourg."

"This information should not be outside of the Foreign Office, and most definitely should not be in France." She closed the folio, rubbed her hands on the smooth leather. "When did you discover it?

"'Twas a fortnight ago." Jem leaned forward. "The trunk was being loaded onto my fishing lugger."

"We didn't know what to do with it," John told her. "We didn't want to go to the magistrate or the customs house, not knowing who wrote it." He took a bolstering sip of ale then wiped his mouth with the back of his hand.

"We didn't know who to trust." Jem gestured toward her. "So we thought: Miss Gracie will know."

But she didn't have an answer as to whom they could trust. Grace secured the folio with the thong. Tucking it away inside her coat, she wished she could hide treason as easily as she could hide the folio. Did she recognize the handwriting? She couldn't be certain. Chilled, Grace pulled her coat more securely around her.

Thomas, the third man, leaned forward. His narrow features were serious and haggard. "It has to stop, Miss Gracie. I might ignore the law for a few extra coins, but I don't hold with treason."

*Treason.*

The word fell between them, a lead weight.

"Who should we tell?" Thomas continued. "And how do we tell someone without explaining how we found it in the quarries? We'd be turning ourselves in for smuggling. I have seven mouths to feed." His voice was full of fear. "I can't be taken up for smuggling."

Grace looked around the table. Three pairs of eyes turned to her for answers. She could feel their anxiety, tense waves that radiated through the air. Each of them was afraid. For themselves, their wives and children, if they were caught smuggling.

"Someone must be informed," Grace agreed, and held each of their gazes in turn. "I don't know who—yet—but I give you my word, when I inform the authorities, I'll protect you. I won't give them your names."

She could see the relief flow over them, a little wave of release that rippled around the table. They'd been living in fear for two weeks and she was glad she could relieve them of some of it. Yet now their worry weighed heavy on her shoulders.

"If we can help, we will." John leaned back in his chair. "Just say the word."

"Thank you." She stood, the men following suit. "I must return to the manor, but I promise to let you know what happens."

She bid them each good night and moved toward the door to the street. She waved good-bye to Jack, who called out from behind the bar, "Are you sure you don't want to stay and have a spot of fun, my lovely?"

"Next time, Jack." She knew he expected a laugh from her and obliged him. The sound was strained even to her own ears. When she turned Demon toward Cannon Manor a few minutes later, she let him have his head while her thoughts whirled.

*Treason.* The word screamed through her mind. She was certain in the general course of things, an official military dispatch would not be in an abandoned quarry used by smugglers. It would be carried by a member of a governmental office, either diplomatic, military or political. An official British dispatch would not end with the phrase *Liberté, Égalité, Fraternité, ou la Mort!*

Demon tensed beneath her. She rubbed his neck and crooned softly to him to calm him. Still, she couldn't calm her own thoughts. She must inform someone in a position of power. But how to do so and still keep her word to the men? The only way to protect them was to conceal their identities from the authorities.

She would not fail in her promise.

Suddenly, the fine hair at the nape of her neck rose. She felt eyes watching her. Demon shifted beneath her and whinnied softly. He felt them, too.

Glancing to the right, then the left, she squinted into the deep shadows formed by the trees. Nothing was visible in the dense darkness. Yet she sensed the other person, like a faint hum of an insect she couldn't quite see.

She raised her chin. Well, this was Cannon land. She regularly rode these lands in the early hours of the morning. She wouldn't run and she wouldn't be afraid. Besides, if the observer meant mischief, he'd had plenty of opportunity to pounce already and hadn't done so.

The small, delicate pocket pistol in her coat weighed heavy. She'd become so accustomed to carrying it at night she'd forgotten it was there. Now, she was grateful for its presence and glad she'd been taught to use it.

She urged Demon into a canter as they broke the cover of trees and entered a long field. She looked behind her once, twice, and although she thought she saw a lone horseman, she couldn't be certain.

When Demon finally entered the stable yard, Grace breathed a sigh of relief. A young groom staggered sleepily out of the stables. After dismounting, she handed him the reins and strode to the rear kitchen door. She knocked softly and waited, looking once more to the trees behind her. She could still feel eyes on her.

"Is all well, Miss Gracie?" A bleary-eyed Binkle swung open the door and let her in.

"I'm not sure. I have to think on it."

"If there's anything the staff can do, please inform us." He secured the door, latching it tightly.

"Thank you, Binkle. I will."

The shape of the leather folio pressed against her side. She needed to hide it while she decided how best to proceed. Only one place came to mind: her stillroom. She possessed the only key.

Grace hurried to her room and retrieved the ring of keys she carried with her during the day. After descending the rear servants' stair, she delicately picked her way through the silent halls until she came to the stillroom. She slid the key into the lock and slipped into the room, locking the door again behind her. Pausing a moment, she breathed deep. The combined scent of spices mixed with dried flowers soothed her. This was her room, her space. She knew every jar, every bottle, every sachet.

Using the pale moonlight gleaming through the window as a guide, she located the tinderbox on her workbench and quickly lit a candle. Lifting the candle high, she peered into the dark corners and perused the shelves and cabinets and cubbyholes. Her gaze fell on a short barrel of rose petals harvested that summer for use in perfumes, oils and potions.

She strode forward and lifted the lid of the barrel. Pulse pounding, she used her hands to dig through the mass. Clouds of sweet, fragrant air floated into the room. She settled the folio at the bottom of the barrel, then covered it with the delicate petals before replacing the lid.

Chased by fear, Grace snuffed the candle and darted from the stillroom. The folio buried beneath innocent rose petals contained a life and horror of its own.

# Chapter 6

JULIAN SURVEYED THE revelers filling Lady Hammond's salon over the rim of his punch glass. Silks, satins and muslins in an array of brilliant jewel tones and soft pastels twirled around the floor, accented by brilliant diamonds, bold rubies and cool sapphires. He did a quick study for familiar faces. He noted a few he'd seen in London over the past few years. But he saw no spies, no foreign agents he recognized. Nor did he see Grace Hannah. The guests appeared to be nothing more than local landowners and gentry mingling over music and food and laughter. Whether the traitor was in their midst remained to be seen.

Terrace doors were propped open to circulate a breeze, but the humid September night intensified the heavy scents of perfumed women and potted flowers. His clothes clung to his skin in the moist air. Drawing a deep breath for fortification, Julian resigned himself to a hot, uncomfortable evening. He pasted on his charming Wandering Earl smile and prepared for the assault.

It wasn't long in coming. His hostess, Lady Hammond, wide of girth and well-endowed, cleaved through the crowd, her bosom leading the way across the congested floor. "My lord!" she called.

"Lady Hammond." Julian bowed over the hand she offered. "I can't say how much I appreciate your invitation."

"Nonsense. I consider it my duty to introduce you. Come."

She took his arm and led him from group to group in a circuit around the room. Almost every group included an eligible young lady. It was the same each time: Lady Hammond would perform the requisite introductions, the young lady would say something witty and speculative gazes would flick his way to see if he approved. Society was certainly predictable. Already the gossips were considering who could be his prospective bride.

He suffered through another round of introductions to a pair of matrons, a Lady Lintell and her companion, Mrs. Parker. He made polite responses to polite questions—are you enjoying the weather?—and fixed his smile more firmly as Lady Lintell's incessant chatter began to grate. Then, abruptly, his attention focused in on their conversation.

"My goodness. Whatever is Miss Gracie doing here?" The words were delivered by the rail-thin Lady Lintell. "It's been—well. I don't even *know* how many years since Miss Gracie joined us."

"At least seven years, Minnie." Lady Hammond followed Lady Lintell's gaze. "Long overdue."

"Quite overdue." Mrs. Parker stood on tiptoe to see over the crowds. Julian doubted it would help, as she wasn't even as tall as his shoulder. "It's a shame she never attends."

"I wonder why?" Julian said, more to himself than to the older matron.

Lady Lintell leaned close, her eyes bright with a conspirator's light. "Now, I don't know, but it's been said Lord Cannon won't allow her to attend. Why, everyone *knows* he just works that girl to the bone without giving her a *thing* in return. Not that Miss Gracie complains, mind you," she added. "She takes her duties seriously and is always willing to lend a hand. Why, just yesterday she sent another bottle of tonic over to my husband for his cough."

"Last week Miss Gracie brought one of her special teas to my daughter, who is in the family way," Lady Hammond explained. "I am glad to see Miss Gracie finally joining us."

"I suppose it *has* been seven years since Mr. Wargell jilted her. Poor Miss Gracie. It really wasn't well done of him, you know." Lady Lintell's fan tapped Julian's arm. "She's a pretty thing, isn't she, my lord?"

"I beg your pardon?"

"Do you see the lady just inside the door wearing the white dress? That's Miss Grace Hannah." She frowned. "Really, if Lord Cannon is going to finally let that girl out of the manor, he ought to outfit her properly. That gown is *quite* unfashionable. Although, what does a man know about fashion, after all?" She squeaked and looked up at Julian. "Oh, my lord! Not you, of course! You're quite well-informed about ladies' clothing. Er, well—"

"Don't concern yourself, Lady Lintell." Julian laughed. "For I can see that no one has such a discerning eye as yourself."

"Oh, my lord, you are too kind." She preened, her long face bobbing on her long neck.

"As it happens, I have made Miss Hannah's acquaintance," Julian said, bringing the conversation back to the topic he wanted to discuss. "Three times."

"Is that so?" Lady Hammond turned shrewd eyes toward Julian.

"She even promised me the first dance. As I hear the musicians beginning to warm up, I believe it is time I seek my partner. If you'll excuse me, ladies." He bowed and left them, though their curious twitters and whispers followed him as he crossed the floor to Miss Hannah.

Lady Lintell was correct about Miss Hannah's gown. The diaphanous muslin was unadorned, the waistline a little too high, the sleeves too long. Still, it was flattering.

She stood beside Lord Cannon while he spoke to another man leaning on a cane. What was the expression on Miss Hannah's face? He supposed she meant to be expressionless. Yet he could see beyond that blank face to the defiant angle of her head, her proud shoulders and the intense gaze that pretended to see nothing. Julian recognized nerves as well in the elegant fingers that clutched a small silver reticule.

Then she saw him, her unfathomable silver eyes meeting his. Her mouth set. Ah. He made her nervous. Good.

"Lord Cannon, Miss Hannah." Julian bowed. "Please excuse me for interrupting your conversation, but I've come to claim my partner for the first dance."

"Are you certain?" Lord Cannon barked. "You could ask another chit. Grace won't cause a scene."

"Why would I ask another lady? I've already asked Miss Hannah." Julian cocked his head. What an interesting development. "It would be ungentlemanly if I withdrew my invitation now."

"She's damaged goods." The second old man leaned forward, cracking his cane on the parquet floor as he spoke. "Jilted. Ruined. *Compromised*."

The hurt didn't show on Miss Hannah's blanked features, but Julian knew she felt it. Her shoulders were nearly up to her ears and if he wasn't mistaken, she'd stopped breathing.

Temper reared up. He grasped his quizzing glass and brought it to his eye, surveying the cadaverous stranger with disdain. "I'm sorry. I don't believe we've met."

"Lord Stuart Paget." Lord Paget's narrowed eyes flicked toward Miss Hannah, then back again. "She has no reputation."

"She's an embarrassment," Lord Cannon added, rocking back on his heels. "It has to be said, my lord."

"No. It doesn't. And as long as Miss Hannah is my partner, I suggest you refrain from discussing any such embarrassment." He wanted to launch his fist into Cannon's face. "Miss Hannah, the couples will be lining up shortly. Shall we go?" He offered his arm. She stared at it as though it were a coiled snake preparing to strike.

She searched his face. Then, with a deep breath, accepted his arm. They moved away, and Julian heard Cannon and Paget blustering and bristling behind them.

"You don't have to dance with me. I won't mind." Miss Hannah stared straight ahead. "I've probably forgotten the steps in any case." Her cheeks flushed.

"I *will* mind," he bit out. Then he realized he was all but dragging her onto the dance floor. Keep it easy, he instructed himself. Flirtation. He waited a beat. "At any rate, if I'm going to compete with Jack Blackbourn, I need to begin consorting with fast women. What kind of smuggler would I be if I consorted with virtuous spinsters?"

She abruptly stopped walking and stared at him. Then she laughed, long and merrily. The delighted sound filled him with a rush of pure lust. The sort that grabbed a man by the throat and refused to let go.

"My lord, you may just compete with our Jack after all." She glanced at the dancers as they began to line up. A smile flirted with the corners of her mouth. "It seems it's time to begin the dance, my lord smuggler. I only hope your reputation survives consorting with fast women."

"If it doesn't," he returned as they took their places, "at least this smuggler will keep his lady consort content." He was rewarded with a faint blush high on her cheekbones.

Whispers rippled through the surrounding crowd as they took their place on the floor. Was it himself or Miss Hannah that set tongues wagging?

The lively violins started a country dance. He and Grace came together, separated, came together again. Her eyes, silver-bright, remained fastened on his.

Woven through the whispers was one clear word: *Gracie*. She must hear it. How could she not? Yet her face stayed blank, her eyes focused on his. It must have cost her dearly to appear so unaware.

"You haven't forgotten the steps, fair lady."

"It's said dancing will come back to you quickly," she murmured.

"And does it?" Their hands touched, a fleeting brush of glove on glove that resonated through him.

"If one concentrates."

"Alas. I'm clearly not distraction enough if you can concentrate so thoroughly on the steps of the dance. I must try harder." They separated again, then came together once more at the head of the line.

"Not wise, my lord. If I stop concentrating I may tread on your toes."

"My boots are sturdy."

"So are my slippers."

He laughed aloud and spun her down the avenue created by the other dancers until they reached the end and took their places once more.

When the song had ended and the couples dispersed, he smiled at her. "Would you care for a walk on the terrace, Miss Hannah? Or would you prefer I return you to your uncle?"

She cocked her head, as though listening to the whispers. "The terrace, please."

They exited through ornate glass doors and walked the length of the terrace, away from the crowded rooms of the manor house.

She withdrew her arm when they reached the farthest end and stood at the top of the steps leading down to the gardens. He leaned against the balustrade and took a moment to search the darkness. No sound out of the ordinary. No shadow that didn't belong.

Satisfied, he turned to look at her. She, too, stared into the darkness. The quiet and serene Miss Hannah with a core of passion. A smuggler and a rebel.

"The moonlight suits you, fair lady." The silver light slanted over her delicate features, turning them into a beautiful study of light and shadow.

"Oh, moonlight flatters everyone. It's soft and vague and smooths out rough edges."

How could such a lovely face show such loneliness? It was her eyes. They seemed lost. Something stirred in him, answering the call of her loneliness. He pushed it away, trying desperately to remember she was only an assignment.

"The night is liberating, is it not?" She tipped her face up to the sky.

"I would have said the night is secretive."

"It's both, I suppose." Looking out to the moon-washed gardens, she continued. "It's the darkness, I think. In the dark, nothing is quite what it seems. Anything, anyone, could be hiding. The possibilities are endless."

She seemed lost in the darkness. He waited, feeling like he was balancing on the edge of a knife, and wondered which way she would pull him. She drew a deep breath, held it. When she exhaled, it was as though some long-forgotten need was being given life.

"Let's walk, my lord. Let's throw caution to the wind, walk the paths and test the possibilities." She skipped lightly down the stairs, then looked at him over one slender shoulder.

He could do nothing but follow.

Her gown was a beacon in the dark, floating around her as she guided him down the garden paths. The night was still, without the slightest breeze to stir the leaves, so that it seemed the only living thing was Miss Hannah. Heat lay heavy on the foliage, drawing out the heady scents of blooming summer flowers. Their sweet bouquet enveloped him, drew him in.

"What do you think is hiding in the dark, Miss Hannah?" He gestured toward the garden. "What unseen delights await?"

She crouched, then stood again with a thin stalk of late-blooming lavender. She twirled the lavender and studied the quiet gardens. "Perhaps a chivalric knight is waiting to rescue a maiden."

"With his sword drawn and ready and his charger prancing among the rhododendrons," he finished, watching the moonlight play over her features. She was a romantic at heart, he realized.

"But perhaps it's a dashing highwayman, waiting to way-lay the guests and steal kisses from beautiful maidens." She laughed.

"Or perhaps a faerie queen waits for her lover among the blossoms and blooms." He stepped closer, whispering in her ear. "Every pleasure, *any* pleasure, may be waiting in the dark."

She tilted her head to watch him through long gold lashes. One corner of her full mouth rose slowly up, then the other. Lust arrowed through him and wiped all thoughts of his assignment from his mind. Had he seen her smile before? Not like that. The slow half smile was seductive and sultry.

Here was the passionate woman he'd kissed.

"Perhaps a smuggling earl awaits in the dark," she whispered.

"Ah yes. My second career." He plucked the lavender from her fingers and held it to his nose, breathed deep. And smelled *her*. He struggled to focus. "Perhaps I'll buy my own ship and hire a crew to smuggle goods from France. Then I would truly thrill the local ladies."

"But you wouldn't be a smuggler as much as you would be a captain, would you?"

"Ah, not just a captain—a *smuggling* captain. And if I were a smuggling captain I could sail the seven seas, collecting gold and riches from the far corners of the world."

"You could, but that wouldn't thrill the local ladies, would it? If you're off sailing the seas and collecting gold you wouldn't be here in Devon to dazzle them with your exploits." She angled her head, pursed her lips in a playful pout.

"I did promise to keep my consort content, did I not? I must impress her with my fantastic deeds." He stepped forward so that they were only inches apart and tried to battle back desire. "I'd come to her in the deepest night, when others slept and they were alone. No one to hear. No one to see."

He saw her breath catch, saw her breasts rise and fall with it.

"What would they do in the night? In the dark?" she whispered.

"They'd *feel*. There's no sight in the dark, only texture, sound. Sensation." He could all but taste her, cool and sweet. He leaned in so that his lips hovered just above hers. "Close your eyes," he breathed. When she did as he asked, her lashes fluttering down to curtain her eyes, he lost the battle with himself.

---

GRACE WAITED, ANTICIPATION trapping her breath. He did nothing, only stood there, a hairbreadth from her. Heat radiated from him, mingled with the humid warmth of the air that dampened her skin. What was he doing? Silent, still, blind, she waited.

"The smuggler and his woman would listen to the night around them," he whispered. His warm lips touched her ear so that she drew a quick, uneven breath. "Tell me what they would hear."

Her hearing sharpened, focused. She listened, and heard the stirring of the flowers. Just the merest sigh on the air. Had she ever heard that sigh before? Had she ever noticed that the leaves in the trees quivered and rustled, even in the still air?

"The flowers, the plants, whispering in the night. A cricket." The insect chirped once, twice, the sound a strident call to his mate. "Laughter and voices and music echoing from the house."

"What would they smell?" His voice was so low she strained to hear. "Tell me what scents float upon the air."

Breathing deep, Grace took in all the scents of the garden. "Lavender and verbena. The faintest scent of roses. Earth. Summer. Night."

Over it all, around it all, was the earl. His scent, man and outdoors. His breathing, in and out, rhythmic. His breath fluttered warm over her lips.

Grace tipped up her own mouth. Would he kiss her? He would. He *must*. Her eyes still closed, her body straining, she waited. Blind anticipation warred with the need to see him. Just when she could bear the awareness no longer, she felt it. The tiniest tickle against her lips. The scent of lavender engulfed her as soft little petals stroked, then trailed across her jaw and down to her collarbone, leaving a line of sensitive skin in its wake.

"I—"

"Hush. Just wait. Just feel."

The petals traced the neckline of her gown, grazing the soft swell of breast that rose above the muslin. A quiver ran through her, set her muscles trembling. Someone moaned softly. Shocked, Grace realized the sound came from her. She started to flutter her lashes open.

But she was stopped when his mouth finally, *finally* touched hers. Firm, warm. He touched her nowhere but her lips. Yet still she felt his nearness, his body skimming just beyond hers. She opened for him, couldn't help but open for him as light poured through her. Rising on her toes, she met his mouth and let need overwhelm her.

When he drew back, her breath was ragged, her heart pumping. For one final moment she kept her eyes closed and savored the brightness within her. Then finally, she opened her eyes and met the intense focus of his gaze. Deep, powerful, his eyes searched her face.

"Alas, fair lady. The night must end for our smuggler and his consort."

"So it must." She struggled to focus beyond the rush of blood and pounding of her heart. "And the smuggler must relinquish his plunder."

"Ah, but that is the beauty of kisses. They cannot be returned and must remain forever with the receiver to be treasured." He rubbed a thumb over her bottom lip.

"You may keep the kisses, my lord." Her lips curved under his thumb at his foolishly charming words.

But reality intruded. She looked toward the bright squares of light that marked the windows of Lady Hammond's manor house. "We should return to the assembly before our absence is noted."

She hated saying it, hated the dread gathering in her belly, but there was little choice. She accepted his offered arm as they wound through the garden and onto the terrace.

Through the open door, Grace could see Lord Cannon standing near the punch bowl, numerous people ranged around him. Even as she watched the group shifted, changed. Anxiety clutched in her stomach as she saw who remained beside him. Michael Wargell and his stunningly beautiful wife.

Her mind raced as they entered the house and crossed the room. She didn't know what to say to the man who had irreparably compromised and jilted her. Nor to the wife he chose over her.

"Where did you go?" her uncle demanded as they approached the group.

"We took a turn about the room, then the terrace," the earl answered glibly. "It's terribly warm in here, is it not?"

"Lord Langford," her uncle barked, impatient as always with polite pleasantries. "May I present Mr. Michael Wargell and Mrs. Clotilde Wargell."

Grace could only stare at the floor. He was here. Worse, *she* was here. Grace had managed to avoid them for years, even in Cannon Manor where they visited so often. Now the moment had arrived and it was in front of the Earl of Langford. In front of the entire village.

"Lord Langford, a pleasure to make your acquaintance." Michael's voice was unchanged to Grace's ear. It was smooth and pleasant, the tone polite.

She frowned. His voice didn't give her the thrill it once had. She stole a quick glance and saw that his face had changed even if his voice had not. Lines fanned out from his eyes and the hair at his temple was gray instead of the same rich black as the rest. Yet he was still handsome. Her heart constricted with a fierce ache.

"Lord Langford." Clotilde Wargell's sugary tone swirled through the hot, scented air. "We've only recently returned from London. I found the Season to be such a whirl I could barely keep up. Did you enjoy London?"

The pleasantries began. Fashion, theater, scandal, weather. No one directed a comment to Grace, nor did she join the conversation. She had nothing to contribute, anyway. She'd probably blurt out something ridiculous such as, *Why did you jilt me, Michael?* But she supposed she didn't need to ask. The answer was standing before her, in the exquisite form of Clotilde Wargell.

"Oh, Gracie wouldn't go to London," Mrs. Wargell said, pulling Grace into the conversation. "She's too attached to Devon, aren't you?"

Grace looked up to find Mrs. Wargell's cunning gold eyes on her.

"Er, yes, I enjoy the countryside."

"And your gardens, no doubt," Michael added. His dark eyes were neither warm nor cold when they looked at her. Pain sliced through her at the absolute disinterest in his expression.

"You spend hours out in the gardens, don't you, Gracie?" Mrs. Wargell shuddered delicately. "I wouldn't dream of mucking about in the dirt as you do. That's why we employ gardeners."

"No need to employ someone when Gracie's right here," Lord Cannon countered.

"Cannon Manor's gardens are singularly impressive," the Earl of Langford noted. "They must be full of delights, Miss Hannah."

His blue, blue eyes met hers and sent heat shimmering through her. She ignored it. Michael Wargell stood only feet from her. She needed no other reminder why she should stay away from the earl.

"A lady gardener," the earl mused. "You have so many hidden talents, Miss Hannah." A knowing smile flirted with his lips.

"It's just a garden." She needed to leave. Soon, before she tumbled deeper into trouble. She looked away, searched for the door. It wasn't far. The Earl of Langford's eyes laughed into hers when she looked back, as though he knew she hoped to escape. She flushed.

"I look forward to seeing your garden in its entirety." The earl brought her hand to his lips. His hand was warm covering hers, his breath fluttered over her skin. Sensation spread from her fingertips through her body to center low in her belly. She knew what those lips felt like on hers, had tasted them only a short while before.

Caught in his spell, she waited, breathless, everyone forgotten. When the earl let her hand slide away from his, the guests, the colors and sounds of the room remained unfocused.

"Until later, then, Miss Hannah." The earl sent her one final seductive smile before he left them.

As he walked away, she wondered if she were dreaming. Then reality rushed back in startling clarity as Sir Richard Elliott, her uncle's bull-like crony, barreled into their circle. His dainty wife, Lady Marie Elliott, followed a step behind, murmuring her apologies.

"I've hired a new steward, Wargell." Sir Richard's broad body angled toward Michael.

"Have you? Is he well qualified?" Michael's eyes lit with interest.

"He came highly recommended by members of the Agrarian Society." Sir Richard clapped a hand on Michael's shoulder and they broke away from the group.

Lord Cannon watched the other men move to a quiet corner then looked at Grace. His eyes were cold and the message was clear: *Do not embarrass me.* Then he, too, left their circle, leaving her alone with Clotilde Wargell and Lady Elliott.

"Well, well." Mrs. Wargell's silky murmur was barely audible over the music. "Aren't you up to your old tricks, Gracie."

"I'm not up to anything, Mrs. Wargell," she snapped. It was past time to leave the assembly.

"I would disagree, given the earl's eyes on you. Wouldn't you agree, Lady Elliott?"

"I'm sorry, Clotilde." Lady Elliott turned her sad dark eyes on Grace. "I don't understand."

"Oh, I think we all understand. We're all of us women, and all of us experienced." Mrs. Wargell's smile turned malicious. "Aren't we, Gracie?"

"*Clotilde!*" Lady Elliott's shocked whisper matched her shocked eyes. "You're being improper."

"Less improper than Grace was all those years ago."

"*Still.*" The word was a hiss.

"What do you want me to say, Mrs. Wargell? That you won?" Weary of the assembly, of pretending, Grace sighed. She wanted to rub her temple and massage away the headache brewing there. But she held back. To do so would only show more weakness. "Fine. You won. Michael married you and I'm a ruined spinster. Is that what you wanted to hear?"

"Grace." Lady Elliott's hand reached for hers, squeezed.

"I believe it's time for me to leave." She patted Lady Elliott's hand. "I'll see you soon."

Willing back the tears that clogged her throat and stung her eyes, Grace crossed the room. When she reached the door to the hall, she looked back once into the room. The Earl of Langford was watching her, his eyes hooded, his gaze unreadable.

Grace straightened her spine, lifted her chin and let out a slow, controlled breath. She might be retreating, but she refused to look like it.

# Chapter 7

GRACE THREW A leg over Demon's broad back and adjusted her men's riding boots. The miserable drizzle that had started as she left the ball continued, soaking the dark countryside as she and Demon rode to the smugglers' quarries.

Nothing remained of the burning tears and sharp ache she'd felt hearing Clotilde Wargell's spiteful words. Studying the white limestone cliffs that concealed the smuggling caves, Grace pushed the lingering wistfulness aside. Those old dreams no longer had any place in her life. She had found her position in the community and was content.

If loneliness occasionally weighed her down no one need know but herself. If the Earl of Langford had dispelled the loneliness for a few minutes, that knowledge, too, was only for her.

The taste of him was still with her, as was the energy that had rushed through her. Her skin hummed where his fingers had touched her, leaving an imprint on both her body and her memory. She'd lost control of herself, and there was no justification for her inappropriate behavior.

She flipped up the collar of the homespun coat she wore and tugged her cap lower. It was little protection against the spitting clouds. The cold rain coupled with the light breeze made the warm September evening feel more like November.

Rainwater slicked the cliff path and muddied the earth

beneath Demon's hooves. They picked their way across the rough ground, each conscious of where the earth dropped away and the surf pounding below. A false step, a stumble, and she and Demon would be over the edge and into nothingness.

She saw the small gap in the rock formations that marked the start of the narrow path leading to the quarries. The cliffs became less sheer here, but still too dangerous for a horse to navigate. She bypassed the path and turned inland instead, traveling another few hundred yards.

At the edge of a wood squatted an abandoned cottage. She tethered Demon in the lean-to and hurried toward the cliff path as quickly as the slippery ground would allow. The rocky slope was treacherous. Its crags and boulders extended stony peaks to slow her descent. She scrabbled down the path, digging her fingers into jagged fissures to steady herself.

When she reached the outcropping that protected the entrance to the quarries, she ducked inside. Crouching in the low tunnel, she pulled the cap from her head and fumbled it into her coat pocket with numb hands.

It was dark at the mouth of the quarry, but she could see light ahead and hear voices and laughter. Bent nearly double, she started down the natural tunnel. The passageway widened, the roof elevated, and finally she stepped into a large, rough-hewn room. The white limestone walls glowed with the light of numerous tallow candles. Their flames illuminated the hewn arches and columns supporting the roof, throwing ancient tool marks into relief.

She breathed deep and let the cool cave air fill her lungs. It should have been damp air, but the quarries and the natural passageways that connected them had always been dry. Perfect for the storage of smuggled goods.

For the first time in hours she began to relax. In the caves, she knew her purpose and how to conduct herself. In this place—with these people—she belonged.

She strode through the cave. Around her, men stacked the casks and crates and barrels that had arrived earlier in the night, dividing and separating them for later delivery. Their laughter and greetings echoed off the walls.

"A bit late, aren't you, Miss Gracie," one man called out.

"Only a little," she said with a wave in his direction.

"We thought you weren't going to make it to count the shipment," another said.

"Word has it our Miss Gracie fancied herself up and went to a grand ball tonight."

Her stomach clutched, then relaxed again when she saw his grin.

"Aye, where's the fancy dress?" That sentiment echoed around the room, accompanied by good-natured laughter.

"Our Miss Gracie doesn't need a fancy dress, do you, my lovely?"

She laughed as she recognized the voice. "I prefer my breeches, Jack."

"I thought as much." Jack Blackbourn leaned against the wall near the small trunk that housed her ledgers, quills and ink. "I wouldn't recognize you in a fancy dress."

"I scarcely recognized myself." She crouched down and opened the trunk to remove the ledger for the night's shipment. "The shipment came early. I wasn't expecting it until tomorrow night."

"Aye. It's lucky our goods were ready to go out. The lugger's waiting in the cove." He gestured vaguely in the direction of the Channel.

"I'm surprised to see you here." She looked up from the ledger. "Not thinking of taking up smuggling again, are you? I promised Anna I wouldn't let you back in."

"Oh, we all three know I'll be keeping my hand in, don't we?"

"I'd say we do, but I don't want your wife after me. So scat." She flapped the ledger at him, without any intention of persuading him to leave. "I've a shipment to tally."

Setting the ledger beside the first smuggled trunk, she kneeled on the rough stone floor and lifted the lid. Silks. Undamaged, she noted. Emerald and ruby and primrose and cerulean shone in the light of the torches.

"Gracie."

"Hmm?" Burying her arms to the elbows, she rifled through the soft, smooth fabric and counted the bolts.

"Rumor is there's a bit more to our shipments than what's accounted for in your ledger there." He crouched beside her and laid his hand on her arm, the light and insistent pressure forcing her to meet his gaze.

"What?" Dread sent her stomach plummeting. She didn't need to ask. She knew. Jack—ever-laughing, ever-smiling Jack—was serious. His eyes were dark, his blunt features tight and drawn.

He waved across the cave. John the blacksmith responded with a sharp nod, crossing the room to crouch beside her.

"We've found another folio, Miss Gracie." John's voice was low, barely audible above the voices and laughter of the other men. Apprehension was etched into the already deep lines of his face. With his graying hair and beard wet with rain, he looked older than his years.

"When?" Grace pushed to her feet, smuggled silks forgotten, and both men followed suit.

"Just this evening." John worried the cap clutched in his workingman's fingers. "'Twas a man from over Sidmouth way that found the folio. The lid on the trunk weren't on tight so it wouldn't latch proper. It were right on top, Miss Gracie. Not even hidden under the lace this time."

"Did the Sidmouth man question it being there?"

"I don't think so. I took it right away, said it was your ledger for counting the goods and you must have forgot it there. He just said as how you'd be glad to have it back and then closed the trunk lid proper." His big hands had wrinkled and crushed his cap.

"Where is it?"

"I have it here. I knew you'd be by to check the shipment." He reached into his coat and retrieved the folio.

It looked the same as before, she noted dimly. The smooth leather cover and wide thong were identical to the first folio. Grace snatched it from John and slid it inside her own coat.

"Thank you, John."

"Aye. When you need help, Miss Gracie, you tell us." Face grim, he rejoined his comrades.

"What will you do with the folio?" Jack murmured beside Grace.

"I don't know." She gripped his shoulder. "What do *you* think I should do?"

"I don't know who to trust, my lovely." He ran a hand through his thick hair, pulling it out of its queue. "Whoever the traitor is must know the location of this quarry."

"I know." She looked around, saw farmers and fishermen and laborers working side by side. Friends. All of them. Her stomach sank. "There are two dozen smugglers that use this quarry. Nearly all of them are here tonight."

"There are more that know of these quarries," he said. "A few of the villagers. Lord Cannon."

"Uncle Thaddeus?" Eyes wide, she whipped her head toward Jack. "He knows about the caves?"

"Aye. As do Lord Paget and Sir Richard Elliott."

"How?"

"Years ago, when I was first smuggling, they used these quarries for some type of club they'd formed." Rubbing a hand across his jaw, Jack narrowed his eyes in thought. "That would have been in around ninety-four or ninety-five."

"What type of club?"

"A Hellfire Club."

Her mouth fell open. "But Hellfire Clubs were for rakes and drunkards. I've heard rumors of debauchery and other indecent behavior, even sacrifices. Uncle Thaddeus—"

"Oh, their club was quite tame, all in all. A lot of drinking and women but none of the sacrifices and the like. They established it when they were at university together. Later, they'd meet in these caves before going down to the village or over Seaton way for a bit of sport." He turned amused eyes to Grace. "I already had a little smuggling business going then. I stored my smuggled cargo here, and they would help themselves to a bottle or two and leave a bit of blunt in payment."

"Ever a businessman, weren't you, Jack?"

"Aye." He winked. "They disbanded their foolish club a few years later and I lost a bit of my income, though I made it up in other ways."

"I had no idea Uncle Thaddeus was a member of a Hellfire Club," she murmured.

"It's old scandal." Jack surveyed the room. "Others know of the quarries, of course. The families of these smugglers, for example. Men share a lot of information with their spouses."

The statement sent her stomach quivering. "Michael Wargell knows of the quarries," she whispered. Heat flooded her cheeks.

"Does he now?" Jack studied her face.

"I—I brought him here when we were—"

"Don't explain, my lovely." His voice was soft, his eyes full of compassion. "I know it hurts you."

"Not anymore. Not really." She couldn't look at him, so she pulled open the ledgers and ran a finger down the page. But her eyes were blind and registered nothing.

"If I were your uncle—if I had any kind of power—I'd have forced him to marry you."

"It's better we didn't marry." The letters on the page swam even as the lump formed in her throat. "We'd be miserable now."

"But your reputation would be intact and you wouldn't be alone. Come to think on it, I should have killed him," he spat out viciously.

"Jack!" The ferocity of his tone shocked a laugh out of her.

"Well. Someone should have done something," he said, mouth set.

Gratitude bloomed within her, warm and bright. "Jack."

"Aye?"

"I've never said thank you for letting me in."

"With the smugglers?" He turned eyes bright with curiosity on her. "I'd say you do more for us by divvying up the blunt than we do for you."

"Not just with the smugglers, though you did give me something useful to do." She smiled. "Well, I suppose 'useful' would depend on what side of the law you're on."

"That it would." He laughed.

"But I meant letting me into it all. Smuggling, the pub, the villagers. Anna. Your family."

"'Twas the least I could do after you saved my life."

"It was only a musket ball."

"I thought I was done for, my lovely, until you came around." He grinned at her. "Aside from that, your big sad eyes reminded me of the sea. The sea will always call to the sailor."

Yes. This is where she belonged. She bent her head to accommodate the few inches between them and kissed his weathered cheek.

"Thank you, Jack."

"A kiss from my lovely lass." His grin flashed, causing the

lines around his eyes to fan out in the most comforting way. "Don't tell Anna."

"It's our secret." She sent him a saucy smile and a wink, just to please him.

"Always lucky, that Jack Blackbourn," someone called out. Answering guffaws reminded her they weren't alone.

She looked up and caught John the blacksmith's eye. The merriment within her faded.

"Who could the traitor be, Jack? Who do we trust?"

"I'd say you can't go to the magistrate, as that's Lord Paget and he knows about the quarries."

"You don't really think Lord Paget—"

"Our list of suspects is short."

"It is." She sighed and nodded toward the others. "Could it be one of our men?"

"I don't know. It bears thinking on."

"I'll finish today's tally, then." She pulled her coat closer around her and felt the weight of the folio. "Then I'll hide this folio with the first and we'll decide what to do."

"Aye. I'll see what I can learn in the pub. If something's afoot, the lads that come down to the pub might know."

"Be circumspect."

"I don't know what that word means. But for you, my lovely lass, I'll do it." With a wave, he sauntered across the cavern and through the tunnel. She heard his whistle echo as he left the quarries and disappeared into the night.

As she compared the contents of the trunks and barrels with her ledgers and ticked them off, her mind turned over the possibilities. The traitor was unlikely to be any of the smugglers, though it wasn't impossible. They all had access to the quarries, but not the information. Lowborn smugglers wouldn't have the contacts in London that would allow them an avenue to the information. Unless, of course, someone from London had approached the smugglers in the first place.

She let her gaze roam the room. Misery and guilt weighed heavy on her heart. These men were her friends. Her comrades. They'd accepted her without a qualm when Jack brought her in. She'd found comfort and friendship and, more, they helped to fill the dark, lonely place inside her.

And they would be the perfect scapegoat if the folio were

discovered. So she would ensure that none of them were taken up for treason by finding the traitor who was using her friends.

Turning back to the ledgers, she finished the count of goods in the smuggling shipment. When she left the cave, she called out to the men as she departed and wished them luck on the water. A moment later, she was in the darkened mouth of the tunnel.

She tested for rain before exiting the cave. The unpleasant drizzle had ceased, leaving the air cool and moist. She picked her way up the slope to the cliff top above.

A shift in the shadows at the edge of the cliffs caught her attention. She waited, watching the jagged rocks, heart pounding. The shadow shifted again and the figure of a man rose up from the cliff edge.

The shadow was well above her, and if it were not for the sliver of moon attempting to shine through the clouds, she wouldn't have noticed him against the horizon. Then the man slipped away from the cliff edge into the surrounding darkness. She continued to wait, eyes straining against the dark, but she didn't see him again.

Who was it? The traitor?

Digging into her coat, she drew out her pistol. The pearl handle was smooth, cool and comforting in her hand. Gripping it tight, she continued her ascent. Reaching the cliff top she crouched, alert, and scanned the horizon for the shadowy form.

When she was certain there was no shadow that did not belong, she turned away from the cliffs and toward the building at the edge of the wood that housed Demon. Once she reached her uncle's estate and ensured Demon was settled for the evening she entered her stillroom, carrying a short candle.

Surveying the shelves, she contemplated whether to hide the second folio in the same barrel of rose petals. It would be better to separate the folios in case of discovery. She looked around for a suitable hiding place, mentally evaluating and discarding various drawers, pots and barrels, until she saw a small trunk in the corner.

Grace strode to the trunk and flipped the lid. Squares of linen and muslin lay inside, ready to be sewed into sachets. Kneeling, she placed the candle on the floor. Digging beneath the fabric, she cleared a space for the folio on the floor of the trunk. After carefully replacing the fabric, she closed the lid and stood. It was as good as any other hiding place.

She strode to the door of the stillroom and put her hand on the latch, ready for her bed, but her eyes strayed to the barrel of roses. To reassure herself that the folio had not been stolen or discovered, Grace went to the barrel, plunged her arm in and felt around. When her fingertips touched the cool, smooth leather she wilted in relief. It was still there, hidden from prying eyes and traitorous minds.

———————

"Miss Hannah is involved in treason up to her pretty neck."

"Hmm." Sir Charles Flint did not look up from the documents spread across his desk. They were free of their leather bindings, which remained hidden among sweet-smelling rose petals and soft linen.

Julian nodded toward the papers. "I'm not privy to Wellington's plans, so I don't know the accuracy of that information." From his vantage point the scrawling script looked like foreign symbols. But he'd read the damning information repeatedly during the hasty trip to London and knew every word.

"It's accurate enough," Sir Charles said. "Are you certain Miss Hannah is involved?"

"I watched her hide this information in her stillroom," he said flatly. "She's involved."

Sir Charles said nothing, but his fingers skimmed the pages as though following the path of his eyes.

Julian waited. Or tried to. Something hot and edgy seethed inside him. The documents were not enough to let him back in. They were important, but they were not enough.

"Give me your report."

It was as natural as breathing. "She met with three smugglers in Jack Blackbourn's pub. They gave her the first folio. Sir, they were nervous. Fidgety."

"Traitors tend to be that way. Come to think of it, so do smugglers." Sir Charles looked up. "Is she their leader?"

"They treated her with deference, from what I could see through the window."

"And the second folio?"

"The second folio she obtained while inside an abandoned quarry used to store smuggled goods. I counted twenty-one smugglers that night. A mix of farmers and fishermen. Blackbourn himself was there as well."

"How did you acquire the folios, Shadow?" Paper crackled as Sir Charles shifted a page to the side.

"I recreated the pages with false information and replaced them in the folios." It had taken days of painstaking work. Nights of hiding in that damn stillroom while Miss Hannah slept a floor above him.

Sir Charles's head jerked up. "She hasn't noticed the switch?"

"I don't believe so, sir. But I could not risk taking the folios altogether and alerting her or the traitor that we were getting closer."

"Let's hope she doesn't notice." It was not a chastisement, but it was close. Sir Charles pointed a thick forefinger at the description of Alastair Whitmore in the first document. "Angel will be pleased you intercepted the information about his true identity."

"It keeps *him* out of retirement." Julian didn't try to hide the bitterness in his voice.

"The accuracy of the information contained in these folios is disturbing," Sir Charles continued. "Whoever the government traitor is has access to sensitive information. Angel's true identity is known only to a handful of people." Sir Charles paused, then continued more softly, "None of whom I would suspect of betraying his country."

"I intend to work backward from Grace Hannah. If I can determine who her contact is, I will follow the channel of communication back here to London."

Sir Charles leaned back and propped one elbow on the arm of his chair. "What's your opinion of Miss Hannah?"

"She's not at all what she seems. It's my experience, sir, that the quietest suspects play the deepest games." Julian gave a short, humorless laugh. "She appears to be every inch the lady, though she is subservient in her uncle's household. I would have guessed she was nothing more than a poor relation."

He wondered if he would have seen what was beneath the surface if he hadn't been looking for it. He was trained to see what others didn't, but she played her role so well he couldn't be sure.

"She is heavily involved in local smuggling," he continued. "I don't know her role within the smuggling gang, but she is accepted as one of them and appears to hold some position of authority."

"It's a leap from smuggler to treason."

"True." A fact that troubled him. "At this time, the only connection I have to the traitor is Miss Hannah and the smugglers."

"We could shut down the smuggling ring." Sir Charles tapped his finger on the documents. "It would prevent any further information being carried to France."

"I thought about that, sir." He had examined every angle during the long, sleepless nights at Thistledown. "Shutting down the ring would alarm the traitor here in London. He might disappear or cease operations altogether until he had safer channels of communication. If he did, we'd lose our connection to him."

"A good point. Although there is a question as to why the information is being held in England. Why would she hide it rather than send it to France?"

"I don't know." It was another fact that plagued him. "I have no method of finding out except through Miss Hannah. We've developed a rapport." The words tasted acidic in his mouth. He swallowed, felt his stomach start to burn. "I can use it."

Sir Charles eyed him. "Do you have any compunction about using her in that manner?"

"There are no other options." Julian forced himself to ignore the burn, ignore the self-loathing, and hold the older man's gaze steadily.

"Very well." Sir Charles tugged on the bellpull beside his desk. "Thank you for bringing this information to London yourself rather than trusting the usual methods of transport."

The door opened to admit Miles Butler, Sir Charles's clerk. He looked as eager as ever. Julian felt suddenly old.

"Mr. Butler, I need these documents messengered over to the foreign secretary immediately." Sir Charles pulled out a fresh sheet of paper and quill. "Just a moment and I will have a short note to accompany them."

"Of course, sir." Mr. Butler brightened as he picked up the documents.

Sir Charles sealed the letter with red wax and passed it to the clerk. "Deliver these directly to the foreign secretary yourself. Don't let one of his clerks delay or obstruct you. They must go to him and no one else."

Mr. Butler straightened, his chest swelling with obvious pride. "Yes, sir. Immediately." He quit the room, leaving Julian and Sir Charles alone.

"I want the foreign secretary to know what information has been leaked," Sir Charles said. "We may be able to isolate the traitor in London."

"Working the information from both directions, so to speak."

"Precisely," Sir Charles concluded. "Do what you must to either gain Miss Hannah's confidence or discover her secrets. Use whichever course seems to best fit the circumstances."

"Yes, sir."

He was a spy. It was the only thing he knew how to be. But there were always boundaries. He was going to cross one.

# Chapter 8

"M ISS GRACIE, ANOTHER invitation has arrived."
    Binkle laid the invitation on the corner of the escritoire in Grace's private sitting room.

"Has my uncle indicated whether he will attend?" She pushed away the household account ledgers, grateful for any interruption from the mundane task.

"The picnic is being held next week by Sir Richard and his wife, Lady Elliott."

"Ah, then we know he will attend." She glanced at the invitation. As usual the invitees were both Grace and her uncle. She took a fresh sheet of paper from a drawer and picked up a quill. "Thank you, Binkle. I'll give the response to one of the footmen to deliver when I've finished."

The butler returned to his duties and Grace dipped the quill into her ink bottle. Hand poised above the paper, she hesitated. She wouldn't attend, of course. She'd been humiliated by Clotilde Wargell at Lady Hammond's ball.

A voice whispered inside her, *Would the Earl of Langford be attending the picnic?* There was no way to know—at least not without directly questioning someone. The voice whispered again, *Does it matter?*

Something about the earl mattered very much. He dispelled

that dark loneliness she carried with her. Perhaps it only meant that she craved a man's touch. She wanted to touch and to taste, to give and to take from him. The sheer enormity of that desire was, in itself, frightening.

She wanted more. More of his mouth on hers, of his strong fingers touching her. Her breath quickened as she imagined the feel of those fingers caressing her own flesh. She wanted the darkness to dissolve in his heat.

Grace let out a long breath and glanced down at the paper. There was a large blot of ink where it dripped from her quill. With a sigh, she decided to write around it. The cost of paper was high and Uncle would be furious if he found out she'd discarded it. She bent her head and carefully wrote:

> *Lord Thaddeus Cannon and Miss Grace Hannah gratefully accept your invitation.*

She wondered if the Earl of Langford wanted to see her again. The neighbors would be shocked to find her in their midst a second time. Uncle Thaddeus, of course, would be furious.

She shuddered and prepared herself for the battle to come.

———

IT WASN'T AS bad as she feared.

It was worse.

"You have no right to attend, Grace," Uncle Thaddeus roared. "You're just a poor relation."

"I know, Uncle." She shrank back against the sitting room settee. She couldn't help it. It was as though her body itself were shrinking. Her fingers twisted in the skirt of her day gown. She'd chosen her best, but knew she would not be as fashionable as the other ladies at the picnic.

"You're nothing but the whelp of a baseborn laborer." He spat the words as he leaned over her. His breath was sour and smelled of brandy and fish. "You're *nothing*."

"I can't help the circumstances of my birth." Her voice sounded weak and she struggled to speak past her dry throat.

"But you can control your conduct." He seemed to swell and grow so that he blocked out everything. "I expect you to return to your chambers. *Now*. Change out of that gown and resume your duties."

Pushing halfway off the settee, she nearly did as he commanded. But something hot washed over her, and she sank back down. It was as if some part of her were starting to bubble and boil and rise up.

He studied her with cold, narrowed eyes.

She swallowed. "I must go," she blurted out. "Lady Elliott specifically asked me to attend one of her children. He's ill." It was a lie. A poor one. She bit back the groan at her own audacity and hoped her deceit wasn't discovered.

A beat passed, then two.

"Very well." His tone was low and menacing. "This time, because Lady Elliott asked for you. You will not attend in the future. *Is that understood?*"

Shocked he'd agreed, she nodded.

"The carriage will leave in ten minutes," he added. "You *will* be ready." He spun on his heel and marched from the room.

Watching his back retreat into the hall, she couldn't quite believe she was attending. Or that she had lied while looking in Uncle Thaddeus's eyes. Why was she suddenly taking such risks?

Because of the blue, blue eyes of the Earl of Langford and the glorious light that filled her when he kissed her.

———

WHEN THEY ARRIVED at Sir Richard and Lady Elliott's country house, they were directed through the house and onto the rear terrace, where the estate's gardens opened up. A trio of musicians was positioned on the terrace so that the breeze carried their lovely music over the gardens.

Uncle Thaddeus shot her one final furious glare, bushy mustache twitching in disgust, before stalking down the terrace steps and leaving Grace alone to face the crowd.

Her hands went damp with nerves inside her kid gloves as she surveyed the guests. Women in pretty muslin gowns dotted the green landscape, parasols angled above them to block out the bright late summer sun, while men buzzed around them like bees searching for nectar. Grace glanced down at her gown

and lamented the dull lavender that edged toward gray. There
was nothing she could do to make it attractive.

Drawing a deep breath, she lifted her plain gray parasol,
opened it above her head and strolled toward the guests. Blankets were spread on the grass before a sunlit pond. Two small
rowboats bobbed on the sparkling surface of the water. Guests
milled about, carrying plates of food and watching the rowers
race their little boats.

She could tell when her presence was first noted. Conver-
sations dwindled, ceased, then began again with overtones of
speculation and surprise. She could almost hear the questions.
*What is she doing? Why is she here?*

Uncertainty plagued her, but she continued forward, drawing on her reserve of composure. Anxiety had her heart
pounding wildly in her chest. Her uncle ignored her arrival,
assiduously keeping his face averted. Would the other guests
speak with her or would they ignore her as well? Would she be
snubbed? Given the cut direct?

Her step faltered. She had been foolish to accept the invitation. She didn't belong there, among the peers and barons
and squires. Uncle Thaddeus was right. She was nothing.

She nearly turned around and fled back to the house, back
to Cannon Manor and safety. Then her hostess, Marie, Lady
Elliott, disengaged herself from the group she was conversing
with and came toward Grace across the lawns.

"Miss Gracie." She offered a welcoming smile. "I'm delighted
you were able to attend our picnic." As usual, Lady Elliott was
sad-eyed and soft-spoken. Shadows of fatigue lay like bruises
beneath her eyes.

"Thank you for including me. And"—she cleared her throat—
"thank you for your support at Lady Hammond's ball. Mrs.
Wargell is—"

"Mean-spirited," Lady Elliott whispered. Her eyes darted
around, searching for eavesdroppers. "We all know she lured
Michael Wargell away from you, and that's why he jilted you.
Otherwise you might have . . . Well." She trailed off, shifting
uncomfortably.

"Thank you." Grace offered a reassuring smile and raised
her voice to its normal level. "You've outdone yourself, Lady
Elliott." She nodded toward tables arranged near the guests.

Platters of food and bottles of sherry and wine crowded the tables. A huge punch bowl stood in the center of one table with tiers of sweets and candied treats beside it.

"You are too kind." Lady Elliott surveyed the tables, evaluating the display with the critical eye of a hostess. Apparently satisfied, she turned back to Grace. "I confess I did not expect you to accept my invitation."

"I'm glad I did." Grace ignored the curiosity in the other woman's eyes. "How are your children?"

"Active, as usual," Lady Elliott responded, and the shadows beneath her eyes deepened. In contrast, her face, already made sallow by the light yellow dress she wore, drained of any further color. "I'm not certain how Richard keeps up with those boys. I'm unable to manage it."

"Because they're just that. Boys. Boys will forever be a little wild and unruly, and certainly full of mischief."

"They're like their father," Lady Elliott finished flatly.

Grace cleared her throat and moved on to Lady Elliott's favorite subject. "Have you taken the waters recently?"

"I returned from Bath over a month ago. It was most restorative, as you can imagine, but with this heat I'm afraid the treatments don't last as long. I'm still so fatigued."

"I know, Lady Elliott." She laid a hand on the lady's arm. "The heat has been oppressive this summer."

"It has," Lady Elliott agreed, bringing out her fan and waving it at her wan face. "I've run out of the tincture you provided for me as well, and that certainly doesn't help matters."

"I'll bring another bottle tomorrow," Grace promised.

"Thank you, Miss Gracie. I don't know what I would have done without your tincture these past few years. Or your company." Lady Elliott squeezed Grace's hand before heaving a sigh. "But enough about my trials. Please enjoy yourself."

She stepped back and gestured toward the other guests. As she moved away, Lady Hammond and Lady Lintell stepped forward, the former cutting across the lawns in her formidable way, the latter fluttering in her wake.

"Miss Gracie, how good to see you joining us," Lady Hammond greeted her with a broad smile.

"Indeed, Miss Gracie," Lady Lintell chirped. "I was just telling Lady Hammond the other evening that you simply *must* join us more often. Why Cannon keeps you locked up in the manor, I just don't know. Such a pretty young girl should get out with those of your own age. You work too hard. I keep saying it to Lady Hammond, don't I?"

"Yes, Minnie, you do keep saying it."

They flanked Grace and drew her into the crowd. It surprised her that it was easier to find something to say to the other guests than it had been at Lady Hammond's ball. She didn't stumble overmuch with pleasantries. It was disconcerting— and oddly exciting—to be welcomed so quickly by the society she'd been distanced from for so long.

The crowd ebbed and flowed across the lawn as groups formed and reformed. Eventually Grace found herself alone near the pond, the tables laden with food and drink set up before her. She moved toward the tables, thinking to fill a plate with the delicate fare to keep her hands busy. Before she could reach for a plate, a broad shadow fell across the table. She looked up and found the Wandering Earl beside her.

"My lord." Unable to help herself, her gaze fell to the earl's lips. She wanted those lips on hers again and felt a rush of heat at the thought.

"I wasn't expecting to see such beauty today, Miss Hannah, and now here you are, gracing us with your magnificence."

"But what of the other ladies, my lord? Don't they deserve such charming platitudes?"

"Perhaps." He cocked his head, gaze steady on hers. "But I've only eyes for my smuggler."

"Smuggler, my lord?" Her heart bumped once, hard. "Don't you mean a smuggler's consort?"

"Ah yes. That was our fantasy, wasn't it? The smuggling captain and his consort." He gestured toward the blue sky. "But there's no night to hide in now, is there?"

"But there are extensive gardens, my lord smuggler." Private gardens. Or nearly so. There would be others wandering their paths or traveling the maze, but there would still be room for private conversation.

And perhaps a kiss. Just one kiss.

"So there are." He glanced across the green lawns toward the nearby gardens. When he looked back at her, his eyes gleamed. "Perhaps we should stroll through Sir Richard and Lady Elliott's garden."

She accepted the arm he offered and angled her parasol to block the sun. They crossed the lawns to the formal gardens where other couples and groups walked the stone pathways between the flower beds. Grace could hear snatches of laughter and the murmur of voices. Parasols twirled and bobbed above the hedges and blooms.

"Perhaps my lady gardener could offer advice on how to rejuvenate Thistledown's gardens," the earl said, directing her away from the paths occupied by other guests.

"That would depend on what you desired your gardens to be. Cultivated roses or wildflowers? Organized and formal, or spontaneous and natural?"

"What would you prefer?"

She studied the surrounding beds. Ruthlessly organized, the colors marched in precise lines through the beds. They were beautiful, of course, and yet they didn't draw her in.

"Wildflowers. Spontaneity. A riot of colors and scents and blossoms to feed your senses."

"I thought so," he murmured, his lips curving in a knowing smile.

"And you? Would you prefer something orderly and neat, or bold and wild?" Had she ever spoken in that coy and seductive tone before? Only once. To the earl, on the dark night of Lady Hammond's ball.

"Bold and wild, Miss Hannah. Most definitely bold and wild." He purred the words and brought her hand to his lips. He turned her hand up and those full, attractive lips settled on the delicate skin of her wrist just above the glove she wore.

Her breath hitched as the touch of his lips sent desire spiraling to her belly.

She glanced behind them, wondering if they could be observed by other guests. But they were lost in the gardens and the picnic was no longer in view. Surrounding them were only high garden hedges, the hum of bees and the sweet scent of flowers.

She turned her gaze back to the earl, who watched her with seductive eyes.

"In my gardens," he said, bringing his hand up to grasp her glove at the tip of her forefinger, "I want secret grottoes and hidden groves." He tugged at the glove until it was loose enough he could draw it off. "I want unseen pockets of lush foliage that two people can hide in, concealed from the rest of the world."

"What would those two people do in your hidden groves?" Excruciatingly aware of every inch of her skin, she waited, breathless.

"Anything they desired." He turned her hand palm up and placed his lips on the center of her palm. The kiss was soft, seductive. "Secret places have infinite possibilities."

"Secret places have infinite uses, as well." One corner of her lips pulled up in a half smile. "Especially for smugglers and their consorts."

"What do you know of secret places and smugglers, Miss Hannah?" The earl brought her forefinger to his lips and kissed the tip. He looked up and she saw in the bright blue what she'd been waiting for. Calculation, sharp and dangerous.

A thrill shot through her. "What better way to use your gardens than as a smuggler's hideaway?" She angled her parasol, effectively separating them from the picnic. Still, she lowered her voice. "There are many things a smuggler could conceal in his gardens."

"So there are." He kissed her fingers in turn, his tongue making hot circles on each before moving to the next finger-tip. "Perhaps he could hide his consort there, imprisoned among the blossoms."

"Imprisoned?" She curled her fingers inward to hold his kisses in her palm.

"A prison of pleasure only." Keeping her hand in his, he drew her down the garden path. "Come with me."

"Where?" Her feet were already moving, seemingly of their own accord.

"To the maze." His eyes stayed focused on hers. "Will you?"

She thought of the light that swirled within her, of the bur-geoning liquid heat that filled her. And of him.

"*Yes.*"

They passed shrubs and beds rioting with color. Every-where were shades of green strewn with brilliant blooms. The hedge maze rose before them. He found the opening and drew her just inside, between the rows of tall yews.

Even though they were only a step into the maze, the voices of the guests dimmed to become background to the drone of bees and the rustle of the hedge leaves. They were isolated. Alone.

She should turn back. She was flirting with disaster. Compromise could come at any moment. Who knew that better than she? Still, when he pulled the parasol from her limp fingers and gently pressed her back into the leaves, she didn't protest. Her heart was thudding, her body hot. Her blood thrummed just below the surface, a needy beat holding her trapped.

"The smuggler and his consort would retreat to their secret place," he murmured against her ear. His fingers ran the length of her ungloved arm, sensitizing her skin. "He would bring gifts to his consort, only for her pleasure. Smooth silk from the Orient to twine about her limbs, caressing her soft skin. Strings of pearls and jewels that could be looped around her neck." His knowing fingers skimmed up to the hollow of her throat, then slid around her collarbone.

She should protest the liberties he was taking. But she wanted to be seduced, to be lost in his honeyed words. Her breathing quickened as she waited for the next flicker of his fingertips. Where would it be?

"The finest scent could be spread along the skin of her jaw, at the pulse beating at the base of her throat." His hands followed his words, brushing gently against her jawline, pausing at the hollow of her throat. Fingers skimmed along the scooped edge of her bodice, and her breasts ached with need.

"Silver bangles would encircle her dainty wrists and tiny bells from India would tinkle at her pretty ankles." His hand braceleted her exposed wrist. He tugged gently, pulling her against him. She let him, her senses heightened by the low murmur of his voice and the touch of his fingers. Seduction by the earl was a heady thing.

She reveled in it.

"A diamond tiara could be tucked into her silver locks." He smoothed the delicate loose curls around her ear. "Ah, fair lady, I have wanted my fingers in that hair since I first saw you."

She smiled, just the smallest movement. "A smuggler takes what he wants."

A groan escaped his lips. His fingers performed the task his voice had laid out, reaching into her hair and pulling out the pins. Her hair tumbled to her shoulders and his fingers splayed through it, separating the long strands until the mass rained down her back.

"Liquid silver," he murmured.

She swore she heard his control snap. Or was it her own? His lips swooped down to claim hers, hot and demanding, even as his hands fisted in her hair. She raised herself on tiptoe and met his mouth with her own. His tongue darted in, stroked.

Gripping his shoulders, she dug her fingers in. *More.* More heat. More light. More *him*. He burned away the black, melting it so there was nothing but the fire within her. The fire of him.

Until the short, distressed squeak echoed between the hedges.

"My lord! Miss Gracie! My lord . . ." The high-pitched voice trailed away, leaving only the twitter of birds.

She looked to the maze entrance and saw Lady Hammond, Lady Lintell, and Mrs. Parker.

They'd been caught. Everything had fallen apart. Her entire life upended in a single moment of passion.

Again.

Grace tried to wrench herself away from the earl, but he held her face steady between his cupped palms, his fingers still tangled in her hair. His eyes stayed on hers, intense, focused, the bright blue burning into her. Then he stepped back and let his hands fall away. But still he stared into her eyes. She was trapped in his gaze, drowning in it, until he looked toward the others.

The earl made a sweeping gesture with his arm toward Grace. "Ladies. May I present Miss Grace Hannah, who has kindly consented to be my wife."

Grace gripped her fingers together. The situation was spinning out of control. It was happening just as it had with Michael. A kiss, the witnesses, the hasty proposal. A weight fell on her chest, smothering her so that she couldn't catch her breath.

"Oh, oh! My lord," Lady Lintell chirped, clapping her hands

together like a schoolgirl rather than the matron she was. "We were just about to invite you to an assembly, but perhaps we'll turn it into an engagement assembly. Really, this is simply *fantastic*! Our Miss Gracie! A countess!"

"Humph," said Mrs. Parker.

Lady Hammond, her wise eyes flicking between Grace and the earl, made no comment at all.

"I simply cannot *wait* to tell Lord Lintell this news." Lady Lintell's hands fluttered in the air as she beamed at the couple. "Why, I haven't heard anything about it! Not a *whiff*! I daresay we're the first to know!"

"No," Grace said. The word was barely a whisper. She couldn't think, couldn't focus. A low, droning buzz filled her head. "No," Grace repeated, louder this time.

"No?" Lady Hammond raised a brow.

"No." She tried to find her composure. Drawing a deep breath, she attempted to regulate her breathing. "I won't marry the Earl of Langford."

Beside her, the earl tensed and jerked his head around to stare at her. She refused to look at him, keeping her gaze on Lady Hammond.

"What?" Lady Lintell's hands fell to her sides, confusion evident in the furrowed brow that marred her thin features. "You're *not* marrying the earl? But . . ."

"Humph." Mrs. Parker added a snort and crossed her arms.

"You have no choice," Lady Hammond said.

"There is always a choice." Her voice must have separated from her body. It seemed to come from such a long way off. Grace rubbed her throat with numb fingers. "I won't let that choice be taken from me."

"There is no choice in this." It was the earl who spoke, his voice low and carrying none of the charm she usually heard there. His tone was serious, even a little dangerous, and his lean face was set, eyes resolute.

"I don't understand!" Lady Lintell squawked.

"Be quiet, Minnie," Mrs. Parker interjected.

"*But*—"

"It will get out," Lady Hammond said. Her gaze flicked toward Lady Lintell, as if to say the other woman would not be able to keep quiet. "Even if it doesn't, the facts remain as they are. The earl must do what is proper. So must you, Gracie. You cannot withstand this a second time."

"Marriage will fix it? Will that restore my reputation?" But it wouldn't come to marriage. The earl would rescind his offer once his mind had cleared.

"Marriage always does," Lady Hammond replied.

"Reputation?" queried Lady Lintell. "But—*Oh.*" Understanding dawned and her eyes opened wide. "Oh dear. Well, really, my lord. You *must* do the proper thing."

"I'm trying," the earl ground out. "Miss Hannah, Grace—"

"No." Blood surged through her so that she wanted to run, to pump her legs to match the frantic beat of her heart. "If you'll excuse me."

She fled. Cowardly, but with the roaring in her head she could think of nothing else to do.

The earl called out to her, but she pulled her skirts up and half ran out of the garden toward Lord Elliott's stable. Thank goodness she knew the young groom well.

"Quickly," she gasped, skidding into the stables. "Saddle one of Sir Richard's horses."

"Miss Gracie?" He scrambled up from the floor and dropped the bridle he'd been oiling.

"It's important. I need one of Sir Richard's horses." Was that hysteria in her voice? She glanced into the courtyard behind her. No sign of the Earl of Langford. Yet. "Hurry," she urged.

"You want to take one of Sir Richard's horses? He'll murder me, Miss Gracie."

"I'll return it immediately. One of Cannon Manor's grooms will bring him back within the hour." When he hesitated, she lowered her voice. "*Please.*"

"Aye." His shoulders squared and he strode away to saddle the horse. When he returned, he was leading a spirited mare. "Be quick about returning her."

"Thank you." Pathetically grateful, she gripped his shoulder in thanks before leading the mare to the mounting block. Settling into the saddle, she clutched the mare's reins and turned her toward the lane leading away from the house.

The Earl of Langford stood there. Tall, lean and formidable.

"Stop," he commanded. "We must talk."

"There's nothing to discuss." The mare sensed her tension and pranced sideways. She tugged at the reins to keep her under control and struggled to work up an indifferent smile for the earl. "I'll survive the scandal and you can return to London. No harm done."

"No harm? Lady Lintell will spread the news to the borders of Devon and beyond within the week."

"That may be. But I'm just a poor relation, my lord. Within two weeks, no one will care."

She spurred the horse into a gallop and rode past him. Refusing to look behind her, Grace kept her eyes on the dirt lane. Even when sobs wracked her frame and tears tracked down her cheeks to plop onto hands fisted in the reins, she refused to look behind her.

# Chapter 9

JULIAN VERY CAREFULLY and very deliberately shrugged out of his coat and draped it over the back of his chair. The knife he'd hidden beneath was removed next. He set it on the desk beside a delicate kid glove. *Her* glove. He'd removed that bit of leather, kissed the tips of her long pretty fingers. Seduced her.

Ruined her.

Was Grace Hannah a traitor? That was the dilemma. If she was, then the scene that afternoon meant nothing. Her reputation meant nothing. His offer of marriage would be rescinded. Not even rescinded, it would be so unimportant it would be forgotten altogether.

And if she was not a traitor? He felt the noose tighten around his neck and heard the click of the lock as fate trapped him into marriage. No, not fate. His own stupidity. Worse, his own lack of control. He'd forgotten where they were when he'd kissed her. The guests, the garden, the investigation had all faded away until there had only been her taste, her scent and his driving need for more of her.

He fingered the glove, rubbing a thumb over the worn seams. The offer of marriage had been unavoidable. Now he sat in the semidarkness of a curtained room and contemplated matrimony.

Spies made horrible husbands. They had a habit of dying. Travers men made even worse husbands. They had a habit of philandering and murder.

The marriage would be a failure.

But he could see Grace. Her laughter, her wit. The slow smile that spread across her face. The quiet composure. Her breeches. He grinned as he pictured her riding astride Demon, her hair whipping around her. Whatever else happened in their relationship, that image would stay with him always.

He picked up the knife, tested the balance. Absently, he checked the blade for nicks. He would have to confront her. Soon. As soon as he could orchestrate time alone with her. There was no other way forward. Yet in the interim, he couldn't leave her unattached and unaffianced. If there was some other explanation for her conduct, he would be doing her a grave disservice.

In short, he would be no different than his father.

He forced down bile and wondered if the sour burn was the taste of deception.

Picking up a quill, he dipped it in the inkwell and began to scrawl across a sheet of paper. The first draft found its final resting place crumpled beneath his desk. The second draft was thrown into the fireplace.

He read the third draft as the ink dried.

*My dear Miss Hannah—*

*I do not regret our relationship, as I hold you in the highest esteem. Nevertheless, I do regret that this afternoon's discovery has placed you in an untenable position. I understand you may have reservations about marrying a gentleman you have known only a few weeks. However, my offer of marriage remains open indefinitely. Please seriously consider your reputation and the consequences of refusing to become my wife.*

*I would be honored if you would accept my offer of marriage.*

*Sincerely yours,*
*Julian, Earl of Langford*

---

"GRACE!" THE BELLOW was accompanied by the crash and tinkle of breaking glass. "Grace, attend me at once!"

She laid the Earl of Langford's letter on the escritoire and pressed her fingertips to her eyes. Apparently her uncle was aware of the debacle in Lady Elliott's garden the day before.

History, it seemed, was repeating itself.

Or perhaps not. This time she'd refused the offer of marriage instead of acquiescing in a rush of shame and embarrassment. Instead, she'd panicked and run, which was embarrassing in itself. Still, the outcome was the same as before. She was compromised, ruined and unmarried. Only this time it would be by choice rather than rejection and betrayal.

Lord Cannon shouted again, accenting the shout with rhythmic pounding. Sighing, she quit her private sitting room. She had no trouble determining her uncle's location. She could hear him thumping around his study.

She paused outside the room, squared her shoulders and straightened the apron she wore over her simple gown. She took one deep, steadying breath and pushed open the door.

Uncle Thaddeus stood before his desk pouring two fingers of smuggled French brandy into a crystal glass. He whirled to face her, the brandy decanter still in his hand.

"What the bloody hell were you thinking?" he roared.

"Uncle?" Folding her hands together, she struggled to stay calm.

"I've just returned from Beer." He slammed the decanter on his desktop. Amber liquid sloshed over the rim and splashed on the expanse of polished oak. "Not only were you caught in a compromising position with the Earl of Langford, but *you refused his offer of marriage!*" He snatched up the glass and began to pace, leaving the spilled brandy on the desktop.

"I'm sorry, Uncle," Grace responded automatically. She stepped forward and used her apron to wipe the surface clean. What else could she say? She couldn't deny his accusations.

"I won't have it." His tone was low and vicious. "*I won't have it.* I informed you when you came to live here that I expected you to abide by certain rules and maintain your place."

"Yes, but—" Strangely fascinated, she watched his nostrils flare.

"You've tried to elevate yourself above your station in an attempt to be something you are not. You're nothing." He snorted and tossed back the brandy. "Rather, you *were* nothing. Now you're a whore."

Grace sucked in her breath as his words sliced through her. He'd called her that once before. She should have expected it again.

"I let you stay after you whored yourself for Michael Wargell," he said in a vicious undertone.

"I *loved* Michael." The words burst from her, sharp blades that scored her throat.

"Love?" he scoffed.

"I would have married him." Bitterness rose like bile. Oh, she'd loved Michael. With every fiber of her being.

"Out of mercy I let you stay, but not this time. You either accept the earl's offer of marriage, or you leave my household." He returned to the desk and refilled his glass, pouring well over two fingers this time. "Either way, I won't have a whore under my roof."

"You don't mean that." Shocked, she gripped her fingers tight, tighter, until the bones seemed to grind together.

"I do." He turned cold brown eyes on her. "If you accept the earl's offer, you may stay here until the banns are read and the wedding ceremony performed. If you do not accept the earl, you will pack your belongings and leave today. *Now.*"

"I—" With numb fingers she gripped the edge of the desk, willing her shaky knees to support her. "I don't know. I—"

"You have ten minutes to decide." Still holding the full glass, Uncle Thaddeus strode from the room, riding boots beating an angry rhythm on the polished parquet floor of the hall.

On weak legs, Grace staggered to a chair and slowly lowered herself into it, staring blindly into the empty room. The earl's note echoed in her mind. *I hold you in the highest esteem . . . my offer of marriage remains open indefinitely . . . I would be honored if you would accept my offer . . .*

If she refused the earl's offer, she would have to leave Cannon Manor. She had no other relatives, no prospects and nowhere to go. Perhaps she could stay in Beer and weather the storm of disapproval. But no, Uncle Thaddeus had thrown her out. If she stayed, she would be without any respectability.

She saw herself walking along High Street. Eyes averted as she drew near. Noses sniffed and whispers hissed. Skirts twitched away as she passed. Even the image made her cheeks burn. She couldn't weather that storm a second time. With Michael, everyone believed she'd been young and naïve and easily led. Perhaps she had been. But she was older now and knew better.

She could not refuse the earl and stay in Beer.

She could go to London and find a position as a paid companion or governess. She could find a new home and start a new life.

A chill crept up her body, icy cold and sharp. She couldn't leave Devon and her friends unprotected. She promised the smugglers she would find the traitor and turn him over to the authorities. If she didn't, one of the men would become a scapegoat for the real traitor.

Her stomach clutched as the door opened. Uncle Thaddeus stood in the doorway, pitiless eyes as empty as the glass in his hand.

"Have you made your decision?"

Grace looked down at her clasped hands. Deliberately she flattened them against her thighs. She'd acted rashly and let herself be swept away. Now she would accept her fate.

She straightened her shoulders. "I will accept the Earl of Langford's offer of marriage."

"I'll begin the marriage negotiations. Obviously, your father did not provide a dowry for you. However, I will, so the earl doesn't realize he's being cheated." With that, Uncle Thaddeus spun on his heel and disappeared through the door.

Grace continued to stare at her numb fingers.

*What had she done?*

# Chapter 10

THROUGH THE LATE-NIGHT gloom, Julian studied the façade of the Jolly Smuggler. Ivy climbed the stone front to the second floor, which he knew consisted of two small and two large guest rooms. Tacked on to the rear was a tiny cottage. Overall, it was a modest building, simple and unadorned, with a sign that made him chuckle. Two men sat in a small jolly boat, each raising a tankard, as the waves rose around them.

As though men drank tankards of ale while sitting in a jolly boat on the open sea. Then again, such a boat was used to convey goods between a larger ship and the shore. It was the perfect size for a smuggler or two to secretly transport their wares and enjoy a pint while they were at it, if they were of a mind.

Whatever else Jack Blackbourn was, he had a sense of humor. The rest remained to be seen. Intelligence from London indicated Blackbourn had retired from smuggling, but he'd done so at least twice before and returned to the game.

The important question was whether he was a traitor.

Julian hoped he was. It would explain why Grace was involved. Perhaps she was pressured into it by Blackbourn, making her an innocent victim taken advantage of by a criminal. Even as Julian had the thought, he hated himself for it. He didn't wish death on a stranger, any more than he wanted Grace to be guilty of treason.

Clenching his jaw, he put those thoughts behind him. He had only one mission for the moment: Find the traitor. Why he wanted Grace to be innocent when her innocence meant he was trapped in marriage was something he simply could not think about now.

He straightened the coarse homespun coat that constituted his disguise. His pistol bumped against his hip. He could not feel the knife in his boot, but he would have noted the absence. His boot didn't fit right without it.

He pushed open the door of the pub. He stepped into the smoky, yeast-scented taproom and took in the scene. A dozen men in workingman's garb sat at tables around the room. Laughter and voices filled the air, as did the scent of good food. In fact, he thought, sniffing again, the food smelled more than just appetizing. It smelled delicious.

Behind the bar stood a short man with untamed hair and square features. He was laughing with a pair of men while he accepted coins for their drafts. That, Julian thought, must be the infamous Jack Blackbourn.

Julian strode to the counter and leaned against it, patiently waiting for his quarry to finish with his customers. When Blackbourn finally came his way, there was still a smile on his lips.

"What can I do for you?" Blackbourn wiped away the spills on the counter in front of Julian with a large gray rag.

"A pint of ale, my good man." He nodded toward the affable patrons. "A lively crew tonight."

"Aye." Blackbourn set a tankard in front of Julian. "But they're regular patrons, sir, and know each other well. I don't think I've seen you in before."

"Do you keep track of your patrons?"

"Well, now, a good publican remembers his regulars and their preferences." Blackbourn leaned casually on the counter. "I'm certain I haven't seen you in before."

"No, you haven't." He sipped his ale. Curiosity shone bright in Blackbourn's eyes, but Julian refused to elaborate.

A young barmaid with long yellow curls and a sassy smile pranced by and leaned onto the counter beside Julian.

"Jack," she said to the publican. "Ned would like another pint and Young Mike would like a bowl o' stew."

"Aye, Mary." Blackbourn turned, pushed open a door a crack and shouted into what must be the kitchens, "A bowl o' stew!"

"How am I doing on my first night, Jack?" the girl asked when Blackbourn returned to the counter.

"Well enough." He passed her a full tankard. "Anyone give you any trouble, lass? No stray hands?"

"They know yer pub don't run to that, Jack, which is why me ma let me work 'ere. I think they all know me anyway." She tossed her curls and beamed at Julian. "Though I don't think as how I've seen you before, sir."

Her innocence was blinding. It made him wonder about Jack Blackbourn. What was he doing employing a young, innocent barmaid and then ensuring the patrons weren't hassling her? A publican hired barmaids to entice their patrons.

"If I'd known such beauty would be here, I would've frequented the Jolly Smuggler before." Julian took her hand and kissed it as he would any lady of the ton.

"Go on with you, sir!" She laughed, a delighted sound full of youth and merriment. Tossing her hair again, she sauntered away, the tankard hoisted on a tray.

"Well, now, you've made our Mary's day." Blackbourn's eyes narrowed in speculation.

"If a man can't make a girl blush with a pretty compliment," Julian said, lifting his pint, "he ought to retire the field."

"The truth if I've ever heard it!" The barman guffawed and slapped the counter. "Your drink's on me, sir, for putting a smile on young Mary's pretty mouth and making me laugh."

"Thank you, Blackbourn, though I have a mind to pay you anyway. For information."

"Information?" He sobered quickly. Took one half step back from the counter. "I don't give out information, paid or not."

"Everyone has a price, Blackbourn," Julian said softly.

The barkeep narrowed his eyes. "Not me."

"No? Let's try this, then." Julian slid a large pound note across the counter. "I'm looking for someone who can ship something across the Channel, no questions asked, for a high fee. I'll be back in a week. Let me know if someone comes to mind." He downed the remainder of the ale, set the tankard on the counter and walked toward the door.

"Leaving so soon, sir?" Mary called out as she flounced by.

"I am, though I think I may be leaving the sunshine behind, for no beauty can shine as brightly as yours." He bowed with a flourish and quit the pub on Mary's happy laughter.

The grin on his face died only a few moments later as he rounded the side of the pub and approached the small cottage at the rear.

Built of wood and covered by a thatched roof, it was attached to the pub at an awkward angle. The windows were dark. He imagined the entire family, however many there were, worked the pub and the kitchens when called for. Blackbourn himself behind the counter, his wife in the kitchen and the children, if any, where needed. Which left the cottage empty.

The cottage door had a useless lock. Blackbourn might as well remove it. It was no barrier to anyone with a rudimentary knowledge of lock picks. Julian's knowledge was not rudimentary. He slid his knife from his boot before pushing open the door. It was a quieter weapon than the pistol, though he didn't expect to need either.

Standing on the threshold, he listened to the night. He could hear the dull rush of the ocean, voices from the pub. But the cottage was silent.

He stepped inside and let his eyes adjust to the darkness. The furnishings were simple, the style spartan. Yet it was welcoming. Curtains hung at the window and wildflowers sat in an earthenware bowl on the single table. Cheerful quilts lay over straw mattresses in the bedrooms.

He didn't light a candle. Searches could be conducted in the dark easily enough if a man knew what he was about. Within a half hour he'd thoroughly searched the simple cottage, including all of Blackbourn's personal documents. He looked for hollow walls, secret drawers and false-bottomed trunks. He found a number of interesting items, including expensive French brandy and other liquors under some loose floorboards.

Then he found the ledgers. Within minutes he knew with certainty just how deep into treason Jack Blackbourn was.

# Chapter 11

"THANK YOU FOR calling, Lady Elliott." Grace watched the other woman sink onto the settee in the front salon of Cannon Manor. Her sad eyes were shadowed, her cheeks thin. She looked as tired as Grace had ever seen her. "The tea should be here in a moment."

"Thank you." Lady Elliott smoothed her skirts. "I heard the news of your marriage."

"You and most of Devon," she said. "Cannon Manor has received more callers during the past two days since the banns were read than in the last five years."

"I'm not surprised. I've heard of nothing else but that Miss Gracie is marrying the Wandering Earl." She laid a gentle hand on Grace's arm. "How are you?"

"I'm fine." Never mind that she wanted to cry. She swallowed the tears clogging her throat. Her course was set and there was no turning back. "It's just going to take some getting used to."

"I imagine so, particularly when you go to London after the ceremony," Lady Elliott said. "Then again, the earl is such a worldly traveler, perhaps he'll be leaving for the Continent soon. Will you be traveling with him?" Curiosity replaced the usual lingering sadness in Lady Elliott's eyes.

"Ah—" Terrifyingly, she didn't know. "We haven't fully discussed our future travel plans," Grace answered. It was the only statement she could think of that wouldn't be an outright lie.

"I see." Lady Elliott sent Grace a commiserating look. "These things do take time to work out."

"Yes," Grace agreed vaguely, her mind already focused on the future. Would she have to leave Devon? Would she be required to live in London? On the Continent?

In the end, she would be at the mercy of a man she knew nothing about.

"My husband met the earl while out for a ride and invited him to tea. He met my boys." Lady Elliott paused, drawn brows and down-turned lips evidencing her bafflement, before adding, "He seemed quite interested in them. I wouldn't think such a worldly gentleman would want to speak with two such . . . active boys, but the earl did. In fact, he went back out to the stables—just after he'd come in from them—to inspect the boys' new ponies."

The tea trolley rolled in with the maid following in its wake. She set out the cups and pot, then added a plate of seed-cakes. Grace offered her thanks with a smile as the girl left. She picked up the pot and began to pour.

"How are Sir Richard and the boys?" Grace asked, passing a teacup.

"Well enough, I suppose." Lady Elliott shrugged her thin shoulders. "Sir Richard seems to be forever closeted with some-one or another about business or his horses. The boys—well, I don't need to go into detail." She stared into her tea.

"I noted Bryan's arm was healing well when I last saw him."

"I've told the boys time and again that a well-bred young man doesn't ride bareback or perform tricks." Lady Elliott's gaze was fixed on the plate of seedcakes. "His father is to blame for that broken arm. He encourages them both to be reckless."

"They seem to have fun, though." Grace reached for a cake.

"That's true." Lady Elliott's transfixed gaze followed Grace's hand as the seedcake made its way to her lips. "I'd hoped by now they would have found a cause. Something to excite them. Something with meaning. Or at least become interested in their studies."

Grace bit into the cake. Lady Elliott paled and her breath-ing shallowed. She swallowed cautiously.

"What's wrong, Lady Elliott?" Grace kept her voice low, as she might with a wounded animal.

"I'm going to be ill." Lady Elliott pressed a hand to her mouth.

"Breathe," Grace commanded. She slid over to the settee and put her arm around Lady Elliott's shoulders. "Breathe through your nose, slowly. Deliberately. One in, two out. Three in, four out."

Lady Elliott gripped her hand and breathed with Grace's count. As the color came back into her face, she leaned gingerly back against the settee. Her movements were slow and careful, as though she were afraid to upset the balance of her stomach.

"Thank you," Lady Elliott said.

"Of course." Grace squeezed the other woman's hand. "What's the matter? Can you tell me? Are you ill?"

Lady Elliott contemplated their joined hands for a long moment. Then she lifted shining eyes. "I'm with child."

"Oh. *Oh*. I'm so glad. So happy for you." She squeezed Lady Elliott's hand again, genuinely pleased.

"I've only known for a few weeks, so it might not—" She stopped and drew a long breath. "I'm hoping for a girl this time. A small, sweet girl." She trilled a laugh. "It's the seedcakes, Gracie. I simply can't stand the thought of them, let alone the taste. It's the oddest thing, really. I wasn't the least bit bothered by foods with the boys, but with this baby the simplest foods make me ill."

"You sound happy." And looked it, she added silently. Lady Elliott glowed with happiness.

"I am. Oh, *I am*. I've waited so long."

"For a girl?"

Lady Elliott opened her mouth to answer, then swiveled her gaze to the door. "Lord Langford, how nice to see you."

Grace's pulse skipped. The Earl of Langford filled the doorway with his broad shoulders and lean frame, elegant as ever in a blue superfine coat and nankeen breeches. "Lady Elliott, Miss Hannah." He flashed a grin and swept a bow in their direction, eyes twinkling. "Lady Elliott, you look lovely today. Your eyes are simply full of sunshine."

The lady laughed, the merriest sound Grace had ever heard

from that sad mouth. "My lord, you are positively foolish." But she beamed at him nonetheless.

"My lord," Grace greeted him, rising from her chair.

"Miss Hannah." He took her hand and brought it to his lips. His eyes stayed on hers, gleaming devilishly.

"How are your sons, Lady Elliott?" He kept his fingers twined around Grace's. She wanted to tug them free, but was afraid to draw too much attention to them.

"Active as ever," Lady Elliott answered, waving her hand dismissively. "But I really should be leaving, Gracie. No, I know the way, and there's always Binkle." She waved Grace back to her seat and was gone.

They were alone. Without a proper chaperone.

Grace could only stare into his eyes, focused so intently on her. Consumed by sudden nerves, she tugged her fingers free and folded them in front of her. She cast about for an appropriate topic of conversation. What did one say to the man that compromised you?

"Would you care to stroll in the gardens?" he asked.

"Yes," she agreed with relief.

He offered his arm. She placed her fingers on it, conscious of him with every fiber of her body. She and the earl would soon do much more than exchange kisses. If he didn't jilt her, of course.

They stepped into the gold September sunlight. The day was still, without a breeze to stir the air, though the chill of autumn hung on the air. Summer blossoms had slowly given way to fall flowers, which bloomed in a riot of rich colors and scents. Grace took a deep breath and let the sweet aromas soothe away the tension.

She raised the first topic that came to mind. "You met Lady Elliott's sons?"

He laughed. "A pair of scamps."

"You sound like you enjoyed them," she said, surprised.

"Because I did."

Grace wondered at the earl's interest in two rambunctious and unruly boys. Children did not seem to fit his charming personality—or the cold calculation that hid behind the blue eyes. How much did she really know about the earl, aside from his powers of seduction?

"I imagine you were a similar scamp at that age," she ventured.

He was quiet for a long moment. "I was never like those boys," he murmured. "With a father like mine, I could never be so lighthearted and carefree."

"Was your father—" She broke off. "I'm sorry."

He continued to stroll casually through the garden, but Grace could feel the tension in the arm beneath her fingers. "It's well known my father was a bastard, Miss Hannah, though not by birth. He was a quintessential Travers male." Derision dripped from the words.

"I apologize. I have no right to pry into such matters."

"No?" He raised a brow. "But I have been well-informed of your parentage."

She closed her eyes, steadied herself. Of course he had. She should have known Uncle Thaddeus would tell him. The need to move rippled through her.

She stepped away from him and bent to examine a bed of purple-red betony blossoms. Gripping a thick weed that hid between the trumpet-shaped blooms, she dug through the cool, rich soil for the root. "I suppose Uncle Thaddeus wanted to make sure you knew exactly what you were obtaining in a wife?" she said bitterly.

"Indeed." His tone was mild. "Lord Cannon thought it only right in the event you provide me with an heir."

"My mother married beneath her." She yanked hard on the root bundle. It burst from the ground in a shower of dirt. "So far beneath her, in fact, that her father and brother disowned her."

"I believe the term your uncle used was 'baseborn laborer.' "

She shuddered even as she tossed the weed away. "Mother had a modest income—a very modest income—left to her from my grandmother, so she and my father moved to Kent where he had some relatives. They loved each other and were happy. *I* was happy," she finished fiercely. She tilted her chin, daring him to argue with her.

"I can see you were." He studied her carefully, his hands clasped behind his back as he stood beside the flower bed she crouched in.

"If you want to cry off—"

"Why would I?" He gently drew her to her feet.

"Because I'm a baseborn laborer's daughter. I have no lineage and no social graces to offer you. I'll make a dreadful countess." She hadn't even realized her fear until she'd voiced it. She stepped back onto the garden path. "It's not as though we're marrying by choice."

"You don't want to marry me? Ah, I know." She knew he was baiting her from the laugh in his eyes. "It's my lack of smuggling experience that has failed to win you over. What must I do to earn your esteem, fair lady? Offer you a trunk of the finest smuggled French silk?" He took her hand and brought it to his lips in a grand, sweeping gesture. "Perhaps then I shall be able to compete with the notorious Jack Blackbourn for your affections."

She was powerless to stop the bubble of laughter that escaped her lips.

"If you want to compete with Jack, you'll have to captain your own ship and go to France yourself. Jack would do nothing less." She let him tuck her hand in his elbow once more as they continued down the path.

"Alas, I have no ship! I suppose I shall always be second in your affections, then. What a way to start a marriage."

"Do be serious." She struggled to keep the smile from her face.

"Must I?"

"Yes. Our conversation has strayed into the ridiculous once again."

"So it has. Very well." He sighed. "Make no mistake, fair lady. I won't leave you at the altar."

She let out a breath. Studying the hard, suddenly serious planes of his face, she thought perhaps she could trust him. But there was much that stood between them. She couldn't hide smuggling from him once they were married, yet how could she tell the truth? She was, in fact, a criminal. She cleared her throat and started with the simplest topic.

"There are items that should be discussed about our future, such as what, exactly, you expect from this union."

"To be honest, Miss Hannah, I expect little. In fact, I expect only what you're comfortable with." He stopped walking and turned to face her.

She frowned. "I don't understand."

"You may live at Thistledown for our entire marriage, or

you may live in London. You may live at any of my other estates for that matter. If you never want to see me again, that can be arranged. You can share my bed"—he gave her a long, hot look—"or not. Whatever your pleasure."

He was silent for a moment before continuing, as though carefully choosing his words. "As I said in my note, I regret that my actions have forced you into this situation, but it can't be changed. I won't force you any further into a situation you cannot abide. I would have us be friends, Miss Hannah. Lovers, if you are agreeable, but friends at the least."

Thoughtful, Grace searched his lean, handsome face and deep eyes, struggling to reconcile this serious gentleman with the laughing would-be smuggler. "I believed there was much more beneath the surface than you show the world. Now I am certain of it."

"There's always more beneath the surface. Take yourself, for instance." He ran a callused finger against her cheek. "All that smooth, white skin and fair hair. The serene expression. And such passion beneath."

He cupped her cheek, a gentle, testing touch. She couldn't stop herself from turning into his hand until her lips touched his palm. Yet their gazes didn't stray and she saw the blue turn dark with desire.

"I want all that passion," he whispered. "But I won't take more than you will give."

His lips swooped down to claim hers. The kiss was hot and hungry, even a little possessive. He cupped her face, smoothed his fingers over her cheeks and ravished her mouth.

She sighed and let her body relax into his, let his passion fill her. Heat curled in her belly as his hands skimmed her neck, her shoulders, then down to her waist. His mouth moved over hers, giving, taking, and just a little wild. She gripped his shoulders, then let her fingers delve into his thick hair. She met his mouth with her own, matching him with her hunger.

When he pulled away, she sighed once more, this time in regret.

"Miss Hannah—"

"Just Grace. There's no sense in calling me Miss Hannah at this point." Not when his arms were still wrapped around her and her lips were throbbing from his kisses.

"Ah." He cupped her face again, and once more smoothed his thumbs over her cheeks, this time with absolute gentleness. "Grace," he breathed. For a moment, regret shimmered over his face. Then it disappeared into an impassive mask that set her nerves humming. "We do have one vital item to discuss. One that might, in fact, change our marriage."

"It's Michael, isn't it?" Her stomach sank. "You're wondering what happened with Michael Wargell."

"Miss Gracie! Miss Gracie!" The panicked call had her jerking away from the earl. She spun on her heel and saw Binkle sprinting across an expanse of green lawn. Alarm and fear lanced through her. Hiking up her skirts, the earl forgotten, she started to run toward Binkle.

When they came abreast of each other, Binkle reversed direction and began running beside her, heading back toward the manor.

"What's wrong?"

"It's Fanny, Jem's wife. The babe's coming."

"It's too early," she gasped, lengthening her stride. "Who's with her?"

"Jem is up Seaton way today, so she's alone."

A vision of Jem as Grace had last seen him flashed through her mind, his face grave and eyes worried as they discussed treason over a pint of ale in the Jolly Smuggler. That was quickly replaced by a vision of pretty young Fanny, heavy with child and full of joy. She prayed both mother and child would live.

"Who brought the message?"

"Farmer Harris's son heard Fanny screaming and went in. Apparently it's been going on for hours and Fanny couldn't get out to tell anyone."

"Have Demon saddled," she said as they approached Cannon Manor. "I'm going for my supplies."

"I've already ordered Demon brought around," Binkle puffed out. "Cook is gathering your supplies."

"Good. She'll know what I need."

"Bring my horse as well," spoke a deep voice at her side.

She whipped her head around. Disbelief rushed through her. The earl ran beside her, barely winded, his trim coat unbuttoned to ease movement. She'd forgotten he was there.

He'd have to wait. She couldn't manage him now. She didn't have the time.

"I'm in a hurry," she bit out, dashing across Cannon Manor's front drive. Her foot skidded on gravel and nearly sent her tumbling.

Demon waited in front of the mounting block, his reins held by a young groom. Cook stood beside them. Grace saw her satchel already secured to Demon's saddle. Thankful for the woman's quick work, she mounted the stallion's broad back and pulled her skirts up to midcalf. There wasn't time to change into breeches, nor to ride sidesaddle at a sedate pace. She needed speed, proprieties be damned.

Demon pranced sideways, tail high. His muscles bunched beneath her and she knew he sensed her urgency.

"Get my mount," the earl commanded to the groom. The young man nodded and sped toward the stables.

"It's not necessary for you to come, and I don't have time to wait for you," Grace said. Besides, the Earl of Langford wouldn't concern himself with a fisherman's wife about to birth a child.

She wheeled Demon around, kicked him into a gallop and flew across the countryside.

A weak plume of smoke drifted from the chimney of the thatched fisherman's cottage. Outbuildings dotted the nearby landscape and the surrounding trees were just beginning to edge from green to gold with occasional hints of red.

It would have been picturesque but for the agonized scream that marred the air.

Grace slid from the saddle almost before Demon stopped moving. Sparing only a moment to secure the puffing horse and retrieve her satchel, she ran to the cottage door and threw it open.

A woman lay on a pallet on the floor in front of the fireplace. Only a few coals burned in the hearth and they cast a red glow over the mound of belly that rose high into the air. Fanny's head was thrown back as she screamed again, her pretty, narrow features contorted in pain.

Grace kneeled on the packed dirt floor beside the young woman, her hands already evaluating the hard belly.

"Fanny, it's Grace."

"Gracie? Oh, thank God you're here," Fanny sobbed. Her

cheeks were swollen from crying. "It's too early. The babe's too early."

"How long have the pains been going on?"

"Hours," Fanny panted. "They started about midmorning, just twinges. I let them go for a while, then they suddenly became horrible. Just horrible." A contraction seized her and she gripped Grace's hand so tightly that bone rubbed on bone. Fanny's body tensed, writhed, bowed up. She tried valiantly to pant through it before she simply gave in to the urge to scream. When it was over she fell back against the pallet, gasping.

"I'm so tired, Gracie," Fanny whimpered. "So tired."

"I know," Grace answered, brushing her fingers over the woman's soft, young cheek. "I'll do what I can." She knelt between Fanny's bent legs, performed the examination.

Her heart sank. *Please don't let them die.*

"You're ready, Fanny," she said, smoothing the girl's hair back from her perspiring face. "But the babe is in the wrong position."

"What does that mean?" Fanny's deep brown eyes clouded. The girl clutched at Grace's hand.

"I have to turn him."

"Oh, God." Tears spilled, tracking two long rivulets down Fanny's cheeks.

Too pale, thought Grace. Too pale, too tired. She was going to lose them both.

The door to the cottage crashed open behind her. *Thank God! Help.*

Whirling, she saw the Earl of Langford filling the doorway, blocking out the pretty fall day beyond. Grim eyes fastened on the laboring woman, then his face set and his jaw firmed. Shocked, Grace stared at the handsome aristocrat as he began to unbutton his coat.

He'd followed her. Even after he had an opportunity to escape, when he had a legitimate excuse not to come, he'd followed her.

# Chapter 12

Fanny moaned behind her, snapping Grace into action. She placed her hand on the girl's belly. It rippled, tightened, and Fanny began to cry again.

The earl crouched beside her. He had removed his coat, cravat and vest, and was dressed now only in his shirt. "What can I do?"

"I need my things," was her only response. She squeezed Fanny's hand and stood, moving away from the laboring woman so she could speak to the earl without Fanny hearing them. He followed, stepping close.

"What's wrong?" he whispered.

"Just go, my lord." He would want to, she thought, moving to her bag and opening it. She set aside a sharp knife, then a needle. Linens to soak up blood and fluid.

"I'm staying." His hand shot out and gripped her wrist, forcing her to stop the preparations. His voice was low, his lips nearly touching her ear. "Tell me what I can do."

She searched his eyes. So blue, so intense. He couldn't possibly understand the miracle and terror of childbirth, or the life-and-death battle about to be waged. He couldn't possibly care.

A feeble sob sounded behind her. There was no choice. She needed help.

"The babe is breech, my lord. She won't be able to birth him unless I can turn him." She looked up, met his eyes, and knew he saw the hopelessness in her face. "I need you to hold her down. It's going to hurt. Badly."

He nodded his understanding as yet another cry was wrenched from the girl.

"She's going to fight you. She'll scream," Grace whispered, her voice breaking on the word. "But it has to be done or they'll both die. They may die anyway." She searched his eyes. They were steely with resolve. She hoped that resolve wouldn't crumble. "I need you. I can't do this alone," she said, placing her hand on his arm.

"You won't be alone." He turned to look at Fanny. "She won't be alone."

The earl went to Fanny and knelt beside her, his back to Grace. She heard him murmur something but couldn't understand the words, only the tone. Calm, gentle. It didn't seem possible that the earl would be kneeling in a thatched cottage in his fashionable clothes, trying to soothe a laboring woman.

Yet, there he was.

Grace drew a deep breath and gathered herself for the agony of the task ahead. Straightening her shoulders, she went to Fanny's other side and knelt. She reached out to place her hand over the bare mound of Fanny's belly.

But a hand was already there.

His. Long, tanned fingers rubbed slow circles over Fanny's belly, even over the silvery marks where the skin had stretched tightly over the growing babe. His other hand held one of Fanny's, her work-roughened fingers entwined with his aristocratic ones.

Rocked to the core, Grace's gaze flew to the earl's face. Their eyes met and held. Filled with an unbearable ache as sweet as it was painful, Grace placed her hand on top of the earl's. Beneath their hands, Fanny's unborn babe shifted and her belly rippled, as if welcoming their joined touch.

The earl blinked like a man coming from some dark place into the light. Astonishment flickered in his eyes. Grace took an unsteady breath as tears blurred her vision. Still, through them she saw the awe on his face.

"I think the babe wants out," he said. Fanny moaned, and he

leaned forward so that his lips were near the laboring woman's ear. "Let's bring your beautiful baby into the world, Fanny."

Fanny's eyes fastened on the earl's face. She squeezed his hand. "Yes," Fanny whispered, the sound harsh as it made its way between cracked lips.

Knowing what was to come, Grace wanted desperately to weep. But she kept her voice steady and strong. "Get behind her, my lord," she said.

Her eyes met the earl's once more, and something fierce and powerful passed between them. He nodded, his face grim with purpose, and she positioned herself to turn the babe.

Fanny did scream. She screamed until she was hoarse, the sounds inhuman, primal and so full of suffering Grace's heart ached. The earl did as Grace had asked, holding the girl down, forcing her to bear the pain. Yet his words were gentle, his fingers light as he wiped her brow with a wet cloth.

An hour later a girl was born. Weak, tired and undersized, but healthy. As her tiny blue body was pulled from her mother's womb and her first cry rent the air, Grace met the earl's eyes over Fanny's exhausted body. There was relief in those eyes, as well as elation.

Grace washed the baby girl, wrapped her in clean linens and laid her in her mother's arms. Fanny cried once more, but the tears spilled from eyes full of joy.

Minutes later, as the sun's gold rays slanted through the cottage windows, the door burst open and Jem hurtled into the room.

"Fanny!" he gasped, stumbling over to the pallet. He froze when his gaze fell on the tiny bundle in his wife's arms.

"You have a daughter," Fanny whispered, exhaustion still etched on her face.

"It's too early. Are you—is she—"

Grace stepped in, laid a hand on Jem's shoulder. "She is healthy, Jem. Healthy and beautiful."

"Congratulations, Papa," the earl said, placing his hand on Jem's other shoulder.

"Thank God." Jem dropped to his knees before his wife and daughter.

"No," Fanny said, reaching out for her husband. "Thank Gracie and his lordship."

Grace let them have a moment, watched the new father's wonder as he gently touched the downy head of his daughter and tangled hair of his wife. The light that shone from Jem nearly blinded her.

"You're crying, Grace. Again."

"What?" She jerked as the earl's thumb brushed her cheekbone. She felt the hot tears now and could taste the salt of them on her lips.

"You cried during the entire birth. Now you're crying again."

"Oh. Well." She stepped back, swiping at the tears. When she looked up, the earl's gaze thankfully rested on the new parents.

"What will you call her, Fanny?" the earl asked.

"Grace. And—what was your mother's name, my lord?"

"Elizabeth."

"Grace Elizabeth, then."

The earl looked as exhausted as Fanny. The lines on his face were deep. Blood coated his hands and smeared the front of his shirt. Dirt covered the knees of his expensive breeches.

A delighted grin stretched across his face.

---

"STARKWEATHER, I'LL BE in the library. I don't wish to be disturbed."

"Yes, my lord."

Julian pulled the door shut and stalked to the low side table that held the crystal brandy decanter and glasses. He poured a short glass, tossed it back and poured another. This one he swirled in the glass.

He looked down. He was still wearing the clothes he'd worn during the birth of Fanny's daughter. The fabric was marred by dried blood and would never come clean. But he considered the loss of the expensive clothes more than worth the life of that little girl. It had been a wonder to see that blue body turn pink with life as she took her first breath. Grace Elizabeth. A beautiful, healthy baby brought into this world by a mother's pain and suffering and the knowledge of a competent healer. A healer full of compassion.

Grace hadn't even known she'd cried with Fanny while she turned the babe, silent tears tracking down her cheeks as her bloodied hands did their miracle work.

In that moment, Julian knew he had never seen a more beautiful woman than Grace Hannah. Whether she was a smuggler, a traitor or an innocent, the fact remained that she had struggled to bring life into the world and had saved both mother and child.

He was a fraud. He should have confronted Grace in the garden of Cannon Manor. Before he kissed her. He knew, he *knew*, that once he kissed her he'd lose his control and the opportunity. But he couldn't help himself. She was nothing but temptation. He couldn't explain why he was drawn to her, even to himself.

His hand fisted around the brandy glass. If she were innocent, he would stand by his decision, do the honorable thing and marry her.

He looked down at his bloodied shirt. Marriage meant children. Travers children. It seemed the ghost of his father hovered over his shoulder, telling him that he would raise his child as a Travers, as his father had, and his grandfather before him.

*No.* Any child of his might be a Travers, but his child would not witness his father beating his mother, or assaulting a maid, or cavorting with his latest mistress.

His child would never once doubt whether he was loved.

Julian left the library, climbing the stairs to reach the carved doors of the earl's chambers. He had yet to sleep in these rooms, instead retiring every evening to a nondescript guest chamber instead of the soft four-poster he had inherited from his father.

Nymphs cavorted across the oak door that marked the earl's chambers. He reached for the elaborate handle and pulled it open.

Ghosts hovered in this room.

The window curtains were drawn, giving the appearance of dusk. The gloom was suffocating, and Julian tugged at his cravat to relieve the sensation. His gaze fell on the bed. His father had commissioned the artist shortly before his mother's death. Heavy crimson curtains hung from the tester. The carved posts were nude women in a lewd parody of a classical pose. Long hair swirled around breasts and thighs. Hips were cocked in a suggestive stance and lips were quirked in seductive smiles.

Fury and hate and shame roiled in his belly, a volatile mixture that strained his control. His fingers tightened on the brandy glass. With a sharp, angry snap he set the glass on a side table and strode purposefully to the bed.

Taking a deep breath, he clutched at the crimson curtains. The fabric was smooth and thick and rich in his hands. Seized by frenzy, he ripped the curtains from the side of the bed frame. Nearly running in his haste, he tore the hangings from the foot of the bed as well, then the remaining side.

Leaving the crimson damask in a pool of fabric on the floor, he moved to the heavy brown window curtains. One sharp wrench and those, too, lay on the floor. Bright, cleansing sunlight streamed into the bedroom, forcing him to squint against the glare. But it was a welcome glare that dispelled the hovering ghosts.

It didn't matter how the room was redecorated, as long as it bore no trace of his father. He would empty it of all remnants of the previous earl and his predilection for infidelity. And violence.

A series of impatient tugs on the bellpull had Starkweather running into the room.

"Get an ax," Julian commanded before the butler could catch his breath.

"An ax, my lord?"

"Now."

While he waited for the butler to return with the tool, Julian stripped off his bloodied shirt so that he stood barechested in the bright sunlight. He began to pace the room, impatient to begin. But the door that joined the earl's suite to the countess's suite caught his eye.

Grace would soon be his countess. Most couples slept in separate bedchambers. She would need a bed, a space to call her own. Something rose in this chest. It lodged there, clawing and howling.

Not that room. The room belonged to his mother.

Julian turned from the countess's chamber when Starkweather handed him a long, wood-handled ax. He took the instrument from the butler and stepped to the bed.

Each nude woman held the curtain frame with one upraised arm, the other arm resting provocatively on a hip. Julian reared back then swung the ax with as much force as he could muster, striking the first post at the juncture of arm and frame. He struck a second time, then a third until the frame was separated from the post. With a grunt of satisfaction he turned his attention to the juncture of post and footboard and began hacking at the woman's ankles. The wooden post fell to the floor with the dull thunk of wood striking wood.

In his peripheral vision, he saw Starkweather standing in the doorway, mouth agape. Julian ignored him, and attacked the second post, the third, then the fourth until the tester crashed to the floor.

When the wooden frame was nothing but splinters he focused on the mattress. He pulled it from the bed with a strength born of rage and began to strike at it with the ax. In seconds the ax broke through the fabric and began to shred the feathers beneath.

He could see his father's face in his mind, the cold eyes and cruel smile. His chest ached with a dreadful emotion he couldn't name, filling his body and mind. He swung at the mattress again and again, trying to ease that horrible ache.

But it didn't. When he flung the ax aside the ache was still there, the pressure of it nearly unbearable.

"Master Julian," came a shocked whisper from the doorway. Julian turned and saw that Mrs. Starkweather had joined her husband in the doorway. Her face was so full of pity, her voice so full of sympathy, that he thought he might shatter.

"Burn it all," Julian rasped. "Better yet, give everything combustible to the poorer tenants for firewood. Let them use the fabric and feathers to make pillows. I don't care. Just make damn sure that this room is completely empty by tomorrow morning. I don't want a single tapestry or table or curtain left in this house."

The ache pressed down on him so that he couldn't draw a breath. He needed to get out. He pushed past the Starkweathers and through the house until he reached the courtyard. He doubled over, hands on his knees, and forced himself to breathe deep.

To just breathe.

# Chapter 13

The Earl of Langford has intercepted our last two com-
munications. The foreign secretary and the prime minis-
ter have been informed of our general location. Extreme
caution must be exercised. Evacuation procedures will be
implemented. Send the enclosed information using the
usual methods, then destroy this note. No further meetings shall occur and no further dispatches will be con-
veyed until said evacuation procedures are complete. At
such time as the evacuation plans are established, you
will be contacted for final instructions.

Our plans must be abandoned, but hope remains.
Liberté, Égalité, Fraternité, ou la Mort!

# Chapter 14

"AH, MY LOVELY! Come to have a little fun with Jack?" The publican sent Grace a playful wink as she stepped up to the counter at the Jolly Smuggler and took a seat on a tall stool.

"Why, Jack Blackbourn, what would your wife say?" She leaned her elbows on the counter.

He looked the same as ever. Tufts of hair sprang from his temples while the back was neatly queued. An apron covered his belly and he'd rolled up his shirtsleeves. "She'd say I have good taste in women, as I managed to snare her."

Grace laughed. "A glass of wine, please. Then I have a few questions for you."

"I have your favorite French wine, as promised on your last visit." He disappeared through a doorway behind the bar and reappeared a few moments later holding a glass of deep ruby liquid. "You know I only stock it for you, my lovely. Else why would Miss Gracie come to the Jolly Smuggler?"

"I'd come by to see my favorite publican, wouldn't I? I wouldn't be able to stay away." Grace placed a few coins on the counter.

"That's what Jack likes to hear." Jack scooped up the coins and replaced them with the glass. "Now, I can tell by the shadows in your pretty eyes that your questions are serious."

"They are." Grace sipped at the wine and let the strong, sweet flavor roll around her tongue before she swallowed. She lowered her voice. "Nothing else has been discovered in the quarries, has it?"

"The men haven't come to me with any new documents." He propped an arm on the polished wood top and leaned forward conversationally. "But I did have an interesting visitor. A man ordered a drink at my bar a few days ago, and while he was enjoying his pint he inquired about any fishermen willing to carry a few dubious items across the Channel, no questions asked."

"Who was it?" She scooted forward on her stool.

"Now that I don't have an answer to. He was tall and young. His hair was covered by a cap, so I don't know the color, but his eyes were blue. He was dressed as a laborer, but that doesn't mean he was."

"It could be anyone," Grace mused, toying with stem of her glass.

"It could."

"But it wouldn't be one of the locals, or you'd have instantly recognized him." She relaxed. Not one of her men, then. Nor one of the neighboring gentry.

"Well, now, I know a few things about disguises, my lovely, given my former line of work." He grinned. "It doesn't take as much work as you'd think to create a disguise. The problem is the eyes. You can't change the eyes."

"True," she agreed, thinking of the sharp light in the Earl of Langford's summer sky eyes. "You can't change the eyes."

"Our visitor will be back in a week for answer. But an answer bears thinking about, doesn't it?"

She tapped a finger on her glass while she mulled it over. "Could you tell him you're willing to courier whatever the items are? We would be able to catch him in the act, so to speak."

"I could, indeed, my lovely."

"Good. Let me know when the man comes back."

A voice rose above the general din. Grace turned and saw that its owner stood in the middle of the room, his hand on his heart and his tankard raised in the air as though making a toast. Drink slurred the off-key tenor.

*Married beauties may yield to a stranger,*
*My rib need not fear such disgrace;*
*Her virtue is never in danger,*
*The moment you look at her face!*

The other patrons roared with laughter as the song ended. The singer took a swig of his ale and wiped his mouth on his sleeve.

Grace snorted. "For heaven's sake, that's John the blacksmith. He's not been married even six months." She cocked her head. "His poor wife. He sounds completely foxed."

John raised his hand and waved at her. "Lookit! It's Miss Gracie. Hullo!" He staggered to the bar and used the counter to prop himself up.

"Hullo, John!" She put a steadying hand on his shoulder. His eyes were bloodshot and his cheeks were ruddy, but he seemed cheerful enough. "How's your new young wife?"

John's face split into a wide grin. "Perfect, Miss Gracie. Pretty as a summer day and fair worships me. Don't know why I waited so long to pick me a girl."

"There now, I told you there was nothing to worry about."

"I was holding out for you, Miss Gracie," he answered with a wink.

"And I told you I'd marry you in June. But June came and went, and you didn't come courting and broke my poor spinster's heart."

"Oh, now, Miss Gracie—" he protested.

"And a spinster I'm happy to be." She laughed.

John raised his tankard and frowned into it, then looked down the bar. "Jack, a drink, please. Mine's empty and so is Miss Gracie's."

Jack took the tankard and set it aside. Easily, he said, "Why don't you head home for the night. You've got yourself a pretty young bride waiting for you."

John perked up. "That I do."

"Though she'll likely skin you alive when you turn up foxed." Grace grinned as John spun haphazardly around.

"True. But I'll make it up to her," he said. "Hey, ain't you to be married? To the tall gent with them eyes? Never saw eyes like that. They'll look right through you."

Behind the bar, Jack's brows rose. Grace ignored him. "You better get home, John, before that wife of yours comes looking for you."

"I s'pose I better. G'night, Miss Gracie. Jack." Listing slightly to the left, John made his way to the door and into the night.

"Well, now, my lovely," Jack said as he refilled her glass. His eyes were bright with interest and laughter. "What's this about a wedding?"

"I've gotten myself into a spot of trouble, Jack."

"It's about time you got into some trouble again, in my opinion. And if you're not going to play with Jack"—he winked at her—"then you might as well play with the earl. I know his reputation and I imagine he knows what he's doing when it comes to women."

Grace choked on her wine. Even if Jack was a dear friend, she was certain she didn't want to have *that* conversation with him. "Regardless of his way with women, it's the consequences that are the trouble now."

"Well, you could do worse than an earl." He wiggled his eyebrows at her. "Or you could run away with Jack, my lovely, and live in sin."

She laughed, but the sound was hollow. If her marriage to the earl didn't work, if they hated each other, she would lose all chance at love. A lifetime was a long time to live without love.

She swirled the last drops of ruby liquid in her glass before gulping it down. "I'm heading back to the manor for tonight, Jack." She leaned over the counter and gave him a quick kiss on the cheek.

"Oh, now, don't be so free with your kisses, my lovely. Jack's already a married man." He'd said the line a dozen times before, so she knew the proper response.

"Then I must remain a spinster, pining for you to the end of my days." She added one more kiss for good measure.

And so he waved her toward the door with a laugh on his lips and a twinkle in his eye.

She didn't recognize the first man that walked through the pub door, nor the second, third or fourth. But a group of strangers wasn't unusual. These were steely eyed and burly, except one, who was young and handsome with tousled curls.

She nearly walked past the group entirely, but she heard one of them ask for Jack.

"Aye, that's me," came Jack's laughing answer. "A drink, lads?"

"Jack Blackbourn, you're under arrest for treason against the Crown."

It was as if the entire world stood frozen. Sound filtered away, the light sharpened and she stared at Jack, horror-struck. It wasn't possible. Jack wasn't a traitor. A smuggler, but not a traitor.

He bolted. In a heartbeat, he'd disappeared through the door behind the counter. Numb, her mind frozen in shock, she didn't understand where Jack had gone or why the newcomers were clambering over and around the counter after him.

Then her whole body jerked and the world rushed back. She jumped onto a stool, then the bar counter, and leapt down behind it. She was through the door to the kitchen a second later.

Chaos reigned. Shouts rang in the air. Jack grappled with one of the strangers. His wife, patient and affable Anna, had ranged herself between Jack and another man, a long wooden spoon and an iron skillet raised high above her head.

Two serving girls cowered in the corner, Jack's son William standing over them, fists raised and ready to defend them.

"Jack!" Grace shouted, leaping into the fray.

A man plowed into her. Her bones rattled with the impact and her breath wheezed out. She hit the floor hard. Crockery rained down, shattering on the stone floor with a crash. She felt a quick sting on her cheek, another on her forehead, as shards bounced off the floor.

The man scrambled to his feet before she could recover. Gasping for air, the breath completely gone from her lungs, she lurched to her knees.

"Get your pistols!" a man shouted.

Jack sprawled on the floor now. Two men wrestled and rolled with him. The third man held Anna around the waist even as she clawed at him to escape. Grace had pushed to her feet, coiled to spring, when the shot rang out.

The tableau froze. All eyes turned to the curly-haired young man. He stood with his back against the wall, a smoking pistol in one hand, an unfired pistol in the other. The acrid scent of black powder saturated the air. She wished she'd thought to use her own weapon. Instead, she was staring into the black hole of a pistol that was not her own.

"Step back," the man said to Grace, his voice unsteady. He cleared his throat, firmed his jaw. "Step over by the other woman." He motioned to where Anna was held captive. The pistol shook in his hand.

Grace did as he commanded. Anna's captor released her so that they stood side by side. The man that had overpowered Anna pulled out his own pistol and aimed it at William and the two serving girls. One girl let out a high-pitched squeak and covered her face with her apron.

"We only want Blackbourn." The curly-haired man motioned to Jack. His eyes darted around the room. "We'll leave the rest of you here."

"No!" Anna cried out, her round and pretty face defiant. She gripped Grace's hand, crushing her fingers.

"Anna," Jack shouted. Two men gripped his arms, holding him captive. Blood dripped from his nose, though he appeared otherwise unharmed. "I'll be safe. I've done nothing wrong this time."

"He's innocent of treason," Grace said. Anger rose in her, hot and dark. "I'm sure of it."

"We've found evidence in his lodgings that he's couriering military information to France." The curly-haired man kept the pistol aimed at Grace and Anna while his companions manhandled Jack out the rear door.

"It's not possible." Not for one moment did she believe them. "You must be mistaken."

"There's no mistake." Still, he looked nervous and uncertain. "I found the evidence myself." He started toward the door, walking backward, with the pistols still trained on Grace and Anna. They were steadier now.

"Wait." She would give them the folios in her stillroom and they would release Jack. They *must* release Jack. She could hear curious shouts from the taproom. Would other patrons start rushing in? Would someone be injured or killed?

She needed to end this. Now. She stepped forward.

"I have evidence—"

But the young man cocked his pistol and pointed it straight at Anna. "You move closer," he said to Grace, "and the other woman dies."

Grace froze, though the blood roared in her ears and her fingers twitched with the effort not to reach for her own weapon. "Jack's not the traitor. I have—"

But he was gone, leaving them alone among broken crockery, the scent of burned meat and the sound of Anna's quiet sobbing.

———————

SHE WANTED TO gallop. She wanted the blood pounding through her to match the rhythm of Demon's hooves. Yet she couldn't. Black, low-hanging clouds obscured the moon and made the road to Cannon Manor dark and dangerous. She couldn't risk an injury to Demon or herself, so she restrained the stallion's pace with the same control she used to fight her own black mood.

Jack was gone. He and his pursuers had disappeared into the night. She'd started to follow, but she couldn't be sure which direction they'd gone or even if they had left Beer. Would they go to London? If so, there was no way to know if they would follow the coastline or stay inland.

Instead, she'd stayed with Anna for nearly an hour before returning home, doing her best to comfort the woman. Full of her own disbelief and fury, she'd done a miserable job of it.

She fisted her hands around the reins. She needed a concrete plan. Jack would no doubt be imprisoned to await trial. She'd take the folios to London. Surely someone would listen to reason.

She shivered. If he was found guilty, he would be sentenced to death.

Demon's pace quickened. His head came up, nostrils flaring. Grace caught her breath as the hair at the nape of her neck rose.

She wasn't alone.

Pines speared high into the air on either side of her. With her fingers clutching the reins, she slowly scanned the dense shadows between the trees in search of something out of place, concentrating on the sounds of the night animals and the scents of wet wood and grass. She could hear, see and smell nothing unusual. There were no hoofbeats or shadows that didn't belong. Still, she sensed another person in the darkness, just beyond her range of vision.

Uneasy, she guided Demon along the dirt track that lay between the towering pines, wondering if the invisible follower was friend or foe. This dense copse served as a well-used shortcut between two country lanes. At night, however, the copse was empty and isolated—and miles from anywhere.

A faint horse whinny met her ears. She pulled on Demon's reins and he grudgingly obeyed, coming to a standstill on the track. She listened, her own breathing suspended. One minute passed. Two minutes. Perhaps she had imagined it.

Beneath her, Demon shifted impatiently and pawed the ground. She could feel his muscles coiled and ready to run. She struggled to keep her own restless urge to run in check.

A shadowed figure emerged from the trees. A man, tall and lean, stood on the narrow dirt track in front of her, blocking her path. In the dark, under the dense canopy of branches, his face was nothing but shadows and indistinct features.

Fear tightened her muscles and sent a line of sweat rolling down her back. Still, she kept her voice cool and steady. "Who goes there?" She narrowed her eyes, hoping to recognize the stranger's features.

"Why, it's Miss Hannah." Pitched nearly to a whisper, the voice was unidentifiable, yet it carried clearly on the still night air. "Whatever are you doing in the woods, alone, at nearly three in the morning?"

"It's none of your concern," she answered sharply, shifting so that her coat fell open. She wanted access to her pistol.

"Hmmm." The man stepped forward. It wasn't a menacing movement, but certainly commanding. "What kind of mischief would a gently bred lady get into in the dead of night? A lover, perhaps?" The whisper became a sensual caress in the darkness.

Her heart thumped once, hard. She knew that voice, felt its timbre resonate through her.

"What are you about, my lord?" she asked coolly.

Langford prowled to the side so that he was on her right, standing just at the transition of trees to path. He seemed to merge with the tree trunks until he was only a shadow among shadows. Still, she knew what he would look like. Lean and angular and handsome, with eyes the color of the sky in mid-summer.

She could not banish the apprehension writhing in her belly. He'd discovered his betrothed wandering the woods in breeches, alone, in the early hours of the morning.

She'd be jilted. Again.

"Is the lady engaging in something illicit?" The words slid over her, a stroke of heat and danger in the darkness. "Smuggling, perhaps?"

Her mouth went dry. *He knew.*

Without warning, he darted forward and snatched her from the horse's back, his strong hands gripping her waist. She shrieked and bucked against him, pushing against his shoulders and chest. How had he moved so quickly?

He slung her over one muscular shoulder, holding her in place with an arm just under the curve of her buttocks. His free hand looped Demon's reins around a thick branch hanging over the path.

Struggling to draw breath past the unyielding shoulder pressed just beneath her lungs, she thumped a fist on his broad back. He didn't react.

"My lord, put me—"

He bumped her body up for a better grip, wedging his shoulder more firmly into her ribs and cutting off her words.

Gritting her teeth, she sucked in air. It was simply too much. Jack, the arrest, the folios, treason and now the earl. Fury erupted in her, sharp and searing.

"Put me *down*." She thumped his back again, harder this time, and was rewarded with a grunt. Good, she thought darkly. She hoped she left a mark.

"You're not in a position to issue commands." His tone was unforgiving. It seemed to belong to another man. A harder man.

Still, he complied with her demand, his movements swift and efficient. Her knees buckled when he released her so that she staggered. He caught her hands to pull her up and manacled both of her small wrists with his own large, powerful hands.

Alarm raced through her. She didn't know this man. This brute. She twisted her wrists, trying to jerk free. But the earl pressed forward until she was pinned against a tree trunk, their bodies inches from each other. He raised her wrists above her head and flattened them against the tree. Even through the coat and shirt she wore, the rough bark scraped against her back.

"Is this how you treat ladies, my lord?" she snapped. "Roughly?" Though in truth, he was not rough. His hands were firm but gentle around her wrists, his body not quite touching hers.

"It's how I treat smugglers and traitors." His voice was low and dangerous, his mouth grim.

"What?" She gaped at him. She tried to push him away, but he pinned her to the tree with his body. His chest pressed against her breasts, his heat all but scorching her. "I'm not a traitor," she ground out.

"No? Well, you are not an innocent. A woman in the woods at night, alone, is not out for a stroll. A woman who meets men at the local pub and smugglers in an abandoned quarry is not calling on friends for tea. And a woman wearing men's breeches is not a lady."

"I've done nothing I'm ashamed of," she returned furiously.

"Which doesn't recommend you, given the evidence." He dropped her hands and stepped back. His eyes remained intensely focused on her face as he reached into his coat pocket and slid something out. Covered in smooth, dark leather, it was frighteningly familiar.

"Where did you find that?" She couldn't quite catch her breath, as though he'd physically sent a blow to her midsection. Her gaze flew to his face, but the tight mouth and blank eyes revealed nothing.

"In a barrel of rose petals in your stillroom." He bared his teeth in a merciless smile. "Now are you going to tell me you're not a traitor?"

# Chapter 15

"I'M NOT A traitor," she said furiously.

"You lie," he snarled, fisting his fingers in her shirt and yanking her to him.

She shrieked—not in fear, but in fury. Slapping her hands against his chest, she pushed with all her might. But he was as grounded and immovable as a mountain.

His face bent close to hers. "Do you know the penalty for treason?" His menacing whisper chilled her to the marrow.

"I do not lie." She struggled anew, clawing at his fist.

He dropped the folio onto the ground and once more used both of his hands to hold her in place, pressing her against the tree. She strained to pull her arms from his grasp, her breath coming in panicked gasps.

"I know you lie because I followed you," he spat. "I watched you go into the Jolly Smuggler and I saw you hide the first folio under the rose petals. I watched you at the smuggling quarries and saw you hide a second folio in your trunk."

"It was *you* I saw on the edge of the cliffs that night at the quarries?" She stiffened. "You were watching me? Spying on me?" Something dark and ugly swirled within her. Her privacy had been violated and it left her feeling as though a layer of grime filmed her skin.

"Since I *am* a spy, yes. It is what I do best." His lips twisted in a derisive smile as his hands tightened on hers.

"A spy," she repeated faintly. She should have been surprised, but it fit. For all his charming and gilded words, she'd seen the predator that lurked within.

*You can't change the eyes.*

She twisted away and this time he released her, sliding his hands down her arms to circle her waist. Now it was the nearness of him that held her in place. The scent of him, man, leather and outdoors, surrounded her. Her pulse started hammering, her skin went hot. How could she feel desire for this man? He was a spy, and nothing she'd thought he was.

"If you're not a traitor, tell me how you obtained those documents." He leaned close so their faces were only a breath apart, his lips just a kiss away from hers.

"Do you think to seduce the information from me?" Fighting against her need for him, she raised her brows.

"You *will* tell me."

"What do you expect from me?" She glared at him. "That I'm going to tell you everything I know? Divulge all my secrets? It seems I barely know you, my lord. Are you the Wandering Earl, or someone else?" She pushed past him, stalking through the thick tree trunks. She could see Demon only a few feet away, apparently unconcerned by their confrontation.

"I'm a spy, as I said. The Wandering Earl is simply a useful disguise." He leaned casually against the tree he'd pinned her to, but his eyes were sharp. "My mission is to locate a traitor passing military information to the French. We believe the traitor is using the smuggling channels in this area to send the information to France. Which brings me to you. I came to Devon in search of you."

"In search of me." Her stomach pitched. It had all been a lie. The ball, the picnic, the seduction, the betrothal. "It's all been part of your mission."

He studied her, his face unreadable. "Yes."

That one word sliced through her. Unable to stand still, she paced a few steps away then turned to face him. "Was it difficult to feign desire?" Bitterness filled her mouth.

"What?" His eyes widened, the whites showing clearly in the dark. He straightened and took one quick step toward her.

"Would you have gone through with the marriage?" She reached out for the thick trunk of a tree for support. Her fingernails curled into the coarse bark when he strode forward, reaching for her.

"Grace." His hands clutched her shoulders and pulled her up to her toes. His eyes focused on her lips.

"Don't pretend," she snapped, jerking back.

"I wish I were pretending. It would be easier if I were." Fury edged his tone. "*Hell.*"

His lips crushed against hers. The heat behind it stunned her, then filled her. *That can't be feigned.* Her mind blanked as his mouth possessed hers, his tongue exploring, his teeth nipping. Sensation burst through her, bright flashes that burned right down to her toes.

He tugged at her cap and tossed it to the ground. Her hair, loosely tucked inside it, tumbled down her back. She could feel its silken weight as his impatient fingers tangled it. Wrapping her arms around him, she leaned her body into his and felt his arousal press against her belly. Knowing she could do this to him, that he wanted her, set something warm swirling within her.

When he tore his mouth from hers, she was gasping for air and clutching his shoulders.

"I'm not pretending," he muttered against her lips. He lifted his head and glowered at her. "I can't change what happened between us, and I can't change who we are."

"You're not just the Earl of Langford. You're a spy." She stepped out of his embrace. She needed to think.

"And you're not just a poor relation." He flicked open her coat and lightly ran his fingers across the outline of her pistol. "You're a smuggler."

She stepped out of his reach. "What do you want?"

"You." A grim smile flashed. "Your connection to the smugglers and Jack Blackbourn are the only lead I have to a traitor."

"*Jack.*" A tight ball of ice formed in her stomach. Through the moonlight, their eyes met. "Jack was arrested tonight."

———————

A WARNING RANG in Julian's head, sharp and insistent.

"What happened?" he asked.

"Four men came into the pub." Her words tumbled out, nearly on top of each other. "They took him by force."

"Who?" He grabbed her arm, held her in place. They couldn't be from Sir Charles. Anyone sent by Sir Charles would have stopped at Thistledown and informed him of the arrest in advance.

Unless Sir Charles considered him already retired. His fingers convulsed. She drew in a sharp breath and he dropped her arm.

"I don't know," she said, stepping away from him. "Presumably they had some authority, as they *arrested* Jack in front of his wife and son. Thank God his youngest children weren't there to witness it." She closed her eyes briefly. "They don't even have the right man. Jack isn't a traitor."

"You can't be certain of that." No, Julian thought. *He* couldn't be certain. Just as he couldn't be certain Grace wasn't a traitor. Even though his gut told him she was innocent.

"I *am* certain." She whirled on him as she said it, her hair whipping around like silver ropes to bind him to her. Perhaps it was desire that told him she was innocent, and not his instincts.

"It's just not in him," she continued. "Jack smuggled for profit and a little excitement, but he'd never engage in treason. I swear he's innocent." Her gaze fixated on the folio, still lying where he'd dropped it. "*I'm* innocent."

He opened his mouth to speak, closed it again. Instinct warred with training. He should keep what he knew about Jack to himself. He had no proof Grace was innocent. Yet her eyes were sad, and a faint line had formed between her delicate brows. She tugged at something inside him so that he wanted to soothe her fears away.

He bent and picked up the folio, turning it in his hands as though the smooth leather would hold the answers to his inner struggle. "Tell me how you obtained the folios." It still sounded like a command, even if he delivered it quietly.

"No."

"You don't trust me."

"Why should I?" She grabbed her cap from the ground before stalking between the trees, long, slim legs moving fast.

"I can't even verify you work for our government and not another."

"I can't prove it. I can only say that you need to trust me." The words sounded ridiculous even to his own ears. He followed her, his longer legs easily catching up to her.

"How silly of me," she scoffed, turning to face him on the path. "*Of course* I should trust the man who lied to me, violated my privacy by spying on me, attacked me in the woods and held me captive. A man who claims to be a spy—not exactly the most trustworthy of careers." She waited a beat, raised a brow. "Does this mean you no longer need to borrow my horse to take up your second career, my lord smuggler?"

Damn if she wasn't amusing. "You have a sharp tongue. I don't know why I like it," he growled.

He claimed her mouth, filled with equal parts lust and irritation. She returned the kiss, her lips firm and hard and equally irritated. Stepping back, he crossed his arms.

"This is treason, Grace. Not a lark."

"And the people involved are not pawns. They don't deserve to be arrested for treason."

"No, they don't. Not if they're innocent. But I can't prove they're innocent unless I catch the real traitor."

Her mouth opened, closed. Apparently he'd taken the wind from her sails.

"I need information," he said.

She tipped her head back and took a deep breath. He waited, knowing she would break.

"Very well," she said finally. "I'll give you information about the folios and the caves, but I won't reveal any names. I promised my friends I would protect them and I won't go back on my word."

"They're smugglers."

She raised her chin. "And so am I."

"A fact that could eventually lead to your arrest."

"Are you going to hold that over my head? What if we marry? Will you arrest your wife?"

"We *will* marry, Grace. I compromised you and I offered for you. I stand by my offer." He could do nothing less. She was his now—his responsibility, and soon his wife.

"You offered me marriage without knowing if I was a traitor?" She planted her feet and faced him squarely.

"Of course."

"I'm going to be a dreadful countess," she said. "You'll be marrying a smuggler."

"And you'll be marrying a spy. I'd say we're a perfect match."

"You may be right," she said with a half laugh. "But I won't give you the identities of the smugglers."

"An agreement, then, and I hope to heaven our marriage is easier than this." He ran a hand through his hair. "Loyalty is an admirable, if rare, quality. While I believe your loyalty is misplaced"—he held up a hand to stop her when she would have spoken—"I promise I won't betray the smugglers. Any information I learn during this investigation, I'll keep to myself. If they come to the attention of the authorities in some other manner—a risk they've already accepted simply by smuggling—I won't intervene on their behalf to see them freed. But I'll keep what I know to myself. Provided, of course, none of them are traitors."

"You'll give me your word?" she asked quietly. Moonlight flitted over her face.

"I won't give you my word as a Travers. It wouldn't mean anything." He swallowed. "But I will swear it on my mother's life."

"I can't ask for more than that."

"I can't *give* you more than that." He stepped back onto the path. "Let's return. I need to walk."

He could hear her footsteps shuffling through the forest floor behind him as they started toward Demon. When he reached the horse, he loosened the reins and began to lead the animal down the path. Grace fell into step beside him.

"The folios were found in the smuggling quarries," she began. "They were hidden within the trunks scheduled to be shipped to France."

"Who found them? Jack Blackbourn?" He frowned.

"Jack didn't find them, though he was aware of them." She reached for Demon's reins.

"No, I have him."

"He's my horse." She sent him a sideways look. He didn't bother to return the reins and she sighed. "Three smugglers came to me with the folios because they didn't know what else to do with them, and because—"

"What?"

"They didn't want to be arrested."

"So they gave the folios to you, so *you* could be arrested? How gallant."

"They gave them to me because I have more social status and will be taken seriously," she corrected. "Perhaps not much more social status, but more than they."

They emerged from the shelter of the trees. The moon shone bright now that there was no canopy of trees to block it.

"What's Jack's role in this?"

"Nothing. He used to lead our smuggling band. When the men found the folios, he naturally became aware of it." She stuffed her cap in her pocket and shook out her hair. "Jack is innocent. I don't know what information the men that arrested him found, but I know he's innocent."

"I don't know what they found either, but it wasn't there a few days ago."

"What?" She whipped her head around to stare at him.

"I did a bit of espionage. I went into the Jolly Smuggler, asked a few questions about carrying items to France and then searched Blackbourn's home."

"That was you asking questions?" She smiled grimly. "Poor Jack. He'd be embarrassed to discover he was taken in by you."

"I'm a talented spy." He returned her smile, just as grimly. "Nevertheless, I found something confirming Jack is innocent."

"Thank goodness." She blew out a breath. "What?"

He hesitated. It didn't sit well to give information to a civilian. "His financial records for the pub. He's in dun territory. His creditors are already circling. At the rate he's going he'll be closing the pub within the year, if not earlier."

"Oh, poor Jack. He and Anna hoped the pub would provide a life for them. They used everything they had to buy it." She sighed, pressing her fingers to her eyes. "But how does that prove he's innocent?"

"Blackbourn is well-known. He smuggles purely for profit and not for any particular political or religious ideals. In fact, as far as we know, he has no such beliefs. Which means if he were couriering information to France, he would be doing so for money, not for an ideal."

"Then he'd have enough money to keep the pub open," she finished. "But if Jack is innocent, then what evidence did the others find and who put it there?"

"A good question. Who else knows about the folios?"

She stared into the dark countryside. "Aside from the three that approached me, the remaining smugglers don't have any idea about them—to our knowledge, at any rate, and we would know. We don't believe any of them are traitors."

"How can you be sure?"

"We can't, but the penmanship was superb and took skill and tutelage. Certainly not the penmanship of a laborer or farmer. The men I know can barely read and write. That writing originated from someone of the upper class. Or at least someone with a tutor or governess and formal training, so at least somewhat well off. None of the smugglers—" She broke off, corrected herself. "None of my *friends* have any such formal training."

"I can agree that the folio did not originate with one of your *friends*, but one of them could have placed the folio in the cave at someone else's direction."

Her shoulders slumped.

"On the other hand," he continued, "a farmer or laborer wouldn't be directly connected with someone in the Foreign Office, and the information in the folios originated there. There must be a middleman with ties to the Foreign Office to transport the information here to Beer, then to the smuggling quarries."

"And the folio?" Grace slid her gaze toward his coat pocket. "What will you do with it?"

"I'll keep it."

"I have a second one hidden in my stillroom."

"No, you don't." He grinned, satisfied she hadn't discovered the switch. He hadn't lost his touch. "I replaced it with modified information within hours of when you hid it. Much as I replaced this one," he added. "I've had the originals for weeks now. You've had forged replicas."

"In other words, I've been worried about someone stealing useless information."

"Yes."

Grace sighed. "All that worry, wasted."

"True," he agreed. "Are the smugglers searching for additional folios?"

"They're checking every trunk, barrel and cask we transport to ensure no more information passes through France. At least not through us."

"Damn." He ran a hand through his hair.

"What is wrong?"

"I've made a tactical error." He glanced over his shoulder as Demon huffed out a breath.

"What?"

He should have foreseen it. He wasn't green as grass, as young Miles Butler was. Though he felt like it at the moment. He'd sent the folios to London, believing Grace was the traitor and he was thwarting her. He'd never considered she had intercepted the traitor herself. Grimly, he said, "You've interrupted the traitor's avenue of communication. If the information isn't received in France, he'll know he's been discovered."

"Will he run?"

It was hard to know. Some men ran. Some went to ground. He might even find a new avenue of communication. "Are there any other smugglers in the area he might use?"

"He could go to any smuggler along the coast," she said as they turned onto Cannon Manor's drive. "There are hundreds of smugglers. Two dozen in Beer alone."

"But he has a middleman," Julian murmured. He wouldn't groom another pawn if this one hadn't been discovered yet. "He'll stay in this area. Perhaps not Beer, but Seaton, Sidmouth, maybe up to Lyme Regis." Somewhere the middleman could travel in short in just a few hours so as not to be missed.

"That's still a great deal of coastline."

"I need assistance," he said. "Another set of eyes and ears with contacts in the smuggling channels that can ask questions without being recognized." He reached out absently, fingering a wisp of her hair. Behind them, Demon huffed out another breath.

"I'd ask Jack, but he's in prison." She shivered when his fingers brushed against her neck. "And the best way to free him is to find the real traitor."

"I know an agent with ties to smugglers farther up the coast toward Weymouth, Portsmouth and the Isle of Wight," Julian mused. "Angel may be able to penetrate the ranks here."

"Angel." She gripped the hand entwined in her hair. "His name appeared in the first folio."

"And he's grateful his name and identity were not given to the French. I suppose he has you to thank for that." His eyes narrowed dangerously. Still, Julian himself had not been spared.

They were nearing the manor house. A groom came running out. He'd clearly been waiting.

"My lord. Miss Gracie," the groom said, nodding politely as he took the reins from Julian. Whatever he was thinking of this midnight assignation, he didn't let on. He led the horse toward the stables.

"The kitchen door is open," Grace said, nodding toward the side of the house. They started down the gravel path leading toward the kitchen.

"The smugglers aren't the only potential middlemen," she said quietly. "There are other men that know the location of the smuggling quarries. *Gentlemen*," she corrected.

He turned to look at her. Moonlight shone on hunched shoulders. She kept her eyes on the pathway and he wished he could see her face.

"I don't understand," he said. "How would others not know of the quarries? They've been mined for centuries."

"We don't actually use the quarries," she answered. "We store the cargo in the natural caves on the sea cliffs and then use a cliff path to take the cargo to the beach. From there we ferry the goods out to the luggers waiting to sail to France. The smuggling caves connect to the quarries through a series of natural tunnels, which lead to man-made tunnels that are part of the quarries. Some of the quarries are still in operation, in fact. Everyone knows of the quarries, but few know of the natural caves."

"Who knows of the natural caves, then?"

She said nothing for a moment. They rounded the side of the house.

"Grace. Tell me," he prompted.

She drew a deep breath. "Lord Stuart Paget, Sir Richard Elliott and my uncle." Her voice cracked and she cleared her throat. "They formed a sort of Hellfire Club when they were young. Jack said they used the caves as a meeting place when he first started smuggling. I'm sure any of them could have guessed that the smuggled goods would still be stored there. It's a convenient spot and, thus far, the revenue officers haven't discovered it."

"Then we have a list of potential suspects." He narrowed his eyes. "I presume you would be able to recognize your uncle's handwriting if you saw it."

"Yes. He did not write the information in the folios."

"And the other two? Would you recognize their handwriting?"

"No. But there's another," she whispered. She folded her hands together and stared at her clenched fingers. "Michael Wargell knows of the caves." She looked out into the night. "He knows *I* store smuggled goods there."

# Chapter 16

"MY LORD, YOU have a visitor."

Starkweather's words shattered Julian's plans of a quiet brandy while he strategized. Irritation flared. He'd spent a miserable morning and the better part of the afternoon in Beer trying to glean information on Jack's arrest. Now he wanted nothing more than to lounge in an armchair beside a roaring fire and think about the information Grace had given him.

He paused at the door to the library, his hand on the knob. "Who is it, Starkweather?"

"I don't know his name, my lord. He refused to give it." Starkweather's brows drew together. "Nervous fellow, actually. He indicated he would wait as long as it took for you to return to Thistledown. He's in the salon."

Julian's hand tightened on the doorknob of his private library, then fell away. It must be someone from London about the traitor. Spinning on his heel, he strode through the halls until he came to the salon. He quietly pushed open the door and scanned the room.

Miles Butler, Sir Charles's clerk, was helping himself to smuggled brandy. His fashionable clothes were dusty and wrinkled. The man's hands shook as he raised the decanter and splashed the amber liquid into a glass.

"Mr. Butler."

Butler jerked, spilling the brandy onto the table. "Langford," he yelped. "I didn't hear you come in." He swung around and Julian saw disheveled and tangled hair instead of the artfully tousled curls he normally sported. Julian narrowed his eyes. If he wasn't mistaken, there were circles of fatigue under Butler's eyes as well.

"What news do you have?" Julian said, closing the door and striding across the room. He raised a brow as Butler downed the brandy in one gulp. "That doesn't bode well."

"Blackbourn has escaped." Trembling fingers raked through Butler's hair.

"*You* arrested him?" His irritation doubled. The boy had no business arresting anyone.

"On Sir Charles's orders, of course!" Butler added defensively. "More or less." He set down his glass on the side table and refilled it. The liquor glowed gold in the sunlight streaming in the windows. "There were rumors in London that Blackbourn was active and willing to transport anything—*anything*—to and from France. I was to question him. But when the agents with me found the evidence in his lodgings—" He broke off, sinking into a deep armchair as though he couldn't quite hold himself up.

Julian strode to the armchair, leaned over Butler. "What evidence? I searched his cottage myself and found nothing." He knew he hadn't missed anything. But a few days had passed since his own search.

"They found documents containing troop and armament counts." Butler scrubbed a hand over his face.

"How were they bound?" he demanded.

"In leather and tied with a narrow leather strip." Wary, Butler stared up at him. "It was accurate information. Or at least as much as I could surmise, since I'm only privy to certain information."

*It was the same.* The thrill of the hunt rushed through him. "Where are the folios now? We need to take them to Sir Charles immediately."

"We can't." Butler propped his elbows on his knees. "Blackbourn took the records when he escaped."

Shock pierced through the thrill, followed closely by disbelief. Julian closed his eyes, breathing deeply in an attempt to refrain from verbally skewering Butler. When he opened his eyes again, Butler had dropped his head into his hands and was staring dejectedly at the floor.

Julian shook his head and lowered into an armchair. Idiot boy. He was no match for the wily Jack Blackbourn. He tamped down on his anger. "How and when did he escape? Did you search for him?"

"Of course!" Butler's head snapped up. "I haven't slept all night or all day today. We made it as far as Dorchester and stopped at an inn. I don't even know how he managed to escape. The others went to the common room and I locked Blackbourn into the room we'd procured. When I returned, he was gone." Butler gulped what remained of the brandy in his glass. "We looked all over Dorchester before starting back to Beer. But he could have gone anywhere!"

"Was the door unlocked when you returned?"

"No. It was still locked." His brows drew together. "I don't understand how he could have escaped."

"The window?" Julian asked drily.

"I don't think so. We were on the second floor," Butler said slowly, entirely missing Julian's sarcasm.

"Just so I understand, Sir Charles did not give you orders to arrest Jack, correct?" Julian pushed up from the armchair and strode across the room. It looked like he would be having his brandy after all.

"No. Yes. Well, that is, I was to question him, and if he—" Butler stared into his empty glass. "I only thought to prove myself. My father, you see. He was a hero, my mother said, and Sir Charles has said the same. He was a double agent working in France." Butler raised unhappy eyes to Julian. "It is difficult to live in the shadow of one's father."

A pang of sympathy struck Julian. Yes, he understood what it was to live in the shadow of another—though Butler lived in the shadow of a hero. Julian lived in the shadow of a murderer.

"How am I going to explain to Sir Charles?" Butler groaned, falling back in the chair. "What am I going to do? I let the traitor escape. We have to find him!"

"Quiet," Julian said. The man was nearly wailing. "You won't find Blackbourn. He can hide for months when he wants to. However, I don't think he's the traitor."

"You don't?" Butler straightened, his eyes bright with combined relief and hope. "But he escaped. Why would he run if he were innocent?"

"Because evidence against him was found in his home," Julian explained, struggling to control his impatience. He tapped a finger on the arm of his chair, considered. "Although if he is innocent, there's a question as to how the evidence came to be in his lodgings."

"Do you think he'll return to Beer? We could assign someone to watch his pub in the event he returns."

"One thing Blackbourn is not is foolish." Julian snorted. "He'll not return to the pub until his name is cleared. Still, I think I may know where to find him," he finished, thinking of the smuggling caves.

"Where?" Butler jumped to his feet. "We must go. Immediately."

"*I* will go," Julian corrected sharply as he stood. He strode to the door, Butler trotting behind him. Did the boy truly believe he would be accompanying him after the Blackbourn debacle?

"But, Lord Langford—"

"Mr. Butler, I have a personal connection and will be able to easily explain my presence." He narrowed his eyes at the other man. "*You*, I cannot explain away."

He left Thistledown at a gallop and traveled cross-country to the cliffs. After settling his mount in the same lean-to Grace had once housed Demon, he scrambled down the cliff path to the smuggling caves.

The rough tunnels were empty of smugglers, not surprising given it was the middle of the day. Still, there were signs that a shipment of goods had arrived. Water pooled in the craggy floor of the cave mouth, still fresh from recent treks in and out. Barrels of silk, casks of wine and trunks of tobacco were stacked up against the walls of the inner chamber.

There was no evidence of Blackbourn. Julian had hoped for the remnants of a small fire, perhaps food or blankets. But if Blackbourn was using the caves as a hiding place, he'd left nothing behind.

———————

GRACE STARED AT the curtains of her centuries-old four-poster bed, listening to the wind wail and the rain drum against her window. She turned over, fluffed the pillow and tried to settle.

Her body felt taut, her skin stretched tight over nerves. Yet perhaps it was only the storm. Bursts of bright lightning flashed outside, the streaks of blue light stealing between the slim crack of the curtains. Riotous thunder and furious winds rattled the mullioned windows and shook the four-poster. The roiling storm echoed the roiling of worry, confusion and fear inside her.

She should be *doing* something for Jack, not lying in bed. Yet there was nothing to be done except find the traitor, and she didn't know how to go about it. Forcing her muscles to relax, she rolled over again and tried to think about something else.

Julian. Of course. What else was there to think about? Anticipation—even excitement—layered over her fear for Jack. She would be married soon. Part of her wanted to refuse, but she'd been over that before.

Yet marriage to the Earl of Langford was not as troubling as it had been. She'd questioned whether she truly knew him. Was he a coldhearted, ruthless spy, or a charming aristocrat? The answer was both. Just as she was both a poor relation and a smuggler.

More, he knew her secrets and still he *liked* her. Or he liked her wit, and that was simply a reflection of her. The true her, the one she'd forgotten she'd buried. During their confrontation in the woods she hadn't once questioned what to say, or held her tongue, or bowed to Julian's wishes. She'd simply been herself. And he *liked* her. It was liberating.

Although she did have one more secret, one that would have to be revealed before their wedding night.

She stilled as a peculiar sound filtered through the raging storm. It was the scrape of something grating roughly against stone. She waited, but the sound did not repeat. Instead, a new sound emerged from the storm, a quiet click as out of place as the scrape. The partially drawn curtains around her bed moved, fluttered, then quieted again.

Someone else was in the room, a shadow beyond the confines of her bed.

Lying quietly, she scanned the darkened room. She thought

there was a movement in the corner, but all she could see were shadows among deeper shadows.

She licked her lips as fear flickered in her belly. She buried it—she had no intention of hiding beneath the bedclothes. With a sharp, decisive movement, she pushed back the heavy winter coverlet. Kneeling at the edge of the bed, she knew she was fully revealed by the bright slash of lightning that lit the room.

A voice purred out of the shadows. "Do my eyes deceive me? Or is temptation personified in my lady smuggler?"

"Julian." Her heart bumped once, then raced. "How did you get in here?"

"Down from the roof. You don't have a convenient trellis or tree near your window."

He stepped forward, his broad shoulders blocking the window. His head turned so that when the lightning flashed she could see the outline of his firm jaw, the lean cheekbones. Even the shape of his sensual lips as they moved in a slow smile.

"It's nearly midnight." She couldn't seem to move. Still kneeling on the bed, she simply watched him prowl toward her.

"Midnight is the time for spying, fair lady. And the time for lovers."

*Lovers.* Her breath caught, her lungs seizing. How could passion strike so quickly? How could her skin be so hot? "You're spying on me. Again."

"Not tonight." He laughed quietly, as though he knew exactly how her body felt. "I have to leave for London. I need to convey information to my superiors but I can't trust the usual methods of communication. However, I need to leave now in order to get to London and back before our wedding."

"What's so important you need to go in the dead of night?" Rain drummed against the windows and she could hear the wind's angry cry as it whipped around the manor.

"Jack has escaped."

"Jack?" She stiffened. "What's happened?" She gripped the bedclothes, her fingers twisting in the soft fabric.

"Calm yourself." He held up a hand as though to stem the tide of her fear. "He's escaped—unharmed. He'll be safe enough. He's escaped from the authorities before and remained well hidden."

"Yes, Jack knows how to hide," she said, subsiding. Julian was right. "But why are you required in London?" She sat back on her heels. Lightning flashed and a moment later thunder rumbled.

"The men who arrested Jack were sent by my commander."

"Oh, God."

"They were acting on their own authority, unfortunately. And the evidence disappeared with Blackbourn, so he appears guilty. The situation is complicated, and I must speak with my commander directly." He stepped forward, his legs bumping against the edge of the mattress.

She wanted to scramble back in retreat, even as her body strained forward. "Do you think you can exonerate him?" Their eyes were at an even height, their lips entirely too close.

"I don't know. And to be honest, I'm not certain he is innocent."

"I told you—"

"And I accepted your explanations. I can't prove them until I find the real traitor," he said. "I need to inform my commander about our investigation."

"I know," she breathed. Inches. Only inches between them. His heat, his scent, enveloped her. Desire filled her, a low thrum that echoed the beat of the rain.

She could hear his ragged breath in the darkness, could sense the rigid control of his muscles. Some force passed between them, powerful, sexual and as elemental as the storm outside.

"Only two weeks, Grace, until the banns are complete and we're married." He reached out, drew a finger across her cheek. His touch was as gentle as the flutter of butterfly wings.

"Yes." She turned into his hand, let her lips drift across his palm. Her lips tingled as the rough skin of his palm sensitized them. "The smuggler and the spy."

"Husband and wife." His palm lay against her cheek, his fingers delving into the hair bound back at her temples. "Take your hair down," he rasped.

Lightning flashed and illuminated the sharp angles of his face. He looked fierce, nearly grim, his eyes intense. Unable to do anything else, she lifted her hands to the pins holding up her hair. His hand fell away from her face, but his gaze never left hers. She could see his chest rising and falling, hear his breathing quicken.

Power coursed through her. Beneath the charming aristocrat, beneath the spy, was a man that wanted her. Desperately. It was heady knowledge that for all his silver-tongued seduction, he wanted her.

She smiled at him, one slow, knowing siren's smile. And let her hair tumble around her.

She saw his control snap even as lightning scorched the sky and thunder roared. His eyes widened, his lips parted on a sharp inhalation. Arms snaked out, fingers grasping her shoulders as he drew her to him.

His mouth was wild on hers, plundering, demanding. She moaned as the taste of him met her tongue. Man, outdoors, rain. And the essence that was Julian.

Opening her mouth beneath his, she wrapped her arms around him and curled her fingers into the thick hair at the base of his neck. His coat was wet and it seeped through her thin nightgown to dampen her skin. Her nipples tightened, hardening under the cool, wet fabric.

His hands skimmed along her torso, her waist. *Heat*, was all she could think. His hands were strong and hot through the nightgown, and when they cupped her bottom they seemed to sear her flesh. Lightning flared, thunder roared and beneath it, she heard his groan of pleasure.

"Grace." His whisper was ragged as his hands roamed her body. "Grace."

There was nothing but the thinnest fabric between her body and his hands, and she wanted that barrier gone. Wanted his hands on her flesh as she had never wanted before. She was already compromised, wasn't she? So damn the consequences.

"Take me, Julian. *Please*."

A heartbeat passed, when time hung suspended. Then, a whispered caress, "As you wish, fair lady."

He pressed her back and climbed the bed himself so that they both kneeled in the center of it. Body to body, mouth to mouth. Even as he kissed her, he reached down to the hem of her nightgown. He drew it up, inch by inch. The cool air touched her hips, her belly, and his fingers skimmed along just behind the fabric. She gasped when he finally brushed his fingers against her breasts. Then the gown was gone and she kneeled naked before him.

She should be self-conscious, even embarrassed by her nakedness. Yet she wasn't. She felt free, unfettered and full of light. Something pulsed deep within her, bright and rhythmic.

Blue lightning filled the room and for an instant, they could see each other.

"So beautiful," he breathed.

Then it was dark again, and they were only shadows.

He trailed a finger across her collarbone, her shoulder, then down along the outside curve of her breast. The rasp of his finger along her skin sent desire shooting through her. When his fingertip drifted across her peaked nipple she gasped and arched back so that her breasts thrust forward against his hand.

His low chuckle floated through the darkness and warmed her.

He cupped her breasts, one, then the other, rubbing his thumbs across her nipples. Her breasts felt marvelously full and heated under his touch. He bent his head and his tongue caressed them, his breath hot against her skin. She moaned and gripped her hands in his hair, needing something to ground her to the earth.

He raised his head and took her mouth with his. She met him hungrily, wildly, ready for something she couldn't quite name. The wet fabric of his coat was pleasantly rough against her breasts and belly, but she wanted to feel his skin against hers, wanted to touch him even as he touched her. Greedy hands fumbled with buttons and pushed at his wet coat. Then they worked on his shirt until that, too, fell away.

Splaying her hands against his chest, she reveled in the sensation of sleek muscle and hot, smooth skin. Dimly, she heard his intake of breath as her hands stroked down until they played over the muscles of his belly. Under her fingers, those muscles jumped, tightened.

Pure female power coursed through her once more.

With a delighted laugh, she flicked her gaze up to his face. His features were vague in the dark, and yet she knew them well enough now to understand his expression. His grin was as delighted as hers.

Amid a roar of thunder, she could hear his boots thump against the floor, one, two. Then he fumbled with the waistband of his breeches and drew them off.

Finally, he was as exposed as she. Fascinated by the lean muscles and sharp angles she saw in the fleeting bursts of light, she ran her hands over his body. Crisp hair, smooth skin, hot flesh. She took his arousal in her hand, tightened her fingers around it and listened to his groan. Smiling into the darkness, she tipped her face up to his and took his mouth.

Oh, how she wanted him. All of him.

His breathing was ragged, the beat of it matching the hammering of her pulse. He tipped her onto the bed as the thunder rumbled. When his fingers caressed that most intimate place, the lightning flashed behind her eyes and the thunder roared inside her. She clutched at his shoulders, felt the liquid heat gather inside her.

When he slipped inside her, when he breached the barrier that proved she was yet a virgin, she stiffened at the momentary pain. He stilled, then pushed himself up to his elbows and looked down at her.

Her secret was revealed.

Lightning flashed. In that instant of bright light she saw the expression in his eyes. Possessive. Satisfied.

And something so deep, so intense, she nearly wept.

"Grace." He leaned down, kissing her gently. "Why didn't you tell me?"

"Would it have mattered?"

"No." He kissed her again, harder this time, deeper. "Tell me if I hurt you," he whispered.

He moved slowly, oh, so slowly. Tantalizing, teasing. Around and between them, the passion still pulsed, brilliant and powerful. Yet he was gentle, and so utterly tender she unraveled beneath him.

She quivered, then writhed as something built within her even as the storm outside built to a crescendo. As the world within her blazed and flared and sizzled, the world outside flickered and boomed and burst into brilliant arrows of blue light.

When her hands slid limply from his shoulders, he laughed. "That, fair lady, is only the beginning."

---

HE'D LEFT IN the early morning hours, before even the pre-dawn light was a faint gray glow on the horizon. She'd lain there, completely sated and limp. His departure was marked by one searing, dazzling kiss that both soothed and stirred her.

Even now, hours later, she could feel his mouth on hers. Her body still vibrated with pleasure at even the memory of their lovemaking and the sensations of flesh against flesh.

She looked up from the tincture she was brewing. The storm had blown itself out, leaving the sky clear and the sun shining. Now, as the last of the sun's rays became vibrant streaks of color on the horizon and her duties for the day were complete, she wondered if she had been changed after their night of lovemaking. She didn't think so. No one had commented that she looked or sounded different.

Except she *felt* different. She felt knowledgeable, initiated, powerful—and hungry for more. Her body was loose, her muscles limber. Even if no one else knew what had happened between them, *she knew*. She was well and truly compromised.

"I'll return with a special license, Grace," Julian had murmured against her lips as he'd kissed her good-bye. "We'll be married within the week."

They *would* marry, because Julian wasn't Michael Wargell. She stared at the final rays of sunlight that reached into the darkening night sky and colored the clouds pink and orange.

She was falling in love with Julian.

Not all the way—yet. But she could feel herself tumbling down the cliff and wondered what lay at the bottom. Passion, certainly. Perhaps contentment, even happiness.

But what of love?

The knock on the door from the garden was light and furtive, and interrupted her thoughts.

Grace frowned at the boiling tincture on the counter before her. She sniffed the fumes and judged she had ten minutes before it was finished. Moving toward the door to the kitchen garden, Grace glanced out the window and saw that dusk had turned to night.

She shot back the bolt of the wooden door, turned the knob and looked out. With a glad cry, she launched herself at Jack. He winced, but returned her embrace, awkwardly patting her back as though trying to comfort her.

"Hush, now," he whispered. "Let me in."

"Yes, of course." Without a moment's hesitation, she stepped back and allowed him to slip across the threshold. Looking out, she saw nothing in the silent gardens but the muted colors and sounds of dusk. She locked the outer door behind him, then the inner doors leading to the kitchens and the hallway. She turned around and scanned his body for injuries.

Dirt streaked his face and a purple bruise marred his cheekbone. His hair sprang untamed from his head and appeared to have the remnants of leaves in it. Scratches covered his hands, and the coat and breeches he wore were rent and filthy. But he was whole. And—

"Jack. You stink."

He laughed. "Aye, my lovely."

"But you're well?"

"Well enough." He lowered himself wearily onto a stool near her worktable. "Have you seen Anna? The children?"

"Yes." She wanted to embrace him again but settled for rubbing his arm. "They're also well. Anna is furious."

"That's my Anna." His smile was both rueful and proud. Then he sobered. "I can't go back to the pub to see her. They'll be watching it, I'm sure. I need you take a message to Anna and let her know I've escaped, but I'm unharmed—mostly unharmed, at any rate." He rubbed the bruise on his cheek.

"I'll tell her." Anna would be relieved, yet Grace doubted the news would alleviate the woman's fears. Jack's escape only ensured he would be hunted with more fervor, unless they could prove him innocent. But practicalities would have to come first. "Have you eaten?"

"I wouldn't mind a bit of ale and food."

"I'll be back in just a moment. Lock yourself in, Jack." She strode to the door, stopped, turned back. Dropping a kiss on his dirty cheek, she murmured, "I'm happy to see you safe."

"Go on with you, my lovely lass." He waved her away, but not before she saw his affectionate smile.

She worked quickly, breaking off a chunk of bread, pouring a tankard of ale, slicing cheese and cold roast left over from dinner. In minutes, she'd arranged a plate and returned to the stillroom. He started shoveling in the food and she wondered when he'd last eaten.

"Where are you hiding, Jack? At the smuggling caves again?"

"Not this time." A bit of roast was gobbled up, swallowed. "'Tisn't safe."

"If not the caves, then where?"

"Old Mick's cabin." He paused, a hunk of bread halfway to his mouth. "It's not very bloody comfortable."

She snorted. "I expect not. Old Mick died nearly twenty years ago, so I'm told."

"Longer. But the cabin is well enough out of the way, and there's two exits and a hidden cellar under the floor if escape is needed."

"Which reminds me, Jack. How *did* you escape?"

"Oh, well now, my lovely, that's a tale. The boy who locked me in was a twit if I ever saw one." He slapped his thigh. "They locked me in the room, alone. So I went up the chimney. When they came back, it appeared I managed to escape through a locked door. I laughed myself silly listening to that boy and his men scramble around. I stayed wedged in the chimney for an hour while they searched the entire inn. Damned dirty place to be for an hour, Gracie."

She laughed until her sides ached, picturing him squeezed into the narrow confines of a chimney, covered in black soot and listening to his captors mounting the search for him.

"I shouldn't laugh," she said, wheezing. "Poor etiquette, I'm sure."

"Bah. Smugglers don't bother with etiquette, as you know well enough after your dealings with the Earl of Langford." He winked. "When is the wedding to take place?"

Her laughter died. "Jack—" She stopped, debating how much to tell him.

Julian's profession was a secret, one she had no right to share. The trust she'd built with Julian was as fragile and delicate as a spider's web. If she revealed Julian's secret to Jack, that trust would be broken. Yet Julian was as close to being on Jack's side as he could be, and was Jack's best prospect of being exonerated.

"Julian—the earl—he's not just an earl." That wasn't quite right. "I mean, he's—he works for—" She swallowed, then burst out, "He's a spy."

A mist of ale rained over her as Jack choked, spluttered and nearly dropped his tankard.

"Lord love you, Gracie." He made a fist and pounded it on his chest. "Don't toy with a man like that."

"I'm not toying with you. I wish I were," she added.

No, that wasn't quite true. If Julian wasn't a spy, he may not have returned to Devon, and he may not have sought her out. She would never have come to know him, and would never have experienced the sensation of his skin sliding along hers, or the way his mouth tasted or the scent of his skin. She would never have known what it was to make love, or to be falling in love.

Still, she told Jack what she knew of the investigation, stopping just short of her bedroom door the night before. But she could see that Jack knew.

"Bastard." Jack half rose from his stool, his blunt features tight with rage. "Seducing you. *Using* you."

"Stop, Jack. Wait." She gripped his shoulders, trying to push him back onto the stool.

"He will answer for this," he ground out.

"Not to you." She kept her voice controlled and commanding, even cool.

He searched her face before he subsided into the chair, eyes narrowed.

"We've come to an understanding, Jack. He's not like Michael Wargell," she added quietly. "*Nothing* like Michael. Julian may be a spy, but beneath that is honor and compassion, the sort I never saw in Michael. I wanted to see it with Michael—pretended to see it—so that I could justify being swept away by him. But he was only concerned with conquests and appearances." Bitterness rose in her throat.

"Are you certain—absolutely certain—that you want to marry this man? This spy? Your uncle—"

"Has given me no choice. I either marry the earl, or I leave Cannon Manor, disowned and disgraced."

"Now there's a bastard," he murmured. He gripped her hand tightly. "You can live with Anna and me. We'll make a room for you above the pub. Well, Anna will. I'm not sure when I'll be back myself," he added ruefully.

"It's sweet of you to offer, Jack." She couldn't stay with Jack and Anna. If Julian was correct about the pub's profits, they couldn't support another mouth to feed. It wouldn't stop them from taking her in, but she would never do that to them. "Thank you. But, no."

So she was back where she'd been when her uncle had leveled his ultimatum. Marriage to Julian, or leaving Devon and seeking her fortune elsewhere. With no reputation or letter of recommendation to gain a post as governess or companion.

Yet marriage to the earl—to Julian—held such promise.

"I want to marry Julian." It was the first time she could say it without reservation. She hoped she wouldn't regret it.

"If you change your mind, go see Anna." He patted her shoulder. "Now, what the *bloody hell* does the earl have to do with my arrest?" His voice rose and he tugged at his unruly hair.

She stifled a laugh. Trust Jack to be concerned with her before his own safety.

"Did the earl turn me in?" he demanded.

"No," she said quickly. "He didn't even know of your arrest until after it happened."

"How much information did you give him? Did you give him names?" He tore off a piece of the roast, wagged it at her. "Did you take him to the smuggling caves?"

"No. Nor did I give him names." She rubbed a hand over her chest to ease the ache there. Jack had a right to ask. He even had a right to the anger he shot at her, despite the arrow of pain it sent through her. After all, she'd taken Michael to the caves. "I think you should meet with Julian."

"I told you, don't toy with a man." He pushed away the empty plate. "I'm not walking into the lion's den."

"He believes you're innocent." She opened her mouth to say more, but couldn't. She wouldn't prick Jack's pride by telling him she knew the pub was failing.

"So he says, but I have no assurances, Gracie. I'm not hanging for this. You may trust the earl enough to marry him, but I won't trust him with my life and my family's well-being." He pushed up from the chair, his forceful movements sending the stool tipping precariously on two legs.

"Jack—"

"You've made your bed, so to speak. I'm happy he's doing the honorable thing and marrying you. That shows his character. But he's not the only player in this. If I go to him, and he sends me to someone else, I may be arrested again." He righted the stool, but didn't sit. "I support you, Grace, in your decision," he continued, his voice softer now. "But I won't stake my life on it."

"I understand." She couldn't blame him.

"Don't tell the earl I'm back in Beer. I don't want him searching me out, or worse, bothering Anna."

"He wouldn't." Her stomach sank as she realized she didn't know if that was true. For all she wanted the man, for all the honor she supposedly saw in him, she didn't know. Which came first, compassion or espionage?

"Don't tell him where I am, Gracie." His shoulders hunched, and the dried remains of a crushed leaf floated to the floor. "Please."

She stared at the leaf, at the dull brown flecks it had become. That single, dried leaf made her want to weep, and she didn't know why. She clasped her hands together, squeezed. Jack would have her lie to her husband about his whereabouts. For surely they would be married before the traitor was caught and Jack was exonerated.

A lie by omission was still a lie.

She saw the dark shadows under Jack's eyes, the lines around his mouth that she'd never noticed before. He looked so weary. The Jack she knew, her laughing Jack, had dissolved into a much older man.

She had no choice but to lie. Even if Julian fought for Jack's innocence, there was no guarantee his commander would believe him.

She closed her eyes, exhaled sharply. "I won't tell him."

# Chapter 17

THE FRONT STEPS of the village chapel loomed before her, wide and imposing. The bright September sun and the sound of birds chirping cheerfully in the bell tower made no difference.

Grace had a vision of herself walking into the chapel, looking down the long aisle between the pews and seeing only the altar. Of hearing nothing but her own footsteps echoing between the stone walls.

What if she was jilted again?

She swallowed hard and tried to take a deep breath. The air caught in her lungs, leaving her light-headed. Instinct had her clutching at the masculine arm beside her. The arm jerked away, leaving her off balance so that she tripped up the first step.

"You'll go through with it, girl," Uncle Thaddeus hissed, bending down so his face was close to hers. "I won't have a whore under my roof."

"I wasn't—I wouldn't—"

But he was gone. He'd stalked up the steps and through the doors before she righted herself.

Embarrassed color flooded her cheeks. She refused to turn around and see if anyone on the street had witnessed the exchange. She simply couldn't look. Instead, she climbed the remaining steps to the huge oak doors that marked the entrance.

Would Julian be there?

It didn't matter. *She* would be there. Tipping up her chin, she straightened her shoulders and pushed open the door.

The interior was cool and quiet, a contrast to the bustle of the street outside. The light in the entryway was dim and it was a moment before her eyes adjusted to it. When they did, she sucked in a fortifying breath and looked down that long, long aisle.

Her heart fluttered, the tiniest beat of delicate wings beneath her breast.

*He was there.*

Tall and lean, his face relaxed and his mouth smiling. His gorgeous eyes focused on hers and everything else faded away. She knew her uncle was somewhere nearby, and she vaguely recognized the Starkweathers to one side. Yet in that moment, they were nothing.

In that moment, Julian was everything.

The sun, hidden behind clouds for most of the morning, now sent brilliant light bursting through the stained glass windows and into the chapel's dark interior. Rainbows painted the pews and aisle with jeweled color. She stepped forward into one of those brilliant patches. It was like stepping into a swirl of color and heat. Flame red, bright turquoise, lush green, sunlight yellow.

Then he was there, only a step away from her. He reached out and she set her hand in his. She hadn't noticed she'd reached the end of the aisle, hadn't realized she'd even been walking toward him. But there he was, close enough now that she could see the color of his eyes.

"Let's get it done," Uncle Thaddeus barked.

The spell broke. Uncertainty rushed through her and sent her stomach into somersaults. They would be married. Julian was going to keep his promise. Then what?

*Dearly beloved . . .*

Julian's hand squeezed hers, his fingers warm and comforting.

*Forsaking all others, keep thee only unto him, so long as you both shall live . . .*

It was forever, or as close to forever as possible. She would be tied to this man for as long as she drew breath. The idea was both exciting and terrifying.

She turned her head so their eyes met. The jeweled light played over his face, shifting when he smiled at her. And oh, his smile was wicked.

Then it was over. The vows were complete, the prayers and blessings uttered. Uncle Thaddeus stalked back down the aisle while the Starkweathers hugged her. Julian led her through the church and out the church door. A few dozen villagers milled around in the street. Shouts rang in her ears, a cacophony of well wishes and laughter.

Julian tugged her down the steps she'd tripped up only a short time before. He responded to the villagers' greetings with a grin and a wave, and she did the same despite the mist clogging her mind. It seemed impossible she was truly married. It was as though she were being washed away by a force stronger than she. Yet it wasn't Julian.

It felt like fate.

She turned and saw Anna Blackbourn standing to one side of the chapel, her children flanking their mother like young, protective sentinels. Anna waved a greeting and Grace responded with a quick nod and a smile. What was it like, she wondered, to know your husband was living within miles of you and yet unable to come home? She stole a quick glance at Julian, standing straight and tall and strong as he helped her into his waiting carriage—their carriage now, she supposed.

They were husband and wife. No longer was she simply Grace Hannah. She was Grace, Countess of Langford.

How odd.

As the carriage rumbled out of the village, she settled her plain light yellow skirts, smoothing them over her lap. Looking out the window, she watched the stone cottages and buildings pass by. Nerves leapt within her. She couldn't quite bring herself to look at Julian.

His presence filled the carriage. She could smell leather and man, could hear his light breathing. Could all but taste him.

It was the first time she'd seen him since they'd made love. And all she could think about was the feel of his skin against hers.

"Grace."

She swallowed hard, met his eyes.

"You can relax now."

"I beg your pardon?"

"Your shoulders are nearly covering your ears and your hands are gripped together like a vise. You're nervous and uncomfortable." He smiled sensuously. "I don't mind making you a little nervous, but uncomfortable doesn't exactly assuage my male pride."

"Um." Where was that witty conversation he claimed to enjoy? Deliberately, she relaxed her shoulders and loosed her hands. Her fingers were cramped. She stretched them out, studied them. "The ceremony was nice."

"The ceremony was boring."

She smothered a laugh, and felt her muscles relax. "The vicar sounded quite monotonous, didn't he?"

"I nearly fell asleep at my own wedding. Though I did perk up at that bit about the wife obeying the husband." He leaned back against the seat and watched her from beneath his lashes. "Any chance of that happening, my smuggling wife?"

"Hm. I think I would prefer to remain silent."

"I thought as much." His eyes laughed into hers.

He shifted against the seat and she saw something press against his coat pocket. She recognized the shape.

"You brought a pistol to our wedding."

"Is that an accusation?"

"No. A statement."

"I'm a spy, Grace." His face was unreadable. "I always have a weapon. More than one, typically."

She shouldn't have been surprised. She probably shouldn't be comforted by it, either. Glancing out the window, she saw they would soon be at Thistledown. "Will there be many people attending the wedding breakfast?"

"A fair number. Your uncle invited an interesting cast of characters." His tone changed, smoothed out and lowered so that it sounded just a touch menacing.

She stilled. "They're all invited, aren't they? All of your suspects. Lord Paget, Sir Richard and Lady Elliott. The Wargells."

"Yes." The eyes that had focused so intently on her as she'd

walked down the aisle were now serious and sober. A predator lurked in their depths.

"I should have guessed," she murmured, shivering slightly
at his abrupt change. "They are his closest friends."

"You have a friendship with Lady Elliott, correct?"

"Of a sort."

"Use your friendship with her."

"I can't." Something hard and acidic settled in her belly. "I
couldn't possibly. It would be deceitful."

"That is, unfortunately, the essence of espionage. We need
to find a connection from London to the caves, and that connection might involve Sir Richard." He paused. "I went to the
caves, Grace."

"What?" She jerked as shock arrowed through her.

"I was attempting to find Jack, but the caves showed no sign
of occupation—beyond some smuggled goods, of course."

Thank goodness for Old Mick's cabin. Her stomach tightened as her promise to Jack rang in her ears.

"He could be hiding anywhere," she said, hoping she sounded
normal. The words were like knives in her throat. But she'd
made a promise. "He may not even be in Devon."

"Perhaps not." Julian's lids lowered. He studied her through
thin slits of blue. "It seemed the most likely place for him to
hide."

*A lie by omission was still a lie.* That fact hadn't changed
in the days since she'd seen Jack.

Pushing away the sickness in her belly, she looked out the
window. "What do you want me to do with Lady Elliott?"

He remained silent. She wanted to turn her head and search
his face to discern what he was thinking. But she was afraid
her mask wouldn't hold and he would see the lie in her eyes.
Instead, she watched the blur of green and gold and orange
leaves fly past the carriage window.

"I want you to find a connection," he finally answered.
"Ask her questions about London, what they do there, even
Sir Richard's family and close friends. Anything that might
tie him to the Foreign Office."

She nodded, but didn't turn. The carriage seemed hot,
despite the chilled fall air outside.

"I'm sorry, Grace."

"About what?" Surprised, she faced him.

"I brought treason into our wedding day. And now your hands are linked together again."

She looked down, saw he was correct. But it wasn't treason on her wedding day that caused the strain. It was secrets and lies.

Suddenly he was there, beside her on the seat instead of across from her. His scent enveloped her as he reached for her hand and brought it to his lips. The gesture warmed her. His lips pressed against her fingers and sent her pulse skittering.

"Ah, fair lady, forgive me."

"It's nothing, Julian."

"But it is. A lady deserves a wedding day free of unhappiness. I've failed in my husbandly duties and it's only the first day. The first hour. Alas, I must throw myself upon your mercy and beg forgiveness."

She laughed, glad to let treason melt away in his absurd words. She wouldn't be able to bear their wedding celebration otherwise.

———

"I FEEL QUITE on display," Grace murmured in his ear as they moved through the crowds in the salons of Thistledown.

"So we are." Julian glanced down at his bride. "We're the latest *on-dit* in a quiet village."

"I suppose it was a shock." She leaned close so the scent of lavender and woman rose to entice him. "The poor relation marrying the earl."

"And with a special license because we couldn't wait for the banns to be complete."

As they paraded through the salons, Julian scrutinized the room, memorizing faces, cataloging groups, couples. Every one of the guests was the potential traitor. Still, some were more likely than others.

One of the men that topped his list stood near the main entrance, stiffly accepting congratulations as guests entered the drawing rooms. Lord Thaddeus Cannon's formal attire strained across his generous stomach, putting great pressure on the large brass buttons of his coat. Julian realized he had rarely seen his bride's uncle wearing anything but hunting clothes, which explained why the formal coat sat awkwardly on Cannon's sloping shoulders. A scowl threatened to form between his brows, and the thick brown mustache that dominated his face twitched. Julian supposed it was the barely concealed irritation and impatience that made Cannon's movements quick and jerky as he shook hands and chatted with the guests.

Julian's attention shifted as a shout of "Congratulations!" boomed into his ear. He swung around to face the well-wisher and was met with another of his suspects, Sir Richard Elliott. His wife, Marie, Lady Elliott, stood beside him, her eyes downcast.

Sir Richard shook back his shaggy mane of hair and offered his wide palm to shake. "Finally caught in the parson's mousetrap, eh?" Sir Richard pumped Julian's hand enthusiastically. "Well, our Miss Gracie is better than most. You've a fine woman there."

Julian glanced down at Grace. She had leaned in, placed her hand on Lady Elliott's arm and was earnestly talking to the petite woman. Lady Elliott's eyes flicked up at Grace, then toward Sir Richard, then back down to her feet. Whatever Grace was saying must have had some effect, as a smile tugged at Lady Elliot's mouth.

"I do have a fine woman," Julian answered, his gaze still on Grace.

"A fine woman is a good thing. Goes right along with a fine glass of brandy and a fine horse." Sir Richard slapped him on the back and grinned. "In fact, I just purchased a new hunter last week. Bought him at Tattersall's for a song."

Instinct tightened his gut. "Ah, you've been to London recently," Julian commented. Beside him, Grace stiffened and turned her head, cocking an ear in their direction. He continued, "What's the news from the capital, then? Any recent social or political scandal—not that I pay much attention to politics, but I do enjoy a good scandal," Julian confided, keeping his manner easy. Too much interest would cause suspicion.

"I don't pay attention to either one—society or politics," Sir Richard said with a dismissive wave. "I leave all that to my cousin. He's an undersecretary of something. For myself, I just went to Tattersall's, spent a few hours at my club, visited my boot maker and returned home." The big man rocked back on his heels, puffed out his chest. "Let me just tell you about the new hunter. This one's a beauty!"

While Julian asked the appropriate questions and traded the appropriate congratulations on Sir Richard's newest acquisition, he struggled to listen to Grace's conversation with Lady Elliott.

"Did you accompany Sir Richard to London?" he heard Grace ask.

"Oh no," the lady answered. "The city air isn't good for my constitution. Especially now. I went to Bath to take the waters instead."

"It seems to have done you some good," Grace commented. "You've got roses in your cheeks."

He glanced over. Grace was right. Lady Elliott's eyes still held the residual sadness she carried everywhere with her, but she looked healthier. Happier, even, than previous times he had met her. The waters must have agreed with her.

Julian turned back to Sir Richard and his new hunter, but he barely heard the man's enthusiastic description. Sir Richard had a cousin in the government. Although he appeared unfamiliar and uncaring about his cousin's position it could easily be a pretense. Undersecretary of what? With a few well-placed questions he could easily find out.

His thoughts were interrupted as another group of guests congratulated them on their marriage. Sir Richard and Lady Elliott moved away a few minutes later, then the new group was replaced by yet more guests. Then they, too, moved on and Julian found himself momentarily alone with his new bride. Once more treason would overlay their relationship.

"Grace?"

"Yes?"

"I'm sorry," he murmured. He looked down, placed his hand over the long feminine fingers that lay on his sleeve. He gave those fingers an apologetic caress.

Silver eyes locked on his. Resignation filled their depths, as did comprehension. "What do you need?"

"Fair lady, you are the most understanding of wives." He

lifted her fingers, pressed them against his lips. His other hand slid around her waist and pulled her close to his side. He let his fingers linger, let them stroke just at the edge of her belly. He heard her breath catch, and smiled in satisfaction.

"I need more interaction with Lord Paget and Michael Wargell while I have the opportunity. Then, when our guests leave"—he placed his mouth by her ear and whispered—"it will be just you and me, Grace."

Her quiver sent lust spearing through him. He knew what she felt like, had touched that delicate skin. And knew that beneath the cool exterior lay a deep well of passion. He wanted it. Fiercely.

"I intend to hold you to that promise." She scanned the room, then nodded toward a corner of the salon. "Clotilde Wargell is on the settee wearing the bright gold gown."

The crowd parted and Julian glimpsed a woman with auburn hair, her head tilted toward a female companion to give the appearance of listening. But the bored and superior expression on the woman's exquisite features told Julian she didn't care what her companion was saying. She was one of a group of seated women chattering to each other while their male counterparts stood slightly apart, conversing on some heavy topic.

"Michael is standing near the fireplace, holding the brandy glass."

Julian looked down at Grace. Her voice was flat, her face devoid of expression. He hated to hurt her, but it had to be done.

Julian studied Grace's former betrothed. Handsome, his dark hair just beginning to gray, and as bored as his wife. He hadn't paid close attention the first time they'd met as he'd only known Wargell as the man who'd jilted and compromised Grace. Not a gentlemanly act, of course, but no reason to suspect him of treason.

"Yes, I remember them," he said. "Do they have any political or diplomatic connections that you are aware of?"

"No, but Clotilde Wargell and I are not close acquaintances. As for Michael—I couldn't say. He never mentioned it."

Which made Julian wonder exactly what they *had* talked

about. Then he thought of his night with Grace, of their love-making. He knew what they *hadn't* talked about—or done. Possessiveness swept through him. For all the gossip about her reputation, he knew the truth. She was his, and his alone.

He caught her hand and tucked it in the crook of his arm. "Let's act as a proper bride and groom and greet our guests."

He escorted her toward the group of seated women, exchanged brief greetings and then joined the men near the fireplace. Julian focused his attention on Michael Wargell.

"Congratulations on your marriage to Grace, Langford," Wargell said smoothly.

"Thank you." He inclined his head, holding Wargell's cold eyes with his own. Not by even a flicker did Wargell convey any awkwardness about his relationship with Grace.

"Will you be returning to London now that the nuptials are complete?" Wargell glanced at Grace, just one quick, searching look.

It set Julian's teeth on edge.

"I can't imagine you'll be able to persuade Grace to travel to London." Wargell returned his gaze to Julian's. "She's too entrenched here in Beer."

"Is that why you cried off? Because she wouldn't travel to London?" Julian kept his voice low. Control seemed a dangerously tenuous thing at that moment.

The men around them fell silent. He could sense their eyes on him, could feel the tension thick in the air.

Wargell said nothing for a moment. He stood there, the brandy glass clutched in his hand, his face devoid of any expression. "We wouldn't have suited," he said sharply. "She's not what she seems."

"No." He narrowed his eyes. "She's more than she seems. But then, a gentleman would know that."

Wargell's mouth opened. Closed. He tossed back the brandy. "Clotilde and I—"

"You look like two bulls fighting over a cow." Lord Stuart Paget slid between them and punctuated his words by the loud crack of a cane on the floor. "Don't make a scene. It's bad enough you hosted this wedding breakfast to flaunt your mistakes, Langford."

Julian's fist clenched, and he barely restrained himself from plowing it into Lord Paget's gaunt face. He swallowed the fury and waited until the roaring in his ears subsided.

"I would suggest you refrain from calling my marriage a mistake on my wedding day." Forcing his fist to relax, Julian smiled at Paget. Or at least he tried to. He was certain it appeared more as a snarl than a smile. "That would be the height of impropriety."

"I'm telling you what I see. Half the guests are trying to hear what the two of you are saying. Keep it polite." He leaned on the cane, narrowed eyes flicking back and forth between them.

Julian looked at Grace. She was watching him, her silver gaze enigmatic, though she was far enough away she couldn't hear what was being said. But her hands were gripped together, their fingers bone white. He became once more conscious of the nervously silent men around him. Good. Let them be nervous.

He turned back to Wargell. "I think we know where we stand," he said softly. "We wouldn't want to cause a scene, would we? Excuse me, gentlemen."

Grace still stood near the settee, listening to Clotilde Wargell. He stalked toward them, temper still pushing at him.

It spiked when he heard Mrs. Wargell's sly tone. "Of course, we all know the earl compromised you, *my lady*. If he hadn't you would still be just Miss Gracie, wouldn't you?"

He reached out, snagged Grace's fingers and brought them to his lips. He kept his eyes on hers, let the desire he felt for her burn from them and saw her cheeks turn pink.

"Fair lady," he murmured over her fingertips. "My world had grown dim without your shining beauty by my side."

Her blush deepened. "My lord, you remember Mrs. Clotilde Wargell?"

Julian gave the beautiful woman a perfunctory nod. "My apologies, Mrs. Wargell. I find myself blinded by my bride."

He wrapped an arm around Grace's waist and drew her to his side.

"Of course." Mrs. Wargell's eyes glittered. "Any man would be."

"Not so." He could feel Grace trying to pull away from him and used the advantage of superior strength to draw her

closer. "I find the men here to be remarkably shortsighted."
He raised Grace's hand and kissed her fingers once more, this
time lingering over them. Then he turned and stared straight
into Clotilde Wargell's eyes.

"I've been to the Continent, Mrs. Wargell. And if other
men in this area spent more time there, they would have recognized my bride for the jewel she is instead of settling for
something . . . less." He sent a pointed look at an oblivious
Michael Wargell.

A titter sounded behind him and he knew his set-down
had been overheard. Temper assuaged, he pulled Grace away
without even a polite good-bye.

# Chapter 18

THE MEAL WAS over, the guests departing. As Julian stood on the gravel drive beyond the front door saying farewell to their final guests, Grace found herself alone in the entrance of Thistledown. She crossed her arms, gripped her elbows and stared blankly around the entryway.

She was mistress of Thistledown, she supposed. A countess. What did a countess do? For that matter, what did a wife do? She turned her head, watched through the front windows as Julian's lean form crossed to the stables. She didn't know what he expected from her. Perhaps he expected her to go straight to the bedroom so he could claim his marital rights.

Her pulse leapt. She could accommodate that demand. She had already, after all, and discovered a range of delights. The feel of skin against skin was so unexpectedly delicious, the taste of him so utterly male. Something fluttered in her belly as she watched her husband walk up the gravel drive toward the manor. He moved with such fluidity, limbs loose and graceful, yet full of purpose as well. The sun played over his features, gilding them, and the autumn wind ruffled his hair. He was so handsome, so strong.

And all hers.

Desire coursed through her, sending a warm tingling low in her belly.

On this day, Julian Travers was hers for the taking.

When he entered the front hall again, windblown and cheerful, she was ready for him. Reaching out a hand, Grace sent him a provocative smile. "My lord? Shall we retire?"

Instantly, his eyes went dark with desire. He returned her smile, though his was full of knowing amusement. "So early, my lady? It's barely three o'clock in the afternoon."

Heat rushed her face. Was she supposed to wait until the evening? "I believe I mentioned this once before, Julian, but a smuggler is going to make a dreadful countess."

He took her hand, raising it to his lips. His eyes held hers as his lips pressed hot against her fingers. The heat shot up her arm and straight down to her belly. Her breath caught somewhere between her lungs and her throat because now she knew exactly how those lips would feel on her most sensitive skin.

"Fair lady," he said, drawing her toward the massive staircase that led to the second floor. "At the moment, I find myself grateful for a smuggling wife. My enthusiasm to retire knows no bounds."

Something within her clutched, then released, and she laughed as he drew her up the front stairs and toward their chambers. He stopped before a pair of doors and pushed them open. Bright sunshine warmed the room and gleamed over Julian's hair.

"Julian, the windows! How—?" They were everywhere. It was as though the walls had disappeared and all she could see were trees and lawn and sky.

No, that wasn't true, she corrected as Julian closed the door behind her. There were certainly more windows than there should have been. And between them, around them, were dozens of paintings of the sea, the tropics, lush gardens, and fields that sprawled forever.

She whirled to face him. He must have seen the question in her eyes.

"It was dark in here." He shrugged. "I had the stonemason and glassmakers put in new windows and bought some paintings while I was in London. But it doesn't signify." His brows drew together and he stepped forward. "Unless you hate it?"

"I love it. It's beautiful, and so—" She didn't know. Liberating wasn't right. Open, perhaps. Spacious.

"Good."

"Does the countess's suite have so many windows? Oh—the bed!" How had she missed that mountain of white and blue and gold? Anticipation flooded her, sharp and sweet.

"Ah yes. The bed. My favorite piece." He drew her to him, his hand coming behind her to rest at the small of her back. "What's your favorite painting, fair lady?"

"There are so many, and each of them a different setting." She looked around, studying the paintings. His hand began caressing small, light circles against her back. Just the lightest touch and yet her breath caught, then released on a sigh. "That one," she breathed, nodding her head.

He spun them around and through beams of sunshine toward the painting until she stood before it.

"An island in the ocean." His voice purred in her ear. He was just behind her, pressed against her back, his cravat tickling her bare neck. His arm came around her, his hand resting on her stomach. His fingers splayed out, hot arrows against her belly. "Not the green shores of England?"

"No." She ran her thumb along the shoreline in the painting, just at the line of beautiful turquoise water and luminous white sand. "It's so exotic. So different from what I know. The palm trees, the greenery, the bright tropical flowers—it all seems so lush and vibrant."

"Perhaps the smuggling captain should take his consort there."

She smiled at the memory of their first kiss, and the smuggling captain he'd claimed to be.

Lips touched her shoulder, pressing against that sensitive flesh where shoulder curved to neck. And now she was breathless, her body taut with anticipation. Aware of his every breath, she tipped her head. Those clever, clever lips drifted up until they were pressed just below her jaw.

"Perhaps," she whispered, "she's ready to be swept away."

"To an island in the southern seas then, where the sand is white and hot and the ocean is blue as a bluebell."

She turned to face him, pressing herself against him. Her lips tipped up of their own accord as she looked up into his lean features. And his eyes. Oh, how she loved those eyes.

"I would say the ocean is the brilliant blue of the sky in midsummer," she murmured.

He looked puzzled for a moment. Then the expression faded as she rose on her toes and kissed him.

Hungrily. She was hungry for him, for his body, for his laughter. For the light. Pouring herself into the kiss, she ran her fingers across his broad shoulders. Even as she touched the smooth cloth of his coat, even as she tasted him, she could feel his nimble fingers fluttering over the buttons at her back. The gown loosened, the bodice slipping and sliding from her breasts. If she shrugged, even a little, the gown would simply slither to the floor.

His gaze flicked down, lingering on the round swells of her breasts. She saw his lips curve, ever so slightly, in pleasure. She went hot. Her skin, her blood, her body. And so she shrugged, letting the gown fall away. Fingers worked at her stays, until those too fell away and she was standing in only her thin cotton chemise.

She could hear his breathing turn ragged as he gazed at her, as his eyes went dark with desire.

"What would they do on that tropical island?" she demanded softly. "Show me."

"He would sweep her away, as promised."

He scooped her up, so quickly she gasped and gripped his arms. He was carrying her, she thought in wonderment. It made her feel foolish to revel in the strength and fluidity of his lean muscles.

"He would lay her down in the waves, just at the place where the warm, salty ocean kisses the shore."

Gently, he settled her on the bed among the plush pillows and silk coverlet. Beneath her, the soft mattress gave way, cradling her body as she watched him disrobe. His clothes fell to the floor, coat then shirt then breeches.

She smiled in invitation. "He would join her there in the ocean, and let the waves lap against both of them," she murmured as she reached out to draw him to her.

"So he would." Then he was there beside her, propped against the pillows and looking down at her. With the tip of one finger crooked under the edge of her chemise, he pulled at the light fabric. "He would bare her skin to the hot sunshine, inch by tantalizing inch, and would kiss that smooth and creamy skin."

His head tipped forward and when his lips touched the skin of her collarbone she sighed. Her breathing quickened as the chemise slipped down her arms and bared her breasts to him. Though she could hear a fire crackling somewhere in the room, the air felt cool on her heated flesh.

Her nipples stood erect, exquisitely sensitive to the air. It was torture when his thumb brushed across the point, then again when his mouth closed over it. Needing something to ground her, she threaded her fingers through his thick hair.

He raised his head, brushed his lips against hers.

"The water would lap at his woman's toes," he said. "Then her calves, then her thighs."

Fingers tickled her toes, then slid slowly up her calf. His touch was so gentle, yet she felt every ridge of the calluses on his palm. He grazed the back of her knee, then moved up under her chemise to skim along her thigh. Her muscles quivered under his touch.

She wanted to writhe, to move against him. She wanted *something*. Spreading her fingers across his chest, she tugged gently at the sprinkling of hair there. Beneath his smooth skin and lean muscle, she felt his heart pounding hard. The quick beat matched her own frantic pulse.

"Can you hear the rhythm of the ocean?" she whispered. Taking his hand, she pressed it against her breasts. Against her frenzied heartbeat. "Can you feel the beat of it?"

"Grace," he groaned.

His lips swooped down to hers, demanding and greedy. A moment later he drew off her chemise. When he ranged himself over her, his gaze locked on hers. Held, even as he kissed her. Mouth to mouth, skin to skin.

Heart to heart.

As he loved her, as their bodies joined, something powerful rushed through her. It filled her heart so that the essence of her seemed saturated with it. The wonder of that sensation, the sheer enormity of it, left her breathless.

She cupped his face in her hands and kissed him with all the tenderness she possessed. Wrapping herself around him, she met him thrust for thrust, beat for beat, until it seemed they were flooded by the thrum and pulse of the ocean.

————————

CURLED AGAINST HIM and warmed by the heat of his skin, Grace woke in darkness.

She'd been wanton—the first time and the second time. And the third time, after their cold supper in his room. Now she lay quiet, exploring the sensation of Julian's skin against hers, his chest against her back. His breath fluttered in her ear, his heart beat slow and steady.

How strange, she thought. Flesh to flesh. So close, so intimate.

The fire had faded to only the faintest glowing of embers in the hearth. Yet cocooned by the silk coverlet and Julian's arms, she barely felt the cool night air. Instead, she felt limber and loose. And oddly foolish.

It seemed as though their hearts had beat as one. But surely that was impossible. Yet in that moment she'd never felt so close to another person.

It was thrilling and terrifying and wonderful.

Julian's arm slid around her belly and tightened, pulling her closer. "Are you well?" The words were thick with sleep and barely understandable.

"Yes." She stroked the arm that held her close.

"Good," he whispered. She felt his lips brush against her bare shoulder, the lightest of kisses.

Content, she sighed and settled herself against him. She'd just drifted to the edges of sleep when she heard the sounds.

A rough scrape, then a thud.

Julian's muscles hardened, his body stiffened, and she knew that he, too, had heard it. He shifted and his lips touched her ear. "Stay here. Stay quiet."

He pushed back the coverlet and moved away from her, leaving nothing but cool night air behind him. She rolled over to watch him slip soundlessly from the bed. Naked, he stalked across the room to the pile of clothing that had fallen to the floor hours before. His movements quick and silent, Julian drew on his breeches. He bent again, paused, drew something from beneath the remaining pile of fabric.

Moonlight flashed on a short, thin blade.

Her eyes widened. Where had that knife been hiding? Had he carried it during the wedding ceremony?

Then she couldn't think at all. He turned to look at her, the color of his eyes indistinguishable in the moonlight, but the intensity in his gaze mesmerized her. Sharp, cunning, hard. Not the gentle eyes of the man she'd married that morning or the man she'd made love to.

These were the eyes of a spy.

He melted into the deep shadows across the room. She heard no sound, not even his breath, and it was as though she were alone in the room. Muscles tensed and poised to leap, she waited. Endless minutes passed where there was no sound beyond the bump of her own heart and the rushing in her ears.

Her breath caught when he stepped to the windowed door leading to the narrow balcony outside their room. His shape stood out in relief against the night sky as he opened the door and slipped through. A quiet click sounded as the latch caught and it closed again. Julian merged with the shadows on the other side of the glass and he was gone.

*Stay here*, he'd said. She understood the intent behind his command was to keep her safe. But she refused to stay in the bed, naked and vulnerable, waiting.

She slid from the bed and crossed the room, trying to be as quiet as Julian had been. In the silent night it seemed she could hear the loud drumming of her own heart. Drawing on her cotton dressing gown, she crept to a window. Inching the drape aside, she peered through the glass at the dark night beyond.

The white limestone balcony gleamed in the moonlight, its shape a sharp contrast against the soft landscape beyond. Lawn and trees were only outlines, black shapes against the night sky. Stars winked from behind gray clouds, and a low-hanging sliver of moon brushed the treetops on the horizon.

She searched the darkness for Julian. Though the balcony was nearly ten feet long, it was only a few feet wide. He could not have gone far.

It wasn't long before she saw the black figure climb over the railing and slip onto the balcony, but it wasn't Julian. It dropped to a crouch, the figure's head moving side to side as though scanning the terrace. She didn't dare move the curtain, didn't dare breathe. She waited, wondering where her trunks were. Her pistol was in the bottom of the smallest trunk, wrapped in a shawl.

Another figure appeared, momentarily silhouetted against the sky. Grace recognized the second figure as Julian. Yet he seemed like nothing but smoke, dark and lean and lithe, a sinuous shadow that hovered above the white limestone and moved with fluid grace.

The shadow leapt.

She gasped as she saw Julian slam into the intruder, knocking him back against the balustrade. The intruder recovered quickly. He pushed back against Julian, raised an arm to strike. Julian dodged the blow before kicking out, driving his foot into the intruder's stomach. The man wheezed but didn't fall. Taking advantage of the intruder's gasping breath, Julian lunged.

The two shadows grappled, arms locked around each other in a macabre dance. They seemed evenly matched, neither gaining ground as they circled and shifted.

Grace's heart thumped in her chest. What should she do? She stepped to the balcony door and reached out, her damp palm slippery on the latch.

Pausing, she glanced around the room behind her. She needed a weapon. She mentally considered and discarded half a dozen objects before settling on a heavy candlestick. Flying across the room, she snatched the candlestick from the mantel. The unlit candle toppled to the floor. She left it there as she ran to the balcony door and flung it open.

Cool September air rushed over her as she darted across the narrow balcony. She could hear grunts, labored breathing, a gasp of pain. Running forward, Grace drew the candlestick above her head, waiting for an opening to strike.

"Shadow." The intruder grunted as Julian's fist connected with his stomach. "*Langford*," he gasped.

They paused, their dance halted midstep.

"Angel?" Julian said. They broke apart and he stepped back. "Bloody hell, I was going to kill you."

The second man rubbed at his belly, wincing. "I thought as much," he answered.

Frowning, Grace dropped her arms to her sides. Who was

this intruder? She could see no more than strong features and thick hair brushing broad shoulders.

"Julian?" she asked tentatively.

"Grace." Julian turned, held out a hand to her. "Let's get back inside. Angel, you'll join us?"

"Of course." Deep, smooth tones. Grace felt the man's speculative gaze on her.

As Julian closed and locked the balcony door behind them, she replaced her makeshift weapon on the mantel. She returned the candle to its place and lit it, then its mate.

Turning back to the room, she glanced at the intruder and nearly gasped. He was the most beautiful man she'd ever seen. Golden and gorgeous, with hair the color of honey and eyes a tawny gold. What had Julian called him? Angel? Not his real name clearly, but he certainly had the face of an angel.

And he was a spy. She was certain of it.

She pulled her thin cotton wrap closer around her naked body and watched as Julian strode forward, his hand out-stretched. Did he realize he wore no shirt?

"You're getting sloppy, Angel. Not only did I hear you, but my wife did as well." He grasped the other man's hand in greeting.

"And you're getting soft. Another minute and I'd have had you on your back." Angel shook Julian's hand, a grin spreading across his beautiful face. "Wife?" Brows raised, he turned his gaze on her.

"She knows who I am, and why I'm in Devon," Julian said softly.

"I see. I didn't realize you were married."

"It's a recent marriage," Julian said drily. "Tonight is my wedding night."

"Ah." Tawny eyes twinkled. "Sorry about that. Pleased to make your acquaintance, my lady."

"And yours." Her heart was still bumping hard against her ribs. She wondered what else she should say. Welcome to my bedroom? Please make yourself comfortable?

Angel gave her an elegant bow, before raising his fingers to her lips. "I didn't know such beauty could be found in the wilds of Devon."

"I suggest you retreat, Angel," Julian said mildly. "She's mine."

"Indubitably." His eyes sparkled gold as he smiled silkily at Grace. "Still, a man can't help but comment upon such exquisite loveliness."

She narrowed her eyes. "I really don't think you're an angel."

"A fallen one, perhaps, my lady." He grinned again, and she was certain that smile had the ladies swooning at his feet. "But I wouldn't want to be a true angel. What fun would that be?"

Her lips twitched. "Not much, I suppose."

"And have you tamed the Shadow, my lady?"

"The Shadow?" She turned to Julian, who waved the question away.

Angel sent Julian a mock salute. "The Shadow was the best of His Majesty's agents—barring myself, of course—until his retirement."

She couldn't look away from Julian. His face was set in stone, his eyes the color of frost. What was the expression flashing in those icy depths? Determination? Desperation?

"I'm not retired yet," he bit out.

"Point taken." Angel held up a hand, his expression turning serious. "Sir Charles sent me, of course," he said, moving toward the banked fire in the hearth.

"Yes, I had asked for assistance." Julian let out one slow, controlled breath.

She studied Julian's back as he picked up his discarded silk shirt. His movements were swift and erratic. Not anything like her normally agile husband. The muscles of his back rippled and shifted as he shrugged into his shirt. She felt the overwhelming need to press her lips against that vulnerable place between his shoulder blades.

Julian tucked the wrinkled shirt into his breeches before turning away to light another candle. When he turned back, his face was still tight. "I would suggest we adjourn to a parlor or sitting room, but we may still encounter a servant and I would prefer no one be aware of your arrival, Angel." He gestured toward one of the armchairs near the fire. "Please, sit. Brandy?"

Angel ranged himself in the chair and nodded his acceptance.

Julian stepped to the table holding the decanter, and Grace followed.

"Is this about Jack?" she whispered, leaning close as he poured two fingers of brandy into a glass.

"Yes. And the traitor."

"I'm staying, then."

He raised his head, met her gaze. His mouth was firmed into a harsh, straight line. But he didn't disagree. "If you'd be more comfortable in a gown we can retire to the dressing room for a few minutes. I'll act as lady's maid."

She'd forgotten she was naked beneath the dressing gown. Feeling vulnerable, she pulled the neckline up. "You stay with your associate. I'll retire to the countess's suite and find a simple gown I can dress myself in."

"No."

"I won't need help." She turned away, but his hand vised around her wrist and held her in place.

"*No.*" The word was low, short and full of command. His grip tightened painfully on her wrist.

She sucked in a breath and stared at his unyielding fingers. When she met his gaze, his eyes were full of fury. Recoiling from the anger, she tried to step back, but his grip held her in place.

"You will not enter that bedroom. *I forbid it.*"

Anger bubbled within her. She could feel it pushing its way out, ready to spill over him. Until she saw something else in his eyes. Panic. Baffled, she searched his gaze. Was the hand that gripped her wrist trembling? Impossible.

She glanced behind her. Angel was crouched before the fire. Sparks flew as he used the poker to adjust the wood. Even though he gave every appearance of being unable to hear them, she knew he couldn't have missed the exchange.

"Very well. I'll use your dressing room," she whispered, tugging her arm free. She glanced again at Angel. "For now."

She retreated to the small dressing room. Her trunks were there, unopened. Having overseen the packing herself, she knew exactly which one housed her simplest gowns. Within minutes she found a clean chemise and a simple cotton gown.

The fire of her temper banked as she dressed. Julian's

reaction had been irrational, instantaneous and therefore instinctual. But the reason was unclear.

She stared at the connecting door to the countess's suite. It was made of unassuming wood and was as mysterious as the night.

She couldn't worry about it now. Another spy was currently relaxing in Julian's bedchamber, and she had no intention of missing their conversation. Treason must come first. More, Jack's freedom came first.

As she'd chosen to dispense with stays, Grace wrapped a thin shawl around her shoulders and stepped into the earl's rooms. Both men looked up from their brandy and rose. She gestured them back to their seats. "Please continue." Gathering her skirts, Grace slid onto the sofa beside Julian. He flicked his eyes toward hers, then back at Angel.

"Do you have any contacts you could employ?" Julian asked, clearly continuing their conversation.

"I have a contact on a cutter that smuggles between Lyme Regis and Guernsey. He doesn't usually come this far west, but as he is the captain and owes me more than a few favors, I can persuade him to find a position for me on his ship. A few nights with the crew and my disguise would be quickly established."

Julian sipped his brandy. "Someone, somewhere, has connections in the Foreign Office. I just need to find the right connection."

"These gentlemen you mentioned, the ones who are in the Hellfire Club and know about the smuggling caves, do they travel regularly to London?"

This question Grace could answer. "Most of them have gone to London recently, in fact," she put in. "But they don't travel there regularly."

"Except you might not be aware of their travel plans," Angel said.

"True, although if they were gone for any length of time I would probably know. It takes at least three days to travel from London to Beer."

"If you're traveling by coach," Julian pointed out. "A single horse and rider are faster."

"A man engaging in treason would keep his actions hidden." Angel set his brandy glass aside and paced to the fire.

"He would travel fast, and he would travel at night if he could. Anyone could travel between here and London quickly if needed. They wouldn't be able to hide it from their household and family, but certainly from their neighbors."

"He wouldn't need to travel all the way to London," Julian added. "A middleman could travel to Beer. Or they could meet at a halfway point. Perhaps even within a day's ride."

"Or a day's sail," mused Angel. "Are you absolutely certain the smugglers who found the folios aren't involved?"

Julian deferred to Grace with a wave of his hand.

"Yes," she said.

"Even Jack Blackbourn?"

"*Yes*." She looked down as Julian's hands came to rest over hers. Her fingers clutched the folds of her gown.

"I do agree with Grace," Julian added quietly as he pried her fingers from the fabric. "It's highly unlikely Blackbourn is involved. Still, I wish I knew where he was." His fingers, strong and solid, entwined with hers.

Her belly twisted, sharp and nauseating. She didn't dare meet Julian's gaze. He might see the truth about Jack in her eyes. Her fingers felt icy between his warm ones.

Disentangling her fingers, she stood. Let Julian make of it what he would. She couldn't hold his hand so intimately while such sickness washed through her. Keeping her back to the men, she made a show of adjusting the coverlet of the bed, letting the smooth silk slide through her cold hands.

"If you're certain he's innocent," Angel said behind her, "then we won't concentrate our energies pursuing Blackbourn. I'll speak with my contact and see if he'll pick up an extra deckhand for a few days. If there's something afoot, his crew may know."

"That may also establish credibility and gain you entry with other smuggling groups we can't access." Julian paused before continuing, and she could feel his gaze on her back. But she didn't turn around. "I'll pursue each of the members of the Hellfire Club and Michael Wargell," he said quietly.

"How?" The clink of glass on wood punctuated Angel's words, then the tinkle of crystal on crystal, followed by the splash and glug of liquid being poured.

"I think a search of their homes is in order—or at least the rooms most likely to hide incriminating documents." Footsteps sounded behind her. Wood crackled and snapped in the fireplace.

"A search of the smuggling caves needs to occur as well," Angel added.

Her head whipped around. "The caves?"

"Of course." Angel broke off, studying her face. "My lady?"

She shook her head, pressing her lips together.

"It must be done." Julian set his hand on her shoulder. "I should have performed an in-depth search of the caves earlier."

"My friends—Jack—they've already searched it. Thoroughly."

"They may have missed something." Angel watched her over the rim of his brandy glass. "They're not trained or experienced in these matters."

"They trust you." Julian ran his hand down her arm, just a quick brush of his fingers. His touch felt like both apology and question. "Introduce me to them. Let me into the caves."

Fear warred with guilt, and both of those fought with the need for truth. "I want your promise. You won't arrest them, nor will you give their information to your superiors."

He raked a hand through his hair. "You know I can't promise that."

"Then I won't do it." She lifted her chin. "I won't sacrifice my friends. Not for all the traitors in the world."

"My lady," Angel began.

"No. I want your assurances." Gripping her hands together, she steeled herself. "If I do this—if I ask them to trust you—then I'm putting my relationship with them and their trust in me at risk. If you betray them, then I do as well. And I cannot live here and look them in the eye if we betray them."

"I have a duty to my country," Julian said.

"And I to my friends."

With a resigned sigh, Julian paced to the window. He flicked the curtain aside, peered out, closed it again. "Very well. I promise—again—that I will maintain their privacy to the extent I can. If they are caught by someone else, I can't help them."

# Chapter 19

EYES CLOSED, GRACE turned her head on the pillow. The dark behind her eyelids became gold starbursts as sunlight warmed her face. It heated her skin, the bright beams soaking beneath the surface. She allowed herself to float in that dazzling moment, caught between awake and asleep, where her only concerns were the cool silk beneath her cheek and the languid heaviness of her limbs.

It couldn't last. She sighed and let her lashes flutter open.

The bed was empty beside her, the bedclothes mussed. The soft fabric was cold against her fingers when she tested it. Julian had been gone for some time.

She sat up, yawned and studied her surroundings. Her dressing gown was draped across the end of the bed. Julian must have placed it there for her. Getting out of bed, she pulled it on to combat the fall chill. Still, the sunlight beamed into the room through the balcony doors. She padded over and looked out. Trees and shrubs, once green and verdant, now blazed with brilliant oranges and yellows, and even a burning red. The bright blue sky above them was a perfect foil for the autumn foliage and, Grace thought, so like Julian's eyes.

Even when they were hard with anger.

She turned away from the unseasonably lovely morning

and stared through the dressing rooms to the countess's door. It seemed innocuous enough. The elaborately carved wood was lovely. Even elegant. Yet Julian had forbidden her to enter the room.

*Forbidden.* It was a compelling word, a demanding word. It piqued her curiosity in a way a less forceful word would not have done.

She bit her lower lip and stared at the door. It was tempting. Very, very tempting. She could open it, peek into the countess's bedchamber and close the door within seconds. Julian would never know.

Her feet matched the anxious beat of her pulse when she rushed through the dressing room. The door loomed ahead of her, both mysterious and daunting. The knob seemed huge, though she knew it was only her mind that made it so. Reaching out, she placed her hand on it. The metal was cool and smooth.

Sweat beaded beneath her palm, slicking the knob. If she pushed, the door would swing open, probably on squeaky hinges, to reveal the room beyond. But she couldn't open it. She *wouldn't* open it. He'd forbidden it—which barely signified.

But she remembered his eyes, clouded with that panicked plea the night before. Panic was not something she'd expected to see. The man she knew—the spy she knew—didn't panic. He cajoled, commanded, and even became ruthless when necessary. But he didn't panic.

Stepping into that room would ruin their fledgling relationship. She knew it instinctively. They'd begun to build something together despite the circumstances of their marriage. If she opened that door, all trust, all affection would disappear as though it had never been, because whatever lay behind that door was at the core of him.

She swallowed convulsively and let her hand slide from the knob. Striding to the earl's room, she went to the wooden stand holding a matching basin and ewer. She splashed her face with cold water, then changed into the simple gown she'd worn the night before. As she slowly worked the buttons marching up the front of the gown, a young girl came around the door from the hall. She beamed cheerfully at Grace.

"Oh, you're awake! His lordship said as how I should check on you before he went to breakfast."

"I'm awake, Mae. And hungry." Actually, she was starving. Apparently lovemaking—not to mention a bit of espionage—worked up an appetite.

"We'll get you ready for breakfast with your new husband then." Mae's gaze fell to Grace's gown. "Oh, you should have rung for me, Miss Gracie. I would have found a better dress for you than that." She paused. "I suppose you're not Miss Gracie any longer. It's 'my lady' now, isn't it?"

Grace started, realizing Mae was right. The words seemed foreign to her ears.

"This dress is fine, Mae." Grace smoothed down the skirt.

"Oh, Miss—my lady! It's your first morning as a bride. It's nearly as important as your wedding day. You must look perfect for his lordship." Mae bustled into the dressing room and pulled open one of Grace's trunks. "I'll press a gown quickly while you wash and you'll be joining his lordship in no time."

"Truly, this dress is fine."

Mae's pretty face fell. "Very well, my lady." Then she perked up. "Well, his lordship gave instructions to unpack your things. By this afternoon you'll have your pick of gowns for dinner."

Grace smiled in thanks. Mae was so enthusiastic she didn't have the heart to tell her she only had one gown suitable for dinner. She glanced once more at the countess's suite and frowned. "Where are my gowns and personal items to be kept?"

Mae's eyes flicked up, then away. "In his lordship's dressing room, my lady," she said, pawing through Grace's trunks.

She didn't press the issue. Where her personal items were kept and whether she had access to the countess's suite was not a matter for discussion with the servants. Not because of status, Grace thought. After all, until yesterday she had been closer to the servants' status than the earl's. It was, however, a matter of marriage.

Grace left the bedchamber and made her way to the breakfast room. Julian sat at the table already, a newspaper spread before him. He looked up when she entered, then set the paper aside and stood.

"Good morning, fair lady." His knowing smile sent her pulse skittering. "I had hoped my breakfast would be made all the brighter with your presence."

"My lord." Oh, he was handsome. Even in the early morning. "I wonder that anything could be brighter than the sunshine today."

"Only you." He leaned down and brushed his lips against hers. She felt the gentle touch all the way to her toes. "Please, allow me to serve you."

She glanced at his plate, which still held a poached egg and broiled kidneys.

"Finish your meal, Julian. I'll serve myself." She walked to the sideboard and began to fill her plate.

She could feel his gaze on her back. She felt awkward, and wondered if it was treason or his mother's bedroom that lay between them. Perhaps it was the fact he'd been inside her the night before—three times. Just thinking of it brought a flush to her cheeks and a tingle to her belly.

She wanted those feelings back. The intimacy she'd felt when he'd been inside her, his gaze on hers, their hearts and bodies and minds entwined.

When she had filled her plate and seated herself at the table, Julian leaned back in his chair and smiled at her. "Did you sleep well, fair lady?"

"Aside from our visitor?"

Julian's gaze scanned the room before answering. "Aside from our visitor."

"Of course, there were the various other interruptions of, ah . . . our wedding night." She bit into her toast and felt the sticky blackberry preserves on her upper lip. Very deliberately she licked the preserves.

"And those interruptions." His gaze dropped to her mouth, focused there with that intense concentration she found so arousing. "Already my wife has turned wanton on me."

"Perhaps she has." She smiled. "Perhaps she's only waiting for her smuggling captain to take her away."

"Then he shall do so, at the first opportunity." He pushed his empty plate away and raised his brows. "I would suggest directly after breakfast."

She cocked her head, as though giving serious consideration to his proposal. "I have heard that strenuous activity after eating is bad for the digestion."

"Ah. Perhaps just before luncheon, then." His smile was seductive. "We can work up an appetite."

She laughed, delighted she could flirt with her husband this way. "What will we do in the interim?"

"I have a few estate matters to see to—much to my dismay as I would rather be with my wife. But you are free to do as you wish. There's always the gardens, of course, as I know you love them. Redecorating, perhaps? There's any number of rooms that require updating. Many of them haven't been cleaned in years."

The mood was light and a laugh shone in his eyes. But she had to ask. "I wondered what—" She stopped, unsure of herself.

"Grace?"

Picking up her fork she fiddled with the poached egg. Nerves jumped in her belly. "What about the countess's bedchamber?"

He went utterly still as a chill settled in his eyes. "That room is not to be disturbed." His voice was cold, devoid of emotion.

"Julian—"

"No. That room must be left closed."

He curled his fingers around her arm. His touch wasn't rough, his grip wasn't painful. Still, his fingers were tight with the force of his command. She shook her arm slightly, and it seemed to bring him back to himself. Shoving back from the table, he stood and began to pace.

Unsure of her next step, Grace stayed seated and smoothed out a wrinkle in the table linens. "Clearly, this subject is troubling to you." She glanced up. "Can you tell me what happened?"

"It's private."

"You refuse to share it with me," she said flatly.

He laughed. A short, harsh and humorless sound. "With a wife of twenty-four hours? Hardly."

Pain sliced through her. "Don't be cruel. And please, don't exclude me. Tell me something."

"All you need know is that you're not to go in there."

"Am I to be blocked from your personal concerns?" Temper bubbled, as did confusion. She controlled the first, standing slowly and carefully, her fingers gripping the edge of the table. The confusion, she knew, was as visible on her face as her furrowed brow.

"You can use whatever room in this house you like, but not that one."

"That's not an answer."

"It's the only answer you'll get."

"I don't understand—"

"You don't need to." Julian strode to the door, looked back. "You only need to obey." Then he was gone.

Fury erupted. It seethed and sparked in her. She wanted to rage at him, to bully him into telling her why she couldn't go in the countess's bedchamber. But he wasn't there. He'd left without a backward glance.

Picking up a piece of toast, she hurled it down the table. It struck his chair with a satisfying *thwack* and crumbled onto the seat.

She stared at it for a moment, shocked she'd done such a thing. Pressing her fingers against her eyes, she dropped into her own chair. She was becoming a raving lunatic, and all because her husband wouldn't tell her his secret. He had dismissed her. Excluded her.

Made her nothing again.

The fury died. Cold to the marrow, she hunched her shoulders. Nothing. It was a dark pit where hopelessness and loneliness would suck her dry. *No.* She wouldn't go there again. She wouldn't fall into that deep hole. Grace breathed deep and pulled herself out of the dark. She wasn't nothing. She had to be more than nothing.

When the door opened Grace whipped her head around, expecting to see Julian. But it was only Starkweather. Concern etched his homely face, turning deep wrinkles into chasms.

"What's happened?" she asked, rising.

"Lord Paget's upstairs maid has been taken ill. A fever, according to the groom that delivered the message."

Grace rose quickly, setting aside all thoughts of the mysterious countess's suite. "Have a mount readied, please. I'll retrieve my supplies."

"Yes, my lady."

She hurried to the grand staircase leading to the second floor. Grasping her skirts in one hand, she pulled them up to midcalf. Skipping steps, she reached the earl's suite within minutes. She threw off her gown and quickly changed into her breeches.

Locating her medicine satchel, she rummaged through its contents and cursed the fact that she'd had to leave so many essential ingredients in the stillroom at Cannon Manor. She knew her uncle didn't need them, of course. But he'd forbidden her to take anything from the manor that she hadn't arrived with aside from her clothes. Now she was missing so many critical herbs and tonics and poultices.

At least Lord Paget's servants would have personal medications she could draw from. The apothecary in Beer would have more. She'd simply have to make do.

When she exited Thistledown she was shocked to discover her beloved Demon saddled and waiting for her.

"How did you get here?" she crooned to the stallion when he nudged her shoulder. "How did Julian persuade Uncle Thaddeus to give you away?" She rubbed his forelock, then his muscled shoulder. Demon nickered softly and huffed into her hair.

With regret, she ended the reunion. A groom was saddled and waiting as well.

"You don't need to accompany me," she said to the groom as she fastened her satchel to Demon's saddle.

"Beggin' yer pardon, Miss Gracie." He flushed. "I mean, my lady."

"You can continue with Miss Gracie, if you'd like."

"Yes, Miss Gracie," he said. "His lordship said as how we should accompany you if you have need to go out."

"I don't need a keeper," Grace muttered as she mounted and settled herself astride the stallion.

"No, my lady."

It wasn't worth an argument. Fighting the groom for following orders would be a useless endeavor. She wheeled Demon around and set out at a brisk trot.

Lord Paget's upstairs maid did have a fever, as well as aches and a general malaise. Influenza was Grace's diagnosis.

The maid was appropriately quarantined, made as comfortable as Grace could manage and given instructions to rest.

Grace left the girl's room knowing she had done her best. Time would tell whether the maid would recover or worsen. Grace sighed and pulled the door to the tiny bedchamber closed. She used the servants' stairs to return to the main level of the house. Intending to leave through the servants' door at the bottom of the staircase, Grace turned right toward the rear of the house. But a thought flitted through her mind, bringing her feet to a halt.

She was in Lord Paget's house. If he were a traitor, this house would hold the evidence. Looking around, she tried to get her bearings. Paget's study was not far away. It would be the logical place to start. She could search it, quickly and quietly, with none the wiser.

Turning on her heel, Grace hurried to Paget's study and was relieved she saw no one during the short walk. Pausing outside the door, she took a deep breath to calm the drumming of her heart. She placed her ear against the door and listened for sounds that might indicate the room was occupied. Nothing. But then, if Paget were reading or scratching out correspondence she wouldn't hear anything.

And the longer she stood here listening, the higher the odds that she would be seen.

Trying not to think about being caught, she pushed open the door and slipped into the room. Relief washed through her. It was unoccupied. She waited only a moment to steady herself, taking in the dark green colors and masculine furniture before rushing to the desk.

She pulled open the first drawer and rifled through stacks of stationery. What was she looking for? She had no idea, but hoped she would recognize it when she saw it. The stationery was blank, however. Beside it lay a wax seal and jack. Stationery waiting to be used, Grace concluded.

She shoved the drawer closed and pulled open the one below. A few scraps of paper lay on top. They were scribbled notes, seemingly unimportant. *Correspond with boot maker* and *Discuss vote with Viscount Lyndon.* She picked one up. Was it the same handwriting as that in the folios found in the smuggling caves? It was difficult to tell without having the original handwriting in front of her.

She stared at the paper in her hand. It was only a few words, a quick note from Lord Paget to himself. A reminder. Something small and easily misplaced. Unimportant.

She tucked it into her coat pocket without compunction.

Turning her attention to a third drawer, she pulled it open as well. It was near the bottom of the desk and deeper than the other drawers. A stack of ledgers lay within. She removed the first ledger, opened it and scanned the long, tidy columns of figures. Frowning over the numbers and descriptions, she ran her finger down one of the columns. It appeared to be related to investments on the Exchange.

It seemed innocent, but perhaps the others were not. She laid the first ledger on the desktop and retrieved the second, once more running her fingers down the long column of numbers.

"And what," a thin, oily voice drawled, "is the new Countess of Langford doing in my study?"

Heart thudding, Grace slowly looked up and directly into the cold eyes of Lord Stuart Paget. He stood in the doorway, elegant in unrelieved black, a walking cane gripped in one bony hand.

"Um. Well. I was just—" Her mind went completely blank. She could think of absolutely nothing to explain her presence.

She should have concocted an excuse *before* she began the search.

Paget strode into the room. Her hand trembled as she dropped the ledger on the tabletop. She retreated a step as he rounded the desk, eyes full of menace. He must be propelled by fury, she thought wildly, as he was barely using his cane.

A bony hand snaked out and gripped her forearm, skeletal fingers pinching her skin. She yelped when he swung her around, pinning her between him and the wall. He brought the walking cane up and pressed it against her throat. Her breath turned to ragged gasps. She stopped struggling, working instead to maintain her breathing despite the pressure.

He leaned in until their faces were only inches apart. She wanted to scream for help, but the cane prevented her from making any sound besides a moan.

"What are you doing here?" His breath was sour and unpleasant and hot on her face.

Inspiration struck. "I had a message, sir," she croaked. The pressure on her throat eased slightly and she took a breath. "From my husband. I was—" What? What? Panic reared its head, but she beat it back and forced herself to think. "I was only looking for paper to leave you a message."

She could see uncertainty flitting behind his eyes. "My husband wants to host a dinner party for my uncle to thank him for caring for me for so many years. We thought—" She swallowed. "We thought to include you."

Paget's eyes narrowed as he searched her face. She did her best to remain impassive, calling on all of her control to keep the suffocating fear from showing on her face.

"I don't quite believe you, Miss Gracie." Paget's gaze flicked to the side and Grace saw he was looking at her medicine satchel. Abruptly, he stepped back, the cane dropping to the floor.

She breathed deep, rubbing the ache in her neck.

Paget scooped up her bag. After a quick flick at the latch to open it, he upended it and dumped the contents on the floor.

Grace couldn't hold back her distressed cry. Vials and packets and bottles scattered. A roll of linen bandages unraveled and a jar of dried herbs shattered, sending up the bitter scent of betony.

She crouched, scrabbling to rescue her belongings. A sharp whistle of wind sounded near her ear and the cane swept down to block her, the point resting close to her searching fingers. Slowly, she straightened and met Paget's gaze. He held her eyes for a moment, then turned back to the floor as he used his cane to push through her belongings.

"Take off your coat," he barked.

"Lord Paget, I—"

"*Now.*"

Her fingers fumbled as she reached for the coat. She prayed he only asked that the coat be removed. If he asked for more, she would run, would scream. Would fight.

Then something fierce and strong washed through her, and her fingers stilled. "No. I will not."

Shock passed over Paget's face, followed quickly by rage. "You *will* remove—"

Locking her shaking knees, Grace dug deep for courage. She lifted her chin and simply opened the coat. "Do you think I've stolen something from you? A set of silver spoons, perhaps? A candlestick? Do you think I need your paltry possessions now that I'm a countess?" She snorted derisively, hoping desperately that he believed her. "You can see the inner pockets of my coat." She ran her hand down the smooth inner lining. "There are no bulges, no lumps. I've stolen nothing."

*Please, don't let him find the note.*

She stood there, the coat open for inspection but still on her shoulders. His eyes searched the surface of the material, leaving no inch unexamined. Then his gaze returned to her face, eyes narrowed.

"Satisfied?" she snapped, surprising even herself with the force of her words. She closed the coat, fighting for calm as she redid the buttons. She prayed he wouldn't see her fingers shaking.

"Not entirely." He threw the bag at her. She bobbled it, but managed to loop a finger around the handle. Dropping to her knees she began to shove the bottles and vials into it. The bandages went into the satchel in a jumble of fabric. Shards of glass nicked her fingers as she struggled to sweep the betony and its broken bottle into the bag.

"Leave it," Paget said, disgust dripping from his words. He stalked past her and threw open the study door. "I don't know why you're here. But make no mistake, *my lady*, I will be watching you."

She fled. Her heart was still pounding when she rode into Thistledown's courtyard.

———

THE DARK MARK discolored the delicate flesh above her collarbone. No matter what accessory she wore, it was visible. The bruise couldn't be hidden. Nor could she hide the truth from Julian.

She glanced at the door to the adjoining countess's suite. It wasn't lies driving a wedge between them. It was half-truths and omissions and secrets.

Leaving their shared chamber, Grace made her way through the east wing until she reached the drawing room. Julian was already there, a glass of brandy in his hand and the fire leaping at his feet. She hadn't seen him since breakfast when they'd parted in anger.

He left his post near the fire when she entered, a smile on his lips. It didn't quite reach his eyes. Still, he brought her fingers to his mouth.

"Ah, fair lady, after a tedious day, your beauty and—" The flattering words and charming smile died away. His gaze focused on her throat and his eyes went hard. "What happened?" he demanded. His fingers flexed, tightening on hers.

Her free hand fluttered up, ineffectively hiding the mark. "We may be able to determine if one of our suspects is the traitor."

"Tell me." His tone went flat, his face grim.

She tried to tug her fingers from his grasp, but they only tightened further. He held her gaze, his eyes a sharp blue. Then his fingers released and she pulled her hand free.

"I went to Lord Paget's." Stepping away, she paced the room and succinctly told him about her confrontation with Lord Paget.

Fear and panic still writhed in her belly.

She heard his breath draw in, then slowly blow out. She turned to face him. His face was impassive, eyes cold. A muscle jumped in his jaw, but it was the only outward sign of his reaction.

"I will kill him." The words were very measured, very controlled. And all the more frightening because of it.

"*Julian.*"

"I will kill him for touching you." He slapped his glass onto the nearest table, sending gold liquid over the rim. He strode toward the door with terrifying purpose.

"Stop!" Alarmed, thinking only of stopping him, Grace darted forward and put herself between Julian and the door.

"Step aside, Grace."

"No. Think. If you go to him now it will only make it worse." She saw his gaze fall to her throat. Stepping forward, she placed a hand on his rigid arm, spoke softly. "Paget let me leave. The damage is only bruises. *Only bruises.*"

"I would have no marks on you, Grace." He stroked his fingers over the purpled flesh, his touch the barest flutter of butterfly wings. "Does it pain you?"

"No," she lied. "I put ointment on it." She studied the angry flush of his cheeks. His gaze lingered on her bruised neck, and she watched as he struggled for control.

Whatever else stood between them, she knew one thing.

"Thank you for caring so much," she whispered, setting her hand against his cheek.

He turned his face into her cupped palm, breathed deep. Something intense flashed in his eyes before he buried it.

"Thank you for caring, Julian," she said again.

"I can't help it, damn it."

The frustration in his voice made her smile. "Let's go in to dinner. We can talk about what I found today and what to do next." She held out her hand, certain the storm had passed.

She was wrong. He yanked her forward until she was pressed tight against him. His mouth found hers, firm and wild and furious. Fire sizzled from his mouth down to her toes, filling her. He walked her backward until she was pressed against the door, pinned by his hard, lean body.

"Mine," he murmured into her ear, just before he nipped lightly.

"No," she answered on a moan. "You're mine." Drawing his mouth to hers, she kissed him with all the desperate hunger she felt. Their tongues danced and their breath mingled as they gave themselves to the power that pulsed between them.

Her fingers delved into his hair, gripped it, as his hands roved over her body. Possessive fingers skimmed over her hips before cupping her breasts. Those fingers delved beneath her bodice, brushed across her nipple—and stilled. He slid his hand from her bodice. She felt something scrape against the sensitive skin of her breasts.

"What is this?" he asked.

"What?" Dazed, she could only stare at the folded scrap of paper in his hand.

"What is this?" He unfolded it and read the scrawl that marched across the page.

"It's from Lord Paget's study."

His gaze skimmed along the edge of her bodice, hot and

intense. Then it flicked down to the note in his hand. "I assume it's intended as a sample of Lord Paget's handwriting, since we don't care whether he has contacted his boot maker."

She ignored the pounding of her heart. "We can compare it to our sample from the folios."

"I'm still angry, Grace." He tucked the note in his pocket. "At you for recklessly searching Paget's office, and at him"— his gaze touched briefly on her throat—"for hurting you."

"It's over. The bruise can't be undone. Nor can I take back the incident," she said. "But perhaps we could return and search again."

"First, I don't want you participating in any more searches." He stalked across the room to the table that held his brandy glass. "Second, I think Paget would be too suspicious. He would be looking for anything out of place in his home. He might even post guards."

"In other words," Grace finished for him, "I've ruined any future searches."

"If Paget is the traitor, you may have compromised the entire operation."

She heard resignation and anger in his tone and felt uncomfortably guilty. "At least we have a sample of his handwriting. If it isn't a match, we can obtain samples from the other gentlemen."

"Unless Paget alerts the others, which is inevitable."

"We don't know that, Julian."

"But we do." He contemplated the brandy glass, swirling its contents. "If you discovered someone snooping through your financial files—that someone being the niece of your old friend—wouldn't you inform him? And your other close friends as well?"

"Yes." She closed her eyes, accepted it. "What do we do now? How do we move forward?"

"*I* search their homes for comparable handwriting samples." He leaned forward. "*I*, Grace. Me. Alone. If I need assistance I'll contact Angel."

"I can help."

"It's dangerous, and you're inexperienced. We don't need you to be discovered again. You won't escape without consequences a second time."

"But if I'm with you—"

"I'll be distracted and worried about you and make a mistake."

He was right. Rubbing a finger between her eyes, she sighed. "Fine. I understand."

"But you don't like it."

"Would you?" she shot back.

"No." He reached out, took the finger that rubbed her forehead and brought it to his lips. "Fair lady, I would only see you safe." His gaze held hers as he switched fingers, kissed the next one, then the next.

"You're trying to placate me."

"You're too clever." He paused, grinned. "Is it working?"

"Yes," she laughed. "For the moment."

---

A SHORT, SHARP cry pulled Grace from sleep. The cry came again, and she realized it came from Julian. He thrashed beside her, pushing the covers away. She rolled over and saw he lay on his side, knees curled into his chest, his back to her.

"No. *Please*—" The fear in his tone was unmistakable. And chilling.

Placing a hand on his shoulder, she leaned over him. "Julian." She shook him a little. When he didn't respond, she raised her voice. "Julian. Wake up."

A shudder wracked him and she heard his breath heave in and out. My God, she thought. What was he dreaming? What horrors did he relive in the depths of the night? She shook him again, harder this time.

"I'm sorry." His eyes were closed and she was certain he was still asleep. "I'm so sorry."

The words were so full of grief she wanted to cry herself.

"Oh, Julian." Heartbroken, grieving for whatever misery held him in its grip, she climbed over him and lay down so that her body pressed against his. She gathered him close.

He turned into her, burying his face in her neck. The shudders continued to run through him. But there were no tears.

"Grace," he whispered into her shoulder. His arms came around her, drawing her in until she couldn't tell where her body ended and his began. "Stay with me."

"I'm here," she crooned, not knowing what else to say. She stroked his back, as though her fingers could smooth away his heartache. "I'm here, I promise."

She wanted to add *my love*, but couldn't. And the pain of that stabbed through her.

# Chapter 20

"WHAT DID YOU dream last night, Julian?" Grace searched his eyes in the weak light of dawn. His face was mere inches from hers and bore no trace of the nightmares.

"Dream?" They lay face-to-face on the bed, his arm draped over her hip and his hand stroking lazily up and down her back. A faint line formed between his brows as he considered her question. "Hmm. I don't remember." A laugh flashed into his eyes, chasing bafflement out of the brilliant blue. "I must have dreamed of you, of course. For such beauty is every man's dream."

"Please be serious, Julian." Still, a smile hovered around her lips. Then it slid away as she remembered how the shudders had wracked his solid frame. "You had a nightmare last night."

"Certainly not. I've a reputation to maintain, fair lady. My second career, remember?" He dropped a kiss onto her lips. "I must, at all times, remain dashing and dangerous and adventurous. A smuggler would never have a nightmare."

She refused to laugh. "Whatever it is, you can trust me with it."

His mouth only tightened.

Running a finger over his lips, she tried to smooth out the irritation. "You were quite upset. I wondered—" Licking her lips, Grace shot a look at the door to the countess's bedchamber, acutely aware that the carved door figuratively stood between them. "I wondered if it was about your mother."

"No." But she saw the flicker of doubt in his eyes. "If I did have a nightmare, it has faded with the morning sun and therefore was of no significance. Now, my fantasies are another thing altogether and are much more interesting."

Hooking a leg over hers, he rolled so that she lay on top of him. She crossed her arms over his chest, then propped her chin on them and contemplated whether it was better to let him change the subject or to press him. Time, she thought. He needed time to trust her. So she smiled at him.

"Tell me of your fantasies, then. Where are the smuggling captain and his consort sailing now?"

"Today, she's no consort. She's a Scottish maid, tall and lithe and strong. High into the hills of Scotland he takes her, where the air is clear and sharp."

"I thought it was cold and rainy in Scotland."

"So it is. Sometimes." He laughed, nuzzling her neck. Rough stubble grazed her skin and sent little shocks though her. "But today it's a soft rain, quiet and pure and cleansing. He would gather purple heather from the fields and make a bed under the trees."

Julian reached down and drew the coverlet up until it was over their heads, cocooning them. Dim light seeped through the fabric and cast shadows over his lean face as he whispered, "He would wrap her in his tartan and warm her with his body. They could hide there, protected from the gentle rain and surrounded by the sweet perfume of heather. Just the two of them, alone, with no one to disturb them."

She ran her hands up his chest, toying with the light sprinkle of hair that covered it. "What would they do under the tartan?"

Cupping her cheeks, he rubbed the rough pads of his fingers along her cheekbones, then across her lips. "He would kiss her. Starting with her mouth, that most kissable place." The lips that touched hers were as delicate as a whisper. "Then her eyes, her cheeks." His mouth suited the words, feathering first over one closed eye, then the other, then moving to her cheeks. Hands began roaming her body, skimming over warm flesh. "High in the hills of Scotland, he would seduce her, discovering her peaks and valleys and secret places."

Moving carefully so the covers remained over them, he rolled until he ranged above her. Propped on his elbows, he lowered his head and dropped a kiss into the hollow of her throat, then trailed his mouth along her collarbone. Her breath caught when his mouth skimmed between her breasts. She arched up, moaning when his mouth moved to one breast then the other.

The air under the blanket heated, warmed by the passion between them. She sighed as his fingers slid over delicate flesh and lingered over the curve of hip and thigh. He seemed to learn her body anew. She was gasping, nearly undone when he finally slid into her. Wrapping her arms around him, she opened, took him in.

Still hidden beneath the blanket, they moved together in a rhythm as old as time. Yet every touch, every sigh, every beat of their hearts was a new discovery. She let her body surrender to the sensations, to *him*, until she was both lost and found in the world he'd created.

———

GRACE TUGGED APART a tight bunch of dormant crocuses, carefully separating the beige bulbs for transplanting. She added them to those already laid out on the turned earth. Engrossed in her plans, she barely heard the gravel crunch beneath approaching footsteps.

"Grace."

She jumped and the crocuses scattered across the ground. With her breath still caught in her throat, she looked around. Fashionable hunting boots seemed to grow out of the grass beside her. Scars and stains marred the leather—scars and stains she recognized.

"Uncle." Feeling disadvantaged on her knees, she stood. Lord Cannon made no offer to assist her. She brushed browned grass from her heavy skirts. "May I help you?"

"You can return whatever you've stolen from Lord Paget." Disgust dripped from Cannon's words.

Grace folded her hands together, lowered her head and stared at the toes of her ankle boots. She could feel herself shrinking. "I haven't stolen anything." The protest sounded weak, even to her.

"You must have. Paget informed me he found you in his study. What reason would you have to be there if not theft?"

"Not theft, I assure you." She shifted, but continued to stare at her boots. "It was an invitation to dinner. My husband and I—"

"I don't believe you."

Grace tightened her already clasped fists and hated herself. He had no hold on her, no hold *over* her. Yet anxiety balled in her belly and turned her mouth dry. "Uncle—"

"I don't trust whores."

Something snapped inside her, sharp and clean. He'd said it before. Many times before. No more, she thought. She'd done her duty to the family—managing the household, acting as governess and nursemaid, washing, mending, menus, accounts. Even becoming his personal secretary. For a decade she'd been buried beneath rules and disdain and what she believed was her place.

And still, in his eyes, she was nothing.

The need to break free swamped her, overpowering and irresistible. She was finished being nothing. The banked fire of her fury roared to life. The pressure that had bubbled and simmered within her erupted and spilled out.

"Did Lord Paget say what was stolen?" She met his gaze and hoped he saw the blaze of hate on her face.

"No." Cannon studied her with eyes full of distaste. His riding crop tapped his thigh with impatient flicks. "The only reason Lord Paget hasn't publicly accused you of theft is because he's unable to determine what was stolen. Yet."

"Then until you have proof, kindly refrain from accusing me of theft." Blood roared in her ears. She raised her chin and kept her gaze steady.

"Don't think you can speak to me that way, Grace." The riding crop flicked more quickly at Cannon's thigh. "You may be called *countess* now, but a title doesn't change the fact that you're nothing."

"No, a title doesn't change what I am." She straightened her shoulders and stepped forward. "I've only ever been myself. It's never been enough for you. Do you hate me because my mother married beneath her?"

"He was a common laborer," Cannon shouted. "You're nothing but a baseborn whelp, and *I'm* saddled with you when your parents die."

"You could've refused," she shot back.

"And refuse the money for your care? Am I an idiot?"

"Money?" Shock rippled through her.

"Enough to make it worthwhile to keep you for a few years."

*Keep her.* As though she were a puppy. "But it wasn't enough money to *care* for me."

"Hardly," he snorted. "At least you were useful."

"Useful." Resentment raised its head. "I suppose I did earn my keep."

"Barely. The entire time you've lived at Cannon Manor you were gallivanting across Devon, waiting on laborers and fishermen and others of your father's class. No doubt you've whored yourself for them as you did with Michael Wargell and the Earl of Langford. *Embarrassing me.* No more, Grace. I forbid you to whore yourself to the villagers and wait on them with your potions and tonics and—"

"What?"

"I won't have your husband divorcing you and returning you to me in disgrace."

Dumbfounded, Grace could only repeat him. "Returning me?"

"You are forbidden to have any contact with those people."

"I'll have contact with whomever I please," she returned. "*Those people* are my friends."

"Grace," he thundered. "*I forbid you to*—"

"You no longer have any right to forbid me to do anything," she said viciously. She rose onto her toes so she stood inches from his face. "I'll do as I please. And hang your commands."

Eyes wide with shock, he raised his hand as if to strike her.

*She would not allow it.* She blocked his arm with her own and gave it a shove. Off balance, he was forced to take a half step backward. He might be physically bigger than her, she thought, but she would not be made small. Not again. She leaned in. His ragged breath was sour on her face.

"I waited on you. I ran your household. I was a governess for your spoiled daughter and nursemaid for your unruly sons. My own *cousins*," she spat. The words arrowed from her, cruel darts she hoped would land true. "I was a servant."

"You're no better than a servant," he sputtered. But his tone held a hint of panic.

Strength and power sang through her. "I tolerated your insults and your abuse. *No more.*" Fisting a hand in his shirt, she leaned close and narrowed her eyes to slits. Their eyes were level, and she could see fear flickering in his gaze. "Get off of my property. Or I will have you removed." The fierceness of her tone filled her with the thrill of satisfaction.

Whirling away, she stalked through the stone gate that marked the entrance to Thistledown's gardens. She refused to look back, not caring where he went from there. She made her way toward the nearest entrance to the house. It was the stone terrace and glass door that opened to Julian's study.

Her hand was steady on the knob as she opened the door. She tossed one final glance over her shoulder—and shrieked when she saw the man at the top of the terrace steps. She braced, certain Uncle Thaddeus had followed her, before realizing it was Julian.

The wind plucked at his hair and coat, but he made no concession to its sharp, cold fingers. He simply stood, watching her with hard eyes.

"I was in the garden." Pressing a hand to her pounding heart, she pulled in deep gulps of chilled air.

"I saw." A muscle in his jaw jumped and she recognized the light in his eyes. Rage.

"Then you saw Uncle Thaddeus."

"I was a few minutes too late to detain him." His eyes cooled to ice. "Did he touch you?"

"No." Her chin tipped up as pride filled her. "No, I touched *him*. I put my hands on him."

"He raised his arm to you." His voice was low and dangerous. "I should kill him for that threat alone."

"You don't need to. I don't think he'll be back." The mem-

ory of the fear in her uncle's eyes lingered. Satisfaction settled
in. "Let's go in."

He hesitated, his eyes scanning the garden as hers had.
"I'm not finished with your uncle."

"I am." She held out her hand to draw him into the study.
"I've said what I needed to say to him."

"I haven't." But he took her hand and followed her inside.
A low fire lay in the hearth and within minutes, he'd stoked it
so flames crackled and danced in the fireplace.

"You're flushed." Cupping her chin, he studied her face.

"Am I?" She pressed her palms against her hot cheeks.

"What did Cannon say to you?"

"Oh, nothing of import, I suppose." She stepped away and
his hand dropped to his side.

"If it wasn't important, you wouldn't be flushed, nor would
your eyes be so bright with anger." Menace shadowed his
eyes. "He wouldn't have tried to strike you."

"He didn't say anything I didn't know already. I was a burden to him. My father was a commoner, as am I. He said I was
nothing." For the briefest of moments, the black hole yawned
open within her and threatened to suck her in. She pushed it
away, filling it with the dark delight of standing firm against
Uncle Thaddeus.

"You can't believe that."

"Not any longer. Or perhaps I had only forgotten the truth."
Looking out the window, she contemplated the dull gray clouds
that mottled the sky and cast a pallor over the gardens. "According to my uncle I'm a baseborn whelp that serves the lower
classes. The circumstances of my birth are true, as you know.
And yes, I serve the lower classes. They're good people."

"The circumstances of a person's birth are an accident.
Only character can be chosen."

"Not a common view of our class." She looked over her
shoulder at him. So handsome, so elegantly dressed, and with
that indefinable aura of wealth and privilege. No one would
ever mistake him for anything but an aristocrat. "*Your* class, I
should say."

"Yours, too." He held up a hand when she started to protest. "I'm not arguing the point with you, Grace. I don't care

who your father was. It's you that matters to me now. And you are *not* nothing." The muscle in his jaw ticked again.

"I'm just—"

"A compassionate woman," he finished for her. "With a deep well of empathy for those in need. You're also stubborn, quick-witted and courageous."

"Courageous?" The disbelieving laugh caught somewhere between her chest and her throat. "I'm not without fear, Julian."

"I didn't say fearless. I said courageous. The two are vastly different. One is foolish, the other admirable."

"I suppose." She looked once more out the mullioned window.

"Don't let him upset you, Grace." In the glass, she saw him step forward. His hands, warm and heavy, slid around her waist.

"He won't upset me. Not any longer." She shivered at the tender touch of Julian's lips on her shoulder. "Let's not think about him. I've already given Uncle Thaddeus too much of my time."

"As you wish." His lips pressed against her neck now, the kiss soft and sweet. "I have a gift for you. I'd hoped for a little more time yet, so it's not quite finished."

"A gift?" She turned in his arms, stared. "Why?"

"You look so shocked." He laughed, and she could feel the tension in his arms melt away. "I'm giving you a gift because you'll like it. Because you need it today." Taking her hand, he drew her out of the study and into the hall.

"I don't need a gift."

"Of course you do. Everyone needs gifts." He led her through the halls to the rear of the house. "And you need some quiet time before our excursion this evening."

"The smuggling caves." She'd forgotten. Breathing deep, she forced herself to think of their mission. "I agreed I would introduce you to the smugglers. I'll keep my promise."

"Thank you." He kissed her fingers and pulled her into the kitchen.

The warm scent of baking bread flavored the air. Elaborately shaped loaves marched in a straight line across a counter, their braided and pinched designs baked to a delicious golden color. Two newly hired serving girls worked at another counter, their hands buried in dough and young faces dusted in flour. The cook, also new, stood over them with crossed arms and called out instructions—the dictator of her territory.

Julian wrapped an arm around Grace's waist. When the kitchen door slapped closed behind them, the serving girls ceased mid-knead to stare.

"My lord!" Cook croaked. Her mouth continued to open and close soundlessly, as though shock had taken her voice away while the rest of her still answered.

"Hello, Cook," Julian answered cheerfully. He leaned over one of the finished loaves, sniffed. "Ah, gingerbread. My favorite."

"Yes, my lord." Cook's eyes flicked toward Grace. "Miss Gracie—er, her ladyship—mentioned you liked gingerbread."

"And yours is excellent. In fact, I've noticed what wonderful breads and cakes and scones have been put out of this kitchen of late. I've taken quite a fancy to them, I must say. Would they be your particular recipes, Cook?"

"They are." Cook flushed, her cheeks turning rosy and round with pleasure. "But I've had help, my lord," she added, gesturing to the girls. One turned ashen with nerves while the other flushed as much as Cook had.

"And fine help you've had, clearly. I've not had such delicious scones in some time, and I thank you for the treat."

All three females beamed at him. Grace studied Julian's face. He meant every word.

"And now," he continued, "I have a present for my wife. If you'll please excuse us?"

He drew Grace toward an ordinary, inconspicuous door set into a corner of the room. He stopped before the door and took her hands in his. He seemed excited, she thought. Even eager.

"Close your eyes," he commanded.

"Julian—"

"Just close your eyes."

She sent her eyes heavenward before closing them. Still, she did as he instructed, tipping her face up so he could see she wasn't peeking through her lashes.

"Now let me lead you," he said.

She could hear the knob turn in the door. Wood scraped against wood just before she heard the quick squeak of a hinge as the door opened. He pulled her over the threshold and as she stepped through the door, a mixture of scents assailed her. Dust, damp, age. The tang of herbs and the sweetness of dried flowers. Yet each scent seemed faint and faded.

"May I open my eyes?"

He brought her fingers to his lips, let his mouth linger there for a moment. "Yes."

Her eyes fluttered open. The gray clouds had cleared and sunlight streamed in through mullioned windows. Bright beams turned the floating dust to glitter. It gilded long wooden tables and tall shelves, and sparkled on glass jars and bottles.

She had visited this room only once, but she recognized it. Thistledown's stillroom was large and spacious, although it had been in disrepair when she'd last seen it. Now it was free of decades of clutter and dust. An ancient still sat in one corner and a large cooking fireplace dominated a wall. Pots and buckets and iron kettles were organized with ruthless precision.

"Mrs. Starkweather and I spent the last fortnight getting it ready for you. It's been at least twenty-five years since this room was used—more, probably, as my mother didn't work in here." Julian gestured toward the rows of shelving. "It took days to clear out the dust and cobwebs, and I added anything I thought you might need or want. There are bottles, jars, two sets of mortar and pestle—I didn't know how many you would like or what type. Mrs. Starkweather indicated that the sets produced by Wedgewood are unlikely to stain or hold odors, so I purchased Wedgewood. If you'd prefer something else we can buy it in the village or send off to London."

He put one large, warm hand into hers. Pulling her toward a corner of the room he gestured to the books and ledgers stacked on a wooden table. "I'm sure you have your own copies of most of these books." His hand rested on the top of one stack. "*The English Physician* by Culpeper, Gerard's *Herbal*," he recited, running his finger down the spines. "Some of them include handwritten notations that I thought you might find useful. Also, apparently one of my long-dead ancestors dabbled extensively with the medicinal uses of plants, as there are several journals containing various recipes. I thought you might like to add your own recipes, so I purchased empty volumes so you could record—"

Tears gathered and spilled onto her cheeks. She couldn't help them. Something in her tightened painfully, then released in a wild burst.

"Fair lady, I hope those are tears of joy." When she sniffled, he offered his silk handkerchief with a flourish.

Mortified, Grace accepted the silk square and swiped at the gathering tears. "I love it, Julian."

"Are you certain?" His brow rose, one dubious question mark. "A lady's tears are a bit difficult to interpret."

"I'm certain." She followed the words with a watery laugh.

He took her free hand in his and raised it to his lips, then stepped forward until the only thing that separated them was their joined hands. His eyes turned serious, all laughter dying away. "I want you to feel comfortable here. It's a simple matter to rearrange it to suit your preferences."

"It's perfect," she whispered.

"Good." He touched his lips to hers. "Now come upstairs."

Her heart thumped, two bright leaps of anticipation. Still, she protested. "It's not yet noon."

"Which has no bearing on the situation." He laughed, punctuating it with a fast, searing kiss. "Come upstairs," he asked again. His hands slid down her arms until his fingers twined with hers, then he leaned in to take her mouth once more, deep and warm and seductive. "Come upstairs and I'll take you away."

So much stood between them, she thought. So many secrets. But still he gave her what she needed.

Drawing back, she smiled at him. "Where will we go today?"

———

THE SCENTS OF hay and animal and dust filled the air of Cannon Manor's stables. Julian studied the stalls and let his eyes adjust to the dim lighting. Nearly all of the stalls housed horses, from yearlings to mares to geldings. Blood tells, he thought. Every one of the animals had the lines of a Thoroughbred.

Grooms and stable boys moved up and down the aisles carrying tack and buckets and sacks of feed. Lord Cannon marched between them, barking orders. He stopped when he saw Julian, his mustache bristling and eyes narrowing.

"A word with you, Lord Cannon," Julian said dangerously, pinning the man with his gaze.

"Langford. Uh—" His eyes slid right, left. "I'm late for an engagement."

*"Now."* Julian almost purred it. "Outside." He didn't stop to see if Cannon followed him out of the stables. He would, Julian thought, because every bully knew when he was bested.

The cold October wind whistled down from the north, clawing at his greatcoat. He ignored it, slipping around the side of the stable. Cannon followed a moment later, rounding the corner belly first.

Julian let his fist fly, propelled by the dark rage that seethed inside him. He snorted, annoyed when one short arm punch set Cannon flat on his back.

"God's teeth!" Cannon sputtered through the blood that poured from his nose as he struggled to sit up.

Julian hauled him up by the lapels of his coat, his rage unalleviated by the lack of fight. *Hit me*, his mind screamed. *Give me an opening.*

"Langford—oomph!" Cannon's eyes rolled back in his head as Julian slammed him against the side of the stables.

"If you touch her—if you even think of touching her again—I'll give you more than that one fist." Julian leaned close, whispered. "I'll hunt you down like the beast you are."

"Grace—" The word was only a croak.

*"Is my wife."* Julian bared his teeth. "Don't forget it."

He let go and watched in disgust as Cannon slid uselessly to the ground.

# Chapter 21

Lord Langford—

*The foreign secretary has granted permission for you to be reinstated. You will be geographically limited in future missions. However, there is some need for you on the Continent at this time. Complete your mission in Devon as quickly as possible and return to London for further instructions.*

*Yours respectfully,*
*Sir Charles Flint*

Exhilaration roared through Julian.

He was back.

He propped the missive against his inkwell and looked up at Angel and Miles Butler, the bearers of good tidings.

"You know?" Julian asked, meeting Angel's eyes.

"Sir Charles told me." Angel nodded and the gold hair that had earned him his code name fell over his eyes. "It will be good to have you on the Continent again. We need you there."

"Sir Charles is quite pleased." Mr. Butler leaned forward and flashed an enthusiastic smile. "I am, as well."

Julian could feel the cage door being opened. He'd been given freedom again. The freedom to travel, to work, to be useful to the government. His mind sharpened, focusing on Angel's next words.

"Sir Charles hoped we'd achieved more progress. He's pursuing some leads in the Foreign Office, but would like us to continue searching for the middleman in Devon. He instructed I return here and continue assisting you."

Restless energy flickered to life inside Julian. He rose and began to pace the estate room. "Unfortunately, there's not much to assist with." Julian recited the details of Grace's failed foray into Lord Stuart Paget's study. "Otherwise, I have little information—though I hope to obtain more tonight. Grace is introducing me to the smugglers."

"I haven't discovered anything from my smuggling contacts farther up the coast, either," Angel added. "There are rumors that someone has been asking questions and loitering around the fishing boats, but I haven't been able to pin down a description."

"We're at a standstill, then. Again."

Frustrated, Julian looked out the window and saw Grace walking the garden paths. Just the sight of her calmed him again, and he let out a long breath. The chill wind whipped color in her cheeks and tugged at the carefully bound hair peeking from beneath her bonnet. She looked so lovely surrounded by the faded leaves and dark evergreen shrubs.

He felt a pang of regret. Of grief. Then panic. When he returned to spying, she would stay behind.

"What are you going to do with her when you return to the Continent?" Angel asked softly, as though he'd read Julian's mind.

"I don't know."

"She can't go with you."

"No," he replied, but his mind was whirring. Grace was no prim society lady—she was a smuggler that wore breeches and carried a pistol. Nor was she faint of heart. Perhaps he could take her with him, at least some of the time. She *must* come with him.

Because the thought of being without her was agony.

For the first time in a decade, he wondered what it would be like to *not* be a spy.

"My father tried to take my mother with him," Mr. Butler

said softly. "They thought it would work well, as he was a double agent and she a French émigré. But it was a disaster. She simply couldn't bear being away from her friends, her life. Her child. The constant strain of maintaining a façade wore on her." Julian could hear the grief in Butler's quiet words.

Outside, Grace crouched beside a flower bed, the material of her heavy skirts pooling around her legs. Her fingers rooted around and came up with a clump of soil and—presumably— weed. Tossing it aside, she stood again and tipped her face up to the sky. He could see her chest rise and fall as she breathed deep. Her eyes drifted closed and a contented smile played around her lips.

No, he could not take her with him. He would have to make a choice.

Marriage, or espionage.

---

MOONLIGHT FILTERED THROUGH clouds and cast a faint glow over the mouth of the smuggling caves. Julian studied the entrance, then turned and studied his wife. She watched him steadily.

"You gave me your word." The line of her mouth was tight and determined.

"I'll keep it." Julian heard the bite in his own voice. She only wanted reassurance, he reminded himself, and leveled his tone. "They're safe from me, Grace. Smuggling doesn't interest me. I'm here to find a traitor."

He caught the gleam of her eyes as she scanned his face. Apparently satisfied, she turned into the low opening that marked the entrance to the smuggling caves. Bent nearly double, he slipped through tunnels cut into limestone cliffs, his eyes on his wife's very attractive bottom.

When the tunnels opened into a large, cavernous space, he straightened and looked around. Only a few meager candles flickered in the cave. The dancing light cast shadows over barrels and casks, but it failed to reach the high ceilings or penetrate the dark corners.

"Jem and Thomas are already here," Grace said.

They started to cross the cave and the two men rose from the low barrels they had been seated on. Julian recognized young Jem easily enough, as he'd brought the man's daughter into the world. The other man was thin and somber. He'd been at the pub the night Grace received the first folio.

Julian performed a quick visual scan, searching for anything that might be a weapon. He saw nothing out of the ordinary. Still, he didn't relax. When a man relaxed, someone slid a knife in his gullet.

"Why did you bring him, Miss Gracie?" Jem's voice echoed through the room. He sent a sharp look in Julian's direction. Apparently there would not be any camaraderie over the birth of his daughter.

"It's all right. His lordship can be trusted." Grace drew a deep, bracing breath. "He's with the Foreign Office."

It wasn't quite the truth, but close enough. There was no office for what he did.

Thomas bristled, his narrow face going taut. "You brought us someone from the government? You brought him *here*?"

"We're caught for certain," Jem moaned. "He'll have us all taken in to the revenue officers."

"I have no interest in smuggling, Jem." Julian angled his body between the men and Grace. "I won't be turning you in to the revenue officers. I make no promises if you get yourselves caught, but *I* won't be arresting you. I'm looking for someone far worse than a smuggler." He met each man's eyes in turn, let them see purpose there.

"A traitor," Thomas spat. "And he's been in these here caves again."

Grace's hand shot out, gripping Thomas's arm. "What's happened?"

"The caves were searched," Thomas replied, placing a hand over hers and squeezing lightly.

"Are you sure?" Julian narrowed his eyes.

"Aye," he said firmly.

"How can you be certain it was the traitor? A common thief could have been here." Grace whirled away, her gaze probing the shadows of the cave. "Was anything stolen?"

"Not even a single bottle of French brandy." Jem shook his head, disgust ripe on his face.

"Which means he's not a common thief. He was here for a specific reason," Julian said softly.

"But if nothing was stolen—and presumably you didn't

find any more folios—how do you know the caves were searched?" Grace asked.

"Things weren't as we left them." Jem gestured vaguely toward a trunk with casks stacked on it. "Two casks were moved. It looked like they were moved so someone could get into a trunk. I checked the trunk and the silks were all mussed."

"The fabric might have become disorganized during transport," Julian pointed out.

"Not like this. These were tumbled about, like someone started digging at the bottom." Jem scratched his head. "What made me notice it was the casks. I put them in front of the trunk last night and had a little rest on one of them while I ate the cold meat and ale my Fanny packed. I was the last to leave the caves last night and first back tonight." Jem gestured toward the wooden casks, stacked now on top of the trunk.

Julian turned to look at the offending items. Just simple, innocuous wooden casks, worn and scarred.

"Have you noticed items out of place before?" he asked.

"I was telling Jem about that before you and Miss Gracie came, milord," Thomas interjected. "I'd not thought about it before. What's a few trunks or barrels moved around? There's men in and out nearly every night. But it *has* happened before—as many as five or six times."

"I haven't noticed it before, but I thought to ask John the blacksmith." Jem frowned. "I passed him in the street and he said he was coming to the caves early. Had a row with his missus and was thinking to hide for a few hours. Though he was looking forward to going home, as his missus always apologized by—ahem." Jem flushed, looked at Grace, then away. "Apologized."

Julian tried to hold back his chuckle. He'd known his share of angry women.

"John's not turned up," Jem concluded. "He's running nearly a half hour behind now."

Julian's instincts stirred, a quick shift of awareness that had something hard settling in his belly. "Jem, I want you to think carefully." He tried not to let his suspicions sound in his voice.

Still, the young father's eyes widened. "Milord?"

"How long ago did you see John?"

"Nearly two hours now."

"Julian?" Grace's single word was full of questions.

He didn't even turn to look at her. He didn't want her to see the premonition in his eyes. "John indicated he was coming straight here, to the caves. Is that correct, Jem?" Julian continued.

"Aye." Jem's green eyes flicked around the cave. "I thought he'd be here when I arrived."

"What do you think—" Thomas began.

"I'm not thinking anything yet." Julian counted the number of tunnels that fanned out from the cavern they stood in. "How far back do these caves go?" he asked, nodding at the nearest tunnel opening.

It was Grace who answered. Although her voice was even, he heard the subtle fear in it. "The natural caves extend about a half mile, perhaps a little more. From there they intersect the quarries. Some of the quarries are still in use, but others are abandoned."

"Search them," he commanded, looking to both Thomas and Jem. "Search the natural caves and the abandoned quarries. Don't concern yourselves with the working quarries yet."

With grim faces, the two men disappeared into tunnels, each with a lit lantern held aloft. Julian reached for one of the dozen lanterns lining the wall and used a candle to light it.

"Grace?" He held out a hand to her. Icy fingers slid between his.

"What if—" she began.

"Don't think about it. Just search." It was the only advice he could give her. "Shut out your fear, shut out the worry. Just do what needs to be done."

He heard her swallow, felt her fingers jerk once in his. Then she tipped up her chin and strode forward.

Lantern light glimmered gold on limestone walls as he and Grace started down one of the tunnels. Though she could walk upright, the ceiling was just low enough he had to duck his head and hunch his shoulders. The air was cool and damp, and settled into his bones.

"Tell me of John. Is he often late?" Julian asked.

"No." She made a choking sound. "He's one of the most reliable smugglers."

*Don't think. Just search.* He held the lantern higher to penetrate small side galleries and offshoots. Water dripped somewhere, pinging against rock. Her fingers began to warm in his.

Then they heard a shout. Another. Her fingers dropped away as they ran back to the mouth of the tunnel. Beside him, Grace's breathing was ragged. Her boots rang on the stone floor nearly in unison with his.

Jem stood in the opening to one the tunnels. All color had drained from his face and his mouth was set in a severe line. "I found John." He spun around and led them through the tunnel.

Julian smelled death before he saw it. Violent death had its own scent, one he knew well. Blood, tinged with something foul and sickly. He stepped in front of Grace to block her view of what lay ahead.

"Stay here," he commanded.

She didn't even answer. She simply raised a brow as if to say, *Are you mutton-headed?* and ducked around him.

He swore, whirled and tried to grab her shoulders—but it was too late. A sharp cry ripped from her throat before she moved two paces. With her face drained of color, her cheekbones seemed to sharpen. Panic edged into her breathing so that it became shallow and quick.

"Breathe, Grace. In and out." Now Julian did block her view, and he saw her eyes were glassy.

"But John—"

"Can't be helped now." He'd only caught a glimpse of the blacksmith's body, but that was all he needed to see. "In and out. *Now.*"

She did breathe. Long, slow, deep breaths. He watched her struggle, saw her throat constrict and her lips press together. But she battled back the horror and the nausea.

*She shouldn't have seen this*, was all he could think. He should have forced her to stay behind until he'd investigated the situation. He'd seen murder many times before. While he never became hardened to it, it had lost its ability to shock him. But she was innocent to that knowledge.

Or she had been.

He studied her colorless cheeks and the eyes that seemed too large for her face. Espionage didn't belong in her life.

When he was certain she'd found control, he left her and went to John's body.

The cause of death was clear. A blow to the head. Julian crouched down and felt the man's skin, then studied the weapon, the wound. The blood. The blacksmith hadn't been dead long at all. The killer could have been in the caves with them.

"Did he fall?" Grace's voice quavered. Her hand touched his shoulder, rested there. "Did he fall and hurt his head?"

It would be better if he lied. Death was always ignominious, but murder was devastating to those left behind. He could spare her the pain of that.

The fingers on his shoulder dug into his flesh like sharp daggers, and he knew she understood the truth. Her mind was only trying to deny it.

"No. He did not fall." Julian gestured to a chunk of limestone tossed a few feet away. Blood smeared it. "Someone deliberately used *that* as a weapon."

The rock had not fallen from the limestone ceiling above. Nor did the killer accidentally hit John and flee the scene. There were multiple wounds, indicating repeated blows. Repeated blows implied purpose. And rage.

But that, she didn't need to know.

"Oh, John's poor wife," Grace whispered. Her breath hitched, a sharp inhalation. "How am I going to tell her?"

"*We* are going to tell her," Thomas said. He stepped beside Grace so that they stood side by side, looking down at the blacksmith's bloodied body.

"We all will," Jem added as he moved to Grace's other side.

Thomas laid a hand on Julian's shoulder. "Let's take him home to his wife."

Julian hooked his hands beneath the blacksmith's lifeless arms and waited for Thomas to take his feet. They carried the body through the caves, Grace and Jem a step behind.

Beyond the caves, clouds obscured the moon and a chill rain fell. They maneuvered the blacksmith's limp form up the rain-slicked cliff walk. Julian glanced only once at Grace and saw tears tracking down her cheeks, although she made no sound. His stomach twisted. He wanted to pull her into his arms and wipe those tears away.

# Chapter 22

THE DARKNESS OF the night lay heavy on Julian. The bedchamber he'd so painstakingly redecorated to soothe and
calm did neither of those things. Beside him in the bed, Grace
lay on her side, her breathing slow and even.

She'd cried herself to sleep in his arms. Powerless to help,
he could only hold her. He knew there was nothing he could
say. Death was final. Murder was an atrocity. No one knew
that better than he.

Beside him, Grace's breathing quickened. She stirred, and
he caught the scent of rain and lavender. He waited, uncertain
whether he should draw her in and hold her or simply let her be.

Making the choice for him, she drew back the covers and
slid from the bed. Curious, he stayed motionless when she
disappeared into their shared dressing room. He heard fabric
rustling, then the thump of something hitting the floor. She
reappeared a few minutes later wearing breeches, with a pair
of riding boots clutched in her hand.

He wanted to curse. Instead, he held himself perfectly still
and kept his breathing deep and even. Through his lashes, he
watched her tiptoe across the room, the boots still clutched in
one hand. She put her hand on the knob and looked over her
shoulder at him.

For a brief moment, he thought she would speak. Regret

flashed across her face before she turned the knob and disappeared into the hall.

The minute the latch clicked, he leapt from the bed and sprinted to the dressing room. He knew how to dress quickly and quietly. Pulling on his breeches, he snatched a shirt, a coat and a cap. He also slid his pistol into his waistband and clenched his teeth over his knife. As Grace had, he carried his boots in one hand. But where she'd tiptoed across the room, he strode through it. He didn't have a spouse to deceive.

He finished dressing as he stole through the silent house, shrugging into shirt and coat, settling the cap over his head. When he reached Thistledown's side door, he tugged on his boots before stepping outside. Taking the knife from between his teeth, he slid the thin blade into his right boot.

The rain had subsided to a miserable drizzle that dribbled down his neck and past his collar. Julian blocked out the chill and scanned the grounds. Assuming she would saddle Demon, he started toward the stables. The crunch of gravel to his left made him stop. He tensed, waited, watched—and saw her. She was on foot, hurrying down Thistledown's gravel drive.

He frowned. Not a particularly clandestine path, as she was out in the open, but perhaps she didn't expect anyone to be watching.

He snorted. She shouldn't have married a spy.

Staying off the gravel drive to mask his footfalls, he followed her from the shadows of the trees. She wasn't traveling to Beer or to the smuggling caves, he mused, as they were too far away to travel on foot. Who could she be meeting? She turned onto the lane at the end of Thistledown's drive, then eventually onto a narrow path, and finally a dirt track barely wide enough for a wagon.

The dilapidated cottage that finally came into view appeared to be crooked on its foundation. The roof sagged and its windows were little more than shards of glass.

Julian surged forward when he saw the barrel of a blunderbuss glinting in the window. He leapt over a fallen log, sprinted across the path—and stopped short when he heard a curse.

"Bloody hell, my lovely. Are you lookin' to be shot?" The

blunderbuss disappeared from view. It was replaced by a square face and wildly springing hair.

"I'm sorry, Jack," Grace called softly. "I've some news. Can I come in?"

"Well, I'm not leaving you on the doorstep, though I'd hoped to have a full night of sleep," Jack grumbled.

Jack Blackbourn's head disappeared from view, then reappeared in the doorway of the ramshackle cottage. "Come in, my lovely. I'll get the fire going."

"There's no need. I can't stay long," Grace responded as the door swung shut behind them.

For an ugly moment, jealousy streaked through Julian. Was Grace cuckolding him? Was his wife of mere days already a cheat? He closed his eyes, forced himself to think past the pressure in his chest. No. He knew she was not. Certainly not with Jack Blackbourn.

He looked through the window and saw Blackbourn pull Grace into his arms.

The evidence was damning. *And I'm just as damned*, he thought as the jealousy swelled again.

He fisted his hand on his thigh and watched the pair through the window, struggling to use his training to observe. Blackbourn patted Grace's back as one might comfort a distressed child. The kiss he dropped on her temple was similarly platonic.

Julian pushed away the jealousy and resentment. When he looked again, he was steadier, calmer. Still, anger burned low in his belly. She may not be unfaithful, but she had lied to him. She knew where Blackbourn was hiding.

He stalked closer to the cottage, using sodden leaves and needles to mask his footsteps. With only a few swift movements he crouched in the thicket of ferns beneath the window. Above him, faint moonlight glinted on the remains of a broken windowpane. Voices carried easily through those broken panes of glass.

"I'm sorry, Jack. I know you and John were close." Sympathy flowed from Grace's words.

An answering grief filmed Blackbourn's quiet, "Aye. He was a good man."

"He was."

"Hell." Something thumped. A fist pounding on a hard surface. "John's wife. Has anyone told—"

"She knows," Grace interrupted quickly. Hurried footsteps clicked across the floor. "We took John's body home to her."

"And the black-hearted bastard that killed him? Did you find him?"

"No. We don't know who he is. But I think—Julian thinks— it was the traitor."

Chair legs scraped against a wooden floor. Footsteps paced.

Julian brushed away a feathery, wet fern tickling his neck. He leaned forward, straining to hear. Grace murmured something, and although her words were indecipherable, the soothing tone was obvious.

He waited. Fury built, sharp and tight in his chest.

She'd lied to him. Not outright, perhaps. Thinking back, he realized she'd never said she didn't know where Jack Blackbourn was. She'd simply failed to answer him. She failed to trust him.

*Why should she?* a voice inside him whispered. Because he was her husband, damn it. Still, that inner voice whispered, and the words stabbed into him. *But you're a spy and a Travers, and barely worthy of her trust.* He ignored that voice—*had* to ignore it—and concentrated on the cottage.

He couldn't understand the words that floated through the open window now. He only heard Grace's smooth tones and Jack's answering rumble. But he didn't need to hear more. He knew enough.

Skittering backward, Julian retreated from the overgrown bushes and stood up so he could see into the window. Two figures huddled over a pathetically low fire emitting just enough light to see by, but certainly not enough heat to combat the chill fall night. He didn't feel any sympathy.

Not bothering to keep his footfalls silent, he leapt to the front door of the cottage and threw it open. Blackbourn was already scrambling for his blunderbuss, but he'd left it at the window. Grace fumbled in her coat but she was far too late.

"Don't. Move." Julian aimed his pistol straight at Jack Blackbourn's smuggling heart.

"Julian! I thought—God, I thought—" she trailed off when he didn't lower the pistol. "Julian?"

Why, in God's name, did he want to pull the trigger? He was certain Blackbourn was innocent of treason. Yet he still wanted to send a bullet into the man.

*Do it. She's your wife. Your property.* It was his father's voice. Not a ghost or an apparition, but that part of his father that lived in him. His finger slid on the trigger as sweat coated his hands. He buried that voice and met Blackbourn's gaze.

"My lovely, I think this is between the earl and me," Blackbourn said slowly, his eyes somber. "Perhaps you should wait outside."

"No." She surged forward.

"Grace." Blackbourn continued to gaze at Julian, unmoving. "Go—" He stopped speaking as Julian lowered the pistol.

"I might change my mind." Julian kept the pistol in his hand, now pointing at the floor. "But for now, you're not in danger."

"Mighty glad I am about that, milord." Jack offered a sardonic smile. "After all my escapes from the revenue officers, I'd hate to meet my fate at the wrong end of a pistol held by a jealous husband."

"Jealous husband?" Grace jumped between them, her eyes wide. "Have you turned crazy, Julian? It's Jack, for heaven's sake. You know I wouldn't—*couldn't*—"

"Which is why you're both still standing." His finger itched on the trigger. He tried to ignore it. "You've known all along that Jack was in this cottage," he said flatly.

"Yes." Remorse moved over her face. Then she firmed her chin and straightened her shoulders. "I knew he was here."

Julian held her gaze. There was no remorse now in those beautiful silver eyes—there was only defiance. "That's all I need to know."

"'Tisn't all. I—" Blackbourn began.

Julian cut him off with one vicious oath. "I don't care. Blackbourn, I've been working on your behalf to clear your name. The traitor is targeting you as a scapegoat. Stay hidden until I say otherwise." He reached past Grace and snagged Blackbourn's dirty shirt in his fist. Twisting, he jerked him up so their faces were only inches apart. "Do not run. If I find you've run again, I'll hunt you down."

He could feel Grace's small hands gripping his forearm and dimly heard her shout. His fist pulsed with the need to strike something. Or someone. Blackbourn's breath was uneven, but his eyes were resigned. Julian could all but feel his fist plowing into the smuggler's homely face.

It would have been undeserved.

He needed to leave before he did something he regretted. Dropping Blackbourn's shirtfront, he stepped toward the door. "I'll notify you when you've been cleared of all charges. Grace, I'll be waiting to escort you back to Thistledown."

The cold night air burned in his lungs. Still, he gulped air greedily, unable to get enough. He was perilously close to losing control. Because of Grace.

Betrayal. The word echoed through his mind, as rough and piercing as a jagged blade. He bent over, wheezing, his hands propped on his knees. It felt as though his chest were being crushed beneath an unbearable weight. He should be able to control himself. He was well trained and well seasoned. He should—

The door of the cabin opened then slammed shut with a sharp crack. He jumped, his body jerking upright. He watched Grace search him out in the darkness and knew when she saw him. She stiffened, her shoulders twitching. He snorted derisively when he saw her chin jerk up. So she was angry? Well, she was in good company.

Temper had him stalking forward.

"Grace."

"My lord."

"Back to formality?" He lifted a brow.

"When you're being high-handed, arrogant and rude, yes."

"You lied to me."

"I did." The angle of her chin didn't change. "And I would do it again. I owe Jack more than I can say." She swept past him, her boots scattering pine needles.

"But you married *me*."

Her feet faltered, paused, then continued their forward march.

So be it, he thought darkly. So be it.

---

THE PRETTILY WRITTEN invitation slid across her worktable, propelled by Julian's large, strong hand. The tension she'd carried with her the last week tightened her shoulders. Taking a moment to school her features, she eyed the stationery as it came to rest beside the small bowl she used to mix tonics.

*. . . kindly request your presence for dinner . . .*

She didn't need to read more. "Another dinner to welcome the newly married couple into the fold?" she asked.

Looking up, Grace met Julian's sharp gaze. His eyes were distant, even cold—as they had been for days. The tiny vial in her hand slipped in her sweaty palm. She gripped it tighter and focused once more on the bowl, pouring the vial's contents into it.

"Indeed." He leaned against her worktable and crossed his feet at the ankles. He looked elegantly casual, and so *male*, that she wanted to reach out and run her fingers over the broad sweep of his shoulders or the hard line of his jaw.

That action was barred to her now, as certainly as if he were on the other side of a closed door.

"Must we attend this dinner?"

"Do you truly need to ask?"

"No." She struggled to keep her voice light and her words natural. "I'm simply weary of the sudden overabundance of invitations. We've attended a picnic, a dinner and a group outing into Beer this past week."

As weary as she was, the social engagements had at least proved a distraction from the cold and dreary halls of Thistledown—and her cold marriage bed. They hadn't touched each other since the night he'd found her at Jack's cottage. Instead, they were two polite strangers living in the same home and sleeping in the same bed.

"We must attend." His tone held no room for argument. "This invitation is from the Wargells."

She jerked, sending the bowl skittering across the tabletop to spill a few drops of the brown liquid swirling within.

"Very well." Deciding her hands weren't steady enough to work with a liquid, she set aside the bowl. Reaching for her mortar and pestle, she started grinding the next ingredient into a dissolvable powder. Her skin prickled. Out of the corner of her eye, she could see Julian watching her. Not moving, not talking. Just watching. She fought the urge to say something.

She *hated* this awkwardness between them. His absence was a physical ache. Whatever tenuous connection they'd created had been severed as though it were an illusion.

"Why do you suppose they would invite us after you snubbed Clotilde?" She cleared her throat. "And nearly called out Michael."

"To maintain the social connection. We'll be crossing paths here and in London regularly enough." He retrieved the invitation and tapped it thoughtfully against the palm of one hand. "I intend to create an opportunity to obtain a sample of Wargell's handwriting."

"How?"

"An opportunity will usually present itself, if one is watching for it. But it can be created as well. I might be able to manufacture a pretense for leaving the group to search Wargell's study." He leaned forward and sniffed at the thick brown liquid she'd been mixing when he'd arrived. "What *is* that?" he asked, frowning.

"Cough syrup."

"It smells like rotten eggs and fermented fruit. Together." He gave a mock shudder. "Disgusting."

When their gazes met and held, something passed between them. She couldn't quite name it, but it felt as though the door had opened just the tiniest crack.

Her hand stilled and the rhythmic grinding faded into silence.

"I owe you an explanation," she said quietly. His smile died and his eyes turned cold again, but she doggedly continued. "About Jack."

"You made your choice." He turned away from her, leaving her facing only the broad expanse of his back.

"Please. Just listen."

"It doesn't matter, Grace." He looked over his shoulder, his eyes unreadable. "You'll be happy to know he's been declared innocent of all charges of treason. I received a missive this morning and have already been to the cottage to inform Blackbourn."

"*Oh*," she breathed. She looked down at her fingers, still limply holding the unmoving pestle. Her knees threatened to buckle as relief flooded through her. "Thank you."

"I didn't do anything to assist. I simply gave my superiors my opinion and the evidence I had."

"Still, I must explain. I—"

"Grace." He swung around to face her. "It doesn't matter to me. It's in the past and doesn't affect this moment. Or the choices you make today."

"Doesn't it? Doesn't your past dictate parts of your present? You are who you are today because of your past." She swallowed to ease her dry throat. He was watching her so carefully, his beautiful eyes guarded. "I owe Jack so much. When I came here after my parents died, I was lost. I'd never been so lonely. Uncle Thaddeus was . . . well, not exactly welcoming. It was years before I met Jack. When I did, it was like finding my place here. Finally. Somewhere I could just be *me*."

She lifted her gaze to meet his, afraid of what she might see there.

Blue. Bright and brilliant and filled with wary curiosity.

"How did you meet Jack?"

"He had to sink his goods to retrieve later because the revenue officers were watching him. They chased him after he put ashore. He escaped—as usual—but he was shot. He hid in the smuggling caves and sent for me, since he couldn't go to the surgeon without being caught by the revenue officers."

"You cared for him. Healed him."

"I went back every day for weeks with poultices and ointments and provisions." She smiled slightly at the memory. "For all his charm, Jack is a horrible patient. At any rate, when the others pulled up the goods and brought them to the caves they needed someone to tally them and divide the payment. Jack usually did it, you see."

"And so you were asked to take his place." His voice was still hard, but he tucked a stray tendril of hair behind her ear. His fingers lingered on her cheek, the rough calluses rubbing gently over her skin.

She wanted to weep. She wanted to turn her face into his cupped palm and let the tears flow. Breathing deep, she blinked them back.

"I just happened to be in the caves when the shipment came in. It was that simple—and it was that significant. Jack and his wife, Anna, brought me into their family. Jack reminded me who I was and where I came from. They saved me from drowning myself in the misery of loneliness." Now the tears did well. She couldn't hold them back.

A handkerchief appeared in his long fingers. Smooth silk brushed away her tears. Then his lips touched her forehead, soft and warm, and his arms came around her. In that deepest place of her heart, something clutched and released.

"When Jack asked me to keep his hiding place a secret, I had to make a choice between old loyalties or new."

"You chose Jack."

"I chose old loyalties," she corrected. "What would you have done, Julian?"

"You should have trusted me."

"Trust?" She pushed at the arms that encircled her until he stepped away from her. "You had another nightmare last night, Julian. Why don't you trust me with that?"

"Because you don't need to know." A muscle in his temple twitched.

"I *do* need to know." She spun away from him. Picking up the pestle, she began to grind the herb in the mortar with sharp, jerking movements. "If I'm going to sleep beside you for the rest of my lifetime and wake up hearing you screaming or sobbing, I need to know what's happened."

"Don't ask, Grace. It's not for you—"

"It *is* for me." She slammed the pestle down, surprised when the stone didn't shatter. "You expect me to trust you. With my friends, my life, my body. Yet you won't trust me with anything."

"That's not true. I've trusted you with my body and my life, just as you have. I've trusted you with my position with the government." His eyes became bright blue flames.

"You had no choice but to tell me about your position. But when it comes to us—to you and me and our marriage—you withhold your trust. There's a wall between us." She let out a furious breath. "No, it's not a wall. It's a door. I lie beside you every night in the chamber we share, staring at your mother's door and listening to you sobbing in your sleep."

He stiffened, and the faint color in his cheeks darkened. "I'll find another room if you can't sleep."

"No, that's not what I want. I want—" Despair choked her.

"What do you want, Grace?"

*Your heart. Your love.* The words caught in her throat. She couldn't possibly expect his heart when she didn't give him hers.

"I don't know," she finished miserably.

"Whatever it is, I don't seem to be it." He ran a hand through his hair, tugging slightly.

"I'm not expecting you to be anything but yourself." She couldn't give him her love, she thought again. Not without exposing herself. But she could give him the tenderness and affection that had grown within her. Swallowing hard, she took the leap. "I care deeply for you, Julian. I can share this burden with you. Tell me what haunts you."

She reached for his hand, but he jerked away so that her fingers found nothing but empty air. He strode to the door, his footfalls deafening in the silent room.

Anger and hurt tore through her, twin claws that stole her breath and scored her throat.

He stopped at the door, his hand resting on the knob. "I'll move my things out of our bedchamber this afternoon." He didn't look her, but opened the door and strode through it, leaving her alone in the stillroom.

# Chapter 23

"I'LL FIND SOME way to get Wargell into his estate room." Julian jerked at his cravat, trying to loosen the uncomfortable silk. His valet must have tied it too tight.

"Very well." Grace's words were polite, her face pinched.

"Don't say anything that might hint that my reason may be pretense."

"Of course not." She looked offended for a moment before her face blanked. She turned away from him to look out the window.

Silence engulfed the carriage and Julian gritted his teeth against the urge to fill it. In the past two days, she hadn't spoken a word that wasn't an answer to a direct question. Even those were single syllables.

Julian shifted uncomfortably on the carriage seat. He'd slept two nights on the library settee and his back had suffered—as had his mind. The dreams were worse. Now it wasn't just his mother, it was Grace as well. He woke up drenched in sweat and aching to touch her. He wanted to see her lying beside him.

*I care deeply for you, Julian*, she'd said. He'd ignored her.

It was better this way. It would only make his choice easier.

At dinner, he watched her across the Wargells' table. He

couldn't look away from her pale cheeks and the full lips she had pressed together so tightly. Her fingers fluttered nervously around her dinner plate. She barely spoke a word to any of the guests.

Beside Julian, Lady Lintell was anything but monosyllabic.

"I'm certain our Gracie is the finest of wives," Lady Lintell burbled. "She'll take proper care of you and Thistledown, my lord."

Lord Lintell leaned across the table, his fork waving dangerously in the air. "Such a bother, all the decorating a new bride does. Especially a young bride!" He cocked his head. "Not that you're all that young, of course, Gracie."

Julian choked on his creamed spinach. Beside him, Mrs. Wargell hid a titter behind her hand. Down the table, Lady Hammond murmured, "Really, Archie. Most inappropriate."

Grace, however, only gave Lord Lintell a small, polite smile. "No. I'm not so young."

"And how is Thistledown holding up?" Sir Richard stabbed a small, round potato as though it were a thief attempting to abscond with his beef. "That old house has been empty for, what, twenty years? Twenty-five years?"

"Yes, Gracie," Mrs. Wargell chimed in. "Being a countess must be vastly different than living at Cannon Manor."

"Not particularly." Grace's eyes remained on her plate.

"Given the little cottage you were born in, I'm sure you've no training to be the mistress of such a house, have you? And, of course, you're unused to a title and all the obligations that go with it." Mrs. Wargell's voice was low and snide. "Gracie."

*Enough.*

"Her ladyship," Julian corrected smoothly, "is taking up the reins as Thistledown's mistress with ease."

"And so she should." Lady Lintell seemed oblivious to the undercurrents. "There's no doubt about our Gracie. I'm sure she'll do fine after you leave, eh?"

He stilled. "Leave?"

Grace's fork jerked in its ascent to her lips.

"Of course!" Lady Lintell sipped her wine. "You'll be going to London soon, I'm sure, and then off to the Continent. The Wandering Earl and all that."

Grace's expressionless face tore at him. She deliberately laid her fork and knife across the plate. It was like watching her surrender her weapons.

She didn't seem to care whether he stayed or left. But without her, there was no reason to stay. He wanted to snatch her away from the table—away from Devon—and go somewhere the rest of the world wouldn't intrude. He could be alone with Grace, with nothing between them.

He struggled to think beyond that vision. This wasn't an innocuous dinner party.

"And leave my wife and her charms so quickly?" Julian met Michael Wargell's eyes. "I think not. Perhaps we'll go to London for the Season, but I believe we'll stay here for now. I've an idea to try my hand at farming."

"Isn't that interesting," Mrs. Wargell murmured.

He watched Grace, hoping for a reaction he could read, but she only continued to stare at her plate.

"Joining us landowners, eh, Langford? Have you had a chance to look at your south fields? If they're like mine were, they're under-producing." Sir Richard leaned back in his chair and noisily wiped his mouth with his napkin. Beside him, Lady Marie winced and turned away as Sir Richard barreled on. "Talk to Mr. Wargell, here. His advice assisted me in increasing production."

At the head of the table, Wargell watched him warily.

"Fascinating," Julian said.

"I have some theories that have proved successful thus far." Wargell relaxed slightly and signaled to the footmen that the meal was over. "I've been corresponding with the Agrarian Society about my theories. They've been warmly received. I've garnered a number of enthusiastic letters from members of the Society."

"I'd like to hear your theories and read the responses." Julian kept his tone neutral. "If you would be so kind."

"Then let's leave the ladies to their tea and take our port in my estate room." Wargell pushed back from the table. "I'll show you those letters. Gentlemen, would you care to join us?"

It was the opportunity he had hoped for. Julian sent a quick look at Grace as he rose from his seat. Their gazes met and he recognized her understanding of the mission—but there was nothing in her eyes for him.

———————

"A LOVELY DINNER, Mrs. Wargell, as always," Lady Hammond said, sipping tea from a delicate pink cup.

"Indeed, indeed." Lady Lintell bounced slightly in her chair. "Lord Lintell and I do so enjoy your dinners, especially the music after dinner. You have such a pretty voice, Mrs. Wargell."

"Thank you, my lady." Mrs. Wargell gave an arch smile. "Though perhaps this evening we shall change the performances, as we have a new guest joining our little dinner. Do you sing, Gracie?"

"Passably well." She truly hoped she wouldn't be required to demonstrate.

"Oh good!" Lady Lintell clapped her hands. "I shall accompany you, Gracie. I am an excellent pianist, though I would never say such a thing about myself."

"No, of course you wouldn't." Lady Hammond's smile was both indulgent and amused.

"I could accompany you, as well, Grace," Lady Elliott said tentatively. "Though I'm only passably accomplished at the piano. Perhaps you would care to join me to pick out an appropriate song?"

Grace's teacup clinked against the matching saucer as she set it down to follow Lady Elliott to the piano. The lady rifled through music and held up a pretty country ballad. "How about this song, Grace?"

She barely glanced at it. "That's fine." They were away from the others, and unlikely to be overheard, but still Grace leaned forward and said quietly, "Lady Elliott, are you well? Your cheeks are pale."

"I'm just tired, Gracie." Paper rattled as she pushed through the music. "This babe is tiring me more than the boys did."

"Are you sleeping well?" Grace laid her hands over Lady Elliott's nervous fingers. "You must take care of yourself before you can take care of the babe."

"I'm trying to." Her eyes were deep and tired, with huge dark circles beneath. "I'm just worried about so many things, including the babe." Tears welled up and she sniffled.

"Oh, Lady Elliott. Marie." Grace rubbed little circles on her back. The poor, poor woman. "The babe will be fine, and so will you. You didn't have any trouble with the boys and there's no reason to think anything will go wrong this time. You need to rest. Have you been to Bath? I know how restorative you find the waters."

"No." She sniffled again. "I haven't been able to go. And Richard—well, he doesn't know about the babe yet." Wet eyes lifted to Grace's. "Please don't say anything."

"I won't, though you should tell him. He may be able to ease your burden."

"He won't. He'll only make it worse," she said vehemently, her voice low and fierce. "I hate him, Grace."

Shocked, Grace studied Lady Elliott's face. It was no wonder she was in tears. To be with child and married to a man one hated would be difficult for any woman. To be in a loveless marriage was miserable enough, Grace thought wearily.

She squeezed Lady Elliott's hand and slid her gaze to the other guests. Lady Lintell was chattering loudly about church flowers and Lady Hammond was sipping her tea and listening. But Clotilde Wargell was staring fixedly at Grace, eyes bright with malice.

"Lady Elliott," Grace said, not taking her eyes from Mrs. Wargell's. "I don't know what to say to you, except that I want to help you. In any way I can."

"Oh, I wish that you could be with me during the birth, Gracie." Lady Elliott's whisper was perilously close to escalating into a wail.

"Why wouldn't I be?" Surprised, Grace turned away from Mrs. Wargell to look at Lady Elliott.

"Because I probably won't be here." Her fingers started plucking at the lace rimming the bodice of her gown. "I don't know where I'll be. London, perhaps. Or Bath. But I don't think I'll be here."

"Have you ladies chosen your music? Are you ready to entertain us with your lovely talents?" Clotilde Wargell's voice drawled as she joined them. Her eyes fastened on Lady Elliott. "Why, Lady Elliott, whatever is the matter?"

"I'm not feeling well." Lady Elliott dabbed at her eyes.

"No?" Mrs. Wargell's gaze moved to Grace. "It seems both of you are having difficult evenings. I see the roses have already faded from your wedding day, Grace." She smiled, clever and feline, as she leaned languidly against the piano.

Grace stiffened, sucking in her breath. "I beg your pardon?"

"It happens in these circumstances when the groom is a worldly gentleman, such as the earl." She waved a hand in the air, the fringe of her shawl dancing against her arm.

"In these circumstances?" Grace narrowed her eyes.

"You were compromised, Gracie. The whole of Devon knows it." She stroked her finger across the piano keys. "There are any number of ways to orchestrate such a proposal."

Anger stirred and Grace's blood began to heat as her pulse hammered. Lady Elliott's small hand brushed her arm, a subtle warning. She ignored it. She was weary of heeding warnings, of pretending she didn't care and tolerating snide comments.

"Is that how you secured a proposal from Michael?" Grace bit out.

Mrs. Wargell's fingers paused in their smooth exploration of the piano keys. A moment later they resumed their path. "I never needed to do such a thing. I had many offers of marriage. So many, in fact, I had my pick of suitors."

"And yet you married a mere mister?"

"For reasons that don't concern you," Mrs. Wargell snapped, her eyes like two dark daggers. "Unlike *you*, at least Michael and I are of the same class. He's the second son of a peer."

"Well, I did one better, didn't I?" Grace raised a haughty brow. "I married the peer."

---

THE ESTATE ROOM was dark and masculine. Instead of the plush pillows and delicate spindly legs of the rest of the house, this room was utilitarian and relaxing.

Michael Wargell poured glasses of port for his guests, all of whom were ensconced in the inviting cushions of welcoming armchairs. Fragrant smoke rose to the ceiling as cheroots were passed around and lit. A fire roared in the hearth, sending out the soothing crackle and hiss of flames.

If there was one thing Julian could say about his host, the

man did know how to make a guest feel comfortable. So comfortable, in fact, that Lord Hammond was already dozing in his chair, his hands propped on his protruding belly.

"Relief to get away from the ladies, eh?" Sir Richard said as he accepted a glass of port. "All that bother with women's sensitivity. Much easier to just speak your mind."

Julian nodded noncommittally and sipped from his own glass.

"There are benefits to having a wife, however." Wargell settled into the chair behind the desk.

"Indeed," Lord Lintell agreed. "Else why would a bachelor set himself up for all the inconvenience of marriage?"

"A good question," Julian said. He leisurely crossed his legs and leaned back in his chair. His eyes scanned the desktop, searching for a scrap of paper with Wargell's handwriting. Damn. He was too far away to see properly.

Lord Hammond snorted in his sleep. All eyes turned toward him, then looked away again when he only slid farther down into the chair.

"For myself, a willing wife is good to come home to after a day in the fields or hunting or talking to tenants," Lord Lintell said. "You'll find the same if you stay in Devon, Lord Langford."

"I'm certain I will." Julian sipped again before steering the conversation back to his mission. "Mr. Wargell, I look forward to your advice on the south fields. The Agrarian Society is receptive to your ideas, you said?"

"Yes." Wargell sifted through a stack of documents and pulled out one.

"It's drainage," barked Sir Richard. "Those fields have a drainage problem, and Mr. Wargell here has devised a solution."

Julian took the document Wargell proffered and skimmed it. The script was thin and spindly, and didn't match the thick, heavy handwriting sample from the folio. Nor was it Wargell's, as the letter was signed by someone from the Agrarian Society. His gaze shifted to the remaining documents in front of Wargell. If he could get close enough to observe the handwriting on even one of the documents, he could make a preliminary comparison.

"Interesting." He set the letter onto the edge of the table-top, gauging the weight and pivot point. Then he let go. The document fluttered to the floor between himself and the desk. "I apologize, Mr. Wargell."

"No need, my lord." Wargell dismissed the apology with a wave of his glass.

Julian stood and leaned over to retrieve the letter. As he returned it to the desktop he scanned the remaining documents littering the surface. Stepping back, he sat once more in the chair. "Did you apply your theories to your own fields?" he asked.

The question sent the gentlemen into a bout of enthusiastic explanations, as Julian had hoped it would. He let the descriptions of ditches and labor and planting practices wash over him.

Michael Wargell had not written the treasonous documents in the folio. His handwriting was barely legible, a mess of scratching and points and vertical lines. It didn't mean he wasn't connected, however.

Julian was unaccountably disappointed. He'd *wanted* Wargell to be the traitor. A vision flashed into his mind, one of himself subduing Wargell and arresting him for treason. The vision vanished quickly. It was motivated by purely self-ish reasons and had no basis in fact.

Shouting erupted in the hall and ended their conversation. The sleeping Lord Hammond jerked upright, his old-fashioned wig askew.

"I'm sorry, monsieur," the butler called in the hall. "Mr. Wargell is not available."

All eyes in the estate room focused on Wargell. He'd half risen from his chair, his palms flat on the desktop.

"*Non.* This is important. I must see him. Now. *Maintenant!*" The swift thud of boots came clearly through the open door.

Heads swiveled to face the hall. Julian could hear the gentlemen's collective breaths draw in and hold as they waited for the unexpected visitor to appear.

"You cannot enter, *monsieur!*" The butler's voice rose to a shout and a second set of footsteps could be heard. "Mr. Wargell has guests!"

The footsteps stopped. Silence. Then, "I will wait. Tell him I am here and that it is urgent, *s'il vous plait.*"

"Excuse me, gentlemen," Wargell murmured, eyes on the door.

Julian studied his host's face. Tight. Drawn. Anger and—something else. Did the line between Wargell's brows and the jerk in his step denote fear?

Wargell hurried into the hall. Unintelligible whispers floated in through the doorway. When he returned, Wargell was full of apology and emphasized the urgency of the situation. He must meet with his visitor.

It hardly mattered, Julian decided. He had the information he had come for, and more. Satisfaction rippled through him. The visitor was clearly French.

The butler hovered in the hall to escort the remaining guests to the drawing room. Sir Richard barreled into the room ahead of Julian. Lord Lintell and Lord Hammond thumped along behind him, Lord Hammond leaning heavily on his cane.

Julian scanned the room. The ladies were scattered on settees and chairs around the room. Discarded teacups with varying amounts of liquid sat on nearby tables. Lady Lintell's curls bounced as she chattered to sad Lady Elliott. Lady Hammond sat back, amusement hovering around her matronly lips. Two spots of angry color rode high on Mrs. Wargell's sharp cheekbones.

And Grace, his cool and lovely Grace, sat perfectly composed in the middle of them. He glanced at her hands. No laced fingers, no white knuckles. One hand lay quietly in her lap, the other absently stroked the pattern on her teacup.

When her eyes met his, something clutched in him. Her eyes had blanked again, as though she hadn't seen him. But she'd never truly seen him, had she? There was something in him she could never understand. Something he could never show her.

"My lords," Mrs. Wargell purred, smoothing back her hair. "Have you finished your business?"

"For now," Julian said, fighting to focus. "Your husband has business to attend to, Mrs. Wargell."

Julian strode to the settee and offered his hand to Grace. She set her hand in his. Her fingers were warm, her skin as soft as petals. The scent of lavender and woman rose with her as he drew his wife to her feet.

"Is something amiss?" Grace asked politely, as though he were a stranger.

"Mr. Wargell has a visitor. One with urgent news, I understand." He turned to face Mrs. Wargell. "Your husband indicated he will be busy for some time, so my lady wife and I shall take our leave."

Similar sentiments were echoed by the other guests.

"Must you all go so soon?" Mrs. Wargell pouted.

"For tonight." Julian reached down and drew Mrs. Wargell to her feet, much the same way he had Grace. But there was no quiver in his belly, no arousing scent to move him. "It's not necessary to see us to the door, Mrs. Wargell. We shall find our way and leave you to your husband."

"I'm certain we'll see you in the capital, my lord. Like you, we just can't stay away from so many worldly entertainments." Mrs. Wargell's voice was shrill. "I'm sure Gracie could spare you from Thistledown."

Before Julian could answer, Grace spoke from behind him. "His lordship and I will see you in London, then, *Clotilde.*"

Turning, Julian looked at his cool and quiet wife. Amused pity filled her gray eyes—and it was directed at Mrs. Wargell.

---

THE BUTLER RETRIEVED their outerwear and they left amid a whirlwind of pelisses and muffs and guests. Grace's curiosity was bursting, but she waited until they were clipping along toward Thistledown in the carriage before she asked about the events in the estate room.

"An interesting visitor arrived," Julian said thoughtfully.

"Yes, I understood that much. Who was it?" Her breath puffed out in silver clouds as she spoke. "What happened?"

"He didn't give a name, nor did I see him. But I did hear him speaking a combination of French and English to the butler."

"French?" She straightened, her anger with him forgotten. The carriage blanket fell away from her. She barely felt the cold air surround her.

Julian tucked the carriage blanket around her again. His hands brushed against her waist and her stomach tightened in response. Time stopped for a breath. When he drew back, she shivered.

"What did the Frenchman say?" she asked, trying to ignore the awareness of his touch. It was like ignoring her heartbeat.

"Apparently the Frenchman entered the Wargells' home without being let in. The butler intercepted him near the estate room. He indicated he had urgent news and would wait for Michael Wargell to be available."

"Incriminating."

"Inconclusive," Julian corrected.

"What did Michael say?"

"Only that it was urgent business. He was full of apologies, though," Julian said. "And quite concerned about something."

"Hmm." She plucked at the carriage blanket. "What do you think the Frenchman wanted?"

"I don't know, but I do want to find out." He pulled back the curtain and looked out at the shadowed hedgerows flying past. "This should be far enough." He thumped the ceiling of the carriage with his fist.

"Milord?" the coachman called from above.

"Pull into the lane just ahead and stop."

"Aye, milord."

"What do you intend?" Grace leaned forward.

"A bit of espionage, of course." He grinned, teeth flashing white and feral in the dark carriage.

"Espionage. How shocking. I never would have guessed."

"Fear not, fair lady. I am experienced in such matters." He flourished his hand in the air, as though he were about to sink into a low bow.

She smiled before she could stop herself, and pushed away the internal voice that whispered of the door that stood between them.

"Do be serious, Julian."

"We aren't far from the Wargells' home. Just out of view, I daresay." He pulled back the curtains as the carriage turned into the lane. Apparently satisfied, he let them fall again. "I plan to return and attempt to observe or overhear Michael Wargell's exchange with the Frenchman."

"How will you observe them?"

"Through the windows." His tone was as dry as the herbs hanging in her stillroom.

"The simplest course, I suppose." She quirked her lips. "I expected something a little more elaborate from a veteran spy."

The coach stopped with the jingle of harness and a call from the driver. Grace studied the shadow across from her. Julian was half reclining, one boot planted on the bench beside her and his elbow propped on his knee. If she didn't know better, it would seem he was enjoying a casual ride through the countryside. He might have been going to a picnic.

But she did know him. The casual position was a study in control. She could sense the restless energy caged in him, could all but feel the power he kept leashed.

"Do you know which window belongs to Michael's estate room?" she asked.

"I have a reasonable guess. It's a simple matter to count windows and memorize the layout of a house."

"Good. Then we can find it easily."

"*We?*" Disbelief dripped from the word.

"I cannot sit idle in the carriage while I wait for you to return."

"You certainly can. And will." All traces of laughter in his tone had died away.

"I know how to move quickly and quietly, Julian. There's no harm in accompanying you to the window." This she could do. She may have difficulty finding the appropriate remark in a salon, but she could sneak around the empty countryside.

"Grace, you're wearing an evening gown and slippers."

"My cloak is lined with fur—as you should know, since you ordered it—and we'll be back in the carriage quickly. I'm not fragile, Julian. It's just cold. It's not even wet."

"This isn't a lark."

"It's also not dangerous. Aside from that, you have no method of restricting me to the carriage. I'll simply follow you."

He was silent and she wondered what he was thinking. She wished she could see his face clearly.

"I'll expect you to be quiet, and to follow my commands without question." His tone was hard, and tolerated no argument.

Exhilaration rushed through her. "I will."

He pushed open the carriage door and let in a rush of

frigid air. She barely felt the cold as excitement sent her pulse pounding.

He helped her out of the carriage before calling up to the coachman. "If we don't return within thirty minutes, come looking for us near the Wargells' home."

To her surprise, the coachman didn't show even a flicker of hesitation. Then again, she mused, he was Julian's coachman from London and presumably had obeyed similar strange requests. She supposed a spy needed a discreet driver.

"Follow me." He pulled Grace down the lane. Dry leaves crunched beneath their feet. Wind rushed through the trees, sounding like so many whispering voices. When they reached the drive connecting the Wargells' home to the public lane, he stopped and looked both ways. As it was late for country hours, there was no sign of any other travelers.

"We'll walk beside the drive as long as we can," he said. "When we come into view of the house we'll need to circle around to the side gardens."

Grace nodded her understanding.

He offered his hand. She hesitated, breathed in. Out. Then placed her hand into his. Even through their gloves, she could feel the heat sing up her arm. Closing her eyes, she forced it out of her mind.

Walking on the grass beside the drive, they made no noise as they hurried toward the house. The sky was clear, the stars brilliant pinpricks against the black, but there was no moon to shed light on their path. Despite her eyes adjusting to the darkness, she could barely make out the direction of the path. Julian must have been able to, however, for he guided them well. Within minutes she could see the candlelight in the windows of the house. The golden glow illuminated the gravel path that rounded the side of the house and led to the gardens. She started in that direction but Julian pulled her away.

"Your feet will make noise on the gravel," he whispered into her ear. "We'll cross the lawn."

They did so, once again striding beside the path but not using it. There were six windows on this side of the house. Candlelight lit four of them and two were dark. Julian passed the first two without pausing. On the third window, he slowed.

Grace looked through the mullioned glass and into the

drawing room. Mrs. Wargell reclined against a chaise much as she had during their visit, except now she flipped through *La Belle Assemblée.*

Julian stepped away from her and moved on to the next window. He crooked a finger, beckoning to her. She lifted her skirts and jogged ahead to meet him. The fourth window was dark, so they moved on to the fifth—and saw Michael Wargell.

He sat in an armchair in what Grace assumed was the estate room, elbows propped on knees, shoulders slumped. A half-empty brandy glass dangled from one hand. Even as they watched, he hung his head so low it sagged nearly between his knees.

"Apparently he did not receive good news," Julian said.

"No." She glanced at Julian. "I'm sorry we missed the Frenchman."

"I thought we might. Wargell was probably speaking with him before we even left the house. If the Frenchman was smart he would conclude his business quickly and leave."

"Assuming his business was illicit, of course."

Michael stood abruptly, interrupting their whispers. He tossed back his brandy in a single gulp and set the glass aside. He strode from the room and turned to the left. Julian pulled Grace in the same direction down the path. When they stood outside the drawing room, they stopped and peered in once more.

Michael Wargell stood in the doorway, watching his wife turn the pages of *La Belle Assemblée.* She looked up and tossed the publication aside. She opened her arms and he was across the room in three strides. Dropping to his knees, he set his face against her breast. She ran her fingers through his hair, twisting the ends around her fingers.

He spoke, though Grace couldn't hear the words. Mrs. Wargell responded by gently kissing the top of his head. She laid her cheek where her lips had been, her face turned toward the window.

Grace gasped as understanding dawned. Mrs. Wargell's lashes fluttered closed, and she murmured something to her husband. The love there, the intensity of it, had Grace's throat clogging with tears. Shock rippled through her. All these years, she hadn't known why Michael had turned from her.

"It's a love match," she whispered.

"So it seems."

Michael tipped his face up and kissed his wife hungrily. She responded in kind, cupping his face in her hands. His drew up and pressed her back against the chaise, his hands on her breasts, her belly. She arched her back to meet him, her lips opening on a cry.

"I believe it's time to go," Julian breathed in her ear.

"I would say so." But she shivered as his warm breath tickled her ear. It seemed like a lifetime ago that they'd last made love.

They ran back through the lawns and out to the road. Just out of sight of the house, Julian slowed. Grace bent slightly to catch her breath.

"Are you cold?"

"I'm fine, just a little winded. We'll be in the carriage soon enough." She straightened and reached for Julian's hand.

*Crack!*

Fire singed her upper arm and burning pain followed a moment later. She barely had time to hiss before Julian leaped onto her and sent her tumbling into the grass. Landing hard on her left side, Grace yelped as pain exploded in her arm.

"Quiet. Stay down."

His whispered words were short and urgent. She obeyed, gulping back the cry that filled her throat. She knew as well as he what the noise had been.

A gunshot.

His weight pinned her to the earth. Branches stabbed into her back and rough grasses scratched at her face. But it was the throbbing pain in her arm that held her focus. How bad? The material of her sleeve was warm and wet with blood, but that was no indication.

She waited, breathless, listening to the woods around them. The flap of wings from disturbed birds, the whinny of their horses down the lane.

Julian rolled off her and crawled toward the lane. Grace gritted her teeth, unable to tell him of her injury as even a whisper could give away their position. She tucked her arm close to her body and followed, digging her fingertips into the cold, damp dirt. It clumped under her palm, a hard ball of wet earth. Using her elbows and feet to propel her forward, she pulled herself toward him.

Renewed pain sang down her arm. But she could move it, she thought, flexing her elbow slightly. No permanent damage to the arm. She bit her lip as her fingers skimmed over the wound. The bullet didn't even penetrate. Just a graze across the skin. A superficial injury, then. Relief warred with the cold burn of pain.

They lay side by side at the edge of the lane. She followed Julian's example and looked right, left.

Shadows. Nothing but black on black stretching on either side, with little moonlight to reveal their attacker. Looking through the trees to the side, Grace could see the lights of the Wargells' home sparkling through the trees and wondered if they should run back that way.

Julian leaned toward her. She could see the grim planes of his face in the night shadows. "Stay in the trees. Stay low. Run for the carriage. If we're separated go to the nearest inhabited cottage or manor house for help, but *don't* go back to the Wargells' home. Do you understand?"

"What about you?"

"*Do you understand?*" Urgency underscored his tone and sent fear threading through her.

She nodded sharply. Julian pushed to his feet. Grace did the same, choking down the faceless fear. He darted into the trees. She followed, staying as low to the ground as she could. Her feet scraped through dry leaves and brush. Small trees and bushes caught in the skirts of her gown, slowing her footsteps. Wishing she wore her breeches, Grace reached down with her uninjured arm and pulled up as much of the gown and petticoats as she could.

Without the moon to guide her, she could barely see the ground before her and hoped no stray root would jump up to trip her. Keeping her eyes on Julian's back, she raced through the trees parallel to the lane. It couldn't be much farther.

Julian curved to the right toward the lane and Grace followed. Her breath was coming in gasps now. He stopped at the edge of the trees and Grace could only be grateful. He held up a hand.

She could hear the swoosh and rustle of dry leaves. Some-one was running through the trees, just as they had.

"The carriage is there," Julian said, pointing across the lane to the small turnoff. The coachman had turned the carriage and it was standing just at the opening. "Run to it. I'll be behind you."

"But—"

"Go, Grace. There isn't time to argue. He's just behind us."

With one sharp nod, Grace leapt onto the road and sprinted across it. She felt naked, vulnerable, running across the open dirt lane. She shot a look behind her. Julian was still standing at the edge of the lane, a tall, lean shadow between her and their unseen attacker.

"John!" she shouted to the groom as she neared the carriage. "Get ready!"

"Aye, milady!" He stood and brought his whip up, ready to snap it.

Grace pulled open the carriage door with her good arm and tumbled inside. Sticking her head out the open door, she squinted into the darkness. For a moment she couldn't see Julian and panic sent her heart into her throat. Then she saw his shadow, racing across the lane.

*Crack!* Another gunshot. Grace prayed Julian wasn't hit. The whip cracked above and the carriage jerked forward. Julian dove through the open door as the carriage careened around the hedgerows and sped down the lane.

Julian slid onto the rear seat and pushed back the curtain that hung at the back window.

"Can you see him?" Grace gasped. She gritted her teeth, willing away the dull throb in her arm.

"Only an outline of a man in the road. It's too dark for even a brief description. I wish I could have stalked him, but I had to get you to safety. I couldn't bear it if you were hurt."

She opened her mouth to tell him of the injury, but he swung back to face her. "It seems someone was spying on us spying on Michael Wargell." Breathing ragged, he propped his elbows on his knees.

"Ah, Julian?" Grace pulled her arm closer to her side. She could feel the blood trickling down her forearm now and knew she needed to stanch it.

"Fair lady, you were magnificent." His head came up and she saw his grin flash. "Not a scream, not a faint. Not a hint of the vapors. A veritable Amazon!"

He reached out in a gesture she knew well—he meant to lavish her hand with kisses. Grace tried to move away, but she wasn't fast enough. He grabbed her hand and pulled her arm toward him.

She yelped as bright agony shot up her arm. He dropped her hand as though he, too, could feel the searing pain.

"Oh, God. *Grace*." Springing across the carriage, Julian slid onto the seat beside her.

"Don't touch my arm. Please," she hissed through her teeth. *Breathe*, she ordered herself. *Don't let the pain turn to panic. It's just a flesh wound.*

"Where are you hit? How bad?"

"Not bad—" she huffed out. "Until you touch it. I need to stanch the blood."

"With what?"

"Anything."

He began to untie his cravat.

# Chapter 24

JULIAN SMASHED HIS foot into the double doors of Thistledown. The panels flew open and slammed against the wall
with a resounding crash.

"Starkweather!" he bellowed into the dim entryway.

Grace weighed nothing in his arms. He pulled her closer
to his chest, encircling her with his arms. To protect her. Even
if it was too late.

The butler rounded the corner of the front hall at a dead
run, his livery flapping behind him. Feet skidded on the polished parquet floor. "My lord?" he puffed. His eyes widened
when he saw Julian's burden.

"Get a fire burning in the earl's chamber," Julian barked.
"Bring hot water and linens."

"Yes, my lord." Starkweather sped into the recesses of the
manor.

"Julian, there's no need to trouble the staff with fetching
items," Grace said. "It's my arm that's injured, not my legs. I
can walk." Still, her good arm tightened around his neck.

"If you insist on doctoring yourself, then you're damn well
going to do so on my terms," he answered. "You're not walking."

Fear lent urgency to his steps as he stalked up the stairs
and through the halls to the earl's bedchamber—Grace's bedchamber now. A banked fire already burned in anticipation of

her return home. Good, he thought. It would be warm. Laying her gently on the bed, he swept his gaze over her body, searching for injuries they may have missed in the dark.

As soon as he released her, she popped up and swung her legs over the edge of the bed. The cravat she'd pressed against the wound dropped into her lap. He could see a bright crimson stain on the sleeve of her pelisse, a stark contrast against the white trim.

His fists clenched. *His fault.* He should never have taken her. Guilt flooded him, violent and heavy. "I'm calling the surgeon."

"That would be a waste of time. It's only a few sutures. I've set hundreds of them." Hair straggled down from her once elegantly curled coiffure and stuck to her face and neck. He pushed aside a curl caked with mud. "I need my satchel from the stillroom."

He swallowed hard. She could do it. He'd seen soldiers stitch their own wounds on the battlefield. Hell, he'd done it himself, though it had been a poor job. And she had been a healer for as long as he'd been a spy.

"We'll send the Starkweathers for it. Here, let me," he said, unclasping the fastener on her pelisse. His fingers felt thick and clumsy.

A quick knock sounded on the door. Mrs. Starkweather opened it without waiting for an answer. She carried a basin of water in her hands. Behind her, Mr. Starkweather held Grace's satchel and a bundle of linens.

"We thought she might need her healing things as well," Mrs. Starkweather said. "Is she well, my lord?"

"I'm fine!" Grace called from the interior of the room. "It's just a small scratch."

The housekeeper peered around the doorframe. She sucked in her breath, then let it whoosh out again. "Lord, Miss Gracie! You poor dear."

"It's nothing." Careful fingers probed the injury. Julian's belly clutched when Grace winced. "Though it is painful," she muttered.

"I'd ask if it was one of the revenue officers that did it, Miss Gracie, but you're not dressed for smuggling." Mrs. Starkweather cocked her head. She was clearly hoping for an explanation.

"I just need to wash up and I'll be fine," Grace said.

Julian took the basin and other items and shut the door again. When he turned around, Grace was fingering the sleeve of her gown.

"I need to get the gown off. At the very least I need to remove the sleeve, which is so tight it must be cut off," she said.

"The vagaries of fashion," he muttered, shaking his head. Propping his boot on the edge of the bed, he slid his fingers in and pulled out his knife. It was short, wide and meant for stealth. He gripped the hilt. The carved ridges were comfortable in his hand.

"Do you always carry a knife in your boot?" she asked.

"Yes. Stand up."

She complied with slow and deliberate movements, keeping her wounded arm pressed tight against her side. He lifted the fabric away from her breasts, pierced the rose silk and began to slide the knife from neck to hem.

The silk split with a whisper. He kept his hands gentle as he pushed open the gown and slid the right sleeve from her arm. But the sleeves were tight and he couldn't pull the one off her left arm without causing her pain. It had to be done, he thought, and gritted his teeth.

Sweat rolled down his back when her breathing became shallow.

"What can I give you for pain?" he asked as she sank onto the edge of the bed.

"Nothing." The word was short, terse. "Nothing for now. Brandy for after, please."

"What next?"

"Set the basin beside me."

She picked up a strip of thin linen, dipped it in the water and began to sponge the wound. Her head was bent over her work, her breath whistling between her teeth.

"Five or six sutures. No more than that." The cloth she had been using plopped into the basin, splashing water over the edge and onto the dry linens stacked beneath it. "My needle and the thread are in the bag."

He retrieved both, then stepped back and studied the

wound. It was a red crease running across her arm just below the shoulder. He'd seen gunshot wounds before and knew this was shallow. Certainly not life threatening. But there was always the risk of a fatal infection. A chill settled over him.

*"The interrupted or knotted suture is performed with any needle armed with a waxed thread . . ."*

He blinked. "I beg your pardon?"

*"The London Medical Dictionary.* I've read it dozens of times." Her breath hitched as the needle pierced skin. *"Carry the needle and ligature to the bottom of the wound, so as to avoid but little chance of matter collecting under it."* She looked up. Her eyes seemed huge in her face. "It's a different thing altogether when it's your own wound."

He could hear her breathing. Deep, deliberate breaths, as though control required great effort.

"Grace."

"Quiet. This is the last stitch." Deft fingers worked the needle. "I need you to snip the thread with the shears in my bag."

Surely his fingers were too large and clumsy for such delicate work. He was used to wielding a knife, a pistol. His blunt fist. Not a pair of small shears.

Then it was done and he could breathe again.

She dropped the needle and thread into the basin and picked up the linen. She started dabbing at the remaining dried blood on her arm.

"Let me." Julian took the linen from her hand.

"I can do it—"

"Just let me," he snapped. Kneeling before her, he squeezed the long strip of linen and let the water run down her arm.

He'd never been more terrified. In all his years of spying, in all the years he'd courted death, he had never been as scared as that moment when Grace had screamed. He had failed in his duty to protect her. His wife.

"I should never have let you come with me." He tried to keep the rage from his voice.

"Julian." She gripped his wrist. "It was a dinner party."

"Not that." He dabbed at a stubborn spot on her wrist. "After. I should have made you stay in the carriage."

"You couldn't have."

But he should have. "Then I shouldn't have gone at all. Grace—" He looked down into wide silver eyes. "It's my fault. You had to flee through the dark, through the woods." He swallowed hard. "You were shot."

"I'm not seriously hurt, Julian." She sucked in a breath as he wiped a tender area. "And we've discovered something useful tonight."

"Nothing worth your life." The cloth dropped into the basin with a light splash.

"Don't be dramatic. We learned Michael is deeply into some game with a Frenchman. Just what isn't clear. We'll have to find out." Grace stood and began pacing the room, her petticoats whispering again as she moved. "How do you settle, Julian?"

"What?" He watched her, studying her quickened step, the erratic shrug of her shoulders. The gracefulness that usually defined her movements had vanished.

"I can't seem to focus." Her restless pacing turned into prowling. "My heart is still racing. I'm on the edge of something and can't quite step back from it. How do you settle down after a mission, or whatever you call it?"

He understood how she felt. Blood pounding from the chase, nerves stretched thin. Alive and grateful to be so. Full of energy that had no outlet. To release that energy he usually turned to alcohol or a willing woman. Perhaps a boxing or fencing match if he could find a partner.

"I find ways." *But she shouldn't have to.*

"I can't tell what I need." She turned in a circle, surveying the master suite. When she stopped, she faced the armchairs that sat before the fire and the table between them. "Brandy."

"It might help." He'd used it himself. So he poured two fingers and listened to her rapid footfalls as she came near.

"Aren't you having one?" The woman who took the glass from him seemed a stranger. Flushed cheeks, hard voice. Her fingers gripped the crystal.

"No."

She raised the glass to her lips, drank deep then met his gaze. Her eyes left him breathless. The quiet silver gray was usually calm and soothing. Now, however, that gray was dark as thunderclouds, raging and wild.

It didn't belong there. That fierce and wild energy wasn't Grace. He had dark secrets within him, and had taken her to dark places with this mission. She'd experienced murder and lies and heartache. His eyes fell to her arm. She'd experienced pain as well.

He could bring her no further into espionage or the secrets he held deep within. It would forever change her. She had no place in his world—or he had no place in hers.

He closed his eyes, breathed deep and let her go.

———

"JULIAN?" CONFUSION FILTERED through the burn of brandy and energy. She reached for him, her fingers brushing against his chest.

He shuddered at the touch. "You deserve more than I have for you, Grace."

"What are you talking about?" Alarm sharpened her words.

"I'm a spy. It's all I've been for a decade."

"I know that." She set the brandy glass aside. "But Angel said you were retiring after this mission."

"I'm not." His tone was flat. "The foreign secretary is reinstating me."

She sucked in a breath and fought against the need to sink down onto the bed. "You're returning to spying."

"Marriage and children and family aren't for me, Grace. We both know that." He strode to the dark window and looked out. "When this is over, I'll be leaving for London."

"And I stay here in Devon. In this house." She spun away, prowled the room. "With only your mother's ghost for company."

A muscle jumped in his jaw and his eyes went cold. She didn't care. Something vicious and ugly was building in her, straining to be released.

"I can't take you with me." Control hardened his tone and he turned away from the window. "I wouldn't even if I could. Have you forgotten your injury?"

"How does that signify?" She ran gentle fingers over her arm. It throbbed with a dull pain.

"This is my life. Espionage, weapons, injuries, unseen enemies." His eyes narrowed. "Secrets."

"Secrets are something I'm learning a lot about," she said,

hating the spite in her own voice. Needing to fill her hands before she began to tear at the rage clawing in her throat, she tossed the remaining linens into the basin.

"We're incompatible, Grace. Our lives are too different. When we catch the traitor, I'll return to espionage and you can go back to your life—a better one, actually. You'll have more freedom." His face was impassive, cheekbones sharp against his lean cheeks. He spoke reasonably, almost automatically, as though it were the most natural step for their marriage. As though his words hadn't scraped a raw wound inside her.

"I should have known you would leave. You're the Wandering Earl," she said icily. Opening the door, she plunked the basin onto the hall floor before snapping the door shut again. "Does our marriage or the life we were building together mean anything to you, Julian? Or was it all for the sake of the mission?"

"I never lied to you about who I was once we were married, Grace." He grabbed her uninjured arm, held her in place when she would have swept past him.

"No. You're a Travers." She spat the words and wrenched her arm from his grasp.

He stiffened, and his eyes went bleak and flat. "Yes, I am a Travers. It's something I *never* forget."

"They say blood tells, Julian."

"And I can never escape mine any more than you can escape yours."

Vicious rage streaked through her, drowning out the pang of grief that had tears stinging her eyes. "*Get out.*"

He watched her steadily, summer sky eyes guarded. She couldn't read what was in them, and it hurt that he was closed to her.

She stalked to the brandy decanter and poured another glass. Liquid splashed over the crystal rim and onto the table. Behind her, there was nothing but silence from Julian. She tossed back the brandy, gulped and let the burn of it fill the emptiness in her.

The sound of the door quietly closing seemed as loud and devastating as the gunshot had been. She whirled, staring at the door to the hall.

She was in the earl's chamber. Her husband's chamber.
And yet she had no husband.

The brandy glass flew through the air. Fragile crystal shattered against the door's wooden panels and shards of glass rained down, a thousand jagged splinters with no hope of coming together again.

# Chapter 25

G RACE STOOD IN front of the library door, staring at the carved mahogany. In twenty-four hours she'd neither seen nor heard Julian. For all their interaction, he could have left for London already.

Except she could feel his presence in Thistledown. The partially eaten dishes on the sideboard at breakfast indicated he'd already come and gone. The embarrassed maid carrying a dinner tray. A solemn Starkweather slipping through the halls just after dark with a candelabra destined for the library.

The hole he'd left in her ached with misery. She wanted to weep and wail and rage at him. But she could do none of those things. Straightening her shoulders, she pushed open the door. She stopped short when she saw Julian's valet, Roberts, pause in the act of brushing off Julian's coat.

"Oh! I beg your pardon, Roberts." Her cheeks flooded with mortified color. Her husband had taken up residence in the library, so much so that his valet attended to him there.

"Please don't mind me, madam." Roberts's vowels were nasal. "His lordship is seated before the fire." He gestured vaguely toward the fireplace.

She heard the scrape of metal on stone. One long, sinister sound that sent the hair on her arms rising. She looked around—and saw the blade.

Thin and much longer than the short knife in Julian's boot, this dagger was honed to a wicked point. Bright firelight reflected on the beveled blade as it slid along the surface of a small whetstone.

He sat before the fire in an elegantly appointed room, wearing a fashionably tailored coat and boots polished to a gleam. He should have been taking tea, or sifting through the numerous accounts and ledgers of a landowner. Instead, he worked the weapon with ease, his movements purposeful, effortless and well practiced. Beneath his tight coat, she could see his muscles bunching, releasing.

She shivered, mesmerized by the moving blade. She'd forgotten this part of him. He so smoothly charmed everyone, but beneath that exterior lived a spy. She didn't want to know what he'd done with that knife.

His brows rose in an elegant, unasked question as he lazily moved the blade over the stone.

"I shall see to it that the coat is properly cleaned, my lord," Roberts intoned as he passed Grace in the doorway. "But do be more careful with your wardrobe in the future."

"I will try, Roberts, but I sincerely doubt I shall succeed."

"I know, my lord." Roberts heaved a forlorn sigh. "I know." He left the room carrying the coat as though it were a precious artifact.

"I assume this isn't a social visit, since you're wearing breeches." The blade rasped over stone like an ominous warning. His gaze was cold, even disinterested, and the look darted into her heart and pierced it.

"I've had word from Jack." She cleared her raw throat. "He wants to meet with us at the Jolly Smuggler."

He carefully set aside the dagger. It was plain, she saw now. A plain, utilitarian weapon, without the scrollwork, engravings or jewels that so often appeared on such a blade. This was no dagger to brag about. This was a dagger for killing.

"He wants to meet tonight," she whispered. "Immediately."

———

LOW LAUGHTER AND the sharp scent of hops spilled out of the Jolly Smuggler. Grace stepped inside, hoping the warmth of the roaring fires at either end of the room would ease the chill inside her. Before she was over the threshold the greetings started. Raised hands, calls, smiles, many of them directed to Julian as well as her.

They strode to the counter where Jack Blackbourn poured whiskey into a short glass. He looked comfortable and relaxed.

"Welcome, milord." Jack swiped a wet cloth across the bar, eyeing Julian narrowly. Then he switched his gaze to Grace. "Are you well, my lovely? You've shadows under your eyes."

"I'm fine." As fine as she could be with her marriage crumbling. She propped her elbows on the counter. "It's good to see you in the pub, Jack."

"It's good to be back." He nodded at Julian. "I owe you for that, milord."

A beat passed, two. In the background, laughter of the patrons and the clink of glasses sounded. Grace flicked her gaze between the two of them. Julian held Jack's gaze for a moment, then each of them nodded, short and sharp, as though they had reached an agreement.

"A drink, then, milord?"

"Brandy, Jack. The good French sort."

"Well, now, that wouldn't be legal, and as I've turned over a new leaf I don't have any French brandy." But his eyes twinkled and he reached behind the counter for a glass and a bottle. "I do have some good brandy that looks and tastes just like the French sort."

"That'll do."

Grace studied Julian's lean features as he picked up the glass. She met his eyes and saw the shield he maintained slide over that gorgeous shade of midsummer. Anger simmered in her, and she blanked her own features. He would get no more from her expression than she was able to read in his.

"For you, my lovely? Your favorite wine?"

"Only if it's the good French sort, Jack."

When he had set the glass before Grace and she'd taken her first sip, Jack leaned companionably on the countertop. "An interesting business proposition was put about these last few days," Jack said casually. "Passage for two to France, at night, with no questions asked."

Wine sloshed over the rim of her glass. "Who's making the offer?"

"Not sure. Word spread in the pubs, as word usually does. Anyone desiring the work was to leave a message for Mr. Smith at the Anchor's Arms."

Beside her, Julian's muscles tensed and coiled in preparation to spring.

"Did you take the work, Blackbourn?" he asked.

"Happens this man offered a lot of money for safe passage. Being a businessman, I considered it."

"Jack." Grace sent him a quelling look. "What would your wife say if you got back into that kind of work?"

"She'd have my head on a platter, and perhaps some of my other parts as well." He took a fortifying gulp of ale. "Which is why I decided against taking the work. But, seeing as how he might be your traitor, I thought to accept the job, set it up and give you a chance to meet Mr. Smith and his travel companion."

"Jack, you're brilliant!" Grace tipped forward in her seat and gave him a smacking kiss on the cheek.

"What would your husband say to your kissing me, my lovely?"

"Her husband is feeling like repeating the sentiment, except I don't generally kiss the cheeks of other men."

"'Tis a good thing, milord, as it would be premature. Seems someone else already accepted the work."

Deflated, Grace sighed.

"Don't be too sad, my lovely." Jack nudged her hand aside and topped off her wine. "I wouldn't bring you out on a cold night for nothing."

"You know something." Julian's eyes turned cold, the blue becoming as sharp as shards of ice.

"I do, indeed." Jack's smile had a self-congratulatory quirk on one side. "I thought to myself, this Mr. Smith, he might be staying at the Anchor's Arms."

"It couldn't be so simple," Grace pointed out.

"It could be just that simple. A traitor needs a bed to sleep in as much as the rest of us." Julian tapped his fingers on the counter. "Get to the point, Blackbourn."

"I thought to inquire of the innkeeper. Unfortunately, there's no Mr. Smith staying at the Arms, and in fact, no man staying there more than a night before he travels on his way. I asked the innkeeper to let me know when someone comes in inquiring about messages for Mr. Smith and to pay particular attention."

"And?" Grace prompted.

"It so happens the innkeeper knew exactly what Mr. Smith looked like, as he'd inquired about messages not two hours earlier."

"Oh. *Oh*." Could they be this close to the traitor?

"Mr. Smith had a scarf over the bottom part of his face so the innkeeper couldn't see his mouth. Had a cap on, too, pulled low, but he could see Mr. Smith's eyes were brown." He raised the tankard and sipped again. "He was a bit on the over-delicate side, too. Thin, narrow shoulders. Barely more than a boy, the innkeeper said."

"Or a woman," Julian murmured.

"Well, hell," Jack spluttered. "That I didn't think of."

"If my wife can go around wearing breeches, so can any other female."

Grace slanted a look at him and decided to ignore the bitterness in his tone, even though it rankled. "It could be anyone, then," she said coolly.

"It could," he agreed. His eyes were distant when they met hers. "But we have the advantage. Passage for two was requested, which means we are dealing with two people. And we know both of them are in or near Beer."

"We know more than that." Jack leaned an elbow on the counter. A cocky brow shot up. "I know when the boat will pick up its passengers."

"When?"

"Tonight."

Energy spiked within her, sending her pulse scrambling. She reached out, gripped Jack's forearm. "Where?"

"Off Brogan's Pointe. There's a narrow cove there at the base of the cliffs," Jack explained to Julian. "The smugglers will anchor at the mouth of the cove and come to shore in a jolly boat to pick up the passengers."

"We can stop them." Grace turned to Julian. "We can stop the traitors before they get on the jolly boat."

"*We?*" One brow rose, very slowly, very deliberately. "You're not involved in this, Grace."

"Exactly how do you expect me to stay *un*involved?" She narrowed her eyes. "This is my fight as much as it is yours. Jack was arrested and John the blacksmith was murdered. *Murdered.*"

"Exactly. It isn't a game. It's real. It's dangerous." His voice lowered to a menacing whisper. "You are not going, Grace."

"I intend to see this through to the end." She angled her chin and squared her shoulders, preparing for the fight.

"You're a liability, Grace." The harshness of his tone made her scowl.

"Aye, my lovely. He's the right of it."

"Jack?" Betrayal cut through her, keen and sharp.

"A man can't be on the offensive when he has to defend his woman." Jack's square chin jutted out.

"His woman?" Fury leapt in her. She turned to Julian, pinned him with her gaze. "I am not his woman. I'm nothing more than a mistake."

"You're still my wife, Grace. I own you. Which means I have the final word."

Jack's hand snaked across the bar and gripped Julian's wrist. "You bruise my lovely," he said evenly, "and I'll hunt down your black heart and skewer it."

"Jack!" Grace choked out. "That's—"

"Understood." A muscle jumped in Julian's jaw. "But what's between Grace and me isn't at issue right now. Capturing the traitor and Grace's safety are."

"We agree on that, then." Jack waited a beat before releasing Julian's wrist.

"Smuggling isn't safe, but I've been doing that for years." She pushed her empty glass across the counter.

"There may be a fight, Grace." Julian's features were hard and grim. "And it won't be honorable. It will be dirty. Hand-to-hand combat, knives, pistols. I'm going to be outnumbered. I'm going to need to concentrate on catching the traitor and coming out alive, not on defending you."

"I can defend myself, Julian."

"The traitor will see you as the weakest one of us. He'll use you to escape. He'd kill you to do it."

"How do you know that?"

"Because I would," he said flatly. The lean angles of his face showed no emotion. And his eyes.

*His eyes.*

They were dead. There was simply nothing there. Is that how he lived with the knowledge that he may not live to see the next sunrise?

She shuddered as bitter, vicious cold pierced the marrow of her bones.

"You'll need someone with you." Jack was already untying his apron. "Someone who knows the land, the sea. I may even know some of the smugglers." A crooked smile flashed. "If not, I'm good with a sword and a pistol. And I always have an escape plan."

"I can't ask another man to accept nearly certain death."

"You accept it." She surged to her feet, fueled by resentment.

"Because it's my profession," he hissed through gritted teeth.

And he valued his profession over his life. Over *her*. She turned away, swallowing her angry words.

"I'll stay, then," she snarled.

She had no intention of following through.

# Chapter 26

G RACE STARED INTO a glass of ruby red wine and let the laughter and camaraderie of the Jolly Smuggler's common room swirl around her. Waiting was like being poised on the edge of a precipice, with her nerves stretched taut and her heart pumping as she stared into the unknown.

Except she was unable to step back from the edge. Nor could she jump off the cliff and end the agony. She could only wait, jittery and impatient.

At least long enough to give Julian a head start.

Gulping the last of the wine, she slid from the stool and strode through the common room. Instructions had already been issued for Demon to be saddled. She'd be less than fifteen minutes behind them.

A hand shot out, grasped her arm and pulled her back. She whirled, ready to strike out—and looked into the tawny eyes of the man with the code name Angel.

"Where's the Shadow?" The words were delivered close to her ear in a low, urgent baritone.

He wasn't dressed in elegant breeches and coat as he had been when she first met him. Instead, his masculine beauty was hidden behind common, homespun clothes. The scent of wet wool clung to him.

"Angel?"

"Hush." He sent a quick glance at the young man working behind the counter. "When I called at Thistledown, they directed me here. Where is Langford?"

"He's—" How to explain? "Unavailable."

"I need to speak with him. *Immediately.*" His touch was firm. Tension radiated from him.

"What's the matter? What's wrong?" Icy fear lanced through her.

"We know who the traitor is. He's on the run."

"Who is he?"

"Someone Langford won't expect." Gold hair slid out of its restraining queue and he pushed impatiently at it. "A person he trusts."

Her mouth went dry and she swallowed hard. "We received word this morning that someone was hiring a smuggling ship for safe passage to France. Julian and Jack are trying to intercept them. Tonight. Now." The sweet flavor of wine still on her tongue turned acidic.

Angel cursed. "Where?"

"The smugglers are anchoring at the mouth of a cove about three miles west. The cliffs are high there, so it's isolated." She sidestepped as a pair of patrons bumped past them, then lowered her voice. "The path is impossible to find if you don't know it. I'll take you. I can show you."

"Langford will have my head on a pike if I let you come."

The words faded from her hearing. She was already striding through the dark toward her horse. When she glanced back, he was two steps behind her.

"I won't let them be ambushed and there isn't time to argue. Get your horse," she tossed over her shoulder.

Demon raced across the lanes and fields, hooves thundering on the frozen earth. Angel's rented horse followed close behind.

Near the cove, Grace slowed as they entered the last stand of trees before the cliffs. Angel moved up beside her. Together, they peered between the branches and tree trunks.

"We need to go on foot from here." Her breath rose in puffs of vapor that writhed on the cold night air. "There's nowhere to tie the horses between here and the cliff edge."

Angel studied the grassy field between the trees and the

cliff. It rolled out before them, ending in a drop into darkness. "We'll be unprotected when we cross the field to the cliff."

"There's no way to avoid it. Only one path leads from the cliffs down to the water. We would have to go another two miles to find a way down, then travel back on foot along the coast. There isn't time."

"Then we run fast," Angel said as he dismounted and tethered his horse.

They did. Grateful for her boots and the freedom of breeches, Grace pumped her legs. She waited for a shout, perhaps the harsh report from a pistol, and was relieved when no sound came.

She clambered over the rocks at the cliff edge, then slipped and shimmied down the jagged slope. The ocean roared and crashed below and she prayed she didn't tumble into it. She fell the last few feet and dropped onto the narrow shingle beach. Angel landed beside her, sure-footed and barely winded.

Boulders formed a rough wall between cliffs and shingle, tossed there centuries before by the relentless ocean. They crouched among them and scanned the cove. Crescent shaped, it narrowed at the opening to the ocean and ended on two sharp spits of land. A clipper was anchored between those points. It rose and fell with the huge ocean waves, an undulating shadow against the night horizon.

The smugglers had arrived.

She scanned the surface of the water in the cove, then the shingle beach. She saw no one. No boat, no smugglers. No traitor.

No Julian.

"I don't know where Julian and Jack are," she whispered to Angel.

"The cove's entrance." Angel nodded toward the boulders that littered the farthest point of land. They were full of shadowy hiding places. "If I were a smuggler picking up passengers, I'd meet them at the point of land farthest into the water rather than come into the cove."

"Then that's where Julian would be as well."

"Follow me," Angel said. "And *be careful*."

He pushed up from his crouch, but stayed low. She copied his movements as they picked their way among the rocks.

When they reached the tiny spit of land, Grace scanned the beach and water.

"Do you see—"

A hand slapped over her mouth, shooting panic through her. She reared back, clawing at the arm that pulled her into shadows of the boulders.

"Quiet." The word was an urgent whisper in her ear.

But it was the scent that revealed her captor. Man, leather and soap. Her body relaxed, but her heart still beat wildly in her chest.

*Julian.*

———

"WHAT ARE YOU doing here?" Julian hissed when Grace crouched beside him among the boulders. "And why did you let her come?" he demanded of Angel.

"I needed to find you," Angel said simply.

"I keep telling you, boy, my Gracie doesn't get left behind." Jack's laughter echoed lightly between the rocks.

Julian pinched the bridge of his nose. Even the scent of her was distracting him from the mission. "Grace, you agreed—"

"Angel knows who the traitor is." Her hand shot out, gripping the front of his shirt.

His muscles tightened and coiled, ready for the verbal blow. He swiveled to face Angel. "Who?"

"It's Miles Butler," Angel spat viciously.

"*Butler?*" Shock rippled through Julian as Butler's face flashed in his memory. Young, fashionable, earnest and eager to please.

"Who is he, Julian?" Grace asked.

"My commander's clerk." A trusted man, he thought. A man who knew how to hide behind a mask.

"How insidious," she whispered.

"Angel, who's the second man operating as the middleman in Beer?" Julian asked.

"We don't know yet."

"Wait." Julian held up a hand. Filtering out the thrum of the ocean and the furious rush of wind, he focused on the sounds above those low hums. Had he heard something?

Yes, there it was again. Pebbles pinging against rock as they fell.

A voice floated out of the darkness. "Be careful, now."

He waited for more but the voice was silent. Still, pebbles continued to clatter and fall.

"Someone is coming down the cliff path. To the left," he whispered.

Steadying his breathing to slow the rhythm of his heart, he waited. His senses sharpened so that everything came clear around him. The rush of the ocean's waves. Jack's heavy breath whooshing in and out behind him. Below that, Grace's quiet, even breath.

He took comfort in the sound of her breathing, the steadiness of it. Even though he knew tonight would be the last time he heard it.

Then he blocked it out and concentrated on the two shadows struggling down the remaining feet of cliff and emerging onto the beach. One was tall and lean, the other petite and wearing skirts.

The second traitor was a woman.

"I can breathe easier now that you're down the cliff," said Butler.

"Darling, we're fine. You don't need to pamper us." The woman's voice was sweet and amused. And familiar.

"You're carrying my babe." The man leaned down and kissed the woman, his hands cupping her cheeks. "I promise, when we reach France, I'll pamper you daily."

"I don't need to be pampered. I only need you." The woman sighed. "Where will we go?"

"Paris. I need to speak with members of the government there. Then my mother's family will help us disappear into the countryside. There's a family farm where we can live for a while." He paused. "I'm sorry we can't return to England."

"I don't care." Her voice turned petulant. "I hate this god-forsaken country and my idiot of a husband."

The woman turned her face toward the sea, and the silver light of the three-quarter moon set her delicate features into relief.

Beside Julian, Grace let out a shocked gasp. He tensed as she clutched at his thigh, her nails digging into flesh. She knew something. He turned his head to the side so he could just see her. She set lips against his ear.

"It's Lady Elliott. Marie," she whispered, her breath light against his skin. "Sir Richard's wife."

Recognition flared, warring with shock. Sad-eyed Lady Elliott? A traitor? An adulteress?

"Look," Lady Elliott said from the beach. She pointed to the ocean.

Beside the clipper, a jolly boat bobbed on the waves. A lantern flared to life in the bow of the boat, creating a small gold beacon across the water. The light blinked once, twice, three times.

"There's the signal," Butler said.

Julian used the lantern light to count smugglers in the boat. Eight. Damn. "It has to be now."

"Agreed." Angel began unbuttoning his coat.

"Jack, are you armed?" Julian asked.

"Aye. A pistol and a dagger."

"Good. Do what you can. Grace, stay here."

"I can count the number of men in that jolly boat as well as you." Grace dipped a hand into her coat pocket and came out with her pistol. "You need me."

Frustrated, Julian pushed the weapon away. "If I stop arguing with you, we can overpower Butler and Lady Elliott before the smugglers reach the shore. We might even come out of this alive. *Stay here.*"

"Hurry up, Langford." Angel was already rising from his crouch, eyes on the beach. "The boat is on the move."

Grace's breathing quickened. "Fine. Go."

The jolly boat was barely three hundred meters from the shore now. They'd argued too long. He hoped the smugglers' fee for the passengers wasn't worth a fight.

He waited one more second to memorize her face. Just the way she angled her chin, the high cheekbones that caught the moonlight. Even the way the wind whipped her white-blond hair around her face. And the pistol gripped in her hand.

He would carry that image with him. For however long he lived.

Julian shifted, muscles tightening as he gathered his energy to rush the beach. He focused on the dark shape of Miles Butler's back.

Fury pumped through him. He rode the rush of it and sprang forward, racing across the shingle. His breath wheezed out as he slammed into Butler's back. Pebbles scattered as they tumbled to the ground.

Dimly, Julian heard a shout go up from the jolly boat and Lady Elliott's shrieks as Angel seized her. But Julian could only see Butler's face. He drew back and let his fist fly, felt it connect with flesh. Pain radiated up his arm as Butler's head snapped back.

"*Traitor!*" Julian spat. He balled his aching fingers to strike again, but Butler bucked him off. Julian thudded to the ground. Stars exploded in his vision as his skull rapped against stone.

---

GRACE BIT HER tongue to hold back her scream as Julian landed hard. His body jerked, and she saw his head snap back. Fear bloomed and she curled her fingers around her pistol.

But when Butler would have leapt on him, Julian rolled away, kicking up pebbles. *He wasn't hurt.* Relief flooded her but it lasted only seconds.

A scream rent the air as Lady Elliott reared back against Angel. Her feet kicked out as she bucked against him. The back of her head slammed against his face. She broke his hold, darted away. Angel reached for her, missed, even as blood spurted from his nose.

Grace could only stand on the fringe of the scene. Her choices had been limited. The argument with Julian would have wasted precious minutes.

But she wasn't helpless, and the battle wasn't over.

Grace raised her pistol and steadied it on the boulder in front of her.

She would bide her time.

---

BUTLER'S KNIFE ARCED toward Julian's throat, so close he felt the rush of air as it passed by. He rolled over, scrabbling across the shingle. Pushing onto his feet, Julian fumbled in his boot for his own knife. The familiar metal hilt fit easily into his hand and he struck out, the knife an extension of his body.

But he wasn't quick enough.

Pain seared across his arm, a line of fire left by Butler's blade. The metallic scent that filled Julian's nostrils was as familiar as the knife in his hand. Blood ran warm down his arm, slicking the knife hilt.

"First blood belongs to me, Langford."

"It's not first blood that counts, Butler. It's last blood." Blocking out the pain, Julian shifted his knife from his dominant right hand to his left hand. The weapon felt comfortable there, but he knew he would be slower.

"It seems you're at a bit of a disadvantage," Butler mocked. "Sorry about that, old man."

They circled, thrust, parried. Evenly matched, Julian thought. So it would be luck that won the fight.

---

EVEN AS JULIAN evaded Butler's knife, Grace saw the smugglers' jolly boat ram the shore. Men scrambled out, their movement like so many insects spilling from beneath a newly turned rock. Footsteps pounded on shingle as they fanned out across the beach.

Her heart slammed into her throat as the report of a pistol echoed between the cliffs. A scream followed and one of the smugglers near the boat crumpled.

*Not one of hers. Thank God.*

Still, there was no more biding her time. Wanting one final glimpse of Julian, she glanced over her shoulder as she clambered over the boulders.

And saw the smuggler bearing down on him, his knife raised high so its keen edge flashed in the moonlight.

---

"RUN, MARIE!" BUTLER shouted, thrusting blindly.

Julian felt the air quiver as the blade slid by him and knew his luck was holding.

"Miles! Not without you!" Lady Elliott shouted as she staggered toward them.

Julian's arm arced wide, the knife only a whisper from Butler's chest. The man flinched, but his focus stayed on the woman.

"Into the boat! The baby!" was all he said.

Lady Elliott changed direction, her feet splashing through the surf as she ran toward the jolly boat.

She was going to escape, Julian's mind screamed. But his body acted instinctively as he drove his knife forward. It slid beneath Butler's arm and into his side. Julian felt the point pierce flesh, then slide out again. *Not deep enough. Not debilitating.* Still, Butler dropped to the ground.

"Come now, boy. It's just a scratch." Julian stepped closer, reaching down to haul the man up. As his fist closed around Butler's collar, Julian glanced to the right.

A smuggler ran straight at him, only feet away, dagger poised to strike. Julian gathered himself to pivot.

It would be too late. He knew it with every ounce of his instinct, every moment of training. Fate had finally caught him. Only one thought came to mind.

*Grace.*

A primitive torrent of need and fear flooded him, even as he braced for death.

# Chapter 27

A SHOT RANG out.
The smuggler fell with an agonized scream. As if in a dream, Julian saw the dagger flash in the moonlight as it dropped to the ground.

Julian jerked his head up and scanned the beach—and his blood froze.

Grace kneeled on the shingle, her pistol braced on her forearm. Smoke curled from the weapon. It still pointed at the smuggler now dead at Julian's feet.

The world seemed to stop spinning. It went silent and black, the smugglers disappearing from his consciousness so that all he could see was her, with her eyes as silver as the moon that shone down and gilded her hair.

Then the world rushed back.

She was in the open. Unprotected.

The hair rose on his neck, drawing him back into the battle. He whirled and ducked when a fist shot toward his face. Kicking out, he felt the heel of his boot connect with bone. The smuggler yelped and toppled over, clutching at his knee.

To Julian's left, Butler staggered to his feet. Over Butler's shoulder, Julian could see Angel's foot come up in a high kick and he saw a smuggler fly backward, where he lay inert.

His gaze flicking back to Butler, Julian advanced.

But his mind was still with Grace. Had she retreated to the boulders? Was she safe?

He leapt at Butler and plowed a fist into the man's stomach. Butler yelped, but returned with a fist to Julian's jaw that sent him spinning backward.

As he righted himself, he saw a smuggler lying motionless on the shingle. That meant four men down. The fifth limped toward the boat, shouting at Marie to get out. Two more battled Angel and Jack.

But one was still on his feet somewhere, and Julian couldn't see him.

*Grace.* He turned to the rocks and saw her. Hair gleaming, face white as death. She stood silent and tall on the beach. The last smuggler stood behind her, a pistol shoved into her back.

The smuggler sneered. "Into the water, woman. You're my freedom. One of your men comes after you, and you're dead."

All of Julian's senses, all of his training, focused on Grace. With a howl of fury, he sprang forward—and was stopped as his head wrenched back, Butler's forearm pressed against his windpipe. He gasped, struggling against the crushing pain.

He wouldn't get to her in time. She'd be lost to him forever. His mind emptied and darkness closed in at the edge of his vision. He couldn't breathe.

Terror for Grace jerked him forward. Butler flipped over Julian's back and landed hard in the rough shingle. The traitor scrambled up to a crouch and braced to leap—then froze as a bloodcurdling cry echoed between the limestone cliffs.

Butler's head turned toward the dinghy, leaving him exposed. Vulnerable. Julian jumped forward, knife poised for the kill. But Butler wasn't looking at him. Instead, he was staring toward the water, his face contorted with raw, stark terror.

Julian withdrew, his knife hand falling away as he followed Butler's gaze. Fear whipped through Julian and he took an unconscious step forward.

Grace and Lady Elliott stood side by side in the stern of the jolly boat. A smuggler pointed a pistol at their backs. More smugglers rushed to set the oars and another splashed through the water, Angel following close behind.

The gold light of the boat's lantern glowed over Grace's

face, highlighting sharp cheekbones. He met her gaze over
the roiling surf, and those captivating eyes held him transfixed. For one moment, one breathless moment, all he could
see were her eyes. Calm. Trusting.

*Trusting.*

Then Julian was running, Butler forgotten. His feet dug into
pebbles as he flew across the beach. Icy water sprayed his face
and chest as he leapt into the ocean. The surf tugged at him,
pounding against his thighs and threatening to pull him under.
He could hear Angel sputtering behind him.

"Stay back or they die!" the smuggler shouted as he aimed
the pistol at Grace's back.

Julian saw the smuggler's thumb move over the pistol's
hammer, though he couldn't hear the click over the roar of the
ocean and the thud of his own heart. Dread clutched in his
stomach. His feet seemed to stop of their own accord, sinking
into the ocean floor.

Angel splashed to a halt beside him.

"Let them off the boat," Julian shouted. The vessel was
too far into the cove. Already water slapped at Julian's chest.
It would be well over Grace's head. With the undertow, she
could easily be swept out to the ocean.

"I think we'll wait a little longer," the smuggler returned.
"Then again, I might just keep these ladies."

Lady Elliott moaned, thrashing against the arm that held
her. Julian could see the whites of her eyes as they darted
around.

"We can't catch you," Angel called out. "You're free."

The smuggler laughed. "And so is one of your ladies." He
pushed, sending Lady Elliott tumbling into the frigid water. She
screamed, one long shrill note that ended in a splash, then silence.

"I've got her!" Angel's voice rose above the thrum of the
ocean. He dove and disappeared beneath the waves.

On the shore, Butler surged forward, shouting, but Jack held
him back.

"Now this one," the smuggler called out, grabbing Grace
around the neck. His fingers dug into the slender column,
pressing against her fragile skin. "This pretty lady is coming
with us."

She winced, one quick grimace. Julian met her gaze. Her eyes flicked toward the water. Then again. He understood and reflexively shook his head. She ignored him, jabbing an elbow into the smuggler's belly to release his hold—and jumped.

Fear rocketed through Julian. Drawing breath, he dove into the numbing water. The last sound he heard before the freezing water closed over him was a smuggler laughing.

He kicked, propelling himself forward, hands groping before him. Nothing. He came up to the surface, gasping for air and treading water. Cold shards of ice stabbed into his lungs so that he coughed even as he looked wildly around. To his right, Angel was diving under the water.

"Milord!" Jack shouted from the shore. "Over there!"

Julian followed his pointed finger and saw Grace only fifteen yards ahead of him, her wet hair a beacon against the black ocean.

*Thank God!* He dove again, cleaving through the water, and came up where Grace had been. Only she wasn't there. A wave crashed over his head, sending him under. He could feel his body starting to shake with cold. He kicked feverishly, propelling himself up so his head broke the surface again. He spun in the water. Where was she?

And then he saw her, only a few feet away. He reached out. His fingers slipped, slid, then found purchase in her sleeve. He pulled her in, pulled her close. Her body was shaking, but she wrapped her arms around him and clung.

They struck out toward the shore, fighting against the waves that tossed them about. He could hear Grace gulping for air. She had to be tiring. Her limbs must be as numb as his, her muscles screaming with effort.

*Please don't let her go under again.*

His foot skimmed the ocean floor. A few more feet, and he could use it for leverage. He pulled Grace with him, both of them sputtering and choking, until they reached the shallow water. He was dimly aware of Angel and Jack pulling Lady Elliott from the water and saw Butler sprawled on the pebbles.

But his only thought was for Grace.

She was on her hands and knees in the shallows, coughing. Her hair hung in wet ropes around her face and her body shook with cold. He crawled to her, fingers and knees scraping against rough rocks.

"Grace," he gasped.

She launched herself at him, clung once again.

"You idiot," she panted. "You could have died."

# Chapter 28

A COLD RAGE SETTLED over Julian as he watched Miles Butler pace the packed dirt floor of the makeshift dungeon,
which was actually an empty cellar with a convenient lock and
no windows.

Julian leaned casually against the wall. He fingered the long
blade of his dagger, running his thumb along the edge. It was
tempting to lock the door. No one would be able to intervene.

There was no sign of the earnest young man that had posed
as Sir Charles's clerk. Butler's face was still young, his shoulders still narrow. But those shoulders were no longer hunched
in docile compliance.

Butler shuddered and Julian realized the man's clothes
were still wet. He supposed he should provide dry clothes. He
didn't want the traitor to die of a chill before he stood trial.

"A far cry from the London, isn't it, Butler?"

Butler pivoted and braced himself, as though anticipating
a blow. When Julian remained leaning against the wall, he
relaxed slightly, rubbing at the bandaged wound on his side.

"Shadow." He nodded, as if they were greeting each other
in a London ballroom.

"I suppose there's little reason to ask why, is there?" Julian
held up his knife, as though studying the edge of the blade. A

dark side of him hoped Butler would need persuading. "Your father."

"It was so easy to deceive you. All of you." Butler's eyes alighted on Julian's dagger, and a small smile played about his lips. "Even scheduling trips to Bath to meet Marie was simple. I just went whenever Sir Charles was out of town, or over a few days when he didn't need me."

"Clever."

"And I all but *told* you," he crowed. "When Blackbourn escaped and I came running back here, ostensibly with my tail between my legs, I told you all about my father the double agent. And you never guessed."

Inwardly, Julian cursed, but he kept his face expressionless. He'd been played for a fool.

"So you followed in your father's footsteps, so to speak, but for the enemy instead."

"This country killed my father, and wouldn't even acknowledge him," Butler spat.

"He was a spy," Julian countered, shoving the knife into the waistband of his breeches. "If a spy is killed in the field, his identity goes unacknowledged. That's a condition a spy accepts when he accepts the position."

"To be forgotten? To leave behind a family?" Butler's eyes turned vicious. "My mother didn't forget. I didn't forget. And I won't let my child forget."

"A child deserves more than a traitor for a father," Julian said softly.

"And my child would've had more. The child was our reason for leaving England." He paused, licked his lips. "*Our* child. I couldn't risk Marie and our child. Not with you and Angel so close."

"How did you persuade Lady Elliott to betray her country, Butler?"

"I didn't have to. She hates her husband enough that it required no effort at all." Butler's breath hitched, one sharp movement he couldn't hide even though he attempted to feign nonchalance. He leaned against a pile of the wine casks and casually asked, "She's well? Marie?"

The offhand questions were too studied, and in complete

contrast with the concern in his gaze. Julian narrowed his eyes. Whatever training Butler had, he wasn't well seasoned. The first rule of espionage was never expose your weakness to an enemy.

"She's been returned to her husband's care, under guard, until Sir Charles determines her sentence," he replied. And then went for the kill. "How does it feel to see your lover with another man—the man who owns her?"

Butler lunged, rage twisting his handsome face. But Julian was ready. A quick jab to the throat, a kick to the stomach and Butler was on the ground, gasping for air, clutching his injured side.

"I'm older and wiser, Butler. Remember that." Julian crouched beside him and leaned over, letting the cold rage in his heart show in his eyes. "How do you know Lady Elliott? Did you meet her when she traveled to Bath?"

"Our mothers—our mothers were both French émigrés. Friends. We've been lovers since we were fifteen. Bath was only our most recent meeting place." He coughed, wheezed. "Marie is *mine*. She only married that oaf Sir Richard because her father forced her to."

Julian stood and watched Butler roll over to his hands and knees. Butler waited there, panting until he caught his breath. Then he staggered to his feet, leaning heavily on sturdy shelves. Through his torn shirt, Julian could see fresh blood staining his bandage.

"It's certainly interesting to finally face you as an equal, Shadow," Butler rasped. "I've often wondered who would win."

"You feel we're equals?" His fist shot out and clutched the front of Butler's damp shirt. "Did you even once think about the men you caused to die? Did you think about *my* life when you betrayed me to the French?"

"Why should I? They're nothing to me, and neither are you." He gripped Julian's hand, twisted. "But you understand that, Langford. You and I, we're the same."

"I don't have the blood of thousands of Englishmen on my hands." But Butler's words echoed in Julian's ears, planting an insidious seed of doubt in him.

"You're a spy." Butler shrugged dismissively. "You have as much blood on your hands as I."

"Not the blood of my countrymen," Julian responded. "Not from betrayal."

But a sly voice whispered inside his head. *You still have blood on your hands. It's just French blood instead of English.* For a moment, Julian thought his hand would wrap around the man's throat and squeeze. Something dark and dangerous seethed beneath his skin, simmered in his blood.

Butler was right, and knowing it sent despair slithering through him. They had both lied, stolen, cheated, even killed for their countries—and they both loved a woman. He was no more worthy of love than Miles Butler. After all, murder ran in his veins. He came by it naturally.

———

GRACE STIRRED AS she drifted out of sleep. She lay on her side in the massive bed, limp from exhaustion and cold. God, she'd been so cold. Even now, with blankets piled on her and the fire roaring a few feet away, her bones were chilled from the frigid ocean water.

She buried her face in the pillows and breathed deep. The scent drifting up from the smooth silk was of her own lavender soap. No scent of man or leather, or the fresh air Julian so often carried with him. Her heart ached, and she squeezed her eyes shut to will back the gathering tears.

He'd saved her, as she'd known he would. Julian had pulled her from the ocean, plied her with brandy and a hot bath and then went to conduct his business. He went back to being a spy.

Despair threatened to swamp her. Forcing it away, she squinted into the gray half-light of predawn.

The doors to the dressing room stood open. Through them she could see Julian, wearing only his breeches and boots. His feet were apart, as though braced for a fight. The sight of him filled her with both the warmth of love and chill of hopelessness. Then she realized he was standing before the doors to the countess's suite.

His mother's suite.

Curiosity mixed with concern and she pushed back the mountain of bedcovers. Shrugging into her dressing gown,

Grace padded across the bedchamber and through the dressing room on bare feet. She was still yards from him when he spoke.

"Go back to bed, Grace."

She ignored his command and pulled her wrap closer to block out the night chill. "Where are Miles Butler and Lady Elliott?"

"Angel is guarding Butler for now. I'll relieve him in a few hours." He didn't turn to face her, but spoke to the door before him. "In the morning, Angel and I and a few footmen will transport Butler to London."

"You're leaving already." Her stomach twisted. It had been a silly wish that their relationship would have changed.

"I must give my report to Sir Charles."

"Of course." It was an excuse. But she was simply too exhausted and too heartsick to fight with him. "What of Lady Elliott?"

"Her husband is going to petition for clemency and ask that he be allowed to hold her under permanent guard at his estate in the north of England. His plea will probably be granted, at least until she's had the babe." He paused, shifted slightly. "Go back to bed," he said again.

Grace stared at the broad expanse of his naked back. She should return to bed. The traitors were caught, so there was no longer anything binding she and Julian together. And there was too much pushing them apart.

She started to back away—then stopped when a shudder wracked his frame. His shoulders shook, and the muscles of his back shifted as he hunched over. The movement tore at her, ripping at the heart she'd been guarding so carefully.

Stepping forward, she raised her hand and flattened her fingers in the warm, smooth center of his back. He stiffened, but didn't shrug her off. Drawing a deep breath, she slipped around him and looked up into his lean face. He looked drawn, haggard. And lost. Oh, so very lost.

Her heart simply ached. Whatever demons haunted him, they were beyond horrible. "Oh, Julian," she whispered, tears already gathering. "Tell me of your nightmares."

He lifted shattered eyes to hers. Grace nearly recoiled from the ripe anguish swirling there.

"Not nightmares, Grace. Memories." His gaze fell, and when she followed it, she saw he was staring at his open hand.

A slim brass key glinted dully in his palm. His long fingers curled around it again and he stepped hesitantly forward. His chest expanded with a deep breath before he fit the key into the lock and flung open the door to the countess's suite.

The room was nothing but shapes and shadows in the gray dawn light. The breeze from the door fluttered the linens covering the furniture as though ghosts, freed from their long solitude, danced to greet them. Dust floated on the air, as did the faint scent of roses.

Julian stood just inside the door, his hands motionless at his side. "She died," he rasped. "And I killed her."

Grace nearly wept at the pain reverberating in his voice. "Julian, you couldn't—"

"I killed her. Or as good as. She was defending me against my father. He'd been drunk, as usual, and raving that my mother coddled me too much." He looked around the room, as though considering. "Perhaps she did, but it was in response to his dissolute ways."

"What was your mother like?" she asked softly.

"Sweet. Shy. Meek, even, which made it easier for my father to be cruel to her." He reached out and ran his hand over the empty surface of the dressing table. "I would come into her room to show her my latest outdoor discovery or something I'd accomplished with my tutor. She would be sitting here in front of the mirror, weeping and putting salve on a bruise to speed the healing."

"He hurt her."

"Often. He drank often as well, and had his regular mistress installed in one of the other bedchambers."

"That's heartless," she breathed. She couldn't imagine the insult. "Your poor mother."

"I didn't know who the woman was until I was older. He went to other women, of course, but he always had one living in Thistledown before my mother's death, and later in our London townhouse. We never returned here after my mother died." He walked to a chaise and pulled off its cover. A quarter century of dust billowed out, clouding the air.

"What happened to your mother, Julian?"

He closed his eyes, ran his hand down the arm of the chaise. "I can remember exactly how they looked. My father, drunk and furious. My mother, terrified yet determined. He was making plans to introduce me to his mistress. Not just then, as I was only eight, but in a few years. It was getting to be time I learned how the Earls of Langford conducted themselves."

Shock sliced through her and she stepped forward. "God, Julian, that's horrible. You were so young."

"Old enough, in my father's eyes. He was telling my mother he'd have to start teaching me earlier to counteract all of her coddling. She fought him. I think it was the first time she openly defied him."

"With good cause." She reached out to put a hand on his arm then dropped it. He seemed oddly fragile, as though he would shatter if she touched him.

"He shook me, telling me he'd have to teach me to be a man. I remember she leapt at him, scratching, biting even. He lost his grip on my arms and I ran. Not far," he qualified. "Just far enough that I could hide behind some tapestries in the upstairs hall. She followed me into the hall and he followed her."

He looked at her now, but his eyes were unfocused and she knew he wasn't seeing her.

"I hid there," he continued, "crouched behind the tapestry, hands covering my ears while they fought. But I still heard my father shout that he would be rid of her, once and for all. I heard her scream as she tumbled down the servants' stairs."

"Oh, God. *Julian.*" Her legs turned weak. She staggered to the chaise and gripped the arm to keep from sliding to the floor.

"I stayed behind that tapestry until the morning, terrified because I could hear my father shouting for me as he stumbled through my bedchamber and the nursery." He looked down at his hands. "I was such a coward."

"You were *eight.*"

"That's no excuse," he bit out.

"You were only a child," she returned.

"Old enough that I could have stood in front of my mother instead of running. Grace, my father killed my mother. He *meant* to. I've the blood of a murderer in my veins."

"But that doesn't make you a murderer."

"It was my fault he killed her. They say blood tells, Grace—

and it did. I'm a spy. My training includes the ability to kill, and I've done so." He turned to face her, and the red light of dawn slanted over his grief-ravaged face. "I have nothing in me to give you. I'm no different than Miles Butler."

Grace's heart swelled, ached, nearly burst from the pressure. She grieved for the child whose innocence was stolen and for the man who didn't believe he deserved love. She stepped forward, reaching out for him. He only shook his head.

He wouldn't let her comfort him. At least not with her touch.

"I killed a man last night, Julian. I stared down the barrel of my pistol, pulled the trigger and killed him. What does that make me?"

"Grace—"

"By your reasoning, I'm a murderer."

He only shook his head.

"Do you know why I fired that pistol and killed a man? Because I love you, Julian." Saying the words sent her heart soaring. And left her belly quivering with nerves. She swallowed hard. "I love you, and I would do whatever I had to in order to protect you."

He turned, stared, his eyes wide with shock. "Why?" he whispered hoarsely.

How could he ask such a thing? "For so many reasons," she answered.

He searched her face, his eyes staring intently into hers. Then he turned away from her.

Her heart plummeted, dropping off the cliff and into the black. She'd taken the step, said the words, and he'd turned away. Again. Despair clogged her throat, dragged at her. It was so deep, so dark that it was beyond tears.

"You can't love me, Grace." He looked over his shoulder at her. His face was hard, his mouth one firm line. But his eyes were unbearably sad.

"Because your father killed your mother? That's not your fault."

"It's—"

"No," she snapped. "It isn't. You were a young child who couldn't have stopped him. And you're not your father. He was cruel and immoral and dissolute. You're not."

"You don't know what I'm capable of."

"I do know. I sat side by side with you when Fanny's child was born. You held the hand of stranger as she labored to bring a babe into the world."

"Grace. Stop it." He shook his head as if to ward off her words.

"And you're not Miles Butler. He's selfish and reckless, with no thought beyond himself and his desires. He's never considered the consequences of his actions on the young men at war for this country. Everything you've done, anyone you may have killed, has been for your country. And I watched you stay your hand last night when you could have killed Miles Butler. You didn't."

"You think too highly of me."

"No. I know you. I *love* you."

"You can't possibly."

"I do," she whispered through the tears that clogged her throat. "And I always will."

He staggered under the weight of her words. She reached out once more, and this time he stepped toward her. Dropping to his knees, he wrapped an arm around her waist and pressed his face against her belly.

He made no sound, only held her there while she stroked his hair and wept for him.

When his grip eased, she cupped his cheeks and raised his face. Those gorgeous summer sky eyes were dry, and the heartbreak in them seemed to rend her in two. She brushed her lips against his. The kiss was soft, tender. Full of light and warmth and love. A meeting of souls.

"Come to our room now," she whispered, drawing him to his feet.

His hand was warm and strong in hers as she led him out of the countess's suite. She closed the door softly but firmly. "Don't lock it, Julian."

"I won't. It will always be open to you."

Now it was his turn to lead her back to their chamber. To their bed. As they sank onto the soft mattress, he pulled back. His mouth hovered over hers.

"Where would you like to go, my lady smuggler?" He traced a thumb over her lips.

"Anywhere." She smiled slowly. "As long as I'm with you."

*Dear Reader:*

*The most difficult and fascinating aspect of writing historical romance is research. I could spend hours (and have!) researching the minutia of daily lives, fashion, food and politics. It's difficult knowing, however, that for every detail I get right, another detail is likely wrong. I hope you will forgive my mistakes. I assure you, I diligently research, but sometimes I am just plain incorrect. It happens more often that I would like.*

*When researching, the best place to start is always primary sources. I owe so much to Google Books! When Grace stitches herself up, she quotes* The London Medical Dictionary, Volume 2, *by Bartholomew Parr, published in 1809. The ditty sung by John the blacksmith is part of a song printed in* The British Minstrel, and National Melodist, Volume 1, *published in 1827 by Sherwood, Gilbert, and Piper, and John Bumpus. I love learning these little bits of history from the original sources.*

*Such a primary source is how I stumbled on Jack Rattenbury, the smuggler I patterned Jack Blackbourn after. Jack was a joy to write, but that is because he arrived in my brain fully formed. When researching smuggling during the Regency, I ran across a book called* Memoirs of a Smuggler. *It was written in 1837 by the infamous smuggler Jack Rattenbury, the self-styled "Rob Roy of the West." I fell in love with Jack and his escapades and decided I simply must include him in* The Smuggler Wore Silk. *Of course, I took great license with his character and life, but as with all fiction, there is a kernel of truth at the base.*

*The real Jack Rattenbury was born in Beer and by the age of age of sixteen had already been a privateer, an apprentice on a ship and imprisoned in Bordeaux. He'd traveled to New York, Copenhagen, France and a few other places. When he returned to Beer in his sixteenth year, he thought to try his hand at fishing, but found it dull and tiresome after his "roving life." As the smuggling industry was booming at that time, he decided to make his fortune that way.*

Jack was cheeky and confident, and seemed to me to have a delightful sense of humor. He was known for his clever escapes, including hiding in a chimney to escape the customs officers—a fact I shamelessly used for this book, but which had no relation to treason. He left the smuggling business briefly to run a public house in 1809. The pub failed after a few years, however, and he went back to smuggling. So that part of the story is true, though the dates might be a bit sketchy. He was not arrested for treason that I know of, though he was arrested multiple times. He usually managed a clever escape, of course.

Jack married a woman named Anna, who was as daring as her husband. She helped orchestrate a number of Jack's escapes, including steering a boat alongside a brig so Jack could jump ship. When the second mate started to shoot at Jack, Anna "wrested the piece out of his hands." A brave woman, was Anna Rattenbury!

With Jack Rattenbury in mind, I crafted my Jack Blackbourn. I tried to do justice to his sense of humor and ingenious escapes. I don't know if the real Jack would approve of my Jack, but I hope so. And I hope you enjoyed reading him as much I enjoyed writing him!

# Prologue

THE WOMAN SHOULDN'T have been in the thick of battle. But she rose out of the acrid smoke, perched high atop a chestnut horse and wearing the scarlet coat of a cavalry officer.

The Marquess of Angelstone staggered through rows of trampled corn, shock rippling through him as the woman raised a cavalry sabre high into the air. A shrill whistle sounded overhead. Instinctively, Angel ducked as cannon artillery pounded through the ranks, blasting into the earth and showering him with dirt and black powder.

The woman on horseback didn't flinch.

He staggered forward, coughing, ears ringing, as soldiers around him fell or scattered. Pressing a hand to his jacket pocket, Angel fingered the square shape of the letter he carried there. He hadn't known he'd have to fight his way to Wellington to deliver it.

The horse turned a tight circle, one of the woman's hands gripping the reins. The sabre in her other hand flashed like quicksilver in the sunlight. Her grip on the steel blade was untrained, her movements awkward. But fury and hate blazed from her eyes and seemed to fuel her sabre as it sliced across the chest of a French soldier. The man collapsed, shrieking and clutching at welling blood.

The woman turned away, already arcing her sabre toward another enemy soldier, and Angel lost sight of her.

Reflex sent Angel's bayonet plunging as a Frenchman reared up in front of him, face contorted by fear. When the man screamed, regret shot through Angel before he forced it away. It was kill or be killed. There was no time for regret.

He surged forward with the ranks of foot soldiers, compelled to look for the woman. The muddied ground sucked at his feet, threatening to pull him beneath thundering hooves and panicked soldiers. Broken corn stalks slashed at his face. The sulfur smell of black powder burned his nose, mixing with the scent of men's fear.

He fought past a charging enemy soldier, spun away from another and saw her again.

Soot streaked her grim face. She grinned at the enemy standing before her but the smile was terrible. The man paled and aimed his rifle at her. He was not fast enough to beat her sword.

When that soldier, too, fell under her sabre, she looked up. Over the dead soldier and through the swirling gray smoke, Angel met her eyes. They were a chilling, pale blue and held only one thing.

Vengeance.

She pulled on the reins and her horse reared up, hooves pawing at the air. Angel planted his feet and braced for impact. But the hooves never struck. The woman kept her seat, her jaw clenched, and continued to hold his gaze.

The battle faded away, booming cannons falling on his deaf ears. The gray, writhing smoke veiled the dying soldiers and hand-to-hand battle being waged around him.

He only saw her merciless eyes. Blood roared in his ears and the beat of his pulse became as loud as the cannons. A high, powerful note sang through him.

The woman's horse whinnied as its hooves struck the earth again. Standing in the stirrups, she thrust her sword aloft and howled. The battle cry that echoed over the field carried with it the sting of rage and unfathomable grief. She wheeled the horse, spurred his sides and charged through battling soldiers, her blond hair streaming behind her.

And she was gone, obscured by clouds of dark smoke and the chaos of battle.

# Chapter 1

*July 1817*

ALASTAIR WHITMORE, MARQUESS of Angelstone—code name Angel—coughed into his gloved hand in the hope of discreetly hiding his laugh. A man shouldn't laugh when a fellow spy was being hunted by a woman.

"Oh, my lord," the brunette tittered. "Truly, you are a remarkable figure of a man."

The Earl of Langford—poor hunted bastard—lifted his annoyed gaze over the short matron and met Angel's eyes. The woman leaned forward, her powdered cleavage pressing against Langford's arm.

Angel quirked his lips. The brunette's fawning was highly amusing, since it wasn't directed at himself.

"If you will excuse me," Langford said, "I must speak with Lord Angelstone about an urgent matter."

"Indeed?" Angel didn't bother to conceal his merriment. "I wasn't aware we needed to discuss an urgent matter."

"It has just come to my attention," Langford ground out. He extricated his sleeve from the woman's grasping fingers and eased away from her.

"Must you go?" The brunette pouted rouged lips. Feathers trembled on her turbaned head as she sent a coy look toward Langford. "I truly feel we should further our acquaintance, my lord. You have been in the country for *months*."

"With my *wife*."

The brunette's mouth fell open. "But, you are in London. She is not here this evening. I thought—"

"My dear lady," Angel said smoothly, sliding between the pair. He might as well stage a rescue mission. "As I'm sure you are aware, his lordship has many demands on his time. Not the least being his wife and new daughters."

"I see." Without even a single remorseful glance, she turned her back on Langford. Sharp eyes flicked over Angel. Subtle as a stalking elephant. "Well. You are unmarried, Lord Angelstone."

"Indeed. But alas, I am otherwise engaged for the evening." Angel raised the woman's chubby fingers until they were just a breath away from his lips. "A pity, for you would have been a most enchanting diversion." He wondered if his tongue would turn black after such lies.

"Perhaps another day, Lord Angelstone." She preened, patting her bosom as though to calm her racing heart. The cloying scent of eau de cologne drifted up, and Angel fought the urge to sneeze.

"Perhaps." Angel let her fingers slide out of his. He bowed. "Good evening, ma'am."

As the brunette waddled away, Langford sighed gustily beside him. "A female predator, that one." He brushed at his coat sleeve. "She was getting powder everywhere."

Angel smothered a grin. "You've been married and ensconced in the country too long, my friend, if you've forgotten how our society ladies once adored you."

"Not as much as they currently adore you."

"True. A title does that. Now, did you truly have something to discuss?"

"No." Langford palmed his pocket watch and flipped open the case. He frowned at the small glass face. "But I do intend to make my escape. I've had enough weak punch, innuendos and pleasantries for one evening. And Grace is waiting at home."

"How is your countess?" With a wife such as Langford's, he could understand the desire to hide in the countryside.

The frown cleared and Langford grinned at Angel. "She is still tired from the birthing, but she shooed me out for an evening when she learned of my assignment." The watch disappeared into a waistcoat pocket.

"Ah. I wondered if you were here for business or pleasure."

"A little of each." Langford's shoulder jerked up in a half-hearted shrug. His eyes roved the room. "You?"

"The same." In truth, it was always business. A spy never did anything simply for pleasure.

Angel studied the ballroom. It was an impossible crush. Guests bumped up against one another as they laughed and flirted. Diamonds winked and painted fans fluttered as women entertained suitors and friends. Footmen threaded through the crowd carrying trays of gold champagne and rose-colored punch. Surrounding it all were the subtle notes of a string quartet and the scent of candle wax.

Such was the glittering and dazzling world of the ton. But underneath the gleaming polish of society were passions and intrigue and secrets. It was his mission to seek them out. And beyond his government assignments, beyond the political intrigues, was the enemy who had assassinated a woman four years ago. *His* woman. *Gemma.*

Cold anger turned him from the scene. "I believe I may follow your lead and make my escape as well." He wanted his own hearth, a brandy and his violin. The constant din of voices grated and the endlessly changing pattern of dancers was visually dizzying. He scanned the room once more. A wave of people ebbed and flowed, came together and parted.

And he saw her. No cavalry coat. No sabre. Instead of wearing steel of weaponry, only a gown of silver netting over white muslin. A painted fan fluttered languidly near her face. No howling battle cry now, only the sensual curving of her lips as she bent her head toward a military officer.

Something clutched inside him as the battleground superimposed itself over the ballroom. Twirling women became French soldiers, the sound of stringed instruments became the whistle of a blade. The scent of gunpowder stung his nostrils and the pounding of artillery rang in the air. The scene swirled around the woman, though she was no longer on horseback.

It had been two years since Waterloo. Two years since he'd seen a bright halo of hair and pitiless eyes full of retribution. He shook his head to will away those memories.

But the woman remained. A bevy of men were gathered around her, jostling for position. The striped waistcoats of the dandies clashed with the brilliant red of soldiers' uniforms. Then, like an echo of his memories, the Duke of Wellington himself approached the woman. She smiled warmly as he bowed over her hand.

The bevy of suitors stepped back in deference to Wellington, leaving him as alone with the woman as two people could be in a crowded ballroom.

"Who is that woman?" Angel spoke softly, nodding toward the woman. "The one talking to Wellington?"

"Lilias Fairchild. Major Jeremy Fairchild's widow. He was killed at Waterloo." Langford raised a brow. "Did you know the major?"

"No." Angel watched Mrs. Fairchild's fan tap lightly against Wellington's arm. A sign of affection rather than flirtation. "What do you know of her?"

"Both Grace and I found her pleasant enough, though one can sense a spine of steel beneath the attractive exterior. She's known for being private, which has only increased the gossips' chatter." Langford lowered his voice. "She followed her husband on the march. They say when the major's body was brought off the field, she was wild with grief. She took her husband's horse and sabre and joined the battle."

The gossips were correct. There had been a wildness in her that day. Across the room, her hair caught the light of the candles and turned a bright yellow-gold. "I'm surprised she's allowed into this ballroom." A woman on the march with soldiers, one so unladylike as to fight and kill, should be ostracized by society.

"There are some doors closed to her. But with Wellington himself championing her, society as a whole has accepted her."

"She should have died." He'd assumed she had. He'd thought about her periodically over the past two years, the way one did with a striking memory. Her face was the clearest recollection he had of that day. He had never considered she would live, and was vaguely sad to think such a vibrant creature had been struck down. Seeing her alive and whole seemed to defy fate.

"If you ask the troop she marched with, death was her intention," Langford said softly. "The French called her *La Dame de Vengeance*."

*Vengeance*. It seemed he and the widow Fairchild were two of a kind.

"I know her just well enough to introduce you." Langford's glance turned sly.

She wouldn't remember him from Waterloo. One soldier meeting another on the field of battle was nothing. Not that it mattered. It had been only a moment. A fleeting breath of time that would barely be remembered. Never mind that he'd seen her wild, vengeful eyes in his dreams as often as he'd seen Gemma's dying eyes.

As Wellington bent to speak to Mrs. Fairchild, the woman angled her head and let her gaze wander the room. She should not have seen him. Guests danced and flirted and laughed between them, blocking her view. But like an arrow piercing fog, she trained her blue eyes unerringly on Angel.

There was no vengeance there this time, but still they seemed to blaze. The color of them, the shape of them, ignited a visceral beat low in his belly. As did the lush curves even the most flowing gown couldn't conceal.

Recognition flared in the widow's eyes. Her lips lifted on one side before she flicked her gaze back to Wellington. The duke bowed his farewell and retreated into the crush.

"Introduce me."

"You're asking for trouble with that one, my friend." Langford laughed. "Which means it would be my pleasure to introduce you."

Langford pushed through the crowd. Angel followed, brushing past silks and satins and elaborate cravats. Mrs. Fairchild's eyes tracked his movements across the floor. It was odd to be studied with such interest, even as he studied her. Flanked by soldiers and gentlemen festooned in evening wear and vying for the position closest to her, she seemed to be an island of calm.

He narrowed his eyes. No, not calm. Confidence. There were no affectations, no feminine vapors. A woman who killed a French soldier in the thick of battle had no time for vapors.

"Lord Langford," she said as they approached. Her eyes flashed briefly in Angel's direction, then back to Langford. "It is good to see you again. How are your wife and daughters?"

"Quite well, thank you. The twins are a handful already." Langford grinned. It wasn't clear whether the grin was for his daughters or Angel, as he slid an amused glance in Angel's direction. "Mrs. Fairchild, may I present the Marquess of Angelstone?"

"Lord Angelstone." Her voice moved over him like velvet, smooth and rich. "But we've met before."

"We have indeed, Mrs. Fairchild." He bowed over her hand. "Though the circumstances were quite different."

Langford's brow rose. The message was clear enough.

"We met in battle." Mrs. Fairchild tilted her head. Candlelight shadowed dramatic cheekbones and full, ripe lips. "I'm afraid names were not exchanged."

"My condolences on the loss of your husband," Angel said.

"Thank you." Her face softened. "He was a good man."

"And a good solider, I've heard," Langford added. "Will you be in London long, Mrs. Fairchild?"

"Through the Season, I think." She smiled, a subtle, feline turning up of her lips. "Will you dance with me, Lord Langford? So I can pretend I'm not too old for all this nonsense?"

"For you, Mrs. Fairchild, I'll brave the dance floor—but not tonight. I must return to my wife."

"A flattering escape."

"Indeed. Now, I see your punch glass is empty. I'd offer to get you another"—Langford looked toward the table holding the punch bowl—"but I have no desire to fight this insufferable crowd."

Mrs. Fairchild laughed, low and throaty. The sound sent desire spiraling through Angel.

"Go then," she said, shooing Langford with her closed fan. "I can obtain my own punch."

"Allow me." Angel stepped in, offering his arm. Langford, the cur, grinned. Angel ignored him. "I would be honored, Mrs. Fairchild."

Behind them, the bevy of gentlemen suitors bristled, almost as one. A pack of wolves defending their queen. Or a gaggle of geese flapping uselessly at a predator.

"Thank you, my lord." She cocked her head to look up at him. A smile flirted with the corners of her lips. "I would be most grateful."

The gaggle hissed in disappointment.

She set her white-gloved hand on his arm. The touch of her

fingers was delicate on his sleeve. As they crossed the room, she splayed open her painted fan and waved it languorously. A lazy ripple of painted wildflowers in the wind. The scent of her skin rose into the air. Clean. Bright. And when she smiled at him once more, his body tripped straight into attraction.

*He wouldn't settle for less than
her unconditional surrender.*

From *New York Times* bestselling author
# MADELINE HUNTER

## The Surrender of Miss Fairbourne

As reluctant business partners, Emma Fairbourne's defiance and Darius Alfreton's demands make it difficult to manage one of London's most eminent auction houses. But their passionate personalities ignite an affair that leaves them both senseless—until the devastating truth behind their partnership comes to light, threatening the love they have just begun to share . . .

**"Hunter's books are so addictive."**
—*Publishers Weekly*

madelinehunter.com
facebook.com/MadelineHunter
facebook.com/LoveAlwaysBooks
penguin.com